Praise For *CHEMICALS*

"When I first started reading *Chemicals* by literary newcomer, Erica Crockett, I had to look up the author's name again to make sure I wasn't reading Charlie Huston or Chuck Palahniuk. The writing is that good. The story about a world devoid of pharmaceuticals is even better. Imagine a world where cartels terrorize society and something as everyday-taken-for-granted as a baby aspirin is a rare thing to possess. This is one of the most intelligent and suspenseful novels by a young, sure-to-be superstar that I've read in a long time."

- Vincent Zandri, New York Times and USA Today Bestselling author of *The Remains* and *Everything Burns*

"*Chemicals* is bound to be a bestseller. Crockett constructed an engaging plot centered around America's dependence on drugs and delivered it in a tight, literary package. Read this book."

- Mazal Simantov, Creator of Audiobook Pop!

"Erica Crockett's debut novel *Chemicals* is a deconstruction of big pharma. It is a masterful narrative that betrays her sly pagan roots. The prose has a decidedly distinct voice—the dialogue and characters are carefully crafted with a dark, biting humor, just enough to pierce through the delightfully foreboding sense of doom conjured by a society entirely overrun by drug cartels and lack of any real political order. A must read for fans of dystopian sci-fi."

- Benton Rooks, author of *TRETA-YUGA*

Corvid Tear Media

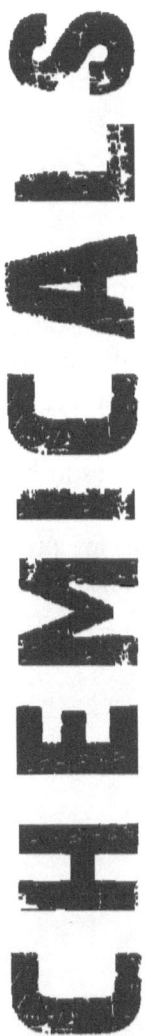

CHEMICALS

ERICA CROCKETT

CORVID TEAR MEDIA

Printed in the United States of America

ISBN 978-1-942300-01-4

First Printing, 2014

Cover Design by quiet wren

Author photograph by Cy Gilbert Photography
www.cygilbertphotography.com

Published by Corvid Tear Media
www.corvidtearmedia.com

For Aaron Sup

CHAPTER ONE

Her lungs aren't working. Not properly. It takes two dreams passing through her sleeping mind, one slipping into the other, for her body to tell her this is so. The first dream is of her talking to an old boyfriend who has creeks of sweat on his forearms. She tries to tell him she must ford his arms without getting her socks wet, but when she strives to talk, she hasn't enough air in her lungs to convey her need. The second dream has her in the position of a human accordion. There are mobs of people to either side of her, pushing with one solid thrum into her and then pulling away. Her torso collapses in seams but no sound issues forth.

Aberdeen awakes and a moment of confusion gives way to the remembrance of asthma. Her lungs are locked. Her body is set on dying. Fucking bronchial sacs, she thinks, and reaches for her inhaler.

Instead of her familiar bedside table, her hand hits the top of a cardboard box sized for books and other heavy things. Her eyes are blurry and lazy and she uses her fingertips like a claw in a plush-toy machine to pluck her medicine from among the bookmarks, lip balms and discarded earrings missing their backings. She puts the L-shaped plastic in her mouth, catching a lock of her black hair between lip and inhaler, and depresses the metal canister. A bitter mist hits her soft palate and she gasps it into her lungs. She does this two more times. The parts of her intent on dying are thwarted. Her lungs go back to being life-supporting instead of life-ending. The wheeze escaping from her mouth and nose is quieted, vanquished.

She shakes the medicine in the container. The liquid inside is slight, a captured bit of chemical fog. Three hits left. Maybe five.

"Time for new medicine," she says to the other side of the bed. Her husband isn't there. She can hear him in the kitchen, swearing at the coffee pot.

She swings her legs out over the edge of the bed, the pits of her knees sweaty from sleep, her flesh aiming to stick to the floral-patterned sheets. She spots her slippers and slides them on. There are no rugs on the floor yet and once Aberdeen's toes are cold, they are cold for the day. Once on the floor, the blood flows down to busy itself with her feet instead of her chest. She kneads just under her breasts with her knuckles and yawns.

Toothbrushing, showering, makeup. Put together, she brushes her hair into a tight ponytail. Sirens outside are clarion through the brick walls of the apartment building. She didn't think of that before they moved in. The sounds of the city. But now they're here, first night in the apartment after dropping off their things earlier in the week and heading to the woods for four days to unwind after the move. She already misses the black knots in white trunks and the smell of humus.

He's still in the kitchen when she emerges fully clothed. The kitchen is bigger and kinder in the daylight, not so oppressive and cold like it was the previous night when they arrived home past ten, eager for showers and bed.

"I'm going to be proactive today," she says to him. He's not looking at her. He's intent on making the coffee pot sit perfectly in its rimmed base.

"Hmm," Hurt replies.

"It's the cardboard boxes, I think. My asthma's been terrible since we started the move. Much worse than usual. And I refuse to believe it's the apartment. That would be too crushing. Nope, it's the boxes."

Hurt swings around and holds an empty mug limply from his index finger. Pouty lips. Aberdeen hates that he's letting everything defeat him since the move. Days ago, before they headed out camping, it was a flat bike tire. Today it's a kitchen appliance.

"Do you want me to do it?" she asks, already moving to take over.

He shifts to let her at the coffee maker, placing the ceramic mug on the counter between a box of spices yet unpacked and a potted basil plant yellow with too much watering.

"Did the pot change or did the base shrink?" Hurt asks. "I've been messing with it for ten minutes."

"Neither," she says, slipping the glass carafe into the base, "you're just antsy to get it perfect. There. Have at it."

Hurt looks at her with what Aberdeen translates as both admiration and annoyance. His brow is lifted, his eyes squinting. She thinks he's mad about last night and the real reason they broke camp late in the evening and headed back to the city. She thinks he's mad about where they've moved, that he hates the change. He hates that she can deal with a coffee pot. Adeptly deal.

Instead, all he says is "thank you" and digs to the bottom of a triple-layered plastic bag and produces a shiny, metallic sleeve of coffee beans.

Aberdeen turns to find a pair of shoes suitable for public viewing but Hurt stops her with a palm to her bony hip.

"You had an asthma attack?" he asks, then drops some of the beans into a grinder and turns it on. The noise prevents an answer from her until the beans are ground. She smiles at him, liking how he presses down on the power button with the gravity of nuclear deployment.

She nods and says, "Like I said, the cardboard boxes around here make it hard to breathe."

He pours water into the top of the coffee maker. Hurt walks back and forth from the sink, flipping on the tap filter and filling his favorite mug eight times. He dumps it eight times. Aberdeen watches what he's willing to do to not struggle with the pot anymore.

"You're getting ready to leave. I could empty some boxes and get them outside. As long as you don't mind me stringing stuff all over the floor."

His words make her think of last night and she can't help but attack.

"Last night you said you always wanted a clean home. Nothing to trip over. No walls to wash clean of marks. No pasta in the floor vents. I think you actually said that. 'No pasta in the floor vents.'"

He lifts his mug up to his tongue and licks a drop of water from the rim. "This isn't anything we need to talk about now, Aberdeen. Just go for your medicine and I'll make a dent in this."

Aberdeen moves to her husband and wraps her arms around his soft torso. His paunch is the product of his thirties and his ceased biking and his increased sedentary studying, but she likes the way his warm torso envelopes her small chest. He taps his cheek to beg a kiss. She pitches up on tiptoes and places one gently and releases him to find her shoes.

The kiss has made Hurt forget his caffeine and crave her instead. She feels him walk up behind her and put his chin on the top of her head. "Can't you just call in the prescription and pick it up later? There's plenty to get done here."

She considers it but ducks her head away from him, dipping her ear to her shoulder. "I need the air, babe. And a walk to a

4

new pharmacy sounds entertaining." She kisses him again, this time on his dry bottom lip and walks out the front door. She thinks it's good to leave him wanting.

It's startling when she's not greeted by fresh air. Unlike their previous residence, with its door that opened onto a dry, xeriscaped front yard, this door opens onto a landing that spins dizzily downward by way of a flight of stairs in the center of the building. Hurt and she are on the fifth floor, the uppermost reaches of the brick tenement building in a part of town she'd never been to until they were looking to save money and downsize.

Before she starts down the stairs, she reminds herself that she is young, only thirty-five. She is fit. She can climb up and down these stairs as long as they need to live here. She thinks about elevators being overrated, metal traps to lift you up only to drop you back down to earth. She thinks these things as her feet slip down the stairs one at a time.

At the bottom of the stairwell and in the echoing, cold foyer of the building, she notices that she hasn't seen any other tenants. And there are the sirens again. Aberdeen can't decipher if they are from ambulance, police car or fire truck. She checks her mailbox not expecting to find anything but checks it anyway. The change of address form hasn't been filled out yet. She imagines whomever is living in her former house is cursing the junk mail as if it was sent from Aberdeen Childress instead of to her.

Pushing on the glass front door, she breathes in the air, ready for it to be cool and clean, but coughs instead. There is an acrid tang to the breeze; sharp and burning, it hits her lungs and they close slightly in response. She nearly turns around and heads back up the stairs, but she's committed. She needs more medicine. She ventures out.

This has yet to become her neighborhood. *Her* neighborhood is miles away, across the city. This street is new and its foreignness is evident. The elm in front of the building isn't a friend. While she walks, she eyes new pads of concrete, street signs with known symbols but individualized with their bent corners and tagged lettering, a brown Labrador tied to the base of a lamppost with a shattered light. She takes them all in, says her greetings and tries to form those bonds.

But the people are strange, she thinks. A man passes. He wears a long duster jacket and his hands are deep in the pockets, his fists either balled up or he's carrying around apples, plums, the fruits of fall. He shakes his head. Aberdeen slows and notices there are tears on his face.

She walks and the man becomes normal in comparison to others. In a car similar to the one her mother drove to her secretarial job in the eighties, sits an elderly couple holding hands. At first, it is simple affection. Aberdeen tries not to stare, but her spirit is fortified by the intimacy of the people. That could be she and her husband in several decades. Full runs of years later, when their current fight would be forgotten.

She stares and the couple begins to grope at one another. There is desperation to the caresses, turning them from something gentle to something primal. The man pulls hard on the thin, white hair of the woman and she responds with a love bite to his ear. Aberdeen looks at the sidewalk and starts to move once again.

The sun is lower in the sky due to the season, leaving the northern hemisphere, dipping back to the Argentineans and Zambians and Kiwis. Aberdeen knows she will miss the light but she loves the warm russet colors of decaying leaves and the look of soil folding up, squeezing, and going fallow. She notices it in the small circles of dirt around the trees otherwise cloistered by concrete and city. She looks to the earth in distraction. She always looks to the things that grow in distraction and thinks of her bags of moss and packets of sand and boxes of seashells yet unpacked in her apartment, their promise as elements of terrariums not yet fulfilled.

Wandering towards her final destination, she finds herself in a pocket park close to the notion of a location of a drug store she has in mind. It could be a street over, she thinks. The acrid smell is still present in the air, yet from where she stands she can see no smoke. She is the only one in the park. A cloth bib lost from the neck of an infant lies near the foot of a bench. She takes a seat and pulls her corduroy coat tight around her stomach. Aberdeen nudges the bib with her red ballet flats and thinks of how annoying that must have been for the mother. Something paid for and then lost. Something meant to be dirty, then made clean will be dirty always. And missing.

Sirens again. Then gone. Still no people wander, like her, into the park. Aberdeen gets to her feet. She leaves the area of sycamore and oak, crunching the cap-less acorns on the ground when she goes. Most are on the pavement of a running trail. They will never find a grip in the ground.

As she walks, things become louder. Before she sees them, she can sense them. It is a biological program all humans have: to know when a mob is forming. It comes to her as a prick of sweat at the divots in her elbows. The hair at her neck becomes hackled. Wild dogs, she thinks. Boar, lions, frilled-necked lizards.

Then, there they are. People. Hundreds, maybe, not quite a thrumming multitude but numerous enough, all at the pharmacy for which she was searching. Aberdeen realizes she has missed something in her days away from media and her phone, some vital clue sent at a time she was unable to receive it, perhaps when her lungs were suffocating her or when she was fighting with Hurt under vivid starlight in the woods.

Something is very wrong.

There are no longer windows in the drug store. People are walking between the outside wall of the store front and the inside as if the lips of the windowsills were door thresholds. Some people, the younger ones, mainly the male ones, have things in their arms or slung about their torsos in bags. One man holds a package of toilet paper high over his head and runs down the street on the balls of his feet.

She should leave; she knows this. She should find out what is happening without putting herself in danger. But she is being called. It isn't curiosity or the desire to see what is occurring inside. The pull comes from the energy of the mass itself. It sings to her genes which in turn tell her it is okay to become part of a pack. *Come play, come see.* And her feet move, with caution and timidity, but they move forward. Into it.

Aberdeen sticks to the wall of the city block, keeping her back to it as she creeps closer to the crowd. The feel of stout brick and the pressure of the building on her spine strengthen her resolve to be in the thick of things. She calls herself a lunatic and immediately her reptilian brain shouts out a *boo!,* turns down its thumb and moves her on. She brushes past those on the fringes of the crowd: pensioners, grade-schoolers, pregnant women. She passes them, moving them out of the way while her back is still held up by mortar and earth, moving deeper in, past the moderates and the meek.

She hears them talking, shouting.

"Don't touch that, asshole. I put my hand on it first."

"What am I to do, then? What am I supposed to do!?"

"Antacids. It's not like I want everything. Please just a bottle. No? No?"

Then Aberdeen is around the corner. She doesn't step inside the raised flooring just beyond the fractured window. The glass at her feet is nearly powder. So many have stepped on this, she thinks. Ground, like coffee beans. Using her fingers to grip at the wooden window frame, she pulls her body away from the brick and takes in the sight of three people red in the face and yelling at one another. She swallows and reaches for her phone to take a picture and realizes it's at home with Hurt.

Under the feet of the looters are greeting cards covered in black shoe prints, crumpled into pleats and sticking to the floor. Pictures of flowers, and cakes, and dogs with balloons in their mouths face upwards to the throng of people inside the pharmacy. It's as if they are watching the madness from a two-dimensional realm, where things like this just don't happen.

The aisles of the store are overrun with plunderers. Everything is being gleaned. This includes the numbered lights over the checkout stands. No one appears to have a weapon, but Aberdeen reminds herself she can't see through fabric. Or a pulsing, moving mass of people.

The mob is denser, louder at the back of the store. She thinks there must be a reason for this, the mass's want and desperation exemplified via screaming and an occasional wolf whistle, clipped and loud, blown through the same lips, on repeat.

She steps inside. She watches a woman hit a man in the face with an umbrella when he touches a package of shower caps sitting on a shelf in front of them both. She reasons that if she doesn't take anything, if she doesn't pose a threat to the others, she will be okay. Don't ever touch a strange dog's toy, she says, over and over in her mind, while walking to the back of the store.

The epicenter is the pharmacy counter. What stops her cold isn't the tight cluster of horrified and horrifying people, but the shelves. The shelves are completely bare. This is what everyone is after, she thinks. Here is what they want. All the other things, the Pringles, the dishes that hold the pennies at the counters, reams of paper, they're an afterthought.

So why are the people still here? Why, she wonders, as a young man with glasses smashes his face against a wall until a short Latina pulls back on his arms, pulls him away, are they still here?

"Why are you all here?" she screams into the crowd.

They don't answer. They are too busy losing whatever it is they each have to lose.

She feels a wetness on her elbow and looks down to see a smear of warm blood just above her joint but no scrape or cut on her skin. The sight of blood – specifically the sight of blood without a known source – pulls Aberdeen back into a place of rationality. She turns her head about, scanning the people around her, looking for the bleeding human. She sees no one that could have marked her.

"Jesus," she says, and wipes her arm off on the sleeve of a man busy yelling obscenities to an empty counter space. She's in self-preservation mode and worries she could be wiping AIDS virus off of her arm and on to someone else. This triggers a flow of sweat down the small of her back. It runs the length of her buttocks, down to her thighs.

Then she sees the blood. It's on the hands of a woman who has pushed her way through the mob and has disappeared behind the wooden door linking the body of the store to the nook meant for pharmaceuticals. There must be a lock on the handle and if Aberdeen was closer, she figures she would hear the click of a bolt sliding home once the woman was inside.

Yet the counter is open, traversable. People aren't hopping over it, like they must have been, to get at the medicine. It's as if they are all using the counter as a barrier. They don't want to cross. They just want to cluster, mob up, display their rage.

Aberdeen feels the remainder of the blood crusting on her arm and pulling at the light hairs on her bicep. She makes her way to the counter and tries to peer over it while dodging the erratic, jetting limbs of several people. There is nothing to see. The raised counter is too high, preventing a glimpse of what is happening on the floor or between the rows of shelves. Using the adrenaline inside her for something productive, she places her hands on the Formica and heaves her body up onto the ledge by straightening out her elbows. A hand grabs at her leg and she instinctively kicks out, using the bulk of whatever she made contact with to help get her knees up to her chest. Then she feels like a four-year-old again, with the elation of climbing onto the countertops of her childhood kitchen and scooting about to locate something sweet.

She drops to the floor on the other side of the counter and her red shoes end up in a miasma of cotton, blood and what could be urine, a waft of ammonia coming from the impact. Instantly she feels more secure having half of a wall between her and the other people. It is only now when she realizes the danger she is in, once she is somewhat removed from it. Though she stands in the spent trappings of trauma, they tell her of past events, not of any future detriment to her.

"Are you okay?" Aberdeen queries to the empty niche. She walks with one foot in front of the next like she's treading a crack. She places her foot in front of each short shelving aisle before looking to see if anyone is there.

She finds the woman with the bloody hands in the third row and she is not alone. A man with a shock of white hair caked in drying blood lies prone on the floor, his arms held straight and close to his sides. The woman tucks a coat under the man's knees. Her hands are shaking so violently bits of blood not yet coagulated are flinging off of her, dotting the white of the melamine shelves. Aberdeen steels herself by looking at the dots. They remind her of the cochineal beetles that get pulverized into red dye, to redden textiles and lips.

The woman uses her employee smock to dab at a large gash on the head of the pharmacist. It is doing little good; the vest's rough, blue fabric is already soaked and dripping. The woman hasn't removed the pens from a plastic pocket near the top of the vest. They clink against the rings she wears on every finger, fat bands of cheap Black Hills gold and garnets perched on sterling silver hearts.

"It's not like I could leave like everyone else," she says to

Aberdeen. The woman with her nametag spelling out Vera looks up at Aberdeen and babbles more. "It's not like this is part of my job. He's new here. I don't even know his last name. But I couldn't leave him here to bleed."

Aberdeen crouches down at the feet of the man and adds her pea coat to the pile under his legs. She recalls something about needing to raise a person's legs above their head. But is that just when they're in shock? Do you want all the blood racing up to a crack in a skull so it can burst forth more quickly? She can't decide what to do so she leaves her coat there, aware of how much medical knowledge she lacks.

"You've probably saved this man's life," Aberdeen says. "Is he talking? Is he conscious?"

The man's eyes are small slits, the tip of his chin tilted upwards to the buzzing fluorescents overhead.

"He stopped talking when he was hit the third time."

"Ah" is the only response Aberdeen can get out of her mouth. The blood on the floor under the man swells in size, moving from salad plate, to Frisbee, to bathmat. It is viscous and more scarlet than the blood left in the Styrofoam trays under Hurt's favorite T-bone cuts. Aberdeen knows this man will die if he is not already dead.

She shakes her hands out. They're stiff and frozen and she doesn't want to touch a dying man with icy fingertips. Straddling him so as not to bump into any wounds on his body, she bends down and touches a patch of cheek clear of blood.

"Sir?"

She cranes her neck backwards to look at Vera. The woman has started humming something which Aberdeen doesn't recognize.

"Is an ambulance coming? Did you call 911?"

"Yes," Vera answers, twirling her rings about her knuckles, turning them rust-colored with blood. "But no one's come. I bet this is everywhere in the city. In the whole country."

Aberdeen wants to ask what she means by this but the man on the ground is her first priority. The lure of the group, the crowd has left her. Now there is a man at the edge of life in front of her. He is stepping out of it. He is going.

"Sir? We need to get you somewhere and get you help. Sir, can you hear me?"

A flip of his stubby lashes, nearly imperceptible, comes as a response.

Aberdeen squats down over him. She's careful not to put any weight on his torso. She uses her thumb and index finger to open his eyelids. The whites of his eyes show, the pupil and iris lost somewhere behind the shelf of his brow.

Aberdeen looks to Vera once more, keeping her fingers on the man's eyelids. "If we don't move him out of here, he's going to die."

It issues forth then – a sigh of words – and a summation of what is happening finally crosses Aberdeen's ears.

"We'll all die," he says, "without medicine."

Aberdeen releases his eyelids then but they don't close. They stay open, stay empty. The man is left possessed with eyes inoperable, globes of white and shocks of red webbing.

And somehow she knows that things won't be coming together again anytime soon. Not the pharmacist's eyelids, not the split in his head, not the city. While she was in the woods, the world changed.

Vera cries now, nods her head, makes the confirmation.

CHAPTER TWO

They lift him by his calves and the pits under his arms. Aberdeen is taller than Vera and she takes his torso so the blood can drain away from his head. She's calm enough, rational enough to realize that's what needs to happen. Vera flicks tears from her face like they're gnats and locks her arms around the man's feet.

Vera unlocks the partition door and they heave his frame through it. They are met with the mob. Moving, pushing people aside. There is a woman in her forties with hair the color of a magenta crayon leaning over the man. She spits onto the pharmacist's chest. The spit hovers on his coat, resisting soaking into the fabric like a clear drop of hot glue. Aberdeen wishes she had a hand to use, to swat the woman away. But they keep walking, pushing, stopping to shift the man's weight between women short and tall.

They pass people with ridiculous loot and Aberdeen considers the thieving might have been initiated by this unknown event but rallied by years of a depressed economy. There is a boy with a stack of unopened plastic bags held tight together at the top with a slightly melted seam. Another child with marker on his chin sprints by with a wad of tiny rectangles and flings them into the air. Numbers rain down and stick to Aberdeen's black hair and sloping shoulders. 2 for $5. $8.99. With nothing to signify any longer, they do more good as confetti. She whips her hair about and sends the price labels flying.

At a place down the sidewalk clear of feet and glass, Aberdeen bends her knees and lowers the pharmacist, feeling the strain in her thighs and ass. One of Vera's hands gives way and a leg clunks to the concrete hitting sharply on the heel. Aberdeen screws up her face at the impact. They get him to the ground with her coat tucked under his head.

There is tightness, solid like an unwanted hug, in Aberdeen's chest. But she figures it isn't caused by the exertion. The air is still harsh, still richer in poison than oxygen. Vera is having trouble as well. Her ribcage shrinks and lifts with a sharpness and speed that indicates physical danger.

"Are you asthmatic?" asks Aberdeen.

Vera shakes her head no and waves off the question with one flapping hand and a fist pressed up to her mouth to stifle a cough.

Aberdeen is happy to not have to share her medicine. It might be all she'll have for awhile. She pats at her purse, looking for the hard outline of the inhaler. It's there. She holds it for a second before letting it go.

It's as if the ambulance comes just to see the spectacle, because it stops on the opposite side of the street and the EMTs do not emerge. Aberdeen lifts her hands in the air and waves to them like she's flagging down a lover. She can see a man and a woman in the front of the vehicle, but they stay seated, the lines of seatbelts crossing their chests, plainly seen from the sidewalk corner.

Then a police car arrives and the paramedics are suddenly yanking open doors and pushing a gurney across the empty road. They are flanked by two officers. The cops have their hands on their riot sticks. Their faces are behind plastic shields held tight at their waists.

"Here," Aberdeen screams. "He's here."

The paramedics are wearing thick jumpsuits and firm boots. They lift the man like he's paper and shuffle him to the top of the gurney. The white sheet on the soft foam tracks an arc of blood with his placement. The police stand tall and quiet. Their eyes move rapidly over the mob, eyes darting as if they are dreaming, as if they are asleep.

"How long has he been this way?" the paramedics ask, both of them in unison, and Aberdeen expects one of them to murmur "jinx." One shines a light in the man's eyes. The other presses his fingers to his wrist and looks down.

Aberdeen looks to Vera. Vera holds her hands pinching at her waist and takes in swallows of air.

"Not sure. I got to him once the crowd parted. I seen him get hit three times. I think it was a metal rod or something like it. But it took me a bit to get to him, once they were done taking all the medicine."

The EMTs nod. A stethoscope is out. A plastic mask goes over the man's mouth and a clear bulb is depressed.

Aberdeen wants to tell them she talked with him, that before they carried him out of the store like the others were carrying out candy bars and car buffing mittens, he was alive. He wasn't well, but he had enough sense to know what was happening.

What *is* happening? she thinks, and realizes her answer may be in front of her.

She steps up to one of the policemen. He has a thick moustache arching over his lip and it twitches lightly when he removes his gaze from the crowd and studies her face. He looks her over as a hostile, a predator, something to be subdued.

"I'm at a loss. What's going on? I've been camping the last few days. Something about medicine? Are we out of drugs or something?" she asks.

But the paramedics are running with the gurney now, letting the weight of the man on the rolling table lift their feet. They make it over the asphalt on tiptoes. One of the EMTs spins in a pirouette when they reach the back of the ambulance, the lanyard about his neck flying perpendicular to his chest.

Instead of answering, helping, the police are backing away, shields still facing the crowd which seems ambivalent to their small presence. They cross the street. They buckle up. They drive away.

Vera smiles at Aberdeen. It looks to be a grin of thanks accompanied by more tears flowing down the woman's face.

"I best go with him, then. Not that I even know him. But someone should be with someone hurt so bad," she says to Aberdeen and leaves, walks over to the ambulance. They let her in the back of the vehicle. With sirens and lights on, they make way up a street with no moving cars, still insistent on announcing their coming and their going.

The soreness in her legs encourages her to sit down on the pavement, folding her legs under her in what they used to call sitting Indian-style but it occurs to her the term can't possibly be politically correct anymore. She's not sure people would care about something like political correctness right now. Aberdeen looks over at the crowd. They seem subdued, bored, the surging emotions of fear and indignation taking flight. Twos and threes are breaking off and leaving, as if the absence of fresh plasma and platelets no longer has them frenzied.

She lets her hands drop into her lap. She has blood on them, which was inevitable, but it upsets her all the same. She drags her palms on the pitted concrete until her hands turn into a swirled pattern of maroon from the iron and beige from the dirt. They won't be clean until she can make it home. If she can make it home.

Aberdeen gazes into the middle distance, until a pair of people materialize and catch her eye. One is old, a bit hunched at the back, and the other is young, chubby with sedentary youth. A grandmother and grandchild, she guesses. And there is something familiar about them.

Standing, she puts her hand to her eyes to block out the sun and gets a better look at the couple. Yes, she thinks, she does know them. Or recognizes them, at least.

Aberdeen raises her hands in front of her and waves them away. They seem intent on making their way into the milling crowd and give no sign of heeding her motions. She is immediately fearful of them continuing forward. What business does a woman in her eighties and a boy without a hair on his lip have in this chaos with the potential rekindling of violence, the possible resumption of rioting?

Then again, what business has she in it?

Her feet pick up and she intercepts them before they cross to the side of the street housing the remains of the drugstore. She nearly falls flat on her face, her foot rolling over a little plastic horse forgotten in the fray of plundering. Aberdeen kicks it away and watches the tiny Palomino skitter across the asphalt and disappear down a storm drain.

The elderly woman reaches into a reusable grocery bag on her wrist and brings forth a wooden rolling pin. The boy steps behind her, not in front her, clearly not a man yet. Seeing him up closer, Aberdeen realizes his size is out of proportion to his evident youth. He's eight, perhaps ten years of age.

She allows herself a bit of a laugh. "A rolling pin? Was that all you had? Why do I feel like I'm in a Tom and Jerry cartoon?"

"You live upstairs from us, don't you?" the woman asks.

"Yes, in apartment 5F. I've seen you both around the building. I never stopped to say hi when my husband and I dropped our boxes and furniture off early in the week. Guess I can say hi now."

"Good day to you then," she says and lowers the wooden roller. "I'm Myrtle Dover. This is my grandbaby, Louis."

Only when he hears his name does he emerge from behind his grandmother like a Sasquatch from behind a whip of an aspen. He extends his hand out to Aberdeen and she takes it. His hand is yielding, the skin on his palms degrees lighter than that of his wrists, arms, face.

"I'm Aberdeen Childress," she says, and for a moment things are cordial enough that she wishes she had a sitting room to escort them into, put them on a sofa, offer them a stale box of Thin Mints.

Louis pulls back his hand at the same time he says his hello. Aberdeen notices the tops of his ears have little points of cartilage under the skin, slight pyramids that make him look elfin, despite his lumbering size.

"You can't go in there. People are acting like beasts. I just helped carry a man out of the store. He was bludgeoned. He might be dying in an ambulance right now." Aberdeen does her best to convey the desperation of the situation. She thinks of her hands and holds them stiff in front of her, like she is showing off a set of nails in need of polish or a cuticle stick. "See? That was blood, until I got most of it off on the sidewalk."

Mrs. Dover nods her head in understanding and then starts to move forward again. "We've got to get in there, see what we can get. We've both got our needs. Ours isn't a household blessed by good health, Aberdeen." She says Aberdeen like she's said it a thousand times before, a warm reprimand on her lips.

"I can save you from making the effort," Aberdeen goes on, "because there is nothing left in there of use. At least there is no medicine left. Nothing. Not an ibuprofen on the floor to step on. Trust me, I've been to the pharmacy counter and back out. It's clean in there."

This does it. The woman stops and reaches up for her grandson's hand, such is his height and such is hers. She squeezes it, milking out a moment of comfort. She looks up into the boy's face and gives a smile replete with yellowed dentures, all the canines, incisors and molars the same molded blocks.

"Guess we'll have to work hard to keep our levels up, son."

"Yes, Gram," he responds.

Aberdeen takes in the pair. The boy overweight, the woman in tight socks and knock-off Birkenstocks, even in the chill of autumn. Diabetic, she guesses. Maybe even the both of them.

Mrs. Dover addresses Aberdeen again, releasing her grandson's hand. "Then I guess we've got a whole bunch of needles at home with nothing in them, doing no good to me. Not sure what I'll do until we can fill them. What do you do with an empty needle?"

Aberdeen shrugs her shoulders, knowing she has no answer for them. "I don't even know what's going on. I got up this morning and left the house without picking up a paper or turning on a radio or television. Of all the days I skipped NPR, this is my reward, I guess. My husband and I were camping, getting out of the city for a bit after moving into the apartment. We were taking some time together, just the two of us."

Louis speaks then, his eyes are lit, disbelieving. "You came out here not knowing what was happening? You went in with all those people over there?"

Aberdeen considers her poor excuse for throwing caution into a very strong wind, a tornado. Primal urges. Pack mentality. She chooses instead to stick to her original goal.

"I'm almost out of my asthma medicine. I thought I'd take a walk, get a new inhaler, maybe stop for black tea somewhere." She drifts off after she mentions the tea, as if tea has relevance here, now.

"It was the terrorists," spits Mrs. Dover.

"Terrorists?"

"Yes, Aberdeen," she says with aplomb, "don't know why we all been having to take our shoes off at the airports for years and letting folks take looks at us naked when they didn't bother with any of that."

This conversation is a waving line, thinks Aberdeen. She's desirous for a straight explanation.

"Could you please tell me what is going on? From the beginning, if you would."

It's Louis that answers. "We don't watch much television at home. Gram's eyes aren't good enough to catch much anyway. So we listen to the radio when we eat our eggs and toast each morning. There is a man we listen to everyday. He's always angry at something, usually how there aren't any jobs and only really rich and really poor people now. But a few days ago he was talking about the terrorists bombing all the places that make medicines. He was even talking about places in other countries that make medicines being turned into balls of fire. I think he said balls of fire, but maybe he didn't. People were hoping things would get better but then last night there were more fires and more bombs in more buildings. He said the bad guys were on round two, but I'm not sure what he means."

"Someone's bombed, what, the pharmaceutical plants? And storage facilities? More than once?"

"Believe so," answers the old woman. She absently touches a silver bracelet at her wrist. It's not meant to be pretty. It has etchings of her blood type, her allergies, and all the things killing her.

"So people are freaking out, grabbing what they can of medicines? That explains things." Aberdeen tells herself she can handle the situation. She tells herself knowing is half the battle. It's cliché, but she believes it now because if she doesn't, she will run home and start planning a trip to Europe or anywhere that still has albuterol and tetracycline.

"Not just in this city. Every city in America, from what I gather," says Mrs. Dover. "The first bombs made people worry. These last ones made them act out. I do believe we are all on our own when it comes to drugs. Our bodies will learn to live or I suppose they won't."

Aberdeen counters. "You're making this sound dire. I'm sure there are stocks of medicines around, warehouses that weren't bombed. Even if there aren't, those drug companies, they have tons of money. They'll set up new shops and have Paxil and Viagra back to the public in no time. Weeks, maybe, but no more. No way."

"Maybe," says the elderly lady and levels a stare at Aberdeen. "The big online pharmacies and the giant super stores with memberships had all their pills bought by rich folks after the first attack. With the one just happened, people without means get desperate, take what's left."

"I just can't believe all of America would be without medicine of any kind. What would I do if I stepped on a bit of tin can? What about all the people locked away in psych wards? There would be disaster everywhere, everyday. We'd be reduced to what we were all born with," and she considers what she has said. "That'd be horrible." Aberdeen checks herself, noticing her voice is rising. She doesn't want to provoke an asthma attack. Her near-empty cylinder may be all she has for a while.

"I'd believe it. The people with money might have enough pills to last them awhile. Don't think that the medicines aren't there somewhere, but do you think they'll waste them on people like *us*?" Mrs. Dover says the word with the similar drawing in of breath that begins a yawn.

"I guess it depends on what kind of people we are, then. Worth something or worth nothing. I guess those are the two options," says Aberdeen.

"The only two," confirms the woman. Louis nods his head in solemn agreement with his grandmother. Aberdeen wonders if he understands the implications of these attacks. She wonders if he would be more worried if all the confectionaries had been blown to bits, all the factories in China that make his toys leveled to smoking ash.

The smell of burning hits Aberdeen stronger now and the wind picks up and moves her hair away from her ears. Her eyes begin to water. It's coming from somewhere, probably miles away, but the caustic breeze is here, strong gales of manmade compositions.

"Look at that," says Louis. His finger is pointing to the crowd coming out of the drug store. They are quieting, coalescing, observing instead of acting out.

Aberdeen turns and sees those people left, perhaps a hundred, are paying attention to a woman standing on a stack of magazines. The tower shifts beneath her feet as the glossy pages slide against one another. She rides the motion by making slight corrections with her knees and her feet. In constant movement, her voice sounds out. Aberdeen is surprised there were magazines left after the looting to create a makeshift dais.

"They won't let us die! We are the hearts of this country. They can't *afford* to let us all die." The woman has her jacket over her head. She's swinging it like a lasso. A button flips off and pings the road, drawing eyes away from her spectacle for a moment before they return.

"There is medicine. It will come. We all need to have faith," and she pauses here. Next off is her blouse, a green cotton piece with lace about the cuffs and neckline. She maintains her perch, the cups of her bra spilling over at the tops with leavened falsity.

Mrs. Dover claps a hand over Louis's eyes and the boy doesn't pry away the fingers.

"But for now, enjoy your freedom from the meds," the woman screams. The crowd responds with hooting and an arm reaches up to her and pulls her firmly back down to the earth.

Aberdeen is feeling the air in her lungs now. Like she can taste it with her bronchial sacs. The bitter burn has nestled in. She needs to go soon, get indoors.

The fear of the crowd is returning with the return of shouting, the return of cacophonous noise. The proper, human fear of other humans. She's left her beastly self behind for now.

"I'll walk you both back to the apartment building. I think we should leave now. Before things get violent."

"Don't you go bossing me about," says Mrs. Dover. But the mention of an escort sends her small feet moving in a tight circle and then she's taking short, shuffling steps away from the road, back home. Louis takes her arms and lifts up with his shoulders, bearing her weight.

Aberdeen thinks perhaps she was supposed to come here and help the white-haired man and stay to intercept these two. She has an image of them in the crowd. The old woman, though substantial in girth, would be pushed under and walked upon by all present. Louis would be rocking under a check stand. Maybe not. But Aberdeen realizes she doesn't have much faith in people tending to themselves. Not now, at least.

"I'll see you all the way to your apartment," Aberdeen offers, but figures that point was implicit in her initial suggestion.

Mrs. Dover gives her a tired lifting of her eyebrows. "Suppose that makes me feel all right."

Wind pushes at Aberdeen's back. She removes her coat from where it's been in a ball under her arm. The corduroy is wrinkled and the channels of fabric are crusted and flaking off bits of blood, a few pebbles dropping from the folds of the coat. There is a small piece of skin on the collar, not hers, ashen and out of place like a bit of tripe in a vegetable stew. She flicks it off with a thumbnail and swings the jacket over her shoulders.

A bit of white catches her eye as they walk. Then more comes in whirling flakes. Louis raises his face to the sky to accept the precipitation. "Snow," he smiles.

The unpleasant tang is heavier now than it's been and her eyes are burning. Snow in early October isn't unheard of, she thinks, but it's not nearly cold enough. Not close.

White is covering the parts in their hair and the edges of their shoes. They all stop and Aberdeen swings around in a circle and sees the blizzard coming at them from their right, following the flow of another empty street running perpendicular to the one they just left. Except the bits of white aren't coming from the sky. They seem to be riding the wind. Aberdeen looks up and she can see where the blue of sky shows above the bits, clear and empty.

She bends down and takes up a handful of the white stuff. It is jagged strips and miniscule spheres all ringed with a crispy black burn.

"It's Styrofoam," she announces to the other two and then hands off the contents in her palm to Louis who gazes at it for a moment before trying to fling it away. Most of it sticks to him with static strength and he picks off the false snow with his fingers a bit at a time.

"Explains the smell, I guess," ventures Aberdeen. She knows somewhere something is burning away. Was it just the packaging for the drugs? The drugs that keep them all sane and alive? Or was the Styrofoam what remained after the fires, taking to the wind, persevering like its design dictated? Perhaps it would last for thousands of years? There would be a strata, a layer of white in the soil for good now. So even when this all passes, she thinks, and when we dig into the earth come spring, we will see it all again.

We'll recall the time we all thought we were going to die.

She smiles. At least the foam will increase drainage for stronger roots to take hold.

They pick up walking again at a plodding pace set by Mrs. Dover. The walk is quiet once they are clear of the crowd and they take their time in getting back to the apartments. Louis moves his head around like a cat watching a laser pointer, full up with potential energy, eyeing all motions and people that come anywhere near the three of them.

The slick soles of Aberdeen's shoes float over the beads of polystyrene all the way back to her new apartment, the woody dust from the packing boxes and her unsettled husband. The spheres bear her up instead of squishing beneath her. They are the backs of chemical ants, fantastically strong, conveying her forward, conveying her home.

CHAPTER THREE

Aberdeen makes sure to walk the Dovers up to their door and see them safely inside. When the door swings wide, she can smell burnt fish and horehound candies. The old woman pats Aberdeen on the back of the hand and Louis gives her a cockeyed smile before closing the door behind them.

Then she's back in her own apartment, calling out to Hurt. She closes the door and stacks three boxes, one on top of the other, in front of it. She cocks her head, looks at it. Instead, she opts for locking the door only and nudges the boxes out of the way with the sides of her legs. Barricading herself in seems fatalistic and self-absorbed. What would someone take if they came into her house? Her terrariums? Her sleeves of Ritz crackers? What little she has, they can take, she thinks, as long as they do no real harm.

"Hurt," she yells out in each room she passes. He doesn't answer but she finds him in the bathroom with a plastic razor dragging over the skin of his Adam's apple. Half of his face is a mask of ivory cream, the other half is pocked with pores wide and red. He taps the razor against the sink basin and rinses it in a trickle of water from the faucet.

"You're just shaving?" she says, knowing there is

something incredulous about her voice, partially due to the current situation, partially due to the fight they had last night.

"Um," he says with lips in a pout to get at the softer whiskers around his smile wrinkles. "Just because I'm not leaving to go to class I shouldn't drop the personal grooming routine, right? Unless you like hair against your cheek?" He winks.

"No, I mean, you're shaving at a time like this?"

"What time *is* this?" he asks back. His stubble decorates the cracked porcelain like bits of Halloween glitter reflecting the trio of lights over the sink. Black, gold, red.

"I take it you haven't turned on the television? Or looked out the windows? Or done anything?"

Hurt stares ahead at the mirror and continues shaving. "I've been trying to log into my student account, look some stuff over before the online class starts in an hour, but their server must be down. Hope they know it. I don't want my grades taking a hit because I can't sit my ass in a virtual classroom."

Aberdeen takes the razor away from Hurt and nicks her thumb on the blade. She tosses it in the sink. Her blood flows readily over her already tinted, tainted, bloodied skin.

"Shit," she cries and bumps Hurt out of the way with her hips. She flips the handle of the hot water all the way to blast and squirts three viscous dollops of soap on her hands. Don't let his blood get in my cut, she thinks. Don't let anything into you that doesn't belong there.

"Aberdeen, what the fuck?"

"See this," she says, nodding downward at her hands. "I've got blood on my hands. And I don't mean my own. I've just carried a bloodied man out of the drug store with his body fluids all over me. Who knows if he's sick or has some disease?"

"What?" Hurt says, a spot of shaving cream on his earlobe. He stands back and takes in his wife, eyes scanning her from top to bottom and then back up again. She watches him appraise her filthy coat, the Styrofoam in the collar of her shirt.

She picks up her toothbrush from its holder and scrubs under her nails with it, circling the cuticles and jabbing at the hangnails and drawing more blood in the process. She can get a new toothbrush from under the counter. That's one thing she has put away: a stack of Oral-B brushes inscribed with a dentist's name who quit practicing when Aberdeen was still in college.

"It's chaos out there. Something has happened to our medical supplies, medicines, I mean. We leave town for a few days and come back to catastrophe. Not that I would trust all the information I've heard, but people are looting, acting crazy. The man was a pharmacist at the drug store. Another woman and I had to get him outside, get him where help was available." She takes another hit of soap and repeats the whole process.

Hurt stands still with his arms at his side. He's got three wrinkles above his nose and his jaw is slack. He shuts his eyes and swallows so hard she can hear him open and close his esophagus over the sound of water flowing.

"Is this your reaction?" she asks. "To just shut down? I'm not accusing," she hedges, "just saying."

"No, what?" is what he comes out with. "No more medicine? For how long? Why?" He rubs the shaving cream off his earlobe and onto his fingers and looks at it like he has no sense of why it's there.

"Mrs. Dover says it was terrorists. They blew up pharmaceutical factories or something. The first strike was a couple days back. And then there were more attacks last night." Aberdeen feels okay about the state of her palms and fingers now and turns the faucet off and wipes her hands on a towel unraveling at its bottom hem.

"Who the hell is Mrs. Dover?" Hurt moves back to the sink and leans against it.

"Our neighbors, well, they live two floors down. She's an old woman raising her grandkid, from what I can tell."

29

"Are they nice?" Hurt asks.

"What, the Dovers? Yeah." Aberdeen lets out a sharp breath, a physical reaction to her husband's penchant for avoidance.

"I could try fiddling with the television. We've got that adaptor box. Might be able to get a channel or two and see if we can get some news." He flips back on the water and cleans his face of the residue from the shaving cream and dries himself on the same towel Aberdeen used, right on the fibers damp with water and her blood and the blood of the bludgeoned pharmacist.

They move into the biggest room in the apartment which will eventually be used for sitting, watching movies, eating, making love. That is, if society doesn't collapse. As a present for Hurt's birthday two years ago, when they still had money to burn, Aberdeen bought him a modest flat panel television. It was an off-brand and the sound tinny from the long side speakers, but it did well enough when they wanted to watch old black and whites. There is a rectangular box next to the television now, never opened. It's a digital adaptor, meant to pick up local signals. Neither of them is too tech savvy. Aberdeen wonders if she should fetch someone like Louis. Most kids know how to make machines work; part of her believed that their DNA was changed if they were born after the invention of the internet.

"How do you suppose it works? Just plug it in?" Aberdeen lifts the lip of the box and pulls out the white plastic bit of technology shaped like a fat magazine along with a three-page operating manual. It seems short on explanation. Somehow reading directions on how to get network television while the country yearns for medicine and stability seems bourgeois and strangely distracting.

"Plug it in to what exactly?" Hurt asks as he takes up the box and turns the cord in his hand. "Wait, there's only one round metal tube with a weird metal prong thing in its middle."

"I've got this," she says, "it is just like the DVD player, I think."

She fumbles about the back of the television, looking for the right hole for the right plug. Looking for a connection to something concrete will make things work and turn on and make sense. She finds it and shoves it in and then turns on the television. The digital doohickey runs itself through set up while they look with passion at the download screen.

Once the channels are up they scan through them all. There is news on each of the 13 channels they get, some of the visuals deteriorating to pixilated scrambles when they move to the left of the adaptor box. They pick the channel with the clearest signal. Hurt folds up in front of the screen balanced on his mother's hope chest. Aberdeen stands, arms crossed.

They watch and they listen.

"Again, emergency responders in all areas of the country are asking the public to stay inside their homes. Police are attempting to maintain peace and are authorized to use riot suppression tactics if groups or individuals are perceived as a threat."

The anchorwoman tugs lightly at a gauzy scarf wrapped around her throat.

"They never touch their accessories when they're on the air. Notice that? She must be worried, too," chimes Hurt, pointing at the television.

The talking head continues. "State and local governments are issuing different laws and curfews based on factors such as population density, proximity to chemical disaster sites and current incidences of reported violence. For now officials are refusing to comment on the number of pharmaceutical warehouses and chemical plants damaged by the apparently coordinated and synchronized explosions earlier this week and the new attacks late last evening."

Aberdeen wonders why they won't put a number on the destruction. She thinks that it must be grand, expansive, a catastrophe so massive that ambiguity is the only thing big enough to mask it.

"Sources linked jointly to the FBI and DEA are claiming while no one group has taken responsibility for the attacks, the federal government has recently received a paper letter signed by a man calling himself Caesar. The man claims he is the appointed representative of a conglomerate of drug cartels with branches in the Americas, Africa and South Asia."

The anchorwoman looks at the teleprompter a moment too long, a pause that reaches between her eyes and mouth and stops her for a moment. Her eyes flicker, she looks down at a sheet of paper, looks again into the camera. The anchorwoman is reading the screen with its scrolling text, but Aberdeen has the feeling she's being stared at by the woman in disbelief, in incomprehension.

"Now, yes, okay we are getting new information about the letter sent to the head of the DEA. We have a few lines to share with you from the correspondence. The man calling himself Caesar claims the attacks on major pharmaceutical factories and storage sites in North America and at other unspecified locations supplying the United States with medical goods were justified."

Aberdeen watches the woman take a breath. Then she says on air, "The lines read as follows: The relentless so-called War on Drugs that the United States Government has engaged in for the past several decades is now brought to American soil. We will no longer play defense. We will bring the war to your citizens and free them of your drugs. Your country has pushed its own drugs for years. Now it will be forced to welcome us with open arms when the masses get hungry for the cessation of pain. And we will sell to your people all the chemicals we have to offer. "

The woman on the screen presses her fingers against a receiver in her ear canal. "The letter itself is over fifty pages in length but the government insists on keeping the bulk of the letter's contents private at this time."

At this announcement, Hurt hurls the remote at the base of the trunk.

"Whoa," Aberdeen responds. "Babe, it's okay."

He's standing up now, his legs extending upward like a bit of scaffolding. He bites his lip and retrieves the remote. She sees the remote has lost its rubber number 4 button but Hurt seems oblivious.

"Who the fuck do these people think they are? Do you know how many people are on drugs in this country? Not pot or meth. I mean antibiotics and fucking Zoloft. We're in big trouble. Big, huge trouble." Hurt pauses and Aberdeen takes him by the shoulders, holds him.

"And you," he says, pulling back and looking at her chest. "What are you going to do without your asthma medicine? What happens if you have an attack and we can't get you breathing again? Huh?"

Aberdeen doesn't have an answer for this. Her lungs have been inundated with Proventil since she was seven years old. If only her bronchia would hold a reserve of it. Or just stop trying to seize up, quit, hang a closed sign on her bony sternum.

She pulls herself in close to him and puts her head on the place where his pectoral meets his collarbone. "I'll be okay. We'll get rid of all the cardboard today and I'll be better off. And I'll have to find a new home for the one houseplant that makes my nose itch."

Hurt smiles a little at this. "You love that fern. We could just put it outside the front door. On the landing. By the time it gets really cold, things will be back to normal."

Her mind tells her to say yes, so she does. But her guts say no, not that quickly. Her lungs laugh outright.

"Good idea," she says. She promises herself when he's not around she'll pitch the maidenhair fern off one of the brick windowsills. It's her or it, and she's the one with opposable thumbs.

And while she thinks of what the fern will look like falling five stories, lacy fronds a green V with a plastic pot as a torpedo head, her chest tightens. She knows unless something is done about the medicine, about the maintenance of life, she will be in trouble.

She releases Hurt and walks over to a box near the hall closet. It's an approximation of a wardrobe with an aluminum rod at the top and a side that peels back in a big L. She's had a thought about possible salvation.

"Are my purses in here?" she asks herself but Hurt answers.

"No idea. And you shouldn't be digging in there and stirring up the cardboard fibers. Let me do it."

Hurt takes over then and she lets him, standing well away from the box with her hand over her nose and mouth likes she's ready to give out a secret.

"Look for my purses at the bottom. If I have a spare inhaler, it might be in there, in one of the bags. I'm not sure, but maybe."

Hurt digs down and flings out a colorful snake of a scarf that coils on the floor. He sighs and looks back at her.

"You have too much winter wear."

"Just find the bags, please."

He's pulling out the purses one by one and dropping them to the floor by their straps and handles. His body is pitched over in the box. He thumps at the bottom with his hand making sure he hasn't missed one.

Aberdeen scoops them up and takes them to the center of the room where there aren't any open boxes to make eddies of cardboard dust about her. There are eleven bags. She only uses three of them consistently. It was stupid to bring them all in the move, she thinks. But she believes that if one gives something away they could potentially use or need, they may not ever get it back.

She checks the side pockets, the little zippered nooks of the main bodies of the hobos and baguettes and clutches. The words for the purses go through her mind while she rips through a bag and tosses it aside when she finds nothing. Pictures of men with soiled undershirts carrying around thick, crusty sticks of bread instead of the clichéd stick and sack of fabric pass through her mind.

The last bag is a thing of the evening, navy blue sequins sewn onto a circular shape with a silken cord for slinging over the shoulder. There is nothing in the purse but the inhaler. The medicine label is faded and peeled away at the top. She lifts it from the bag and Hurt comes over to look.

"Check the expiration," he says.

Pulling the canister out of the yellow plastic holder, she spins the cold metal in her hand and reads the black number out loud. It's years in the past from the current date.

"That's very expired," he points out and takes the metal out of her hand. He rolls it around in his palms like a prayer wheel against a shrine. He cups his hands around it. Holds it up to his heart.

Aberdeen puts her hand out for it and he gives it back gently like it's a final specimen of human reproduction or the last diamond ever mined. She pushes the canister back into the plastic delivery system careful not to depress too hard and have any of the off medicine escape into the ether.

"It will still work, Hurt. I've used expired medicine before. It may just not be as effective is all. Plus, it's probably a third full. It's something."

Hurt picks up the shiny clutch and hands it back to her. "Put it back in there for now. Just in case people come stealing. They won't be looking for medicine in a sparkly doohickey."

Aberdeen smiles at this, tucks her backup inhaler in the slight wave of the satin liner, zips the bag up. "No, they'll only be going through my purses looking for money to buy medicine on a black market, babe."

"I'd never let anyone in here to take what we have, Aberdeen. I'd protect you."

Aberdeen says sure and thinks of Hurt in a bathing suit this past summer: thin arms, red speckles on his torso, hopping up and down on scalding pavement because his feet are tender, uncallused.

"I believe you'll always protect me," she says and kisses him on the nose, right above a pock mark left by a torrent of chicken pox scratching when he was five.

He takes the purse back to the cardboard box and tucks it at the very bottom. He covers it with the other bags, the scarves, jackets and hats. He buries her hope under a mountain of knitwear.

"I will protect you," he says, closing the box with one hand and picking at his chin with the other. "As long as I'm here."

Aberdeen wants to ask him what he means by this. But then the shouting starts from the center of the building, somewhere outside their front door. It has the pitch of anger, low and guttural.

Hurt cocks his head to his shoulder and then sticks a finger in his ear. "I'm not the only one hearing that, am I?"

"No," says Aberdeen and she moves towards the door and the landing.

"Why," she asks, her hand on the doorknob, "would you think that?"

CHAPTER FOUR

"Don't go out there," Hurt says and reaches for the back of her pants like a father would catch the belt loop of a child about to step into traffic.

"I've got to see what's happening. We can't just barricade ourselves away." She reaches behind and pries his fingers away.

The landing outside looks the same as it did when she came back earlier from her sortie with herd mentality. There are three other doors on their floor besides their own. There is one to each side of the square layout and Aberdeen realizes she doesn't know the residents behind any of them. The one across from them, over the hole of the stairwell, has a faux-concrete rabbit sitting on a welcome mat deprived of the W and the M from years of scuffing feet.

The hollering is louder out on the landing. Immediately she knows that it's drifting up from below them, possibly from the bottom-most floor with its heavy glass door and rows of brass mailboxes.

Hurt comes out after her, shutting the door quietly behind him. He folds his arms about his stomach and hunches over slightly.

Aberdeen shakes her head at him, unsure at what she's

trying to communicate but certain of the need to be quiet and listen. She walks to the railing around the central stairwell and leans her head out over it. It is the second time today she feels she's reduced to skulking about, snooping and checking for signs of predation.

She can't see anything, but the yelling continues. It's definitely a man, but his words are distorted and bounced off walls and concrete and metal for five stories. He's not directly under the hole gaping upwards to her ears. This man, she thinks, knows nothing of using acoustics to help deliver a message.

Aberdeen turns and looks at her husband. He's barefoot and in his lounge pants, the bottom part of a track suit missing its jacket, frayed at the heels from him walking on the fabric instead of rolling it into cuffs.

"You're not dressed to go and see what's up. But I'm going down there."

"No," is all he says but doesn't move to stop her. He knows better, she thinks.

"But you should take something with you," he adds and opens the door back into the apartment. He returns a moment later with a stubby grapefruit knife with an orange handle. He hands it to her and she takes it and places it in the gap of her pants at the hips. The dull teeth make their presence known on her pelvic bone.

She says, "I'll make sure he's thoroughly segmented if I have to," but Hurt is in no mood to laugh.

Aberdeen knows he could have just as easily gone into their bedroom and put on some shoes as he retrieved a bendable hand-me-down knife from her mother's cutlery drawer.

"You okay?" she questions him. She'd like an honest answer. She thinks of pulling the knife on him in jest, but wonders if it would rip at her skin upon flourishing it about. A morbid silliness has taken hold of her and she welcomes it in the chaos of the strange, fall day.

"Why do you need to go down there? Who cares what that dude is saying? He's upset, I'm sure. Like all of us." Hurt rubs at a solid line of wrinkle about his eyebrows. "He could be psychotic. Do you even know how many people are fucking crazy, Aberdeen?"

Gobs. All of us. Or is he looking for a number? she wonders.

"The man is just scared, I'm sure. He probably needs someone to talk him down. Plus, even if he's a crazy, he can't have been off his meds for more than a few days. It'd be an unlikely event he ran out right at the time of the first terrorist bombings but I guess it's possible."

"It doesn't take a pharmaceutical apocalypse to make some people drop their medications. Haven't you played super hero already today? You saved a man's life. Can we leave this guy to someone else?"

"I can't," she says and she means it.

Hurt throws his hands and arms back like he's bungled a catch and lost a game.

"If you get shot, they won't waste pain killers on you at the hospital."

"I love you, too, Hurt," Aberdeen smiles. It is said in earnest.

Down the stairs she goes. On the third floor she catches a face looking out of the thin crack of an open door. It closes lightly as she passes and as soon as her feet are back on the stairs it creaks back to a slit.

She gets a glimpse of the man from the second floor before going down to the very bottom. She's concerned, but she's not dim. She checks his hands for anything shiny or metal or heavy. She sees nothing when he passes in front of the stairwell other than he hasn't the use of his legs. His pacing is done with wheels holding up a leather chair.

If I can't escape someone crippled, Aberdeen thinks, then I

deserve to get my ass handed to me.

His words are clear now. He yells about lambs and slaughter and addiction and normalcy. His wheels move back and forth on the black-marked linoleum of the entrance.

"I'm coming down to talk," she says aloud. It isn't the most inspiring lead in, but it is better than surprising him.

The man looks around and then looks up the flight of stairs. He tries to locate her face and lifts his nostrils. His face is maroon, bearded, weary. His reaction is to a disembodied voice.

"Who do you think you are to stop me voicing my opinions? You God? Are you one of the crazy people who will come and kill me, one of the so-called normals, when you don't get your medicines every shitting hour and you start thinking I'm an alien or a pot roast to carve? Eh? Is this just the pinnacle of shit, the tip of the crap pyramid that this country has become these last few years?"

She holds her hands up in front of her and doesn't proceed down the stairs. The man is off. Is it the crazy ones who worry about crazy ones losing control? She's more worried about her monthly cramps when she doesn't have Pamprin. She worries about running out of hydrogen peroxide and the Tums Hurt eats after a mound of sautéed peppers.

"Just came down to see if you want someone to talk to. You're probably scaring the people in this building more than they're already scared. If that's possible."

The man uses his hands to maneuver his wheelchair to face the stairs. He has a decrepit red bandana around one of his wrists. It seems ephemeral; if Aberdeen were to touch it, it would fall away to pieces.

"I don't give two shits about that," he goes on. Aberdeen isn't sure he can see her from his vantage point and she gives thanks to the god of stairwells if he can't. "All the good Americans, the ones who don't need drugs for everything are the victims in this. Do you see me crying like they do because they can't afford a new car every other year even though they've got the good jobs? I don't need to hide my anxiety in pills. No I don't. And for that I'm gonna be a lamb. A lamb for the slaughter."

"Well, I'll stay up here. We can talk with some space between us." Aberdeen tries for distraction. "What apartment do you live in? What's your name?"

"Why the hell would I tell you? You and your husband haven't been here long. I've spent more time taking a single shit on my toilet than you've spent time in this place. You two new to slumming it and you want to come down here and tell me what I can say in my god-damned apartment building that I've been in since it was built and I got my subsidy? What's my name," he laughs. "What's *your* name?"

"Aberdeen," she answers and then wonders if she should have given him another name. She'll only feel okay if he gives up his name. Otherwise he'll have all the power. At least she has the upper ground. Literally.

"Which city you named after?"

"Not sure I was."

He lets go of the wheels and runs his hands along his thighs. He has white hair with a few streams of black that hits just above the nape of his neck. Aberdeen guesses he's a veteran, most likely from the country's stint in Vietnam.

"Were you in the service?" she says and takes two steps down the last flight of stairs and sits on a step. The sharp edge digs into her ass and her knees are thrust up to her chin.

He can see her now. He looks her over. She wonders if he does this to all people, wondering if they could lift him if he were to tip out of his chair. Or maybe just to women, whether they could find him sexual and enticing enough to straddle his broken legs? The set of his lips doesn't supply a clue.

"Nah, just worked at the Army/Navy Store for thirty years, girl." He laughs at himself and Aberdeen gives him a grin. It was a stupid question.

"What do you do?" he asks and she's thankful he's not too angry to be waylaid by small talk.

She's almost embarrassed to say it. Her work isn't exactly as epic as service to the motherland. "A little of everything. I teach classes on crafting. I sell terrariums online and in stores."

He snorts the way an old man can with ample phlegm and malcontent. "The hell is a terrarium?"

"Uh," she prepares to explain the absurdity of her occupation, "it's a container, usually glass, with a bunch of small plants in it. Like a miniature biome. They're very delicate and pretty."

"A bunch of nature under containment, eh? I guess I could see why people would like something like that." He rotates the bandana on his wrist around and around, bringing the knot back to the top of his spotted hand.

"We do what we can to make a bit of money and still stay happy, don't we?"

The wheelchair man looks behind him, twisting around his spine like it's soldered in place. It might be, Aberdeen thinks.

"So you the self-appointed guardian of this building while we all run about screaming and crying about the sky falling?" He sniffs again, clears his throat and swallows away whatever was giving him problems.

Aberdeen hasn't thought much of taking on a role. She's doing her best trying to be her. She's not sure she could ignore the problem, the people, lock herself away inside her tiny apartment to watch her husband struggle with building a career and her own dying slowly from lack of need, want. She thinks if what's happening with the drugs keeps happening for a long while, she'll need to do something. It might as well be helping.

"I think we can all look out for one another, don't you? I bet you've had all kinds of experiences where you've had to watch the back of others." Aberdeen rubs her feet on the stairs making swirls out of the dirt and grit from the outside world.

They sit in the quiet of the building. Someone opens and shuts a door floors above. If Aberdeen really tries, she swears she can hear her husband breathing hard five floors over her head. She doesn't look up; she doesn't want the man to feel like he's being monitored. Paranoia is the problem at hand, she thinks.

The man looks at her some more, takes her all in. He spends a minute or two on each part of her body. He nods to himself and says something that sounds like "suitable" under his breath. She has the queer thought not to appear hostile or Vietnamese. Not that she could be mistaken as anything other than muttish European, but still, she sits still, tries not to squirm while she's under intense observation.

"Well," she says at last, "what do you think?"

"Bout what?" he says, still looking.

"Me, I guess."

"You'll be okay, I think. At least you have the sack to come down here and get me to shut up."

Her arms are aching from the events of the morning. It isn't just from carrying an adult male around. It's where she keeps her stress. She weaves it into the fibers of her triceps and shoulders and the bits on her wrists that ache with carpal tunnel when she digs too long in hard soil. There is a smile on her lips when she stretches her arms out in front of her. Relax your body, she reminds herself. The situation is just beginning. You can't hold it all inside. You'll be more nerve than muscle and bone.

"That's a compliment I'd like to take," she says. "So, if you need to talk, you can come get me. You don't need to holler yourself hoarse for everyone to hear."

"You live upstairs, girl. How am I supposed to get up there? No elevator."

Aberdeen remembers now. She's not even sure how the building is allowed not to have one. It seems like it's in defiance

43

of codes or statutes. Maybe that's why the rent is so dirt cheap. She doesn't want to give the man her phone number. There must be a way to communicate.

"I suppose you could just yell up the stairwell for me. I'll come if I'm at home. I bet I will be. I bet we'll all be staying in more, now."

"I'm old but I still know a man or two in the military. Fucking cartels hit plants, storage centers, everything they could screw with a bomb. Won't surprise me if this is just the beginning. They won't stop what they've started." He pulls his bandana around again and changes subject. "I'm the only one on the first floor. I hear everybody get their mail. My family room wall is just the sound of people putting metal keys into little metal doors, all thunking and slamming."

"I'll close mine quietly," Aberdeen gathers her feet under her and stands. "So do I get to know your name or not?" She uses the appearance of height to her advantage. She finds herself placing her hands on her hips, raising her chin.

"Nope," the man says and rolls away from the staircase and out of Aberdeen's sight.

She leans her head back and sees Hurt leaning over the stairwell, his torso giving against the rail and his shirt crinkled up about his chest making him look busty. Aberdeen waits until she can hear the man glide his chair into his apartment and shut the door. She speaks to Hurt, using a voice that is half whisper, half annoyance.

"Good support. I felt like I had a fucking gargoyle behind me!"

"What?" he yells down. She can see the dark hole of his throat.

She shakes her head and climbs the stairs, staying silent until she's back in front of Hurt. He goes into the apartment first, an odd smirk on his face. Aberdeen follows and locks the door.

"You're in contention. You're in the running to be the new

Mother Teresa," Hurt hugs her and pushes against the door to check the seal.

"Nice, babe. Don't think I do all of this out of moral concerns. I'm scared shitless about this and I don't want my fear to be cultivated in a place where some nutter is hollering about slaughtered baby sheep all day long."

"I'm not buying it," he says. "You really do care."

Aberdeen releases the hug and moves to the edge of the couch. She swipes a roll of paper towels off the armrest and sits on it with her legs in front of her. She looks out the only window in the room, a double pane of glass. It's two windows, really. A strip of drywall, a stud between the clear rectangles that open out over the front of the building. It also frames the view of the back of a billboard. The metal struts and cakes of pigeon shit give no indication of the advertisement on the other side, the vertical surface that faces away from the apartment.

"Maybe I do," she says.

Hurt sits next to her. Their thighs touch. "You think he's on medication? He was yelling about how he's fine and all the crazies will take out people like him."

"What's that quote from Shakespeare? Something like blah blah doth protest too much? That's him. He's afraid of himself. I bet he's on something. The man's in a wheelchair. He's not the picture of health. Physically or mentally, most likely."

Hurt takes his wife's hand and holds it in his own. "Distraction might be the best way to deal. I know I'm going to do my classes online, go to work at the vet, watch out for you. Just you and me, sticking together and letting the wilds pass outside our door." He stops then and Aberdeen can see him thinking. He licks his lips when he's taking something under consideration. "I guess I'm going to just go on with life for now. That's my plan. Be normal. I'll be as normal as I can possibly be."

Aberdeen watches the floor at the bottom of the door and

sees the light from the landing move about and then go out. Feet in front of the door. Then there's a knock.

Hurt is the one up, the one looking through the peephole and then looking back at Aberdeen with a crease in his forehead. "You can't see out of this!"

"Someone painted over it," she says, recalling it was just one thing she had listed in her 'con' column about taking the apartment. She vows to take a scraper to it tomorrow but knows she might not have any luck. They might have a window in their door meant for the eye, allowing nothing to be seen.

"Just open it, Hurt."

He pulls it open wide and catches his elbow on the wall with the violent swing. He holds it with his palm, trying to cup away the pain of a pissed off funny bone.

Louis and Mrs. Dover stand there. Louis has his body touching that of his grandma's, just as he posed earlier in the day. She is his life support system. Love and security flows through touching of skin on skin. Aberdeen can see it in how the fine hair on his arms mingles with the yarn of the woman's sweater. Charge. Like attracting like.

Mrs. Dover holds a thick paper plate of tan cookies in front of her chest. She eyes Hurt.

"You okay? Nothing makes me madder than smacking my bones on things. You scream if you need to."

Hurt holds up a finger and flaps his elbow around at a sharp angle, finishes a funky little dance of nervous pain. "I'm okay, thank you."

"Hurt," says Aberdeen, "this is Mrs. Dover and Louis. From this morning."

"Oh," he responds and then thinks on it. "Oh!"

Louis checks out the boxes in their house. "I made a fort once out of all the empty boxes I had when I moved in with Gram."

A fort sounds good, thinks Aberdeen. Except she wants one

made out of stone, with arrow slits and a big cast iron pot for boiling oil.

"Brought you cookies to welcome you to the building. Now that we know who we've got up here, it's time to act neighborly," Mrs. Dover explains while pushing the paper plate into Aberdeen's hands. The cookies are still warm and the moisture seeps through the thick wood pulp and wets Aberdeen's palms. She smells peanut butter.

Aberdeen smiles and turns her body to welcome the couple inside. Hurt puts on his best face for guests, a look of placation and aloofness.

"Come in," Aberdeen says. "Take a seat on the couch. I love that you brought us cookies when the world is breaking outside. I appreciate the normalcy."

Mrs. Dover moves into the apartment, Louis holding on to her shoulders like a human backpack. "Can't let the terrorists win," she echoes from a speech she heard years ago.

"No," Aberdeen says, "we really can't."

CHAPTER FIVE

Hurt's furiousness is the color of tomato soup. His cheeks hold the hue for a month. The days are colder, darker, but it isn't the temperature that keeps him rosy. Aberdeen thinks it's his biggest tell; a blushing of red that matches his favorite stocking cap. He has become anger in forms of crimson; skin and knit hat and principles all a violent red.

More has transpired. Red Cross tents had been set up in major city centers and the unified cartel had laid them to waste in a coordinated attack involving fire, bullets in do-gooders, and absconding or destroying of medical supplies. A semi-truck laden with medicine from Canada was hijacked at the border. Rumor was an official in border control was diverting medicines somewhere for his own profit. Three temporary chemical plants set up to pump out basic pharmaceuticals were bombed, regardless of the military presence surrounding them, and the media was reporting the government was shy to try again for fear of further loss of life.

Yet the well-to-do kept literally level heads with stores of chemicals hidden away in safe caches. It was those unable to stockpile before the cartel's constant barrage who were keenly feeling the effects of missing medicines.

Hurt is yelling again. She wonders where her mild-mannered husband of thirty days ago has gone to. She knows he left and hid behind the anger when the veterinarian hospital he works in as a vet tech was raided and robbed while he and the other employees were there. The group had worn plastic masks over their faces. They were the flimsy, brittle kind made out of the same material as plastic cups; they were the masks of cheap masquerades and smeared mascara after a Mardi Gras night in New Orleans. The entire time they threatened the employees, threatened her husband, he watched their noses and their mouths. Hurt came home swearing that half of them had harelips, the other half misaligned teeth. After, he'd become defeated, talking about how the animals didn't have any drugs anymore either. There would be unspayed cats in heat for good. There would be rats without antibiotics after getting tumors removed.

"We're all dead in the water now," he had told her and gone to bed in his dirty scrubs. Aberdeen had picked carnivore hair from the sheet fibers that night and tried to hold her head away from Hurt, tried to avoid an asthma attack, her lungs more sound once the moving material had exited their home, tried to let her husband get some rest.

The day after the crowd ransacked the vet's office for iguana anesthetic and heartworm medication, Hurt had taken to carrying his shoulders with a scoop to them, like a yoke had been placed there the day before. No matter how Aberdeen rubbed them out, they curved forward as if they were trying to hug his ribs, lungs, heart. And then came the anger. And with the anger, the flushing of his face.

"Calm down and tell me what's wrong," Aberdeen says. She's lifting a spoon up from the bottom of a mayonnaise jar and dropping it back down to watch the emulsion wiggle. Since the first attacks on the pharmaceutical industry and the continuing chaos around the nation, interest in her in-home craft classes and online sales of her terrariums had ground to a halt. She didn't blame people; people saw such things as luxuries, or even dangers. Prick your finger on a bit of floral wire and you could end up with an infection. Lose the finger. Lose your life. Things like crochet coin bags and moss in glass become gauche. Very fucking gauche, she thinks.

Hurt picks up the unfinished sandwich in front of his wife and takes a bite. He makes a face like he's eating paste in school. He opens the bread. It's devoid of cold cuts, of spinach or crisp disks of pickle.

"There's just mayo on this," he says. His face gets brighter. It flames.

Aberdeen takes it from him and sticks a corner of it in her mouth. "I used to eat bread and mayo when I was a kid. With our finances the way they are, I'm getting creative."

Hurt pulls it away. "We aren't that poor off, Aberdeen," he says and tosses it in the sink. It lands on a dish full of tan water, its rim caked with bits of dried egg. She looks over at the sandwich and then levels her husband with a stare. Zen, she thinks. Don't get the lungs pissed off.

"Start talking," she says as she notices something in his hand. It's a piece of bright yellow paper.

He holds up the sheet to her face like he's administering an eye test. It's so close she has to uncross her eyes and snatch it away from him so she can see what's scribbled there in a looping, wide mess.

Written in a black Sharpie and then photo-copied so that the letters have dots of missing pigment, the gist of the flyer is this: A call to arms! The government is demanding hospitals and medical doctors, counselor and psychiatrists, anyone who works in the health industry, who has access to drugs, who dispenses them to others, these people are to give all medical records of the American people to the government. They say it is for the safety of all, to see who needs what, when, why. The truth is that they want this information for suppression! Subjugation! Invasion of privacy, life and liberty! Come! Protest!

Aberdeen puts the paper on the countertop. A wet circle blooms and grows on the paper from a bit of liquid on the Formica. What comes from below rises to the top, insides out, bottoms up.

"You aren't going to this protest, babe. No way. This isn't your style. I know the raid at work got you upset, but this is a perfect opportunity for getting yourself killed. Besides, what kind of librarian in training does something like protest against the government? You'll be working at the local library someday and city hall will be writing your checks."

Hurt picks up the yellow paper and folds it twice before shoving it in his front pants pocket. "The government didn't steal the medical supply at work. That was a group of desperate assholes. That's got nothing to do with why I want to go."

Aberdeen can smell the mayonnaise. She looks down at the lid. It's a month expired. Shit, she thinks, and brings a fingernail up to her mouth and scrapes a bit at her tongue. She leaves her mouth open and questions him with adeptness akin to a de-tongued heretic.

"Then why?" she asks but it comes out sounding more like the mewling of a cat before fighting or copulation.

Hurt understands her. There are benefits to living with someone for two years.

"Because medical records are private. I swear our government has been dying for this scenario so they can put tabs on us all, especially the angry folks and the poor people. Just because we're feeling the fallout from lack of medicine and these terrorist assholes keeping the country on high alert does not mean all the branches of government can start pushing through legislation to open everyone's personal business to the authorities like it's the next bestseller!" Hurt says open and bestseller like books are opened anymore. Maybe with a click or a press of a finger.

Aberdeen thinks of her medical record. She's never seen it. In fact, she figures that most people have no idea what's in their medical records. With visits to doctors over her thirty-five years of living, she's not sure of what is in the file, even if it is a paper file anymore. Is there technology to convert shitty medical doctor handwriting to typed text? Does her record show she was stung by a wasp when she was six and her skin turned violet and itched for days? Does it record her first Depo shot when she was fourteen? Is there a place where all medical records go, mingle, coagulate into a new mega-record of things wrong, things never fixed, and one or two things righted?

"Okay, I agree," she says, "but what about you and me, huh? You know, us sticking together, keeping our noses down to the ground. Wait, no. Heads down."

The clock Aberdeen finally got up on the kitchen wall clicks with each move of the second hand. Hurt smirks. "Don't use that now. I think you've befriended everyone in this building since that day you were running around being the superhero. Talking down angry cripples. Being the booming voice of reason."

"I've got to have something to do. And I don't know the person that lives in 4C. They've eluded me, but I'll get them eventually."

"Right," he says and picks up the dish towel dirty with a brown stain so he can throw it back down to make a point. "Make jokes, keep hiding."

Aberdeen knows he has her on this. Maybe yelling in the streets will do him some good. Marching about, waving poster boards perched on broom handles missing their brushes could bring the blood out of his face and into his hands, balls, dick. They hadn't had sex since their fight in the woods the night before the public rioted, Tylenol became golden doubloons, and people would trade their sofa or Geo for a single pill.

"We'll go, then," she says.

"We will?" he echoes.

Aberdeen makes her way to their bedroom and calls over her shoulder, "What's in for government protests this season? Pantyhose on the head or Guy Fawkes masks? I don't want to commit a fashion faux pas."

She disappears around the corner. She hopes her husband is laughing at her and that the blood is dropping out of his face, sliding back down the cords of his veins and back to his heart.

The protest carries a sense of irony for Aberdeen. It begins on the same street the drug store occupied. She can see the boarded up windows and door over the heads of the people lining the middle of the street. She wonders if there are still dried pools of the pharmacist's blood on the vinyl floor, decaying in a dark, silent room. Then she wonders about the pharmacist, whether or not he lived, whether or not Vera told him about the strange woman in tortoiseshell glasses and a banged bob who hopped the counter just to see what was what.

There are thousands of them. She thought the group that raided the pharmacy was big, but it was like a baby mob, one that was still learning to crawl, that spit up more things than it swallowed and still cried out when frustrated or startled. This rabble, this slew of people is all grown up. They carry signs, rocks, and wear handkerchiefs over their mouths and noses. Adults at play.

Hurt and Aberdeen stand off to the side of the flow of people and wait for a spot to jump in, a sinister Double Dutch. For a time, it is like a sedate running of the bulls. There is anticipation, the image or thought of a presence bearing down on them keeping them moving forward, step by step. Corners make for bottlenecks. The step by step becomes inch by inch at the choke points, but then the crowd fans out, makes room, gears back up.

The signs are scrawled with things like, "My body is MINE" and "Stay out of our medical records" and some are direct to the point with "Fuck you, government!" Those are the ones Aberdeen likes the best. They are the earnest ones. No need to explain why you're mad. Just choose an expletive and go with it.

Aberdeen doesn't carry anything. She keeps her hands in her pockets, keeps her arms tucked in and to herself. Everyone is playing bumper cars but she doesn't want more parts touched than necessary. Hurt doesn't have a sign, but he does have a can of spray paint. Aberdeen called him a wannabe thug when he pulled it out of their utility closet that morning. She'd bought it for stenciling on corkboard years ago. It was a metallic bronze color. Hurt swore to her he used to tag when he was younger. If he did so now, it would be pretty tagging, glittery and shiny.

She pushes up against her husband's side and links his arm in hers. "Don't take out that spray can. See how everyone else is playing nice, babe? I haven't seen anyone looting, breaking things or doing violence to one another. Have you?"

"No," he says and keeps facing forward. Aberdeen can see the outline of the can in a messenger bag slung over his torso. It could be a sub sandwich or a torpedo. It could be a tall bottle of pills.

They keep pace with the crowd, going with it, moving with the herd. Thirty minutes pass, then ten more. Then they hit the wall.

It's made of humans, just like them. Except these are wearing the uniforms of cops with the same riot shields and batons that Aberdeen got so close to a month ago she could see the scratches on the Plexiglas frames. They stretch the width of a major thoroughfare. They hold a line against the protestors crossing into another part of the city. What they must want, thinks Aberdeen, is an illusion of control and containment. This will be bad. She knows it in her gut and head. Both drop a physical inch in agreement.

Those at the front of the protesting mass stop short of the

police by several yards. They stop their screaming and shouting and the effect ripples back to the end of the mob, the now silent head of the snake making the tail still. A hush accompanied by an energetic buzz moves over clumps of the crowd, cruising through the spot Aberdeen and Hurt maintain and moving on. It's the exact sensation Aberdeen always feels during that space between a firework mortar being shot into the sky and the instant it crackles alive in gold, green, red chemical fire.

It is like this: stillness for one minute, maybe a minute and a half.

Then, chaos.

Aberdeen can see an arch of an arm near the miniature DMZ and a projectile looking a lot like a chunk of broken concrete crashes against one of the police shields. And the noise is back. Growling, shouting, an occasional trilling of tongues at the back of throats like an Arabian war cry. She looks at Hurt and realizes this last sound comes from him. His chest is thrust forward, his mouth agape, a fleck of saliva pinging past his teeth like a bullet.

The police give as good as they take. They give better, even. From somewhere behind the first line of officers riot suppression guns are produced and thuds of blunt pain from bean bag rounds hit the crowd. Aberdeen can smell the sweetness of gasoline and her eyes are rewarded with a flare of fire tossed against a brick wall to her left side. She instinctively reaches for Hurt. But he's not there anymore.

He's pushing forward. He's going to the frontline.

"Hurt!" she screams but with the fighting there is no reaching his ears over the sounds of desperation, rage, and weariness. He gets past several people in front of her; their bodies are as good as blockades to her light frame.

Instead of pursuing, she does her best to move in a slant through the crowd, like she's being swept away by a rip tide and making diagonally for the shore. It seems to take several minutes to get to a side of the street, but she's aware time is doing its own thing here.

She's lost sight of her husband. She needs to gain elevation and take in the situation. There. A trashcan, rectangular with hard, plastic wheels. She'll take her chances and squat on it. Anything to escape the flow.

She can see him now, the red of his stocking cap popping over the swell of people like he's at a concert, in a death metal mosh pit. Determination does a lot for him; he's near the front and pulling his spray can from his bag.

No, she thinks. Are you going to spray them in the face, babe? Are you looking to get killed?

And then he's in the frontline. He is the frontline.

As he removes the cap from the spray can, an officer steps to him, turning his body and a barrel of a shotgun painted a vivid, bright orange emerges from the depths of the ranks like a battering ram. She can't hear the shot, but she can see the way Hurt's torso folds like a thumb and index finger are running a fine crease into his midsection. Just like the first fold in a piece of origami. His legs go out. He's on the ground.

Fuck. Fuck. No.

And then she moves.

The edges of the crowd are easier to move around, as if the protesters are like a solid mass, molecules getting close and tight together. Now time is not just slow, but has stopped. Yet Aberdeen still moves. She wonders how her body can continue on in space, but not time.

She can't see his cap. What she can see is a new force behind the police. Men in camouflage. The military is tossing in their hand and standing up from the table. Time to fight.

Time to fight, she thinks. Time to fight to get to Hurt.

She uses her elbows to nudge people out of her way. They don't react, like they can smell her, scent her as one of their own. She passes a man with a bloodied face and makes herself keep going.

She doesn't see him before she trips over him.

"Hurt!" she yells down at his fallen body. He's no longer at the front of the crowd. It has moved on without him. His hands are out and above his head to ward off trampling. She hooks her arms under his shoulders and heaves him to his feet.

Hurt takes in shallow breaths. "It was a bean bag round. My ribs might be bruised. One might be broken."

She puts an arm under him and she's surprised when the crowd moves aside to let them get at the edges. They're back to the sidewalk when the crowd breaks the police line and the military boys in the back join the fray.

Hurt can't draw himself up to his full height.

Aberdeen kisses his top lip. "No more playing in the street. Time to go home."

"And lie down," he answers as they move through a side alley and away. His hands are stained with bronze paint, blowback that never reached its canvas.

The stairs present a difficulty. Hurt can hobble, but when he needs to bend at the waist, he pulls his hands in to his chest, trying to clutch something stabbing him deep within. His breathing is still labored and licks of sweat dampen his hair though the air outside and in the stairwell is biting, cold.

Aberdeen is beginning to think their new home resonates with noise. Sirens have started again, farther away than when she heard them the day after they had emerged from the forest to find out America was being held accountable for its drug war. But these aren't the calls of blue and red flashing lights. These are the sirens of war; the sound of wahs growing and fading, of bombs coming from the sky. She imagines it was the sound played when Dresden was rolled over with balls of flame.

For her, it is the same siren sound she heard in a video game her little brother used to play years ago. When the noise came, the world the game character was in would morph and change. It would go from being a bad world to a terrifying world. From a plane of disappearing children and endless mist to one of grates coated in human innards and dark, bulging things with their forearms filed into sharp tips like those of garden spiders.

As they climb, one stair at a time, she wonders if the world is changing outside right now, moving along a scale of awful from a seven to a ten. The sound of the sirens should be the one thing that hits a Pavlovian response in all humans and causes them to dig trenches, flee countries or pick up something that can kill.

"It's pretty bad, isn't it?" she asks him when they reach the third floor.

Hurt gives her a wan smile. "I don't think my lungs are damaged. No blood in my mouth, anyway."

"Good," she says, "only one of us can have lung problems at a time."

They make a pass around the landing to get to the next flight of stairs and Aberdeen can see feet sticking out across the concrete. They're capped with sneakers of black, striped in yellow and attached to Louis who sits slumped against a cold wall.

He lifts his head and takes a look at Hurt. He doesn't seem to notice the man's bent frame, labored breaths. He's playing with the lines on his palm, scooting a finger around them like they're race tracks and he's younger, just learning that things with wheels move.

Aberdeen holds up Hurt and causes him to stop for a minute. He looks at her, gives her a lift of the eyebrows but she ignores him and kicks the sole of one of Louis's sneakers.

"Hey, kiddo. You all right?" she asks.

Louis does his best to smile, but his bottom lip vibrates and his cheeks start to pull back. That's where it stops though; his emotions are suppressed, flattened.

"Gram is sick," is all he says.

Aberdeen looks to Hurt. He needs to get upstairs and lie down while she looks up how to tend a bruised or fractured rib. She doesn't have time to play nurse to everyone. Just one patient at a time, she thinks. She can only stand that. And she has promised that to Hurt. That it's just them against this pharmaceutical apocalypse.

"She's sick with what, Louis? Does she have a cold or did she eat something bad?"

"Nah," he says and drops his finger from his palm. "She's just not feeling good lately. She's acting different, too."

Hurt squeezes the ball of Aberdeen's shoulder and looks over at Louis. His fingertips are depressing her skin; she can feel the rigidity of his finger bones on her muscles. She wonders if what Mrs. Dover has is contagious. But it doesn't sound that way. It sounds like she's old, this new world is defeating her, and she's choosing to go, maybe.

She doesn't look at her husband before answering with her gut and her heart in agreement.

"Let me get Hurt upstairs and taken care of and I'll come back down and visit with your grandmother, okay?"

Louis's left eye drops out a bit of water. He nods his head and begins drawing again on his palm. She watches him outline the form of a fish. Or a torpedo.

"I promise I'll be back," she says.

And even though Louis knows nothing of her promises, he responds with, "I know."

CHAPTER SIX

Blood does not come out of his mouth. Hurt coughs again. Again. Testing. He pushes a thumb against where the bean bag round took him in the ribcage. He winces, pulls in like he's plunged a needle there, and takes his hand back down.

"Don't think there's a punctured lung. I think we're in the clear," he says.

Aberdeen must accept the vet tech knows more about these things than her. If a bit of fern was suffering root rot due to lack of charcoal packed into the bottom of a glass container, she could do something about that. But this. She defers to him.

She binds him with tan strips of masking tape, pulling five pieces as long as her forearm off of the roll. It sticks to his right side, the side that took the brunt of the force and he winces when she catches a bit of his chest hair in the stickiness. She mumbles a sorry and stands back to look at her work. If she had a bit of paint with her, she could decorate him with stripes, pull the tape away when he was healed, and she'd have a new piece of art to look at. Then she thinks of the spray can. You're a moron sometimes, Hurt, she thinks, and then kisses him where his forehead meets his golden hairline. He smells of gasoline.

The tape buttresses his side. He lowers himself onto their

bed as if he has a hinge at his waist he can't un-stick. Aberdeen stays standing and checks out his side with lips puckered. There is a redness creeping around his floating ribs. She suspects it will travel from crimson to blackish and leave eventually with a yellow the color of a steno pad.

"It's not that bad, Aberdeen," he says.

She smiles and taps her foot on the wooden floor.

"You can go. I know you want to go check on them. I'm fine, really. Just don't bring home the plague if you think she's contagious. I'll put you through a round of thorough scrubbing in the shower."

Aberdeen touches his shin bone. "You promise?"

"By the rib you sprung out of I do. Aberdeen, we've got two stories to tell now, one about a bruised rib, one about the start of martial law."

She ignores his quip about the military intervention and smiles. "I won't bring home any strays. Not this go around at least," she assures him and lifts her black hair away from her neck and lets it fall back down.

"Me and you," he says.

"You," she says, "and me."

She doesn't use the brass knocker hanging on the door. Instead she walks in and calls out, like every apartment in the building has become just another room in a large, brick house. The smell hits her; a mix of menthol rub and the sweetness of canned chicken broth.

"Louis," she says. He wasn't on the landing waiting to escort her to his grandmother.

She looks around the place. It's the first time she's been all the way inside instead of standing at the door threshold every couple of days to see how the Dovers were faring. The effect of the place is one of immovable decades. The carpet is brown; the easy chairs in the front room are covered in a thin, orange velour.

She likes the place. It calls her own childhood to mind with days spent on her play rug, green and yellow with a yarn owl knit into the middle of it.

"Louis," she says again. He comes then, lumbering out of the kitchen. He has the remains of a chocolate bar on his fingers. He licks at the dark fudge and then wipes his hand on his pants.

"Where is she?" she asks.

He stays silent and leads the way down the hall. Aberdeen's apartment is the same floor plan of this place, just in reverse. She knows they're going to the bedroom with the small closet and the single, high window that lets in the sight of clouds if you crouch and look up.

The door is closed and Louis stops and turns to Aberdeen before opening it. His shoulders are creeping up to his ears like jaws coming down on prey.

"I want to tell you something."

"Okay," she says and looks at the knob to the door behind his back. It's brass and flecked with pink paint. "What?"

"She smells bad. She hasn't had a bath in a while."

Aberdeen can already smell the scent of stale urine and sweat left too long on bed sheets mingling with the odor of artificial mint that makes her throat tickle. She chooses to play dumb.

"I'm sure she's fine. The house smells fine."

His shoulders drop slightly. "You sure?"

"Sure am," she says and Louis steps away from the door, letting Aberdeen enter.

She pushes it wide, hanging onto the handle, and immediately realizes the tiny window must be open. The effect of this causes the stench in the room to rush her, hit her like the bean bag round hit Hurt, air making way for the nearest flow, the nearest escape. Just not fresh air. Air that smells of things settling back to earth. The room is occupied by a prelude to death.

Aberdeen is surprised to find another woman in the room besides Mrs. Dover. The light is low, the overhead fixture switched off, so she can't see the face of the person in bed. She has the irrational hope that it isn't Myrtle under the dirty bedclothes. The other woman, however, she can see. She's middle-aged with long hair twisted up into a mimicry of a hen's comb, skirted with a purple scarf. The woman's arms could be as long as her legs and she holds them hovering over the small of Mrs. Dover's back.

"Sorry. Hi," Aberdeen says. "I've come to see how Myrtle is. I didn't know she was sick."

The woman answers after pausing for a moment, pulling her hands back to her body and waving one of them in front of her face, clamping her fingers tight against her thumb like she's asking for silence in the room.

"Hello. Please come in. You knew she was sick, you just didn't know how sick. You are here. That's important."

Aberdeen steps into the room. She looks back at Louis but the boy doesn't come in after her. She winks at him but he stares through her at a picture above his grandmother's bed of what looks to be a bowl of fruit, a still life. She wonders if he, too, thinks it's someone else in that bed. A wolf in his grandmother's clothing; a force come to devour him after it devours her.

"I'm Aberdeen," she introduces herself and walks to the foot of the bed. Mrs. Dover is on her side. Her eyes are closed and she doesn't speak. Aberdeen gets the feeling she's not asleep, that she's there, listening, just focused on something, somewhere else. "I live two floors up from the Dovers."

"Sani," says the woman. She lifts the scarf from around her head and takes it down, still wrapped in a ring like a fabric donut. She puts it on the bedspread, brings her hands up to her hair and runs her fingers through it. It's a little damp, like she's been exerting herself.

The woman stands then and places her hand on her back

and allows herself a stretch.

"Should we go out and talk?" asks Aberdeen.

"No need to go out. Myrtle knows what's happening to her. She's a woman of spirit. Very in tune."

Aberdeen feels strange talking about Myrtle's illness with Louis at her back and the elderly lady prone in front of her. But she already trusts this woman. Anyone who could sit in a darkened room with a woman passing from the world earned her respect. Automatically. Intensely.

"If you think that's okay, then, okay," Aberdeen says.

Sani smiles at her and reaches out a hand for Aberdeen to take. She leads Aberdeen around the side of the bed to where Mrs. Dover's head is facing, her eyes shut tight.

"It's due to her diabetes. It's nothing new, really, but her kidneys are under duress. I don't know if they're at the point of failure yet, but that will come. Undoubtedly that will come."

Aberdeen is silenced by the earnest assessment of the woman while her grandson is within earshot. She takes a moment and finds her voice.

"What about insulin? She's not managing it?"

"She's doing her best. But what insulin she had for herself this past month she's been saving for Louis instead."

Aberdeen sees Louis in her mind, licking the chocolate off his fingers. She wants to lecture him or take him into an embrace. Or both.

"Are they both Type 2, then?" Aberdeen asks, not even really sure about the differences, but always equating Type 2 diabetes with heavy people, like the Dovers. Mrs. Dover has her soft chest that expands wide like the barrel suspenders of a rodeo clown. Louis has a roll of skin and fat where his neck meets his skull. It looks like a mouth set in seriousness. All Aberdeen really knows is that insulin is involved, sometimes too little, sometimes to no effect. Diabetes as a problem, as a disease, often slips her mind. She knows there are two kinds: both bad, both can kill.

Sani looks to Louis. "No, actually. Louis is Type 2, but Myrtle has been Type 1 since she was a teen. She needs the insulin to survive but she'd rather save it for her grandson, in case his diabetes worsens and he becomes dependent on taking insulin. He doesn't need it. Yet. But she knows how precious those shots are. None of us know when more drugs will be available."

Then Mrs. Dover's eyes open, just small moons of jaundiced white. Aberdeen reaches up and pinches her lips, as if the words of negativity are leaving her mouth and not Sani's.

Sani notices the old woman tucked in to three layers of blankets that mound about her like snow drifts is there now, cognizant. Yet she still speaks for her. "Myrtle wants to make sure Louis is okay and he'll make it through this whole catastrophe without undo harm. She's just being a grandmother."

"She's killing herself," Aberdeen notes.

"She's been on half doses for a year, unable to afford more. She's had a long life. It is not up to us to say how long she stays on earth or tell her she cannot go."

Louis comes into the room then and takes a seat on the end of the bed. He's careful not to touch his grandmother, a distinct change Aberdeen sees in him. At all other times, they have been latched at the hip, a constant connection both gentle and intimate.

Myrtle keeps her eyes on the plane of bed sheet in front of her. She blinks rarely. Aberdeen has visions of starving people in Somalia or India and how they let flies land on the globes of their eyes. Myrtle would do this now. She would invite the pest in, as if the body knows the carriers of decay are wont to come. Welcome, the open eyes say. Stay awhile.

Then Louis speaks up and manages to eke out a statement with a tight voice. "She told me she wouldn't last much longer with or without the insulin. She told me I had to save it for later, if I got sicker. So I told her I could be alone while she goes to see God."

Sani moves to Louis's side. She rubs her hands together and then places them on top of his shoulders and finally they drop down, slope even, and Louis is once again an awkward, man-sized boy.

Aberdeen considers all three people in the room. She wonders if Louis will get sicker, if he will die if he doesn't have the insulin or if diet and exercise will keep his problem in check. She doesn't know. She hopes it can be managed. Because even if his grandmother is willing to sacrifice herself for the boy, if the medicine doesn't return soon, it won't matter.

Mrs. Dover blinks again slowly and then lifts her head a little and turns it so she's looking towards the ceiling. She locates Aberdeen with her eyes and flares her nostrils. Aberdeen notices the fullness of her face. It reminds her how her own face used to look when she'd have to go on steroids to control her asthma, back when it was more severe and Aberdeen was a child. Bloated, full up of swelling tissue, tender and pliant.

Then she speaks.

"Pretty darn tired and can't go the bathroom so not much use getting out of bed. Sani's hands help, though. She's been touched by Jesus to use them the way she does."

Aberdeen's curiosity takes hold.

"What's it called, Sani, what you do?"

Sani answers, "I heal people with my hands. It's that simple."

"Won't be healing me," chimes in Myrtle and her addition is met with Louis finally inching forward on the bed and carefully laying his head on his grandmother's hip bone. "But the heat that comes off those palms is good enough for me."

Sani grins at this. Aberdeen assumes the healer's ability to give any comfort to a chronically ill person is a victory in a simple way. The small triumphs over the sickness in bodies have become precious. Events worthy of smiles and renewed hope.

Yet Aberdeen thinks alternative medicine is well and good only if there is a backup of Western medicine. No one runs to an herbalist when they're holding their intestines in their hands. Nor do they trust in needles poked into so-called energy meridians when they're dying of alcohol poisoning.

She decides to side with the devil and make his position known.

"Have you taken her to the hospital? Or at least called a doctor?"

Sani is blasé about the comment. Louis doesn't have a response. But Myrtle speaks up. Aberdeen can see liquid in her mouth, excess salvia. "Doctors can't do nothing unless they have plenty of medicine. And if they don't have that, how do they fix me, Aberdeen? If there are no drugs used on me to stop the pain when they cut me open, no kidneys to put in me, no way to force my body to take them as its own? No drugs to keep me ticking and watching Louis? No. No doctor can help me in all their white coats and coldness with people."

"But," Aberdeen goes for an objection and is stopped by Myrtle. The woman is shuffling her buttocks in reverse on the bed, pushing herself upwards. A metal headboard, brass and similar to what might have been found in a hospital when Myrtle was born, holds up her heft.

"No buts that I'm dying. No hospital will take me. We tried already, Aberdeen."

Aberdeen gives her head a little shake. "Wait, you've already gone to a hospital? And they sent you away in your condition? They can't do that!" She's aware her voice is an octave higher, pinched, lilting. "What, you have no insurance?"

"No, we don't. But that isn't the problem right now. I'm not a priority person. They take a look at me and think they can't waste medicine they've got on an old woman that's going to die soon from kidney failure. She don't do nothing for society

67

anymore. No job. Just raises a boy because his parents chose not to."

"So what?" Aberdeen asks, not expecting a real answer, "they give what you need to live to someone younger or richer or more productive?"

She gets an answer from Sani.

"Yes," is all she says.

Aberdeen can feel her chest seize, tighten. She looks down at Myrtle. Her breathing is shallow as well. It might be from the war going on in her body. The woman's curly, short hair poufs around her face, a dense cloud of backlighting. An angel, thinks Aberdeen. Bloated, wrinkled and worn and she's amazingly beautiful.

She sounds weak when she says it, but Aberdeen whispers out, "It's not fair. They can't do that. Where do they get the right? How can they pick and choose?"

And it's Louis who answers from his spot on his grandmother's thigh. "Adults get to choose everything. Sometimes I wish I could choose something. I wish that I could choose for Gram to live. But I guess I can't."

The smell of the room is still there. Aberdeen has been trying to ignore it, but with the news of Myrtle's resignation to death, it hits her nose again and the air from the window at the top near the ceiling just circulates it in and out of her lungs. It smells of organs slipping to waste, blood gelling, ammonia caking and crystallizing.

The three adults and one child pause for a moment. No one talks. Breathing seems to be on everyone's mind. Just take some in and then let it out and that's what keeps things going. Thinking beyond the action sets one up for failure.

"What can I do?" Aberdeen finally says and rubs at one of the ovular bed knobs by her hands.

"You're doing it," answers Myrtle and the woman lays a hand with thick, yellow nails on her grandson's head. Louis tries to blink back tears that get away from him and darken the green bedspread. Sani just smiles.

Aberdeen thinks of her husband aching upstairs. She gave him ibuprofen for the pain, but even as she was dolling it out, she was wondering if she should keep it for something more serious. As if a fractured rib wasn't serious. But it didn't seem to be. Not right now.

"Do you need any medicines? I have your typical over-the-counter things and I might have some old antibiotics from when I had a sinus infection last year. You're welcome to any of it."

Myrtle massages the boy's head and his tears come freely. She rubs them out of him, her touch saying it's okay to use water in that way.

"Keep it for the living, Aberdeen," she says and then closes her eyes and opens her lips into a smile.

For the living. Then, thinks Aberdeen, Mrs. Dover is already dead.

"I'll check on you both every day, now that I know what's going on. But if you think of anything, and I mean food, someone to clean, an ear to chat to, you just say it when I come. Because I'll be coming every day. I swear to you."

Myrtle keeps her eyes closed but dips her chin slightly in acknowledgement. Aberdeen can sense Louis is gone from the room, he's away in a place where his grandmother isn't dying, his parents are with him, stupid but remarkable things like chewable vitamins and tetanus vaccinations are in his future.

Sani takes Aberdeen by the elbow and Aberdeen feels a bit of what Myrtle and Louis must have felt when she laid hands on them. Her palm is warm, hot even, like she's been holding onto a mug of cocoa. Nothing else radiates but her palm. And when it touches the space between bones and ligaments and tendons, a release hits Aberdeen and the tightness she carries in her arms dissipates, gone.

"I'll walk you to the door," Sani says, still holding on to

her. Aberdeen impulsively places her hand over that of the
healer's so it looks to be centuries past and Sani is escorting a
genteel Aberdeen into a ballroom.

They head back down the hall. Aberdeen doesn't bother
with goodbyes. She'll be back in the morning and it's already
late in the day. Myrtle won't go before then, she convinces
herself. The woman will decide to stick around as long as she
can and see her grandson through this period, to a time where
medicine is back and abundant.

Sani releases Aberdeen's arm and Aberdeen feels a shock of
loss. It's as though the woman's hand was always meant to be
there and when taken away, Aberdeen is left feeling off. The
healer pulls open the door and smiles at Aberdeen, waiting for
her to take her leave but Aberdeen has more to say.

"We're all grateful, well, I am grateful for people like you.
Right now. And I'm sure the Dovers are as well. You're a good
friend to them."

"I'm not their friend," says Sani without a hint of
maliciousness or explanation in her voice. It is a statement of
fact.

Aberdeen touches her elbow to make sure it's still there.
Her arm is so relaxed, so at peace it reminds her of how it is to
pet a chinchilla. The animal's hair is so light and downy you
have to look to see if you are touching anything at all. "Then
how are you here?"

"I'm friends with a few of the doctors at the hospital. In a
past life I was an ER doctor. Since all this started, when I have
the time, I go down to the hospital to wait for people. I wait and
find the ones I know the doctors won't be able to help, whether
it's because they're too far gone or because they don't have the
medical rations to do so. And today, Louis came in with Myrtle.
He told me it took them three hours to walk to the hospital. With
no car and her needing to take breaks every few yards, it was
quite the feat."

"Then the doctors told you they wouldn't help her?"

"They told me nothing. I could see it after she waited three hours to get in to see someone only to be released within fifteen minutes. I could see the removal of her energy from her body when she walked in the automatic doors. I could see it coming off her, like mist sprays off a waterfall, when she came out of the backrooms. That's when I offered my help. She's the type of person that needs me most."

It was hard for Aberdeen to believe Sani. She believed there was something about a dying person that set off alarms in the guts of the hale and hearty, but to think that she could actually see her energy, maybe her spirit trying to peel away from her physical form? No. That kind of claim had to be an exaggeration, hyperbole born of swirling dust motes and plays of light. Sani no doubt took that as evidence. Aberdeen, however, would not.

"You talk of her dying like it's okay," she says and then shares more with the ex-doctor turned alternative healer. "When I saw Myrtle's eyes, I thought, if there were a fly in that room, it could land on her eyes, lay eggs and maggots would emerge from her irises and pupils. Such is her state. Such is her state to just be done."

Sani still holds the doorknob and Aberdeen thinks of the metal of the handle heating under her grasp. There is a tranquility to the woman's face that makes Aberdeen both indignant and jealous.

"Maggots," she says again for effect, "coming out of her eyes."

Sani takes in a breath.

"Ah," she says in a sigh, "new life emerging from what's no longer living. How beautiful. How good."

CHAPTER SEVEN

Because days weren't spent on work, because work was not productive, did not bring in money, did not fulfill, days were spent doing rounds. And Aberdeen was the apartment nurse. And her favorite patient to visit was Myrtle, a woman dying of urea building in her insides, building and building like a rain gauge never emptied.

There was three weeks of this: running cold plates of chicken and beans down flights of stairs to Louis, rolling the old woman out of bed and onto a folding camp stool of Hurt's so Aberdeen could scald the bedding clean, watching Louis weep, watching Myrtle smile, doing things that don't do anything – not really.

Now in winter, when the snow comes for real and isn't just bits of burnt Styrofoam, Aberdeen is exhausted, but jubilant in her own health. Whenever she tires, she smacks her own cheeks, pinches them until they redden, reminds herself that she's *needed*. Not everyone is so lucky, she thinks. Some of us are dying. And by us, she means her charges, her wards and her, bundled together. A package.

Wheelchair man hasn't let her in his apartment yet. She's tried four times. Each time she's met with a locking of the door from the inside. But she knows he'll come around. He's a man in need of attention. This was made evident the day he screamed of doom in the foyer of their shared brick tenement.

Right now, Myrtle is the focus. Louis and Myrtle. Myrtle and Louis. One dies and the other will too, in a way. She's sure of it. But she's determined to see to it the body of Louis is still standing, flexing, processing things it shouldn't be like chocolate bars and doughnuts with vivid green sprinkles over white icing. Once his form is intact, once he can get past the loss of his sole parent, then he can eat healthy, try to care about his own body, about a future.

Today she comes to their door with a clear plastic bag of spinach and carrots. The prices on fresh vegetables have rocketed with the impact the economy has taken with everyone missing their drugs and the continued threat of further violence occasionally carried out, either by terrorists or soldiers enforcing martial law in the more unruly areas of the country. Add to the situation fewer jobs and national depression and the future becomes questionable.

Over two months in to devastation now. The talking heads reassure. The men in combat fatigues always present now since the protest secure. The people beginning to babble in the stores and the lines at the hospitals defy. End in sight? No, she thinks. Not in sight. Not on the horizon. Not before the curve of the earth hides it from detection.

But humans need fresh veggies. Louis needs veggies. A bit of beta-carotene, some iron infusion from the spinach. It's not comfort food, but the boy is past comfort.

She enters without knocking again, the formality lost before it even took hold. Sometimes Sani is there, checking in on Myrtle, putting her hands that issue forth the warmth of a cookfire on the woman's back, legs, head. But as Aberdeen enters into the apartment she doesn't sense the woman. If people leave a mark of energy, Sani is one of them. And as non-receptive as Aberdeen is, she can tell when the woman is around.

The apartment is dark but the odor is under control thanks to Aberdeen using a concoction of lemon juice, vinegar, baking soda and water on the surfaces of the home. She was shocked at how quickly bleach disappeared from the shelves. After all the meds were gone, people got smart, started thinking of what else was out there they could use medicinally. Bleach, garlic, alcohol; all provisions with new value, new costs, new scarcity.

Moving across the living room she catches her toe on the underside of one of the orange loungers and lets a curse fly. She reaches the pair of windows like the ones she has in her own apartment that face outwards to the backside of a billboard. She pulls aside the drapes embroidered with blossoms in red and cream and light smacks her in the face. The Dovers have a view of sorts; the frames with their peeling paint and broken latches outline a bit of frozen dirt and river rock in an empty lot next door. There is discarded black plastic pocking the lot in mounds soft and rubbery like the bodies of beached whales. She doesn't know how they would have gotten to this landlocked place, if they had been alive, and reaches down to rub at her toes.

It's early yet and she knows Louis is still sleeping. He sleeps at odd angles in his twin bed: hands hanging to the floor, a hip pointing to the ceiling and his eyes behind his lids still and dead. Aberdeen wakes him every day she comes. At first she would touch him on the arm or head and say his name. But then she realized his body had uncontrollable spasms when wrested from sleep and he had put a fist in her thigh the second time she'd gotten too close.

Now she stands in the frame of his door and says his name once to see if he will rouse. Nothing. Let him sleep, she decides. It's his winter break from school. His grandmother is dying in the other room. He's probably dreaming and processing and growing. He's busy becoming. Rest is good.

Aberdeen closes his door and faces the room that contains

74

Myrtle. Rather, it contains the body of Myrtle, that composite of decaying bits. The woman herself, she's been leaving by bits and parts for the past month. There are days she doesn't talk. Other days she speaks about her favorite times spent in a car: drive-thrus, drive-ins, going through the trunk of a redwood, fucking on vinyl until her ass was red and sore. Aberdeen takes any day that Myrtle is still breathing as a good one. Talking or no talking.

She listens at the door before entering, her ear pressed up against the cheap, hollow-core wood. She can't hear anything but this doesn't surprise her. She's not sure what she would expect. Ecstasy at the point of death, a rattle of the breath?

"I'm coming in, Myrtle," she says and enters. No matter how many times she sees the woman prone on the bed, bloated and wet with sweat, she casts her eyes downward until she becomes accustomed to it again, the bright light at the end of the tunnel, the hard luminescence of a body's last flaring, dying.

When Aberdeen allows herself to look, Myrtle is propped up on a pillow forcing her neck into an odd angle. She's wearing the same satiny nightgown Aberdeen helped dress her in three days ago. A collar of lace dancing right across her sternum has gone yellow and curly with the excretions of her skin. Her cheeks are the size of Aberdeen's knees, her knees, under the blankets, are the size of Aberdeen's breasts.

The old woman shakes her head, answering no to a question not posed.

"What is it?" Aberdeen asks.

"I thought I was ready," Myrtle says, "but not yet. Guess I'm not."

She's lucid, Aberdeen thinks. Then she wonders if she should be, if it wouldn't be easier just to let the dark take you when you aren't aware that the lights are being dimmed.

Aberdeen has to ask, though she knows the answer, has to offer, has to be able to say she asked. "What can I do to make it easier or faster?" She pauses and gathers her thoughts. "How can

I help you get ready?"

Myrtle's chest rises and sinks like a bobber in a river, jerking and heaving with a force coming from underneath, all around. She places a hand over her doughy breasts and lets it ride the motions. Aberdeen has done the same while riding out an asthma attack. There is comfort in putting a finger, or a hand on the problem, holding it and acknowledging it. Like that's what it takes to make it go away. Recognition.

"We have to talk about this?" Myrtle questions, her hand still to her chest. Her fingers are red like unearthed worms.

Aberdeen nods her head. "I think so."

"To business, then," and Myrtle takes her other hand, the one that isn't busy trying to will her lungs up and down and points to a dresser on the wall behind where Aberdeen stands. "Bottom drawer. You got to dig below my underwears, but it's in there somewhere."

She looks at the light switch on the wall and raises her eyebrows, points.

"Go ahead," Myrtle says and Aberdeen flips it on. The switch leaves her finger sticky and she makes a mental note to scrub it later on.

The handles of the bottom drawer are shaped like the heads of lions and their brass composition gives them a tawny countenance. Aberdeen grabs their faces and tugs, the drawer sticking on the tracks and needing a bit of jiggering to get it pulled out completely. She puts a hand to her mouth and bites her finger, the sticky one, on accident, and tastes a hint of raspberry jam.

"Um," she says, having expected a blanket of large, cotton underclothes. But instead there are thongs, tangas, boy shorts, briefs, bikinis in tangerine, chartreuse, indigo. One pair has a bit of leather running the length of the top elastic.

"There's my good pairs," is all Myrtle says.

"Right."

76

Aberdeen slides a hand to the bottom of the drawer and feels around for something, realizing she doesn't even know what it is she's looking for. Her fingers run into paper. She catches it with her middle finger and the top of her index and pulls it out. It's a three by five index card in faded pink. The lines are nearly gone. As is the ink.

Aberdeen holds it up. "This it?"

Myrtle doesn't look. Her chin is on her chest. Her eyes are closed. "Can't remember what it looks like."

Aberdeen doesn't look at the writing on the card. She moves closer to Myrtle. The woman is smelling sour again, akin to pickle juice and runny cheese. Aberdeen holds out the card to her, positioning it under her face, above her pillowy chest.

Myrtle opens her eyes, looks at it. A frown.

"Read it for me. But do it quiet. Don't want the boy to hear it."

Aberdeen looks out the door. She wonders if Louis is awake yet or if he's still safe in his dreams.

She reads out loud. It's a tease in ink so old it's turned sepia:

George P. Dover
P.O. Box 97183
Helena, Montana 59625

"That's Louis's daddy. My son. Left Louis with his mom and went to what he always called the "big sky" country to be a ranch cowboy. I told him not to go, not to leave no child with a woman like Fatima, but he did. To think that my son, a city boy, never grew out of playing cowboy."

Aberdeen places the card on the bedside table and looks away.

"So he's still there?"

"Don't know," Myrtle says. "Suppose you could send a note to that address, see if anyone answers. Just address it someone, say you're looking for the tallest, blackest man in town. If he's still there, that's probably him."

"Where's the mother?"

"Dead," is all Myrtle says, looking up finally. Her eyes are glossy and watery, like a new set of membranes have grown there. "At least I hope."

The card, inanimate and worn, succeeds in currying Aberdeen's attention. She picks it up, flips it over, turns it about in her fingers. She uses it to fan at her face.

"So this is what I can do? I find your son and get Louis to him. That's what you want?"

Myrtle takes her hand off her chest and puts it on Aberdeen's, snatching the card away. She holds it in front of Aberdeen's face this time, as close as she can get it to the tip of her nose.

"Hell no. This man left his son with me to raise. I've always been a sick woman. But sometimes I think George wore so many pairs of tight Wranglers it squeezed the brains right out of his balls. I don't want Louis going to him. Besides the fact that his father was fond of riding more than one type of horse. But what choice do I have, Aberdeen? He's the family Louis will have left."

There is a choice. She could choose Aberdeen. But Aberdeen says nothing and part of her womb and her mind balk at the thought. She thinks momentarily of the venomous, hard quarrel she had with Hurt near their spent campfire, inside their tent wet with the humidity brought on by an approaching storm.

"I better go get Louis up. He can help me clean the bathroom."

Myrtle pushes the card into Aberdeen's hands again. "Take it with you," she says and Aberdeen puts it in her back pocket. It's soft and malleable against her backside.

She starts to leave the room but the woman clears her throat.

"Louis got his name from his father's favorite author. I never read any of his books, but he's called Louis L'Amour.

Writes Westerns. But I swore I wouldn't call him no *loo-ee* and I never did."

"I guess you're his parent so you can call him what you want," says Aberdeen. She turns to the door, looks to the room with a sleeping Louis in it. "You were a good parent."

"To this second one, maybe. The first one, he took cows over my boy Louis. You can't love cows like you can a son."

Aberdeen looks at Myrtle, smiles, leaves to bring Louis back to the world of the living.

CHAPTER EIGHT

Myrtle dies.

Louis is there when it happens. He is the only one there. Aberdeen knows it has happened when she finds him outside her door with his pillow in his hands. The pillowcase has stars on it, some big and silver, others tiny and golden. He hugs it tight to his thighs.

"Thought I would need to bring this up," he says.

And that is how Louis comes to live with Aberdeen and Hurt.

There is no money for a funeral. Funerals aren't just twenty thousand dollars anymore. When Aberdeen talks with a funeral home director in a straight navy tie and a fat ring on his thumb, he tells her there is a queue, a healthy demand for funerals. So many people are dying, he says, so many suicides, so many people without life-saving medicines, that the economy is changing. Supply and demand, he says. Everyone wants the bodies they're responsible for in the viewing parlor. Too many bodies, too little space. Cost goes up. He says, you understand, don't you? It's that way everywhere, not just his place. He's not being ungentle. He puts a hand on her hand. She pulls it away.

They decide to put Mrs. Dover in a cardboard box, cremate

her, give the ashes to Louis. He stores them in her old cookie jar. It says 'cookies', is tan and brown, and could cause a problem someday, for someone who doesn't know that it's Louis's way of a highest honor.

Hurt is good with the boy. His claims of not liking children are proven wrong when he only allows Louis whole wheat toast and then puts a streak of butter on it for him. "He's capable," Aberdeen says, but Hurt does it anyway and Louis lets him. There are other things too. When Louis isn't despondent, which is perhaps the same number of hours a day that a cat would sleep, the boy has bursts of innocent energy. Hurt talks with him about how comics have changed from the seventies. They go outside and throw snow at one another, Hurt using a limp wristed fling instead of pelting Louis. On occasion, Louis laughs. On rare and mystifying instances, he shows joy.

And Aberdeen, through all the trouble and death and uncertainty, brings back up the reason they fought months ago. The reason they still haven't made love.

"See?" she says when Louis is in the family room scanning the television channels, a chapter book spread open on his stomach forgotten. "You're so good with him. I bet you'd be the same with all children. Admit it. You'd be a good father."

Hurt pushes Louis's twin bed between two card tables laden with glass jars, odd bits of drift wood and Ziploc bags of shells, mica and dried moss.

"If he stays, we'll have to re-work this room. You can't use it for your terrariums anymore."

Aberdeen knows this. As much as she loves her work with little biomes it no longer brings in money. Besides, she is learning to love Louis more.

"Seriously, you are good with him. But none of our own? The feelings would be more intense. You'd love them even more," she pushes the bed with her hip making sure it's snug up against the wall. "I'm sure of it."

Hurts scratches at his wrists and then shakes out his hands. He leaves the room and comes back. Then he leaves again, comes back again. This time he has a glass of water in his hands. He downs it and holds the empty glass to his thigh like he's about to play telephone with his leg. Or ask Aberdeen to.

"There's no medicine. People are starting to lose hope. And the riots are getting worse. Our society is just beginning to see the effects of this trauma, our government all scrambled, the private sector moving in to take over in the midst of the chaos." He lifts the cup back to his mouth and accepts another drip to his lips. "And you're thinking about having kids? Right now?"

Aberdeen wants to tell him how she passes babies held in slings on the fronts or backs of moms and dads and her nipples ache. She doesn't think they ache. They really do; they grow tender, then hard, sharp, pointing out what they want.

"I just thought we could talk about it again. We never resolved anything last time, at the campsite."

Hurt tosses the glass on the bed and a sprinkle of water hits the bare mattress. "Sure we resolved it. I said no. Resolved." He winces a bit, grabs at his side. The fracture still needs healing.

Aberdeen looks at the cup. She picks it up and sets it on the floor. She rubs the water spot with the back of her sleeve. Suddenly she rethinks the conversation. Too soon, she thinks. Too stressful, she knows. She withdraws.

"Okay," she says.

But Hurt isn't placated. He's on a roll. He's going on with or without her.

"Nope. Don't give me an okay. You're pissed. Well, so am I. When we got married you said no to kids and I was fine with that because I didn't want them either. But you can't go switching horses midstream with babies." He's yelling. Loud.

Aberdeen envisions riding a toddler across a stream, her legs wrapped around a head too large for the accompanying body, downy hair like moss on a rock underwater. She's the only one above the river; the child is somewhere below.

"People are allowed to change their minds, babe. I'm not the same person I was when we got married. I'm older. I want kids."

Hurt holds his hands, flared, up to his head. It's his sign language for intensity and frustration. He looks like a man pretending to be a buck, a bull moose. What he really is is a boy, pretending to be a man, thinks Aberdeen.

"You're just over a year older, Aberdeen. You're telling me," he says and then says again, "me, that you want to bring a kid into a world full of disease and crazy fucking assholes without the promise of a cure or a shield or something to keep them safe?"

She doesn't say anything. She knows there will be more.

"And labor? Have you thought of the delivery of the baby? Shit, they aren't even letting terminally ill people into the hospitals unless they have gobs of cash. I mean, you? What, are you going to trade them a bowl of moss for helping? Or am I going to promise to wave their library fines once I get through this fucking degree?"

Aberdeen thinks of Sani. She would ask the woman for her help. Women helping women bring new people out of them and into the world. It's been done for millennia, maybe longer. Aberdeen knows she doesn't need hospitals or men. Well, she needs a man, but just for a few seconds.

Hurt puts his hands down. He swallows hard. His face is red. Again. It's starting to be his normal skin tone.

"There's no guarantee the baby would be healthy or that you would survive the labor. The pain alone..." and he trails off before he finds his thought and grabs it again, "...could be something wrong. You could bleed to death. You could deliver a baby stillborn."

Aberdeen nods. He's right, but he's not. Not really.

"You could kill you and me. A baby could kill us both."

Aberdeen steps into her husband. She doesn't hold him or kiss him. She merely touches him on the shoulder and leaves the room.

Later on that night, she wakes to the figure of Louis in her doorway. He has that pillow against his body again. Aberdeen flips the sheets off her and walks him back to his tight quarters, his mattress fresh with new sheets he hasn't crawled into. There is a Louis-sized indent in the bed, a maze of little folds and divots where he's tossed and then grown still.

"Back in bed," Aberdeen says lifting the blankets up for him.

He doesn't move. Keeps holding the pillow.

"I had a bad dream," he says.

"Tell me."

"You were pregnant and the baby was coming out of you and it was him."

"Him who?"

"Hurt."

"Oh."

Louis rubs his hands over the pillowcase and catches a corner with his thumb and forefinger. He winds the fabric between his fingers.

"And he was as big as he is now. And when he came out…"

"Louis, it's okay."

"When he came out you split in half. He tore you apart like in a movie or in a video game with monsters shooting out of people."

Aberdeen shakes the blankets in her hand and this does it. Louis climbs in, lies down. She tucks the quilted comforter around his body like he is being packed for shipping. Fragile. Breakable.

Then she lies down next to him. Half her body is on the bed and the other half is suspended above air. Gravity tugs at her. But she thinks she can balance for now. Louis relaxes a little with Aberdeen pressed tightly against him.

"Go back to sleep," she says.

She stays awake until she can smell Hurt making coffee, ashamed of what the boy has heard and then dreamed up.

CHAPTER NINE

The index card plagues her. It sits on the only bookshelf they have in the living room, on the very top of the case, square against the cheap, wooden lip of the thing. If someone didn't know it was there, they would never run a hand along the particleboard and find it. Unless they were crazy about dusting. Aberdeen wasn't. There was enough dust up there already, just a few months of living in the apartment, to plant a seed in, watch it set its milky, soft foot down and struggle to take hold of something. Dusting gave Aberdeen asthma attacks. Better to leave it alone. Let it be so it would let her be. That was her plan with the name of George P. Dover on the pale pink card, too. But it doesn't let her rest.

She's sitting on the couch messing around with a skein of charcoal gray yarn soft with bits of smooth, slick fur spun into the twirled fibers. She can't tell if it's fake or not. For the price she paid for it, she hopes it came off a baby kitten. And then she hopes it didn't, not really. She feels foolish turning the fiber into a hat someone in a production of The Great Gatsby would wear. She plans on putting a green leaf, crocheted to have veins and ribs, near the sloping brim. It was expensive yarn, but she had bought it back when she had money. Back when she was teaching several classes each week and when Hurt was just okay being a vet tech.

Now the classes are no more. Hurt is restless for what he calls a "definitive career." And it is the three of them in the house all the time: Aberdeen, Hurt, and Louis. And the fucking card. That card, she thinks, will grow legs, walk itself into Louis's room, squat on his bed, wait for him. Then she will have a problem.

But she can't bring herself to act on the information, to send a letter to a metal wall of PO boxes in Montana. Once she scrawls out the number, then it's a matter of addressing the thing to a Mr. Dover. Then comes the bit about telling someone through the post that their mother has died. And the worst part would be the offering up of Louis. She doesn't know George P. Dover. Would the man say no, thanks, but no, or would he draw a knife, cut Louis out of her life, not stay long enough to see the blood dry on the rock?

Aberdeen recalls Myrtle talking about her son riding more than "one kind of horse." She wonders if this means he's a promiscuous man or perhaps fickle and brash when making choices. Or, he could be on heroin, could have been on heroin. That kind of horse.

The man could be on methadone, she thinks. Or rather, he could have been, but now that it's hard to obtain, he could be back on heroin. Heroin, crack, pot, cocaine; all these things are still available. They have not disappeared. They have flourished. Exactly what the cartels must have wanted. They are ubiquitous; bountiful supplies of illicit drugs dependent on the burnt remains of pharmaceutical factories, abandoned aid tents, derailed trains, thousands and thousands dead.

She projects her imagined Mr. Dover on the back of a horse with the foam of exertion in its mouth, head low, hooves barely clearing the ground like the earth is taffy. All of this because the man is high, never sleeping or eating, just riding, riding his charge to death.

Or, she considers, the yarn moving through her hands and on and off the fat blue needles without direction, he could be a child molester. Or a man who shows his penis to young women. Or the type of liar who can't help but lie about the mundane, falsities about the weather in another part of the world or what he had for lunch. Or he could just be mean. Plain mean. Mean enough to break a quiet, warm boy like Louis.

He could be pleasant and normal and older, wiser and ready to take on his role as a father.

But she thinks this last thing he could be is an unlikely thing.

She knits her hat. She decides to do nothing. The card can continue to bother. She needs to think more. She needs more time with Louis.

Louis comes in the room with a set of plastic robots in his hands. He doesn't call them robots; they are Japanese and tall like buildings and people can ride inside of them, he explains to her. He calls them *mecha*. Aberdeen follows suit and thinks of a giant black rock full up on prayer and sin whenever she says it.

"Are we going soon?" he asks.

"Downstairs? Sure, let me get this row of stitches on the other needle."

He plays with the toys, making one giant robot fight the other giant robot. His wrists bring them together and smash them head to head. Aberdeen watches and thinks he's too old to be playing with toys this way, but then she has no gauge of normalcy for Louis. She has never seen him at this kind of play until a few weeks ago. She has only seen him absorbed by the reality of a dying grandmother.

Then he asks, "Is Sani coming today?"

Sani has become a regular in their apartment. She is a restless woman; she is like Aberdeen in her proclivity for doing rounds. But Sani's healing and help is more powerful than

Aberdeen's and Aberdeen is thankful for the healer in their lives. She is helping Louis lose weight. She teaches Aberdeen to control her breath by holding a candle in front of her and having her blow it out. Then moving back a step, making Aberdeen extend out her breath, squeeze her lungs empty, ribs hugging tight to her innards. Moving. Blowing. Blowing until the weak air of her lungs can't make the flame flicker at all.

"No, not today. She was here yesterday, remember?"

Louis looks at his Japanese robots and lets them fall, clutched in his hands, to his legs. His lips turn downward.

She finishes moving the stitches from one needle to the other and scoots the yarn down to the bottom of the metal rod so it won't slip off. She digs her winter jacket with the burnt orange trim and down fill out of the closet. It hangs next to the jacket she was wearing the day she saved the pharmacist. There is still a rusty stain on one of the sleeves. She grabs Louis's coat as well. He puts it on and she sees how the sleeves only reach midway between his elbows and hands.

"We've got to get you a new coat," she says, swinging on her own like she's a matador going in for another chance of defeating the bull.

She walks into their bedroom and finds Hurt at his computer desk. He wears squishy, pleather earphones over his ears. They are the size of the earmuffs she would wear as a child, on her walks, her puffy moonboots crunching fresh planes of snow. He doesn't hear her come in. He clicks on various buttons, talks into a microphone that springs off the headphones and dips down towards his chin. He holds his spine stiff in the wooden school chair Aberdeen got from a dumpster outside her college dorm room. His spine is like one of the spindles of wood holding the frame together.

"I don't think that's the right system," he says to the computer or rather, the people listening to him through the computer. More librarians in training. More people wanting to wrangle books for a living.

Aberdeen waves her hand in front of his face when he pauses to listen to someone else. He presses the headphones up against his head to get what's being said. He doesn't look at her hand. He stares through it, trying to see what's detailed on the computer screen.

"Bye," she whispers and waits.

Hurt holds up a finger for her to pause and then slips the headphones down to his neck.

"Rounds?" he asks.

"Just to see the man in the wheelchair," she answers.

"Waste of time, Aberdeen," and he puts his headphones back on. "We're all fucked anyway."

Aberdeen turns and lets her hand trail out behind her, her middle finger erect and pointing to the ground. She catches the tail end of Hurt trying to explain away his comment to the people over the mechanical box.

"My wife," he says, his voice lower now, "thinks she's on the track to sainthood."

He's still called Wheelchair Man. At least that's what Aberdeen and Hurt have called him since the afternoon in the stairwell with his hollering about end times. Louis has dubbed him The White Soldier. When Aberdeen asks him why, he doesn't explain. Louis just mimes rubbing at a beard and lets out a small giggle.

"Don't ask to push him in his chair," says Aberdeen as their feet slip down the stairs.

They pass the apartment he shared with his grandmother. He still goes there on occasion, the landlord absent, no missive sent about the missed rent payments or imminent new tenants. When Aberdeen notices the rising or sinking of his shoulders, she knows it's time to let him go downstairs and be alone with his grandmother's earrings and boxes of stale sugar-free spice drops, none of which they've thought to pack up or put away. He goes to stay with her ghost. And when he's ready to live again, he walks up the two flights of stairs and finds Aberdeen in the kitchen or living room, leans against a doorframe, kicks at the floor.

"I only asked that one time," Louis counters. He slides his hand along the metal railing and slaps at the corners when they pass one landing and start down the next flight.

"And he didn't like it. Just a reminder. I don't want him to yell again."

Louis nods in obedience.

They reach the man's door and Aberdeen tells Louis to give it a knock.

"Hit it with your knuckles, not your fist," she coaches and he does it well and loud.

There is no indication the man intends to answer to their knocking, but Aberdeen can sense he is there on the other side of the door. She hears a squeaking reminding her of the hamster she had when she was in junior high and the metal, urine-caked wheel it ran on while she tried to sleep. It must be the wheelchair.

The door doesn't open. The man doesn't issue a sigh, cough or groan.

And Aberdeen had thought they'd been making progress. He'd let her in his apartment twice since Louis had come to live with her. She was sure it was Louis. The boy mollified the man. But she knew there was a chance the effect would wear off and the old war veteran would go back to his hole, deep and complete in its ability to hide him. That day might be today.

"It's us," she says to the panel of wood. "Louis and Aberdeen. Just checking in to see if you need anything."

The door is unlatched, the chain coming away with a rattling clink.

"Open it," he says and Aberdeen can hear the squeaking

moving away from the door.

She pushes it open and the man is in his hallway. It's another entry hallway like the hallway of Hurt's and Aberdeen's and the hallway of dead Myrtle's and Louis's. This one has black lines of scuffed rubber on the vinyl designed to look like faux parquet flooring.

His cheeks are sinking into his bone structure, two pools of baggy skin under a sharp precipice of bone. His eyes are rimmed pink. There is a speck of paper, orange construction paper, in the deepness of his long beard. Aberdeen wants to lean in and pluck it out. She does not.

Louis crosses himself from forehead to navel, shoulder to shoulder. It's something Aberdeen figures he's picked up from television. There were no crucifixes in the Dover apartment. But again, she wonders what she really knows about the boy. So she checks.

"You're religious?" she turns and asks him, but the man cuts off any answer.

"Don't be acting like I'm on my death bed. Just been having a rough few days. That's all."

Louis drops his finger and looks to the floor. Aberdeen can only imagine what he's thinking. He's probably there, at his grandmother's death bed. She puts a hand on his arm and squeezes before releasing him and clearing her throat.

"Is it your old war wound?" she asks, not even clear on what it is that put him in the chair.

"Nah, I've got the gonorrhea," he says as if he's telling his doctor what ails him.

Aberdeen looks at Louis but Louis doesn't ask what the word means. The man studies their faces and then sniffs one of his long, drawn in breaths and lets out a chuckle. Aberdeen bites the insides of her cheeks to keep from smiling.

"Yeah, the wound, my soldered spine. Hurts something bad, for sure."

"No pills left for the pain?" she asks.

He eyes her. She knows he remembers telling her he didn't need drugs; he told that he was one of the okay ones. He was one of the ones who would be swept away by the waves of crazies breaking against his apartment door. Eventually breaking it down, sweeping him out into society, out into the world.

Aberdeen doesn't tell him she suspected he was on something, like everyone else. "Why don't you go out, see if you can get some sort of priority at the hospitals. How about the VA?"

He sniffs again and turns his chair around in the hallway with a deft three-point maneuver and wheels away from them.

"I'm not going out in the streets so those fucking boys playing soldiers in our own country can hassle me because I don't look right to them. No thank you," he says and says again, "fucking boys at play."

Louis takes a step towards the man. He's eyeing a bench in the corner of the main room, a wooden, unwelcoming thing the man might have for the guests who get past his manners and are determined not to leave without sitting down and feeling they have done *something*.

The man's face gets hard. "Whoa, son. Where the hell you going? I invite you to take a seat?" His eyes are on the boy's stomach, like he's punching at it with his pupils.

Aberdeen shoots an arm out in front of Louis, stopping his progression.

"You're in pain. I get it. But don't talk that way to him. Not with what he's been through. He doesn't need more shit in his life."

Louis whispers *shit* under his breath and takes a step back.

The man rubs his hands over the wheels of his chair. He then grasps them and wheels back and forth, not moving, but rocking forward and back. A loose spoke is what makes the chair squeak. It rubs against another spoke and it makes the metal sing, pitchy and high.

"It's just bad. I don't mean anything right now with the way I am. I'm hurting is all."

Louis speaks up. "We've got a friend named Sani. We could have her come down here and try to help you. She's helping us. She helped my Gram, well, she tried with her hands. Sometimes help just doesn't...help."

Another sniff and he rubs at his red eyes. "Voodoo doctors. Hell no."

"That sounds like a response you'd hear on television. Form your own opinions," says Aberdeen, emboldened by her defense of Louis.

He shakes his head like he's defeated or sad. "Only certain things are gonna be able to help me, girl. Hands ain't one of them. I bet I can find someone who can get me something. I've just got to learn to brave the toy soldiers outside. The pain in my back keeps up and I will."

Aberdeen has heard the rumors as well. There are drugs in the city. The government is keeping them beneath city hall. Dealers under the supervision of the cartel conglomerate causing the chaos around the nation have illegal drugs and stores of the most desired pharmaceuticals as well. Part of her wants to believe there is an inhaler sealed in metal foil, tucked in a crisp cardboard box waiting for her, ready to deliver relief to her defiant lungs when, not if, she should need it.

"Is the pain going to kill you," Aberdeen asks but it comes out as a statement. Her voice is cold. She knows it; she doesn't care.

The man quits his rocking. "Not likely."

"Then I guess you'll live," she says and turns back to the door. Her eye catches a framed sheet of paper on the wall. It's a bit of text in a calligraphic hand and a coat of arms. She doesn't leave her eyes there too long, thinking the man will notice and object. But she can see that his surname starts with an H.

She opens the door, walks out and Louis follows after politely saying goodbye. Louis pulls the door shut and runs another grandiose X across his torso.

The sidewalk outside the apartment is slick with runners of ice. A gap in the front door leaks in freezing air. She goes to the door and pushes on it but can't get it to seal. She thinks of the letter H as a couple of kids run by the front of the building and glide on the heels of their shoes down the slick ground. A middle-aged woman in a long, calf-length quilted jacket watches as well, smoking a cigarette. Louis watches the children, too, bites his lip, places his hands on the glass of the door.

"I'm not going to call him The White Soldier anymore," he says and his eyes shift from the children to Aberdeen's reflection in the glass door.

Aberdeen nods at him. He pulls the door open and joins two other boys, all skating on concrete.

H. She thinks of Louis's dad, thick like his son with calluses on his palms and a wide hat over a short bit of an afro. She imagines him riding that horse until it begs to bend to its knees and pass away and then the man taking a syringe of brown liquid from a saddle bag and shooting it into a vein the length and breadth of a garter snake in the hide of the animal.

How it would buck then. How it would run until it dies and keep on running until the muscles get the last message sent from the brain and then they would cease just as the soul had already done.

H is for horse, she sings to herself, envisioning a preschool Louis watching a segment on Sesame Street while his father is gone west to play at his own Manifest Destiny.

H is for heroin.

Horse is heroin. Heroin in the horse. Keep it moving. Keep us all going, running.

She can envision toddler Louis tickled, giggling.

The draft, the cold settles at the part in her hair. She wishes

for her hat to be done, on her head. That she can do, can control.
She walks up the stairs, heads to something she can complete.

CHAPTER TEN

Two days later the woman in the long, puffy jacket is still outside. She hasn't moved. Aberdeen knows this because she has been watching her from her window that looks out over the front of the building. And the woman is always there when Aberdeen looks. When she goes for a pee or to eat is a mystery to Aberdeen. And then Aberdeen realizes she is becoming obsessed with looking out the window at the woman with ratty brown hair and a new cigarette to her lips every ten minutes, until it turns into a cherry ember followed by a snake of ash and is replaced by another and another. She realizes this woman is just the foreground of a terrifying background.

There are others outside as well: a young man with a Caesar haircut and all the color stripped out of his hair and the same boys, twins with mittens hanging from their wrists, who Louis plays with on occasion. On the day after the second round of bombings in early October, a day people in the city have nicknamed LTP (Losing The Pharm), people hid away with guns and bottles of Mylanta under their mattresses when they weren't in some riotous protest. But now the ones who didn't have jobs to go to or dreams to chase were back to the streets. Aberdeen watched them emerge, the way that zombies in horror films always seem to wander out into the open eventually, searching for things to consume. The people of the city were doing the same. And if they weren't looking for something to take the edge off of reality, they were looking for camaraderie and more reasons to be angry.

There are plenty of others to watch. But it is the woman who draws Aberdeen's eyes down to the street, her hand lifting the slats of the blinds with fingers in the position of a peace sign. The woman is another project, she tells herself. And then she asks herself whether she needs another project. She has a broken boy, a wounded, erratic husband, an unnamed man with possible PTSD. The woman would make four. Three is enough, she tells herself, and resolves to keep her focus on counting to three.

She claims them for her own over and over, under her breath: Hurt, Louis, Wheelchair Man. They are the ones she can help. She knows if she can help them, she can distract herself. She can keep away the chaos and the possibility of death by stopped breath. Hurt, Louis, Wheelchair Man.

But still.

When Aberdeen does go outside, the woman doesn't look up, stays hunkered down near the front door. Her focus is on the concrete and her thick boots with Sherpa-lining sticking out the tops. Aberdeen remembers looking at sidewalks when she was little, focusing on the smear of a flattened bug or the shine of mica locked forever into a block of off-white solidity. She wonders if this woman is looking at the same. Perhaps it brings her comfort, taking the world down to the microscopic. Because right now, the macroscopic is pretty fucking scary.

The day is bright and cold. The soldiers still walk their street at random points during the day. At noon, when the sun tries to peak in the sky, they come with guns at their sides and set jaws. A bloody hit on a rural hospital several towns over has everyone on edge. Aberdeen keeps Louis in. But she goes out for air. She leaves Hurt inside talking to his homework and scratching his side where his ribs are knitting back together. She leaves Louis bored and picking at the fibers of their couch, singing in infrequent bursts songs from the 1950's, a residual trapping of life with Myrtle.

Aberdeen feels like walking. So she chances the people outside, the ones who don't live in her apartment, her domain.

The walk is unremarkable. It is a strange thing, she thinks, to walk in a city adapting to a new reality, new paradigm, and not see *more*. She watches ducks land on a frozen pond and take off when their feet can't penetrate the water. She passes a Chinese restaurant with three specials, all noodles, written on a white board propped on an easel, each dish priced as though it's topped with filet mignon. She hears the sound of a radio above her head when she walks past a building trimmed with fire escapes and a disembodied voice divines new worries and a world devoid of improvements.

As she walks, she wonders if other countries are struggling like America. She knows other places aligned with the United States and its crusade against drugs had been hit in some way, but most governments were still staying mute about the trials on their own soil. Only America openly suffers in its un-sedated reality.

Soldiers are her walking companions. She passes them coming and going on their comings and goings. She waves at one. He smiles at her and puts his hand on his weapon.

Her toes are numb, the circulation leaving as the cold seeps into the open mesh of her tennis shoes. Time for home. No new revelations. Fresh air had.

The woman is still there. But she has moved. She is on her feet, her hands above her head, lifting up her hair and pulling it out over the breadth of her shoulders. There is a man in front of her. He wears a three-piece suit and shiny, black shoes. Aberdeen can't remember the last time she's seen a vest under a suit jacket.

The man is yelling. The woman is yelling back.

Then she's close enough to hear, but not close enough to touch either of the people. She's learned to keep her distance. She thinks of Hurt, how that bronze paint stayed on his skin for days.

"Fucking crazy," screams the man, "You're the kind of person who got us into this mess." He balls his fists and holds them at his hips.

"How the hell is this my fault? What, did I order those beaners and chinks and pakis to blow up all our fucking chemical plants and keep beating the shit out of us after we're down? Why are you even standing here, asshole? Keep walking," she shouts. "Keep walking."

Aberdeen doesn't recognize the man. He's not part of her watch. She figures he's just a businessman having a bad day, one of the dwindling numbers of American society that still believes in the two-car garage, the mortgage and the pension. Maybe he's seen the woman staring at the ground for days now and is angered she doesn't believe in the dream anymore, like him. He wants to see her do something. He makes her lash out so he has someone to yell at. He is a man losing his world, looking to be justified in his pissy mourning. Or his stockpile of drugs is dipping, disappearing, and he fears he'll become just like the woman he harasses.

"It's all the psychos and fat people and sick, old people that make my taxes go up, my cold cuts cost fifteen bucks, cops and military eyeing me every fucking day. What the hell kind of life is this for us normal people? I don't need medicine to live. You need it to operate, don't you? You can't live without it and now that it's gone I have to deal with the drug dealers, protestors and religious nuts." His balled fists become loosened. He points a finger in the woman's face. His lips are pursed.

Aberdeen wants to tell the man he's wrong. The cartel terrorists are to blame. She thinks the woman will lash out then.

But the woman retreats within. Her head turns to the ground. Her jaw shivers and a moment later a drop of water hits the sidewalk. In a few minutes, it will freeze into a microscopic lake for the lady to look into.

"I'm depressed," is all she says as she cries. "It's not my fault I can't control it now. I had it under control. I did what the doctors told me. I took the Paxil and Zoloft. I had a life. Now it's gone."

But the man doesn't seem to sense the shift in the woman's posture and tone. He's still yelling, the finger bearing down on the crown of the woman's head, like he's trying to poke a revelation into her skull.

"Deal," he screams and jabs, "deal or end it. What the fuck are you waiting for? Huh? Deal or end it."

His command becomes a chant. His ears are red. His finger moves faster. "Deal or end it. Deal or end it."

The woman shakes her head and lifts her feet up and down like a child gearing up for a tantrum. The man stops his assault, steps back a bit and reaches down to pick up a leather briefcase at his feet. Aberdeen senses he's had enough. His job is done. He's defended the old pluck of Americans and their bootstraps, perhaps even thwarted a vision of his own mental future, and it's time to move on.

Then the woman grows still. "End it," she says and plants a foot in the man's crotch.

He crumples, holding his groin in his hands. When his knees hit the icy ground and he raises his face up to the sky squinting and grunting, the woman brings her hands together in a ball and hammers him in the place between his neck and right shoulder.

That's when the soldiers come back.

Aberdeen reminds herself of her duties: Hurt, Louis, Wheelchair Man. But she finds her feet moving between the woman and the man. She tries to screen the incident from the soldiers, but the men are high on adrenaline and they've sniffed out the fight.

Aberdeen takes the woman by the biceps. She thinks she should say something to comfort her. The woman lays limp hands against Aberdeen's arms, uncaring about what is holding her up.

"It's not your fault. He's wrong. You didn't do anything wrong."

Aberdeen looks at the man on the ground. One hand has left his groin and moved to his neck. He flexes the muscles there over and over. Her eyes lock back on the woman. She's never seen someone depressed act with such aggression. But the stressors around them are plentiful, enough to make anyone, even those deemed safe and sane, lash out when pushed.

"You need to get yourself together," Aberdeen says as the soldiers make their way to the women embracing as if they are about to dance. Aberdeen looks at the lines on the woman's forehead and a red vein that scatters over the woman's left eye.

This could be me, she thinks, and then hugs the woman close. The woman responds in kind with a tight squeeze.

"They will take you. No doubt. Tell me your name. Tell me who to contact."

The soldiers are there now. Three of them. Three like Aberdeen's three charges. One stoops to pick up the man by his armpits. The other two pry the woman's arms from around Aberdeen. The woman tries to hold tight for a minute before letting the men take her away, to cut in on the dance.

"What's your name?" Aberdeen asks again.

The soldiers have her on her knees. One man with a mole over his eye produces a zip tie from his pocket and secures the lady's wrists together behind her back. The woman looks up to Aberdeen but doesn't meet her eyes. She stops at her chest and stares. It's like she can see into Aberdeen's lungs.

"You have your own problems, I'm sure," she says.

"Your name," insists Aberdeen.

"Why? Who I was is gone when those pills ran out. Now I'm back to the other me. The name I had doesn't signify anyone anymore. She's dead. Until the drugs come back, I might as well be dead."

The woman will not give up her name. Aberdeen doesn't push. People are starting to hold onto what they have. Names are one of the things people can keep. Wheelchair Man. Depressed Lady. These are the names they are given because they will not give any more away. She understands.

The soldiers keep their hands on the woman's shoulders and she goes back to looking at the ground.

Aberdeen thinks of the names she does have: Hurt and Louis. And her own.

The soldiers use a cell phone to make a call. Aberdeen is asked to stand against the wall of the building. She is told if she moves, if she interferes, they will dig out a zip tie for her as well. The soldier who calls says a few words and relates a code over the phone followed by his location. He folds up the phone and looks at the man with his briefcase. The man is told to go. He does.

It's quiet. Aberdeen expects them to ask the woman questions. But they stay silent, their hands on her shoulders, their fingers wrapped in thin, textured gloves.

Soon, minutes later even, a sport utility vehicle comes down the street and stops in front of the building. Two people exit the car. One of them is a female soldier. The other is a man in plain clothes with black-rimmed glasses and a sling cradling his forearm.

The soldiers guide the woman to her feet as the man approaches and the lady soldier stands by the vehicle, her eyes squinting out over the road ahead. The lady in her quilted jacket and resigned aura says nothing. She keeps her head pointed down.

The man reaches her and says something under his breath. He hunches down to get a look at the woman's face without touching her, his knees popping loudly. He gives the word to take her to the vehicle.

Don't, Aberdeen tells herself, but she pushes herself off the building with her hips and clears her throat.

"Where are you taking her?" she asks.

The man holds his wrist with his opposite hand and smiles at Aberdeen.

"Do you know this woman?"

"I think she lives in my apartment building, but I'm not sure. I don't know absolutely everyone inside."

"How long has she been violent," he says and releases his wrist.

"Oh," she starts and can't help herself, "about thirty seconds in total when the suit decided to take his anger out on her."

He raises an eyebrow. "So violence is justified when you're off medication?"

"No, but she's not healthy. She's depressed. Clearly."

He smiles again. The soldiers are at the vehicle now. They bend the woman's head for her as they place her in the back seat of the SUV and buckle her in. She droops forward and her forehead touches the back of the driver's headrest.

"We're taking her somewhere she can get help. She can't stay out here. She's dangerous to herself and others," and touches his wrist again. "Clearly," he mocks.

"Somewhere?" and she takes a step towards him and stops. He looks at her feet and puts his fingers into the pocket of his button-down shirt. He pulls out a crisp business card and proffers it to Aberdeen. She doesn't move any closer to him. She stretches her body across the distance and he drops it into her open hand.

She reads it. Then she looks at the man. "What is this?"

"We're taking her to a psychiatric facility. That's it. If you find out who she is or ferret out some of her family, they can contact us there. We can tell them why she's been interned."

The word "interned" hits Aberdeen. Maybe his diction is just strange, she thinks. Or maybe he knows exactly what he's saying. She looks at the card again. *Plains View Ward: Health Camp 894.*

"This isn't an actual hospital, is it? What, is this some kind of holding pen for people?" She looks again at the card. "And there is no address. Just a phone number."

"Yes," is all he says and starts walking back to the vehicle.

Aberdeen has visions of Bergen-Belsen which she visited on a trip to Europe in high school. It's enough to keep her asking questions.

"So you're taking her to an internment camp for crazies. Can't medicate them into falling in line anymore so you've got to put them away? Imprisonment? That's not constitutional," her voice rises. "No way."

He doesn't look back but answers. "Things are different now. And we don't call them *camps*. It's a *facility*."

Aberdeen is standing over the woman's shed tears. They've become dollops of ice.

"It says 'camp' on the card."

And then he's in the car and the car is soon gone and the soldiers wander off following a patrol circuit only they know, like ants following the chemical scent of other ants.

She puts the card in her coat pocket, goes inside, finds the two people she can name clearly and tells them what has happened. Then she gets in bed in the middle of the afternoon and cries her own tears which slip through the bed sheet, into the mattress. Tears that never freeze.

CHAPTER ELEVEN

Christmas lights indicate the health of a community. Aberdeen heard of this a year ago, when her craft classes were well attended, still brought in money. The fact came from a woman with earrings that brushed her shoulders. That was all Aberdeen could remember of her. That and the trivia, that Christmas lights, their abundant application or lack thereof, demonstrates the morale of people.

She doubts the fact. Even now, just to be obstinate. She feels when things are hard, the lights will go off. No strings on the conifers or garish strands mimicking icicles over peaked garages. But it is the opposite. When people are sick, dire in mood, fatalistic, strings in white and multicolor go up sooner, stay longer, and dot the night with stabs of light gone muted with snowfall.

Currently, case in point. Fact now proven.

Even with Christmas months behind them, the lights stay up.

Aberdeen knows they'll stay up as long as the trouble stays. They are mutually inclusive from now until the ground thaws soft, hot asphalt divots under tires, the acorns shed their cross-hatched hats, and the cold comes again.

It could take that long, she thinks, looking at Hurt. It could take that long and longer for things to normalize. With drug conglomerates declaring bankruptcy, others consolidating, slow rebuilds of medical manufacturing plants foiled by monkey-wrenching and promises of greater attacks from the omnipresent cartel, the wealthy and powerful still using up the only extant pharmaceutical supplies, and the lack of aid from America's allies because of cartel threats of violence on their own turf in retribution, it could take years. By then, the color will be coming off the tiny, glass bulbs in rubbery peels.

And she thought she was the one who was traumatized by the woman being taken away. But since the day she came in and took him by his hands and led him to the sofa and told him what she had witnessed, Hurt had gotten stoic. Not quiet or scared. He was hard in the face, not letting the lines in his forehead and cheeks crease and give away emotion. Gone was the anger, the red skin.

He's that way now, with his fingers tracing the words in a textbook. He runs his fingertips over and over the same line *...and the reference numbers for the specific genre will not be replaced by...* and then he picks up the same finger, the right index, and does it again. Aberdeen moves to his side and touches a line as well, expecting to find the ink raised, like the thick welling up of fat on the surface of a skillet. But the page is smooth, the font non-tactile. She frowns.

"Learning through osmosis?" she asks.

"Learning through trial," he answers.

"Like the old days," she says, not knowing what days she refers to. Then she envisions young men smooth of chest throwing spears into the bulk of a mammoth.

He nods, doesn't look up from his book. "Sure," is all he says.

Trials for everyone. She thinks of Louis. He talks each day of his grandmother, bringing up the way she stirred a swirl of maple syrup into the top of his oatmeal or the way she cleaned the bathtub with a pair of his old underwear. Aberdeen notes how observant he is; she hopes he'll be a writer, different from his namesake, but a storyteller of renown all the same. He's never mentioned writing and Aberdeen considers she might be in the process of becoming his de facto parent, adopting dreams for a child she can't see fulfilled herself. When she thinks this, the pale index card appears in her mind as well and she shushes it though it cannot speak.

Louis is in his room. Aberdeen rubs her finger on another line above where Hurt is reading. She sees his eyelashes flick and follow her hand. But he doesn't look up.

"What are we going to tell him about school?" she asks and recalls the letter sent to the Dovers' apartment. It was addressed to Myrtle, Aberdeen neglecting to tell the school she was Louis's caregiver and she was functionally kidnapping the boy away from social services and an absent father. The letter relayed a story of a cafeteria set on fire and budget cuts and the disappearance of a troubled principal.

He still rubs the same line. Again. Again.

"That it's closed indefinitely. There's no reason to hide it from him. He's a kid, Aberdeen. He might *like* the fact he won't be sitting in a classroom all day."

She thinks of Louis skating on the ice out front, on the same place the woman held personal vigil before they took her away. Sometimes he skates alone on his thin-soled shoes. But when other kids come out, his wide cheeks lift, he looks at his feet, and then he asks them to play. They always do. But she recognizes his look. It's a look of starvation for friendship, attention, the affirmation one is present and alive.

"He's getting bored," she says, "and I don't think we're the best playmates for him. School would keep him occupied, babe. I just hope they don't keep it closed too long or can place the kids in other schools. I think they're overreacting about the climate out there," and she indicates the world outside by nodding her head at the nearest window. Even she doesn't believe what she's just said.

"Overreacting," he repeats. His finger stops moving. He looks up, dark moons under his eyes. "Even the supposed normal kids are off their Ritalin. Schools must be pits of energy and disease this time of year, nearing spring. I think the teachers and administration know what they're doing."

"He'll be okay," he adds and goes back to his page.

No he won't, she thinks and goes to check on Louis. He's in his pajamas, a fleece two-piece with a superhero logo in primary yellow. He's reading with his finger on the page and Aberdeen watches him and wonders if he's seen Hurt doing it and adopted a bad habit. Or perhaps he started the bad habit long ago, in the life he led before her and before the chaos.

"Why don't you get dressed and go outside? You could see if any of your friends are out."

"Don't really want to," he says and folds his book up and puts it behind his head like a pillow, leans on it, pushing it against the wall. "Mason keeps rubbing his nose when it drips and then not washing his hands. I hate that."

What boy would hate that? she wonders, but then is proud of Louis in a strange way, like the glimmer of OCD is a shield against the illnesses out there. His cleanliness could keep him healthy and un-needing of antibiotics, a commodity vanished months ago. But it could also keep him lonely and friendless.

"Don't let him touch you," she says and means to say "don't let anyone ever touch you if they're ill," but she smiles and opens the closet in the room and waves her hand in front of his clothes. Under his shirts are the bits of her terrarium business. She doesn't look too long at them. It makes her throat close up to see what should be on sunny tables on the surface of a dark, wooden floor.

"He chases people, Abbie."

"Then don't let him catch you," she says and pulls a shirt off a wire hanger. The hanger goes spinning off the rod and pings one of the glass bowls as it hits the ground. Abbie. If it were anyone else, she would protest. The name is too soft. But, then, so is Louis.

"Put it on, grab some jeans, and go be a boy. I mean it. You stay just outside the front door and if the soldiers pass, you wait in the foyer until they go."

Louis leaves once he's dressed, picking up his gloves from the coat closet shelf. Her purses are in there. She checks when he opens the door. It's become a habit for her to get a visual on that sparkly clutch. Her salvation is in it.

"I'll check on you from the window," she calls down the stairwell and he hollers back up at her an assent, his voice filling the landing, reverberating.

She goes back in to Hurt and closes the book with the flat of her hand. He doesn't protest when she takes his elbow and guides him to stand up. She leans in close to him and puts her lips to his chin, kissing.

"Want to?" is all she says.

And he does. And they do.

And Aberdeen isn't trying to trick Hurt, but Hurt leaves the thrall of the sensations to have a realization before entering her. She might not have any more birth control pills. She might be off them. He doesn't ask, but it's been months since they've made love, since before the first fight about children. He squints his eyes and holds his naked torso, his side nearly healed, above Aberdeen. Then he shifts his pelvis away from her own, tilting it to the ceiling.

"Do we have any condoms?"

She points to a wooden box on the dresser and he goes to it, opens it, and pulls out a single shiny square. He flips it over and finds the expiration date.

"It's old, but I'm sure it will work." He puts it on. Comes

back to Aberdeen. Slips inside.

Don't work, she thinks.

"Bust," she mumbles.

"Break," she screams. "Break!"

After, he's at her side on his back, taking in air, holding his ribs.

"New word of passion, Aberdeen?" he says in between sighs.

She props herself on her elbows and looks at his penis. The clear sheath is there, the white liquid a puckered sphere in its tip. Shit, she thinks, and gets up, uses the bathroom, gets dressed.

Hurt stays in bed and falls asleep. She watches him for a moment, satisfied in what they just did and the way his lungs keep rising and falling. Her birth control pills have been gone for two months. Her periods are long and sharp but she loves the way they come on like a rainstorm, unpredictable and wild. She holds herself just below the navel and squeezes.

Then she goes to the window in the living room that looks out over the front of the apartment and searches for the boy. She sees him immediately, his dark hair without a hat. A mother would have remembered to make him take a hat. But she's trying.

He's not talking to the two boys he usually hangs around. Those boys aren't in sight. Instead he's standing next to the young man Aberdeen noticed before, the one with the haircut seen on Roman busts, the hair crispy and white. Where does he get the peroxide?

And then she sees how Louis is holding the sole of one of his feet up against the brick wall just as the guy does. The young man rubs his hands together briskly. Louis does the same.

One to watch, she tells herself.

And she watches; she watches the days Louis leaves the apartment and goes outside without her. The man is always there. Louis has told her over and over his name: Janos. He likes to say it to her, proud of his pronunciation. The J is a Y, the S makes the same shushing sound given to crying children and theater-talkers. It's Hungarian, he tells her. She tells him he's said so before. He tells her seven or eight times over and so Aberdeen shows him the country on a globe that can be plugged in. Yellow light flickers in the center of the earth, backlighting countries in brown, red and green.

"How old is Janos?" she asks.

"Not that old. I think he's out of high school."

She nods and touches his head. "I'd like to meet him."

"Sure," he says, "but say his name right," and then he makes her practice with him in the bathroom mirror, their mouths pursed, awaiting sloppy kisses from their reflections.

The next day she goes out with Louis. She remembers to put a blue stocking cap on him and puts the gray hat she's finished on her own head. The blue cap is an old thing of Hurt's and she decides then and there she'll make Louis his own hat in yellow with red stripes. The stockinette stitch of the old cap is flecked with pills of rayon or polyester and she picks at them and flicks them away as the pair winds down the stairs and out to a day of fog at the tops of the trees, hovering, a seal of mist and gray.

Janos, as always, is there. His hands are deep in his pockets. He brings them out, bare, blows on them and then sticks them back in.

Aberdeen thinks back. The woman with her ratty hair and swollen eyes tried to always be here, stay here. Not as successful.

Then she's in the present again. Janos. He's maybe twenty-three, if that. His skin is scarred by acne cysts but his eyes are perfect circles and his nose has the angle and termination of a ski jump. He smiles at Aberdeen. She smiles back.

She extends a hand and he takes it. His fingers are bits of hard cold.

"You're Janos," she says and then looks at Louis who nods

in appreciation of her pronunciation. "I'm Louis's..." and then she hesitates, searching for the right term. Caregiver? Friend? Adoptive Parent?

"...I'm Aberdeen."

"Yeah, cool," he says, pulls back his arm, plunges his hands past the zipper of his jacket, into the warmth of his armpits.

She looks for signs of depression or paranoia or psychosis or illness and decides signs are not clear on these things, especially within seconds of meeting a person. If signs show, they are in the distance, headlights not hitting them directly, some of the letters scratched off, a tag in loopy red paint scrawled across one of them, a bent side obscuring the message on another.

Who needs signs? she thinks and then speaks.

"You're okay, right? Nothing wrong with you? I have to ask. I'm responsible for Louis."

Louis hears this and it makes his shoulders lift up to the lobes of his ears. "Abbie," he mumbles and then walks down the sidewalk to a patch of ice and starts slipping around. She's a parent here, now, because she has caused embarrassment. And she doesn't care. She'll take the milepost.

Janos laughs and watches Louis feign preoccupation with the slick pavement. He bobs his head up and down like he can hear a beat Aberdeen can't.

"Nah, no worries. I'm okay. I keep myself healthy. And I'm not a psycho. I'm not fucking around with Louis or anything." He pauses, looks down at Aberdeen, "How about you? Crazy or sane or dying of fucking tuberculosis?"

She likes him.

"Ha, no, nothing like that. I'm lucky. Just an asthmatic, but it's under control. I practice breathing techniques, keep allergens out of my apartment."

His hands move around under his jacket. He lifts them back out and places them back in his pockets. He winks at her. She turns away.

"Well, you let me know if it ever becomes a problem. If you need something, I'm down here."

He's hitting on me, she thinks, and she reaches up and smoothes down her hair and then hates herself for being so girlish at the attention of a younger man. Not that he's that much younger. Maybe twelve years.

She doesn't want to ask what he means. Then he's forward; he makes himself clear.

"If you need *anything* I've got it. I'm holding. I've got product."

And he steps in close to Aberdeen. His breath smells like lemon drop candies. He whispers.

"Probably no smoke for you. But opiates, shit, they relax the lungs. Keep that in mind, would you?" and his voice lilts up, like he's asking her to use a coaster or go back to his dorm room.

"Drugs," she says, glancing over to see Louis center himself with his arms outspread like wings, correcting a potential fall. "You have drugs."

"I have drugs," he laughs. "I have drugs."

CHAPTER TWELVE

She figures out the code. But she doesn't understand it. When people walk by Janos, the young or thin or old with walkers, lovers with hands clasped, people with scarves wrapped around their mouths, he says two words, two words that tell that person or people their salvation may come from a man who looks like a David Bowie impersonator.

"Kiss kiss," he says. He always leans his body towards them, out across the sidewalk and into their trajectory.

Then the ones who know and don't want to partake swing wide around his woolen jacket. The ones who don't understand what he's offering don't make eye contact. The ones who know and respond to the call stop, dig about in their purses or pockets for money and when they hand it over, he hands them a ticket. It's the same kind of ticket a person could rip out of a skeeball machine, soft and pink. Aberdeen thinks of them as kin to the index card on her bookshelf.

Then the people leave. Some of them hold the ticket up to the sky, look at it like they can see the sun flying through it, like it's a faceted gem, spitting out light that dazzles and charms. Most tuck the ticket away to keep it safe.

Where they exchange it for product, Aberdeen can only

guess.

No potential customer is walking by now and Janos wolf whistles at Aberdeen to get her attention, like her attention was elsewhere, really on the tree she's leaning up against, her head cocked up to look at the bare branches crisscrossing the white atmosphere. He knows this. She knows he knows this. But she keeps her head gazing up for a moment longer and then walks over to his space on the apartment wall.

"I hate to say you're bad for business, because I don't think most people give a shit anymore about buying out in the open, but damn, could you at least look like you aren't spying on me?"

She shakes her head and thinks of Hurt and Louis inside. She told them she was going out for air while they finished their lunch of tuna sandwiches and fat, bumpy pickles. She'd been going out for air her whole life, whether the smog was thick, the pollen was wafting or the air was so cold it made her lungs seize. Outside air was the best kind. And it was the best of excuses to just…leave.

"I keep debating whether or not I should keep Louis away from you. You know he's enamored with you, right? He's been trying to talk me into letting him dye his hair. The only way I hold him off is by telling him there's no way I can even get peroxide right now, and that won't work forever, I'm sure."

Janos smiles and taps his foot on the concrete. "Tell him black dudes don't look good with peroxide hair. Not racist, just too Demolition Man."

"I don't know if he knows who Wesley Snipes is," she responds.

"Dennis Rodman?" he asks and then turns his head to spit out a bit of creamy phlegm.

"Probably not."

"Shit, I guess we're just old, then," and he laughs and Aberdeen laughs with him because he's so very young.

"Why are you doing this?" she says, easy, and levels him

116

with a look. It's her best mother look. She opens her eyes wide, fixes them on his, folds her arms across her chest.

He gives her an answer she's not expecting.

"Because I want to help people."

She tries to think of a diplomatic response and remembers the time in high school debate class when she called one of her classmates arguing the merits of drug legalization a retard in front of the teacher. That was her argument; the kid was a retard and she was fine with the political incorrectness of the word. She didn't think it would hold up here, either. Besides, a pharmaceutical apocalypse sort of changed things.

"Enlighten me," she says and lets her arms relax to her sides.

He spits again and she watches it smack the ground.

He starts with "people are in pain and afraid and trying to deal and they will take any help they can get" and transitions to "besides the fact I'm only shelling out the product available, even if the product is directly benefiting the very mega-cartel still terrorizing us" and ends with "we're all fucking going to die from this thing anyway, so why not do what I can do?"

She's listening but still watches the naked branches of the tree. They move when a semi-truck drives by, limbs trying to catch the flying vehicle. But they just barely move. You have to be looking, really looking to see it.

"You do what you can do?" she repeats back at him. She can't invalidate the points he's making. Perhaps she can. But she sees some of herself in him and suddenly she's not interested in debating. She feels like entertaining new ideas right now. Someone, she thinks, say we'll all be okay at the end of this absence of medicine. Say it now, she thinks, and she might believe it.

"I help people," he insists. "It's my path."

"Your calling? You have a calling to sell drugs?"

"I have a calling to be a social worker when this shit blows through and I can kick up some fucking dust out of this city. Go to college, get a degree, sit in a room putting people's problems into file folders. You know, a calling."

She takes Janos in, ignores the tree for a moment. She can see him making home visits to dirty trailers maligned with too many children in too few rooms, boxes of cigarettes on the highchair, a dog, a pit bull chained outside to an iron stove with its pipe reaching up to the sky, hooked to nothing. And he fits there, not because of how he looks. Aberdeen can see him slouching into a chair, clicking a pen to ready and talking things out.

Why she thinks this, she cannot say. But she does.

"I believe that's what you want to do. Why not? I'm sure you will when this is all over."

"But," he prompts.

"But selling drugs is still illegal, at least I think it is. Laws are changing so fast, I'm not sure it's illegal anymore."

He takes the roll of numbered tickets out of his inner jacket pocket and fingers the perforations made into each one, moving the roll through his hands like a rosary.

"Nope, still illegal. Not that the police care. They've got the protestors, crazies and sickies to watch. And those people are further down on the shit list. The terrorists are up at the top, first priority. The last thing they want to do is take away the drugs and have millions of Americans coming down off their meth and cocaine and opiate highs. Adds to the problem."

She knows it but she has to ask it. "So the government is letting the dicks responsible for attacking us take over medicating Americans with stuff cut with rat poison and joints and grams of heroin? And that's okay?"

"Not okay. But after LTP, it's just reality, Abbie."

"Aberdeen," she corrects him and he nods but she smiles all the same. He reminds her of an old boyfriend, the one who used to always lay his hand on one of her knees while they talked.

"Besides," he says, looking down at his own shoes and then at hers, "there aren't any other *real* jobs right now for kids without degrees, just temp positions leading nowhere with crap pay. No way would I work the sanitation crews, get exposed to human fecal matter. I might as well dig my own grave if I get some crazy disease from other people's shit. My constitution isn't strong, never has been. Had pneumonia three times last year. Least there were meds then."

"Plus, I can put the money away for college," he says and Aberdeen thinks this young man, this boy, isn't ready to consider college might not exist in the same way by the time he's ready to go.

And he finishes with, "he pays us well. Just have to do this and other theatrics."

Aberdeen looks at their shoes, too, and notices they are both black leather with pencil laces. She should have called him, she kids herself, to see what he was wearing that day so they weren't so tacky, wearing the same things, on the same sidewalk, one of them slinging, the other searching.

The word "theatrics" sticks when he says it. She wants to ask for clarification, and she'd probably get an answer, but she decides not to know, as if knowing would make her ravenous for knowledge, always wanting more and more. She shakes her head. Drug lords becoming the pillars of the community. Propping up the masses with highs.

She moves her feet around, gives them some blood, kicks them into the air making a mockery of a famous Russian dance.

She stops kicking and smiles. "*He* pays well. So the boss is a man? How many folks work for him? I could use the money," and then she laughs because the part of her sick of tuna fish and bulk, generic cereals wishes she had the balls of Janos to milk the current crisis.

He doesn't play with her. His face goes still. "I'm not going to talk about him. That'd be stupid. But there are plenty of us.

Everywhere. We're something of a family. We're so big and fucked up."

Family. Hurt and Louis. She looks up and can see the edge of the window of their apartment and suddenly she misses them. She wants to smell her husband's hands after they've done the dishes. She wants to tease Louis and pinch his elbow in between her fingers.

"At least you have a support system, I guess," she says and then waves at him, moves past him to the front door.

He bumps the sleeve of her jacket with his shoulder. It's a light knock, gentle. "Don't keep Louis away, please. He's so smart. The things that come out of his mouth," and he lets his thought drop. He shoves the roll of tickets back in his pocket.

"I don't think I could," she says. "He's had too many losses already."

Janos purses his lips, slides his hands in and out of his pockets.

Aberdeen goes inside, the last thing she catches is the sound of him saying *kiss kiss* to a passing pedestrian. Not to her. And her cheeks redden.

Upstairs the boys are sitting on the living room floor with their legs out at angles to their torsos. They are playing a board game, moving little plastic amalgamations of people from one box to the next. She doesn't recognize the game. Must be one of Louis's from the vacant apartment two flights down. She couldn't say what those boxes stand for, where they head to, how one could win.

"Talked to Janos," is all she says and she goes into the kitchen to find the dishes unwashed.

Hurt and Louis ignore her and keep playing.

So she decides to play her own game with Louis the next day. He's late to rise and she knows he's not taking the school closure well. He says he misses homework. This worries her.

"We're going out today. Just you and me. We're going to go on a scavenger hunt."

Louis's eyes widen. He dresses so quickly his socks are mismatched, one an orange thing fading to yellow, the other an athletic crew.

"Ready," he says and they go, leaving Hurt at his books, drumming out a rhythm with his highlighter on the kitchen table.

They hit the street and Janos isn't in sight. Louis says nothing about it so Aberdeen decides not to bring it up.

"What are we looking for?" he says, moving his shoulders back and forth like he's prepping for a game of football. He'd be a linebacker.

"Actually," says Aberdeen, and she takes his hand in hers, "it's not really a visual game. We're going to be listening instead."

"For what?"

"For people saying *kiss kiss.*"

"Just like Janos," and he smiles.

"Perfectly right," and she lets Louis pick their direction with a tug on her hand.

They wander for a few blocks, skirting the soldiers when they can. Louis cups a hand to his ear on occasion, as if he can capture the sound of those words from miles off. They pass a hillock of dirt piled high in front of an office building. There is no hole that would explain the dirt. And sticking out of the mound are the broken bits of a wooden reindeer. An antler flaking paint. A bit of a two-dimensional bell that cannot ring.

They keep walking and they pass a young woman with a lavender shawl wound about her neck and over her head. She whispers to them the words they are seeking and Louis stops to talk to her but Aberdeen looks dead ahead and pulls him after her.

"One," he says.

"One," she repeats.

Another gap of street and space and Louis jumps on a manhole cover that's been spray painted with two round eyes and a wide grin, the face a neon green. He jumps on the smiley face twice and then returns to her to take up her hand again. She wonders if she should hold onto him this way. Of course she should.

Another block, another thrown-out call. A few to the south, more pleading for lip on lip. Affection. They keep walking and the words *kiss kiss* come quicker, said loudly, clipped, whispered or in monotone.

"I lost count," Louis says as they head into an area of town Aberdeen isn't too familiar with. It's industrial; there are Quonset huts, metal roofs and garages tall and wide. And it bustles with people.

"Strange," she says aloud and Louis takes it as a reply.

"There's been a lot of them," he says and then adds, "sorry."

She bites her lip, shakes her head and squeezes his hand. Why all the people in an area of town out of the way of storefronts and restaurants and homes?

Engrossed in thought, Louis lets go of her hand and brings her back to him with a question.

"I'm getting tired, Abbie. Are we done counting the drug dealers yet?"

He's known all along. She's discounted the cleverness of the boy that she's taken into her home. The same one that knows to hide candy wrappers from her by shoving them to the bottom of the wastebasket, layering tissue over them, sheets waded up and placed just so.

Then she realizes something else.

"How old are you, Louis?"

"Ten. I'll be eleven in the summer."

She never thought to ask his exact age before. She sticks her hand out, fingers flared and wiggles it in front of him. He takes it in his own. She looks down at their fists. Black and white. 10 and 35.

"Yes," she says, "we're almost done."

And then she sees ahead of them, a man in his fifties is handing a ticket, the same kind that Janos rolled and re-rolled in his palm, to a woman with a stomach so sunken her torso might be just back skin, spine, belly skin.

What the hell? Aberdeen thinks. They might be close.

Hand in hand, Aberdeen and Louis walk forward and the lady without any fat, rolls back on her heels, gains her center, and walks off with her ticket tucked into a pocket over her flat chest. She talks to herself in a voice small, the rhythm of her words staccato.

They walk several steps behind her. Louis is done counting the sounds of *kiss kiss*, curious about the new game but not asking for the rules. Aberdeen figures he probably knows what they're doing.

Where do the tickets go?

Follow the ticket holders and see.

The woman is beyond gone. Whatever high she's on takes away her ability to perceive a boy and a woman following her.

A half mile later, still in the section of town meant for metal smelting and drywall fabrication, they turn a sharp right and the lady speeds up. They speed up, too. And then it's there, in a field surrounded by barbed wire, what must have been a pasture for horses or cattle before the land went to mechanization.

A white tent. A tent the size of something that could hold a trapeze and a baby elephant. But no striped roof in alternating red and yellow. No signs of any kind.

The drugged woman lifts her legs high but Aberdeen pulls Louis to a stop. They watch her move in a circle around the tent, avoid the entrance, and head off behind the tent, her thin frame swallowed up by a movement of the canvas fabric.

But this is not the oddest thing. It takes her a moment to see it, but there are two types of people here, in the field of brittle grass and wet footprints. Some of the people are like the thin woman: tweakers, potheads, men rubbing their noses, women stumbling in stilettos which sink into the soft ground. A variety of addicts on parade.

But not the majority of the people. Most of them are clean, wearing nice coats with pintucks and pleats, hair fixed. There are families. There is a man carrying a young girl, her legs over her father's shoulders, her chubby hands clasped against his forehead.

And the opposite types of people ignore one another. They do not overlap. They move around one another in a dance of avoidance making the groups of people appear like circles, the middle one the widest, composed of the normal folks, the other one a rim of addled souls.

The families, the people who look more like Aberdeen and Louis are moving to the main entrance. They do not disappear behind the tent. They go into it.

"What is this? A carnival?" asks Louis.

They still have their hands intertwined. She doesn't answer him. Instead she gets quiet, listening for something just louder than the sound of the people moving into the tent or around it.

She catches words: *holy, praise, to the highest.*

She hasn't ever seen such a thing in person. She wasn't sure such things existed in the present day. But all the people, the masses, are here to get the same thing, just in a different way. In a time when help is most needed.

Louis asks again, "What is it?"

Pressing her palms together, she names it.

"A revival."

CHAPTER THIRTEEN

Hurt spoons up a dollop of cream of mushroom soup and dribbles it back into the bowl. A gray blob clings to the dip in the utensil.

"It's the dark, I think. It's that steady dark. Not just dark. Steady, steady," he says and cleans the spoon with his tongue.

Aberdeen rubs at a knot in his back smack between his shoulder blades. He's often morose this time of year, when light is scarce and the air is a capped jar of car exhaust and wood smoke.

"We're well past the winter solstice. Look at it this way, babe," she assures with a firm knuckle into the meat over his spine, "the days are only getting longer, not shorter. We're walking out of the woods. We're on our way to an equinox, soon half dark half light."

Hurt puts down the spoon and his head nods back. He looks up at Aberdeen and pouts for a kiss. She lays one on him and watches his back relax as she takes away her fist. He puts out a hand and she takes it and he sweeps her around to face him like a man leading a lady out to the dance floor.

"Where are you going dressed like that?" and he spins his finger in the air and she spins her body accordingly, her pleated dress lifting then falling back to her knees. "If I didn't have work at the vet clinic and then studying, I'd be going with you, wherever you're going. You're a fine looking woman, Aberdeen. Fight off my competition for me, would you?"

She doesn't say she hopes to get a longer look from Janos when she steps out the door, but she wants that. No more. Just recognition of her small waist and slight curves by someone male. It's Hurt she wants; it's Hurt she has always wanted, since they met in Brussels, two people lost with maps unfolded. They looked at one another, laughed, and compared the situation to a scene someone might read in a cheap romance novel. Then they switched maps, read one another's, like it would help them become found. It had worked.

"I'm not getting into fisticuffs for my own honor. If you want to defend me, come with me. Please?"

Her dress is the blue of flax and her black hair is pulled back in a wide clip. She wears gray sweater tights and slouchy boots and the best accessory she can think of is Hurt on her arm.

"Louis wants to go. Take him," Hurt smiles.

She listens for Louis; she tries to get a sense of what he's doing in the next room. It's quiet. There are no clues. But she knows now, knows she must be careful around him. What she says. What she does. He soaks it up, analyzes it as a ten-year-old boy, spits it back out as night terrors and insecurity and friendship with a drug dealer.

"Adults only," she says, hoping it will be enough for Hurt. "He wouldn't be interested."

Hurt gets a bit wiser. "Where are you going again?"

The tent.

But she can't say it. Louis could hear.

"Come with me and I'll show you. We'll have an adventure," she hedges, tugs at one of her boots that doesn't want to ride her calf.

"Adventure doesn't have the same appeal anymore."

"Ah," comes out of her in a hiss.

"Don't do that, Aberdeen."

She exhales again and pulls at the barrette in her hair. Part of her wants Hurt to come. The part that says she might be an idiot, walking into a place she knows is surrounded by drug addicts. But part of her wants to go alone and come back with answers. Moses into the wilderness. Moses into a big, white tent.

She looks down at herself. She's dressed for church. Or at least she thinks so. She's never been into one.

"I won't do *that*, Hurt," she says and wonders what *that* is and spins again and again without reason until she has to hold a chair back to steady herself. She lets the room whirl around her. Hurt laughs and she's glad her moments of silliness have power.

"Sit down before you fall down."

So she does, right on the linoleum floor of squares filled with egg-yellow sunbursts. And when the spinning stops, she stands and pulls on her coat, places her iPod in the inside zipper pocket and walks out the door.

Janos isn't on his wall, isn't there to give her a look over. She's dressed for no one but herself now.

She has two companions as she walks to the tent, passing all the things she has seen before, the hunger, fear, despair of humans, just displayed in new ways. Someone screaming instead of crying. People fighting instead of embracing. Right now they are of no interest to her. The two companions are the things on which she focuses.

Her asthma, roused with the spinning, the exertion in an attempt to have fun. No fun for her. A rattle emanates from her mouth, so she shuts it and lets the wheeze squeeze out her nostrils and into the freezing air. My companion for life, she says and places a hand on her chest.

Her music, specifically a symphony she has fallen in love with in the last month, keeps her mind busy. It was a downloadable gift from a college friend who had majored in music composition. The friend was prone to giving gifts of song to others in times of hardship. Aberdeen hadn't spoken to the man in years and found the link to download the symphony in her email inbox one day after LTP with a note simple, sincere: *Take the pain away with this. I adore it. Remember the night you got drunk on sweet plum wine?*

She didn't remember the night, but she thought it a testament to the human condition that a friend lost to her for years, knew enough to send her comfort. But hell, she thought, he probably sent the symphony to everyone. It was probably his way of comforting himself.

She loves it, though. Gorecki. *Song for the Sorrowful Souls.* That we are, she thinks as she passes waste bins overflowing with refuse and the occasional calling out of *kiss kiss*. The music builds, morose, then hopeful, orchestral emotions pounding, ebbing, building into a crescendo.

The voice of a woman, the soprano singer, hits its high just as Aberdeen arrives at the edge of where the tent is posted into the frozen ground and she has to stop and consider her hands, how they vibrate at the confluence of music, the weaving masses of humans seeking comfort, and the white of the tent billowing with its own apparent breath.

She wishes her lungs could catch the wind the same way. Then she could be the one singing, high and crystalline in some Slavic language, arms open, chest out, sustaining joyful noise. She wipes a bit of moisture off her eyelashes and shuts the music off, pulls ear buds from her head, steps forward into the fray.

It is the same as it was when she was here last with Louis. Two disparate groups of people meander, ignoring one another, out for their own different kind of drugs. She falls in behind a group of young women. All of them have hair down to the small of their backs, thin at the bottom from years without trims, high-collar shirts and sleeves buttoned at the cuff poking out of long, frumpy jackets. She tries to blend in with them. But she is a raven to their flock of house sparrows.

She sees a man with a dog to her left. The dog's neck is ringed with a choke chain. He lifts the dog on its back hind legs as he walks, tugging high on the leash with disregard. They disappear to the back of the tent, the man walking faster than his dog to get at his drugs and a dog with no designs on the world at large.

Then she is moving, getting funneled to the entrance of the tent. The music is there, so different in beat and rhythm to her symphony. There is call-and-response, the sound of clapping and the occasional shout in an unknown syllable.

Two men flank the tent entrance. One holds a dark, wooden box with a thin slit in the top of it. The other has a mask over his nose and mouth as if he is about to sand down joint compound. This man halts the people, asks them questions, his jaw working behind the spongy, white mask. Then he looks into eyes, mouths, noses and ears without instrumentation. Everyone seems to be waved in. Even a small boy with a cough that sends him inching backwards each time he hacks.

That is, waved in after they put money in the box.

Aberdeen tries to remember what she has for cash in her bag. A five, maybe. She hopes it's a donation. But it could be a suggested donation. As if donations should ever need suggesting.

And she's there, at the tent flaps, daylight on her back and the light of lamps and candles falling on the fabric of her dress from within the tent. It turns the light blue dress into an Impressionist painting, all pastel and soft.

The question is muffled behind the mask. A question asked a hundred times a day, if not more.

"Are you sick?"

Aberdeen smiles and then covers her teeth with her palm. "Do I have to be?"

And then the man prods at her a little and shoves his face close up to hers. His eyes are yellow with flecks of brown and she can't help but think this man is a disease vector, poking into people's bubbles. She thinks she'll be sick after this visit. She prays for a head cold if she must fall ill. Nothing more.

She opens up her purse and finds a ten dollar bill. There isn't a change bag hanging near the donation box so she sucks it up, tells herself canned pasta isn't so bad, and shoves the bill in the hole. The man holding the box clutches it to his chest with both arms. He nods at her and she goes inside.

Standing room only. What chairs were folded out at one point, hard and metal, have been leaned against the perimeter of the tent. It's degrees warmer inside, though she can only see hanging lanterns and no real heat source. The use of actual fire instead of LEDs or traditional bulbs surprises her. It's an element of unnecessary danger. People clap and sway and raise arms high and holler like simians. The cacophony makes her yearn for the sound of her symphony. It smells of old body odor and something resinous and sweet to cover it up. It smells as if she's stepped into a bath of hot water and apple cider vinegar.

There are hundreds in the tent. All she can really see are heads crowned in hats, bowl cuts, widow's peaks and bangs. Brown and red and blonde. Wiry and straight. The crowd is all hair, done up, done right, done for the spectacle of what's happening in the tent.

And this is what's happening in the tent: healing.

Or the crowd would like to think so.

Above the heads bobbing and jostling for a better view, a stage stands high up against the back of the tent. It's made of planks of subflooring and it gives a bit in the middle as a man well over six foot with skin the color and texture of chocolate mousse walks back and forth, a Bible held over his face. He taps the edge of it on his forehead and looks down as his feet move back and forth, the wood still giving a bit, the wood yielding to his weight.

Aberdeen pushes her way to the middle of the crowd.

There's a group of younger children in the center and she knows if she can reach them and stand behind them, she'll be able to see the show taking place. And she does and she can see the man more clearly. He wears an overcoat with tails and a thin, red tie. He looks like a Republican lion tamer. She laughs.

The music stops then. And seconds after, the crowd's babbling stills to a hush. The man speaks with his face hidden behind the Good Book.

"Now a healing for you penitent folks. Now a healing for the children of our Lord Jesus Christ whose Holy Spirit was at work at Pentecost and is at work now in our time of need. For you all are the poorest of the poor. Even if your clothes may still be fine, your wives with you, your husbands still with work, you are the poorest of poor because you all have been given this test. Do without medicine. Do without our nation's guaranteed safety. Yes, you are all so poor and meek and this is His holy way. Amen."

And amen is screamed, sobbed, wailed from the people below the stage.

The man pulls the book away from his face and Aberdeen sees he only has one eye. The empty socket is un-patched, the eyelid sinking concave into his face.

He turns and places the Bible over his heart and beckons to someone at his feet, the stage as high as the heads of the people. Two strong men pull a scrappy, unwashed man from the audience and walk him up the raw wooden stairs to the stage. The dirty man blinks and eyes the crowd, his mouth opening and closing like he's chewing something.

In the quiet of the tent she can hear the man pulled onto the stage chirp and whirl his tongue in mimicry of some sort of bird.

The preacher speaks. "This man, this son of Jesus comes to us today for healing, to receive our Lord's blessing, and he will receive. This man is sick of mind and the government and country that should be tending to his needs are fallen to the wayside. What he has now is the power of the kingdom of God, eternal and right. Amen."

The people say "amen." So does Aberdeen, who doesn't think she's one of the people.

"And because this poor soul cannot pay," and the one-eyed man puts his hand on the birdman's shoulder, "he shall not be turned away. Others will pay for him. Alms for the needy."

Then the preacher sticks the Bible into the air and calls forth the healers.

Three people walk up the same stairs to the stage and the wood dips under their moving feet. Aberdeen can guess as to their purposes. A man in suspenders has his shirt sleeves rolled in cuffs to his elbows. He rubs his hands together and then folds them in prayer. Faith healer.

A fat woman with tight ringlets embraces the crazy man and hugs him tight. Then her torso begins to shake and her eyes roll back in her head. Words come from her mouth, but they are not English and Aberdeen can't be sure if they exist in any dictionary, anywhere. Speaker of tongues.

And the last man on stage makes Aberdeen bring her hand up to her mouth. His hair is slicked back, his white shirt is buttoned to his throat and a cluster of thin snakes in greens and browns drips from his hands like roots from an unearthed tree. Snake handler.

But not just a snake handler. It's Janos.

She hopes he doesn't see her. She's sure he can't, not with the dim light and chaotic crowd.

The trio and the preacher set to work on the birdman. He's placed in a chair and the faith healer puts a palm to the man's head and one to the back of his neck. The large woman's tongue slips in and out of her mouth as her large frame convulses and heaves. And Janos, the drug dealer, the wannabe social worker, the snake handler, holds the snakes out to the man. But birdman does not touch them. He sits and coos and clucks and trills.

The preacher does his work last. He stands in front of the man and brings his Bible down on the man's chest and says, "May the love and power of the Holy Spirit give this man healing and peace and bring him back to a place of sanity. Amen!"

Assent comes from all as the preacher pushes on the book with his palms and the man jumps a bit in his chair.

Silence. Even the woman in her throes of glossolalia quiets.

The bird noises are gone. The man is now slumped over in the chair, breathing evenly, his chest lifting and lowering under the leather-bound tome over his heart.

This is sanity? Aberdeen asks, as the tent comes alive with crying, wailing and clapping. They are the sounds of perceived salvation.

"Who is next?" the preacher asks, reaching up and touching the place where his eye used to be. "Who is ready to receive the healing of Our Lord?"

They come to the stage and raise their hands up to the feet of the preacher and he picks them out with a dip of his book over their heads. And she watches for hours, until her calves get tight and itchy. A woman with a red complexion and watery eyes. Fraternal twins, a boy and a girl, each with their right arms broken, tight smirks on their faces. A man that only shakes his head side to side and weeps.

There are more still. So many who look healthy with no apparent malady. Others with grave injuries.

The only thing they all have in common is their belief.

That and the white envelopes bulging with cash they hand to a small boy wearing a bowler hat who stands at the base of the stairs. Once they hand over the envelopes, he disappears out a back tent flap, into the fresh air and returns minutes later to take back up his post.

At one point, Janos loses a snake and it slithers to the edge of the stage and pitches over the edge like dripping mercury. He doesn't go after it. He goes on with his show.

And as the people continue to flow on and off the stage, none of them miraculously cured as the birdman, Aberdeen begins to wonder why she's still in the tent, enraptured by a spectacle put on for the sake of making money.

These people sell drugs and sell false hope and she is suddenly furious. Her hands ball up. She feels sweat bead up on her back. She no longer cares about what happens in the tent or behind it. Her curiosity is sated. She wants to go home, go back to her husband and her Louis and tell them she has found nothing in the cold field in the industrial section of town.

Getting out is a problem. The crowd is always pushing to move forward and be closer to the stage. These people don't intend to leave, not until all the healing is done. Not until the preacher says the work of the Holy Spirit is tired out for the day. She shuffles around the people, having to move aside their bodies with her own body's gentle presses and nudges. Most don't respond with anything more than moving, but some take their eyes away from the stage for a moment to frown at her, at the Judas leaving the dinner table.

She can see the main entrance, the same two men are still outside the flaps but the daylight is gone, replaced by their breath in misty puffs against the dark sky.

A well-dressed man with a goatee and hair to his shoulders leans against the canvas tenting, the fabric swaddling his ivory suit. He files his nails with a bright emery board, as green as a willow in spring. He cocks his head as he looks at his cuticles in the lamp light.

Aberdeen tries not to stare, but his behavior is odd. All the other people in the tent are enthralled by the energy of possible rescue. Not this man. Not the manicure man. Not the man that must see the show every day.

Leave, she tells herself, leave now before he sees you. He'll know you know he's someone. Someone special. The realization is on her face, in the lines of her forehead and the sloping down of her mouth.

The tent opening is ten feet, maybe twelve away from her. She looks dead ahead and walks forward. The man continues to file his nails and she can hear the scuffing sound of rough on rough.

She's almost there when the woman on the stage lets out such a set of syllables it makes Aberdeen turn to see what has set her off.

And it's as if she can't help herself, but after she sees the speaker of tongues shake over the seated body of an old woman, she looks back at the man in the suit. And he stops running the rough stick over his fingers and looks back at her.

His head tilts and he runs his fingers around his mouth and over his goatee drawing attention to his lips pursed in a tight bow.

The entrance. She moves then, walks through it and takes a breath, the cold shocking her lungs after hours in the sultry tent.

She feels a hand on her shoulder and when she cranes her head around she sees the man with the respirator on his face. He holds her shoulder with a strong pinch and uses his other hand to move the mask down to his chin. He brings her torso around, squared up to his own like he's about to chide her for doing a wrong.

"Were you healed, ma'am?" he asks.

She says nothing as she watches the other man put the wooden donation box down at his feet and walk over to stand directly behind her. He smells like clove cigarettes.

And from the wide, welcoming gap in the tent, framed by the canvas, she can make out the form of the suited man backlit in the yellow light.

She feels a sickening push on the back of her neck. A needle. Her vision goes hazy and soft.

And then all she can see is the man with the fine nails

pursing his lips again, bringing his hand up to his mouth, and blowing her a kiss goodnight.

CHAPTER FOURTEEN

She comes to in the backseat of a van. The dome light is on and her eyes are fixated on the shine of the plastic cover radiating out lines of white on the metal of the car roof. She dips in and out of consciousness. There are moments where she thinks she is entirely back, only to feel her neck go loose and her head fall upon her breastbone. But when her senses return, there is just the light and her weak form on a leather bench seat with her seat belt pulled securely about her and fastened.

The van is empty. She can't see the front seat but she hears nothing and feels certain no one sits there. When she feels a tingling in her hands and out through her fingertips, she decides it's time to move them. They are sloppy and uncontrollable at first. Her mind snaps back to the tent, to Janos with his handfuls of snakes. Her fingers are just as unwieldy and wild having been out of control of her mind for God knows how long.

She reaches over and pushes the buckle latch. It comes free. But the slight movement makes her stomach cartwheel and she folds over and lets loose a stream of bile and foam onto the metal at her feet. It must be the drugs. It must be her typical reaction to anesthetic, she thinks. Even in this situation she has the swelling hope of a possibility of pregnancy. But she's sure it's the drugs.

There is nothing within her but those chemicals they stuck in her, the present fear, and the broken lungs.

The purging helps and she reaches out for the handle on the van door. It's locked so she turns her attention to the windows. They're tinted and sealed without latches. Except for one. It's to her left and as she moves to it, she throws up again, this time getting some of her sick on her blue dress and it spreads outwards like a slick of algae on a clear pond.

She focuses, wills her fingers to pry up and out the bar on the window's edge. But all it does is open the glass an inch at most. Not that this matters. She figures it's good enough, it's something to get her started. And then she shifts onto her back, brings her legs up and thrusts her feet square at the glass.

The impact runs up her shins into her knees and she cries out and holds her kneecaps in her palms. The glass isn't broken, not even a crack. After the sharp pain goes, she looks at the latch. She's loosened a tiny screw holding the entire structure together.

So she kicks at it again. And again. And then the window falls away from its frame and her eyes take in a rectangle of dark sky with illuminated clouds.

There isn't time to see if her shoulders can be folded down enough to fit through the window. A key turns in a lock, the van door behind her swings wide open. She's hit with the smell of clove cigarettes again and the visual of three men with hands in their pockets.

It's the two men who flanked her and the man in the soft, ivory suit. He gives her a smile and then the men crawl in over the seats and pluck her up in their arms, swearing about the smell of sick on the floor, the seat and her.

She goes limp. She knows if she struggles, she will lose. They have hundreds of pounds on her. Still, something primal in her pushes for a fight, but it's ruled out by the simple, small voice telling her to submit. If she submits, there may be a chance to run later. Run now, fight now, die now.

The man who wore the white gauzy mask, the one with the yellow eyes, covers her head so she does not knock it on metal as they pull her out of the back door. They hold her up like she's next to the stage, next for healing in that big, white tent.

The man in the suit smiles and nods. She tries not to look him in the eyes. Instead her eyes dart around quickly to take in her surroundings. They're somewhere with lots of trees, away from the sounds of dogs and cars. A park is her best guess. What she can't determine is which park it might be in the omnipresent atmosphere of night and terror.

The man with smooth nails in his overcoat speaks. The words come out in a saccharine Spanish accent. Maybe Castilian.

"You are Abbie, are you not?"

She swallows hard. She wants to say to him, "it's Aberdeen, you effeminate motherfucker," but she does her best not to nod, or jerk or acknowledge he has some semblance of knowing her.

"You look very, well, like what Janos told me about you. It is not hard to miss you. Your hair is very blunt and black and you looked like a lost child in my big tent."

She doesn't respond, looks to the dark ground under her feet and quakes a bit with a shiver brought on by the cold.

"You have a look for the stage," he tells her, "a real *something* for theatrics."

Theatrics. Had Janos seen her then? He must have and somehow pointed her out. He claims he wants to help, she screams internally, and his help is in getting her drugged and abducted. If she sees him again, she'll get the rolling pin from Myrtle's apartment, get it from her kitchen smelling of mold, take it downstairs, dent in his head.

She might say something juvenile when she attacks him. "Snake handle your dick in whatever sewer you crawl into to die."

This thought gives her the ability to smile at the Spaniard.

He smiles back and puts a hand on her neck and guides her into the dark towards a line of trees and the faint outline of a cluster of buildings.

The smell hits then. Animal musk. Wet hay. She knows where they are heading.

The zoo.

The wall around the perimeter of the zoo is stacked limestone crowned with wrought iron spikes placed there when buggies used to take turns around the park and lovers would picnic with real wicker baskets. A modern steel door is plumb to the rectangles of stone. The suit man pulls a key from his pocket, unlocks the heavy door and shoves her forward.

It leads into a hallway that branches in a T from where she stands. He nudges her forward, down the long hall with dim emergency lights running along the fluorescent light casings. She shuffles her feet, takes her time, anything that will draw out her getting to wherever he wants to take her.

She walks and he walks behind her, his palm hovering over the small of her back like he'd catch her if she fell.

They pass several doors. From one she can hear the sound of some ungulate, snorting and huffing in its stable. Another is marked with a thick, red marker right on the metal. It's a giant X and it sits over the doorknob.

At the end of the hall is another metal door with a deadbolt turn on the outside of it. There is also a sliding metal hatch at eye level. The man steps forward, holding onto Aberdeen's back, and pulls the view portal aside. He presses his face up to a metal screen, scans the room and turns to his men at arms.

"I'm not seeing anything wrong," he says in calm vagueness. Then he throws back the bolt and they enter the room.

Except it's less of a room and more of a cage within a room. A snow shovel leans against a wall, its edge caked in brown muck, next to gloves the size and thickness that someone might find in a blacksmith's workshop for reaching into a forge of fire and oozing metal. The only solid wall is the one to their backs; the other three walls are grating overlapped twice, making the holes between the weave small as honeycomb. Beyond the wire is the black of night.

The man in the suit pulls from a pocket inside his coat the key he used on the zoo perimeter door and tosses it to the man with the yellow eyes who wore the respirator. He takes out a metal key ring in the shape of a penis and threads the key on the ring that hangs like a piercing from the tip of the cock. He puts it in his pocket and pats it while staring at Aberdeen.

The man who held the wooden box outside the tent closes the door but does nothing to lock it. Aberdeen lets her eyes become adjusted to the dark. The only light comes from a glowing *exit* above the door through which they've just entered. The man stops touching her and takes up a position against the solid wall and merely watches her. Aberdeen steps forward and looks out past the metal caging and sees nothing.

But she smells something. It's similar to the scent of her old pet, Alabaster, the one she had to give away at the age of ten due to her asthma. That scent. That smell of cat urine.

And then comes the rumble, a purr amplified a thousand times over that of a domestic cat. It issues from the chest of a tiger, lion, leopard. Something big with paws the size of her face and claws the size of her lips.

She looks at the man in his designer suit and then checks out the other two men that stand at the ready, apparently absent of thought.

The absurdity of the situation hits her then and she laughs. She laughs so hard she has to put her hands on her sides and pinch them, bite her lip, shake her cheeks out. All the while the man watches her. Her humor doesn't seem to upset him; he remains calm, pets his facial hair.

"Are you fucking kidding me?" she finally says. "Is this

really happening? A goddamned cage *inside* of a big cat cage for some sort of interrogation room with two grunts and a man who spends more time on his personal hygiene than most women I know?"

She holds up a finger, not letting him respond, and allows herself a round of laughter that lasts several minutes. She wants it, needs it, feels it helps distract from the fact that she's pissed herself a little out of intense fear and can feel the hot wet dribble down her left thigh. Laugh before they kill you, she thinks. It's better than crying.

"You do not like cats?" the man asks. He walks up to the caging and sticks a pinkie through one of the holes. "I thought it was clever and frightening. I suppose I was wrong. Ah, well, there won't be a next time. Let's enjoy this while we can, Aberdeen."

She stops laughing, wipes at her eyes and hopes the men don't notice the liquid flowing to the floor, coming from underneath her dress.

"I can't be," she says between gasps of air as she struggles to get her breathing back in line.

"What can't you be?"

"That important," she answers.

"Oh," he says, releasing the grating. "You are not. But when Janos told me about you, one of my men, a good man, that Janos, no matter his upbringing, I put it on my steno pad so I would not forget. And then I see you in the tent and I wonder if it is you and wonder why you would be so stupid."

Her breathing is erratic but she does her best to calm herself even with the adrenaline mainlined into her heart, veins, arteries.

"So he pointed me out?" She thinks of Janos. She thinks of pulling the white hairs from his scalp.

"No, he shared information with me at a meeting. I am not so dumb I could not know it was you. You are not the type of person who comes into the tent. Or comes around to the back of the tent."

"You people have meetings? What, like staff meetings where you share success stories about how much crack you sold that day or is it more practical stuff, like whether you should get a popcorn machine or a new coffee maker for the break room? Or both? I bet a man like you could afford both. Janos said you took good care of your people."

"Janos said nothing to you."

Aberdeen looks to the ground, the inkling to poke at the man waning. "Yes, nothing."

"And you think you are cute, no? That you are a clever woman in everyone's business?"

Aberdeen blinks hard and looks at the man.

"I'm just trying to get through this, just like everyone else. Just like you."

It's his turn to laugh then. His guffaws are low and throaty and he runs his fingers over his moustache and goatee again and again, drawing attention to his mouth.

"You are not like me," he says. "We are not the same. I will not try to get through this. I will make this stay. I will make this last. This is how I profit. This is what I know how to do."

Her appeal to humanity is lost on the man. She knows he won't let her go unharmed. The bit of her that lives in her medulla oblongata, the part of her reptilian brain that was never shut off but is merely hushed by the cortex, that part tells her what she is. What she will always be. Prey.

Why talk, she thinks. Just stay quiet. What happens will happen. The cats might eat well tonight. Her black hair might dance through the intestines of a lioness.

The man comes to her and lifts her chin, looking into her eyes. She lets him. His hands are warm and soft, just like Louis's.

"What the fuck do you want?" he asks her gently and runs a thumb over the dimple in her chin.

Her answer is immediate. "I want to go home."

"That is not my meaning. You know this. What do you want, poking around my tent? You do not want drugs. That is clear. And you do not believe in the healing power of the Holy Spirit!" At this he raises his arms into the air in supplication, ready for a divine gift.

"You don't believe in it," she says.

"No," he answers, "I believe in money."

"So," she says and rubs her thighs together. The wet on her legs is drying and causing her tights to stick to her skin.

He puts his hands down and smirks so wide his molars show. "An answer, please, Aberdeen?"

She rubs her arms with her hands but none of the men take it as a sign of her trying to flee and press her to stop her fidgeting. Her coat is too thin for the nighttime cold and she's beginning to shake, more due to the frigid temperatures than the sense of danger. She's starting to become numb to fear, and it surprises her how quickly she's become accustomed to the fact she is going to die.

There is no clever response to the question. But there is an honest one, though she's sure it will leave the man in the soft, woolen suit a bit crestfallen. Fuck him, she thinks.

"Why did I come to the tent? Why did I ask Janos about the drug dealing stuff? Well," and then she realizes she doesn't know his name and her jaw clenches because he's going to end up another nameless person she meets before her death, "I'll tell you. I'm lost and bored and curious and fucking scared shitless about the absence of vitamin E tablets and living for some semblance of purpose or goal or adventure is better than me sitting in my shitty apartment, listening to my angry husband and thinking of all the ways I'm messing up the future of a young boy."

She stops, takes in a breath, and starts up again. Her hands drop to her side. Suddenly she's warm enough.

"So I went to your tent. I didn't go for pot or meth or whatever the fuck you sell in the back or your own approximation of spirituality. I went to the tent because I fucking wanted to go to the tent." She's screaming now. The man in the suit maintains his grin. His incisors are dull white in the glow of the emergency sign. "I just wanted to see what was happening! I just wanted to see what the fuck was, no, is, going on!"

The boss doesn't offer his name. He closes his mouth, puts his lips together and continues to pet the circle of hair around his mouth. Aberdeen wants to shave it off with the lid of a tin can, rusted and jagged.

"And did I answer that for you, Aberdeen?"

"No, of course not. Of course you didn't."

He keeps rubbing. "Was the tent going to tell you when America will get its drugs back or when the people will stop dying or when martial law will end? Because I have an idea. There are things that I know that I could share with you, if you like."

Her nostrils flare and she owns her situation. She owns the piss on her tights and the growing ache in the back of her neck that signals a migraine coming. She owns the way her skin throbs where they stuck the needle in her and how she yearns to reach a hand back and cup the place of pain.

Aberdeen is done. No hope. Myrtle dying. The responsibility of tending a child not her own. These things build in her, taking over her toes, then quadriceps, moving up into her innards and onto the tips of her ears. The pressure is striated pain across her form. And if death is to come, she doesn't need to hear anymore sad bullshit.

"No," she says in a plain, but forceful tone. "I don't care what you have to say. I'm not standing here for an expository villain speech."

The man drops his ear to his shoulder and considers her. He moves back to the caging and shrugs his shoulders.

"What is this?" he asks her and the men. The men don't answer, but she can't help herself. If it's a chance to point out this man's mortality, she'll take it before they bury her under the big white tent in the cold, cold field.

"You're like the rest of us," she says, "people who will die of tuberculosis or the flu. You are fragile and human and your life means shit no matter how you spin it."

"Ah," he exclaims, "do you see how you are set for the staging of a great play? Your whole person is dramatic performance. I could make you the lead protagonist. We could act against one another."

Quiet takes over the cage within the cage and the sound of the cats somewhere in the dark comes like a vibration over the three men and one woman.

The Spaniard leans his body against the metal mesh and lowers his head.

"There are still medical drugs in this city. Many of them are mine. The big men of the cartels, I work for them. They put me here to do many things. Drugs are one thing I do. If you had the money, they could be yours. So no, I will not die of these illnesses. I am thinking you might need drugs, not the kind that come from Laos or Mexico, but the stuff in pill bottles. If you want it, you just need to ask. If you can't pay with money, there are other ways."

She speaks without thinking. "I assumed you were gay."

"I am," he says, no pause, "but payment would not be with that kind of performance."

And it is like her lungs take his words as a cue and they begin to grow tighter. She takes a deep breath and tries to imagine Sani standing in front of her with the scarf around her head. Sani holds a candle and tells Aberdeen to breathe in and release slowly. Blow out the flame. Take in air and do it again and again until the suffocating stops.

Her logical mind asks her what the point is in trying to

reason with the lungs when the body will soon be dead anyway. But the body pushes on. The body pushes for life.

She can tell her lips are going blue by the way the man stares at her face. She's gasping now and she looks around the cage. She doesn't have her bag; it could be in the van or back at the entrance of the tent being stepped on by hundreds of holy rollers.

With her back to the solid wall, she slides down to the concrete and feels the heat seep out her tights and silken dress as her knees fold under her. She scratches at her throat. Her nostrils pump open and closed like small, insignificant bellows.

And then she watches the man who held the donation box bend down and press something into her hand. She looks and sees her asthma inhaler in her palm. She empties the last few puffs it contains into her mouth, breathing it in as deep as possible and then throws the empty canister at the Spaniard who doesn't move and lets it slap him in the shin.

Air comes back. Life comes back. Aberdeen swallows to push back the tears on the verge of sliding out her eyes.

When she's fully returned, the man picks up the empty inhaler and tosses it between his hands. "We looked in your purse and found this. Did you think we would not find a way to know you and know what you need? So sad this is all gone. What is it that you will do now, Aberdeen? Maybe you will come to me? Maybe you will come to the back of the tent of healing?"

She shakes her head no, but she doesn't mean it. He might be right. She might have to go to him. But for now she thinks of what he has said. He's talking of her like she will keep living, that there is a future for her. Does it mean she won't be killed tonight? She closes her eyes and sees Hurt's face in front of her own. His light hair, sullen set of his mouth. I'm coming home, she thinks to his visage.

"I mean you are not special when I say you are not special," he speaks to her and all she can focus on is the white of his teeth in the dim light. "But my work in this city is many layers deep. I exchange a show for those who need one and it keeps people hopeful. I sell drugs, but this you know. The soldiers do not bother me because I pay them and more importantly, I am not part of the big terror. Do you understand this big terror?"

"The bombings, the attacks on aid workers, terrorist threats leveled at countries who try to help America, all of the shit that keeps happening," she gasps.

"Yes, the big terror. But I have quotas. This is my work. In all jobs, there are expectations. One of mine is small terror. I think Americans have a term they use. Homegrown. Or is it grassroots? That is one of my layers. They tell me to terrify individuals. They tell me how many. Five, ten, fifty. It is all part of their big terror. Many small terrors can equal one big terror. You are part of my job, Aberdeen. But it is me, not my bosses, who sees your potential for the stage."

The boss drops the inhaler back to the floor and snaps his fingers at the man with the yellow eyes. He pulls a long, heavy flashlight out from behind the snow shovel and hands it to him. It is the sort that police use. It is the kind that could be swung as a bludgeon. He fingers the switch and tests it by clicking it on and off, the sphere of light causing Aberdeen's eyes to shut and then burst in red retina burns when it goes out again.

He turns to the grating and places the flashlight under his chin like he's going to tell them all a story of a haunting or of exorcism. He presses the flashlight on and waves it around his face, illuminating his head so it seems to be the only thing in the room, a floating visage of decapitation.

Then he clicks the light off and turns back to face Aberdeen. Her eyes strain to get the upper hand on the dark, to adjust before they are awakened again by the light.

"They are ready," he says, "would you like to see?"

She doesn't say no, so he flips the light back on and shines it through the metal caging out into the all encompassing black.

And right up against the grate are six pairs of yellow eyes reflecting the unnatural light. They are glowing rings, shimmering and glossy and absent of the dark centers that let them see. They look at her. They look at meat.

He clicks the light off again and she can sense the big cats are still there, that they will not leave until their curiosity has been satiated. Aberdeen and the cats seem to have that in common.

She needs to know if she will be going home tonight. So she asks.

"Is it feeding time for them? Am I it? Am I the food? Is this how you mean to terrify me?"

Her eyes are coming around again, making out the men standing about her. The man with the goatee hands the flashlight back to the man with the eyes the same yellow as the cat eyes and bends down next to her, balancing on his toes.

"You are not food. I would never discard someone who might one day grace my stage. No, you are a brand new customer, Aberdeen. How could I make money if I didn't attract new people to consume what I supply? How would the small terror work if you were not alive to tell people to be afraid?"

And she envisions him eating her when she hears the word "consume," but she knows this is not what he means, while the two grunts lift her off her feet and Suit Man, a name she's adopted in her mind, stands up with her. He kisses her on the forehead, his lips yielding and plump and the door is opened to the long hallway and closed again, with her and the two men outside and the man with the nails and hair and suit left behind, still in the cage within the cage.

She walks with the two men. They don't take up her arms. It's as if they know she won't run. She passes the door again with the red X. She will never know what is behind it. She will never come back to the bowels of the animal house.

When they get to the metal door set into the outside wall, both men take up an arm and escort her out so she cannot bolt at the promise of open space, and walk her back to the van sitting in an empty parking lot, its shape the likeness of a great beast itself.

The back is opened and she is immediately enveloped in the smell of her own bile on the floor and seats. They climb in behind her and shut the doors and she looks up at the dome light, still on, the battery not yet dead. She hopes it will die soon but it remains incessant in shining. A false moon.

The entrance men, the escorts, the guards, they stare at her. Then the man of the respirator and the yellow eyes slips his leather belt from its buckle and pulls it off his waist in a sharp jerk.

"Rape?" she asks with her eyes closed. "Are you going to rape me?"

She opens her eyes to find them smiling and the beltless man rolling up the leather and placing it on the seat next to her.

Yellow Eyes says, "No. Fuck no. You aren't my type."

Donation Box says nothing.

And like that, these men now have proper names, too.

Then Yellow Eyes reaches under one of the bench seats and pulls out a duffel bag in bright turquoise. It's ruched at the sides and dirty with water marks. He digs around in it as he talks.

"I've fucked a lion," he says.

Aberdeen flattens her lips. "What?"

"I tend the lion enclosure. It's my other job. The vets take the cats out and put them to sleep every couple of years so they can get in their mouths and scrape all the shit off their teeth. You wouldn't believe those teeth. Big as my hand and caked in dead flesh turned to rock."

He demonstrates the veracity of his claims by knocking on the floor of the van. The plaque is that hard. He pulls a smaller, zipped bag from the larger duffel. It looks like something a man would carry in a valise to hold his razor and his toothbrush and his fine-toothed comb.

"So I find out when they are putting one of the bitch cats under. And I've watched before and I seen how they leave the cats alone to come out of the stupor without humans around. They put them in a room all alone and sometimes the cat will wake up quick and be mean, but other times it takes hours and they wake up like they've been drinking straight Everclear and trying to burn out their guts with it."

He unzips the bag and pulls out a syringe, a spoon, a bag of brown powder, a squeeze bottle of murky water and a wad of cotton.

Aberdeen's eyes get big. She can see Louis's father on that horse in Montana. The horse is coming, she thinks. The heroin.

Yellow Eyes goes on. "The lioness goes down, gets her teeth chipped at and they put her in one of these cells." He stops to mix a bit of the powder in the spoon with some of the liquid and balances the concoction on the seat in front of her. She bites her lip. She wonders what it will feel like despite the fear rising again, the adrenaline returning.

"I've got to be quick, because like I said, there is no telling when she'll wake up and what mood she'll be in. I get my pants down and I swear to God, I fucked that cat as hard and quick as I could and then left with some of her fur on the tip of my dick. I pulled it off later. It was stuck good."

He picks up his belt and uses it to cinch just above his bicep. He preps the cotton and the syringe.

Thank you, she says in her head. It's for him, she says again and again. It's for him.

He drops the needle into his skin, hits the vein, and leans back against the van doors with a dumb smile on his face.

"It was for bragging rights," he says, "because who the fuck else could say they raped a lion? That cat could kill me anytime if I'm not careful shoveling out their shit each day. But she don't. Because she knows. Somehow she knows what I did. I dominate her now."

Then Yellow Eyes is gone somewhere else, floating in ether, dreaming of sex with giant felines.

Donation Box takes the belt off his partner and catches the syringe before it falls to the metal floor. He sets up another round for another injection. Him too, she thinks.

When the syringe is primed once more he stops and looks at her. "Do you know what skin-popping is?" he asks. It is the first time she's heard him speak. His voice is a wisp of soft noise.

"No, not a clue."

"It's how you deliver the dope when your veins collapse and you can't find a good way to mainline anymore. So instead, you just take the syringe and jab it into fatty tissue. Most of the time you just stick it through your clothes."

She thinks of the needle, long and silver, how he hasn't cleaned it and how he doesn't seem to care. They are drug addicts, she reminds herself. And if they get high, then she can figure out a way to get home. Do it, she thinks. Put it in you and let me go.

"You're one of his check marks, a tick on a report for his superiors, another citizen terrorized. But Beso thinks you'll come to him for medicine, eventually. And he clearly thinks there is something special about you, perhaps for the stage. He's good at seeing the levels of potential in people. But he can't be sure that you'll come back to him. On account of the fear."

He lifts up the syringe to the dome light and squeezes a drop of liquid out the end of the needle.

"Could be you do it because your veins are shot, but sometimes skin-popping is just easier," he says in the same calm whisper, as he brings the needle straight down into the flesh of Aberdeen's thigh and pushes in the plunger.

He leaves it there; a cylinder of plastic looking like it's balanced on a center-point, the metal deep in her, the clear plastic tube hovering above the filthy pleats of her nicest, sky blue dress.

Her head drops back and the dome light is there again. Still not dead.

"Die," she says to it aloud and thinks of the name Beso and remembers her Spanish and remembers it means *kiss.*

And then the warmth comes. The warmth takes her. Her eyes shut and so the light, in a way, does finally die.

CHAPTER FIFTEEN

She doesn't mind when Donation Box nudges her from the van, shuts the back and drives away. She doesn't think of Yellow Eyes, the lion fucker, his body in the back of the van but his mind where hers is, in the same stratosphere made of down feathers and heat and the smell of cinnamon. She doesn't notice the van moving away. It was a beast that bore her to a place of terror, only to become the place she was delivered.

Delivered. Salvation at hand. She knows that she was scared, frightened before, but now she only has the sense of security. She stands for a time she cannot measure, moving her body slightly with the change in the movement of the trees, dark shadows in the distance. Then she lets her legs go soft and opens her thighs like a blooming lotus, sitting back on the asphalt parking lot with the soles of her feet pressed together.

Looking down at the space between her pelvis, legs and feet, she's reminded of a yoni, wide and holy. Then she forgets this immediately, lies back slowly feeling her vertebrae come into contact with the tiny rocks dropped by the treads of hundreds, thousands of cars' tires that have been here before her body.

She can feel everything she wants to feel and nothing she

does not want to feel. There are no hallucinations, but instead sensations she hasn't experienced in months. Peace. Relaxation. Stability.

The moon catches her eyes. It lies on its back like her, its belly up to the rest of the universe, like a dog in submission or a woman in heat. It makes her want to live up there on the moon, but not the moon of science with its rough, dead rock and vacuum atmosphere. She instead dreams of sinking into the moon of romance, made of cotton and love and throbbing with bioluminescence.

She is there, for awhile. Her bit of time is indeterminate.

Then she feels a pinch in her stomach and a swelling forth and she turns her head in time to vomit on the asphalt. She vaguely recalls vomiting several times today, but she doesn't care enough to count. She stares at the bile. There was nothing left in her to give. It glows green in the moonlight. The moonlight!

And like that she's back, deep in the moon.

Eventually rest gives way to a surge of life in her soft muscles. She stumbles getting up and takes her eyes from the white, cupping moon and looks around. Ah yes, she recalls, she's in a park. Aberdeen was at the zoo. She watches her breath curl up as a fog and dissipate into the air. Then she touches the silky material of her dress. So thin. She rubs at the bile spot with her thumb and forefinger. She should be cold. She should be frozen. But her skin is radiating heat, the back of her neck dampening the hair that hangs loose upon it.

She wonders where she should go. There is an insistent voice inside her head, speaking quickly and with force, but it seems to be coming from somewhere too far away, from the pharmacy or the apartment building or the moon. She thinks it's telling her to go home. But she can't fathom why. There is nothing wrong with where she is. Her arms aren't tight with stress. The park is lovely when it's empty and covered in dark.

The active energy rises in her and she moves. She heads for a glow of light that illuminates buildings in the distance. Playgrounds and picnic tables and beasts caged but untamed are at her back now. She decides she is done with the park. Somewhere close there should be somewhere even better than where she is now.

She walks. She walks and does not see the things around her for awhile. She is content in the flexing of her calves and the muscles that run the length of her foot and the ones that link her knees to her ass. The triceps, the abdominals, the pectorals, they all get involved in the moving. Contracting and relaxing, they move her forward, back into the city.

At one point she says "thank you" aloud and realizes she meant to say it to her body, and she could have kept it in her head.

The city she walks in is her own but she doesn't recognize much of what she sees. If she weren't high, she would feel concerned now, about how much of her own city she cannot name or place. It would be similar to the concern she felt of being denied the names of people. Wheelchair Man. Depressed Lady. She decides she can call people whatever she wants. And that she can walk the streets like a conquistador in euphoria from a pulp of coca leaves presented to him by the natives he has come to kill.

At least she is not dead. They did not kill her.

Then she considers what they did give her. A gift, a reprieve from the stress and fear and concern that flooded her body and mind months ago and never left, the black mold and moisture just growing higher up the walls of her insides.

But Suit Man, Beso, wants her to want this feeling. He terrorized her and then alleviated that fear briefly with heroin. She is smart enough to know it. But she is not willing to say no to it, not now with the way her lungs are lifting and lowering in slow rhythms, set to rights, and the way the street lights she passes radiate a vibrancy of color that catches her attention at each intersection with enlightenment in red and green.

"Fuck," she says aloud, "I feel like butter left out on the counter."

She moves her head slowly to the sound of a voice, an unexpected response.

"What?" it asks.

A man in urban camouflage with a sidearm at his hip considers her with his eyebrows cocked so high they seem to blend in with his hairline.

Aberdeen looks at him and tries to pry her eyelids upwards. They feel like they're weighted down with silver coins, payment for the ferryman. The ferryman isn't coming for me tonight, she thinks, and pulls her eyes open wide and smiles.

"Nothing, soldier," she answers, unaware of how her voice raises an octave and she dips her hip to the side. It is a bad line; it is a line from a woman with nothing in her repertoire but sexual distraction.

The man doesn't respond to her femininity. Instead he puts his hand on his sidearm and grimaces. He takes a step into her and Aberdeen doesn't move. He comes closer, inside her personal space, but it doesn't concern her. Act normal, she thinks, but then realizes she isn't blinking.

He gets his face up to hers, eye to eye. He gets so close she can see some of his eyelashes are white and there is a red sty on the rim of his left eye. She forces herself to blink.

Eye to eye, he winks at her, then pulls away.

"Nice pupils, lady."

And the words come out of her unwanted and unbidden.

"I'm high. I'm really high," she says.

"No shit," he replies.

"No shit," she echoes and then pleads, "don't take me in."

He laughs a bit and it sounds sweet and right to her. So she laughs a bit, too.

"Where the hell would I take you? *In* where? You're already in it. This city is a giant holding tank for people whether they know it or not; crazy, sick or wild, doesn't matter. Sane. That really doesn't matter. Take you in," he says and shakes his head. "As if there are secret facilities for the ones that break down. Ha!"

Because she wants to, because he's there and nice and honest and stupid, she puts a hand on the tight muscles above his heart and smiles. There are no boundaries for her now; she knows this and leaves the fencing behind.

"You're a really cool person," she says and maintains her smile. "You're not going to do anything to me, are you?"

"No," he says and gently lifts her hand off of his chest, and gives it back to her keeping like it isn't attached to her by pressing it to her breast.

She wobbles on her feet a bit. It might be time to sit down again, but she does her best to stop her frame from going slack.

The man watches her. Aberdeen's body circles slowly, her torso on a pivot point.

Finally he asks. "Do you have any more? Another pop?"

She keeps circling and shakes her head no.

He shrugs his shoulders and says, "You look animatronic like that. You know, like one of those plastic people in store windows come Christmas, mouths in permanent O's with fake hymn books. I loved those things when I was growing up. If you got really quiet you could hear the motor inside of them making them crank around. That's what you look like. Like you've got a motor inside you making you work."

Then he adds, "That's fucking cool."

She likes his description of her so much she kisses him on the cheek and then looks to the ground not because she's embarrassed but because something has caught the light and drawn her focus. The cap of a pen, smashed and drained of color.

"I didn't take the drugs intentionally," Aberdeen says. "Just so you know. I wasn't trying to break the law. Someone made me do it."

The soldier runs his thumb along his gun holster and eyes a group of people in the distance. His eyes narrow. "I wish I had a friend like that," he says and then waves a flipper of a hand in farewell to Aberdeen and is gone into the dark to pursue new things.

Aberdeen thinks he was a very nice man as she starts down an alleyway three blocks away from where she talked with the soldier.

There is dim light from apartments above her. Nothing is fully lit; trashcans are mounds of undefined plastic and awnings over backdoors into businesses look like black blobs.

Time to rest, she thinks, and picks a spot she believes safe: a gap between part of a brick wall outcropping and the metal side of a big, blue dumpster. She lets her body settle in the crack, her legs out straight in front of her, her back on the wall. She closes her eyes, appreciates the way she can breathe slow and steady and the way the cold air doesn't seem to slip past the rips in her tights from their rough treatment since she walked into the big, white tent.

There is another curious thing happening to her. A wet bloom of fluid seeps out of her and into her underwear. She is not aroused, not preparing for sexual contact. Nevertheless, the warm wet comes forth and keeps coming. All she can think of is the strangeness of the dampness without the familiar companions of throbbing, swelling and pricking.

In her space, snug and content, Aberdeen believes she is encapsulated in a force field. Nothing can touch her. From outside or from inside. Her body is tidied up, relieved of pain on any and all levels. And the night is not so bad. It is currently her truest, steadfast friend.

When her eyes stay open long enough, they adjust to the dark. Her sight is limited by the blinders of wall and dumpster, but she can tilt her head back and look to the sky. The moon isn't visible; the stars are blocked by smog and lights from the entire city. But she can see something above her about a story or two in the air. It hangs from a fire escape.

It turns and she can hear the creak of metal as it moves above her. She knows this means it has some mass to it. It keeps her attention, an undefined, unnamed thing that moves like a mobile above her crib, her spot of rest and comfort.

Here she stays. Again, time is indeterminate.

And again, life comes back to her body and she resolves to stand, using the wall and the side of the dumpster to shimmy herself upright. Let's see what this thing is, she thinks, and scoots out of her den.

Standing back in the alleyway, she has to get all the way to the other side of the path, up against the brick of those buildings to get a semblance of what's hanging in the air. She still hears the whine of the metal and now smells whiffs of decaying plant matter. She wonders if this is because her head is higher in the sky since standing, in the strata of air that holds and maintains the odor of rotting lettuce and tomatoes long since gone to sugar, then vinegar.

The form hangs long and heavy and covered in something that doesn't reflect the scant light that exists there, in the alley. There is a bar coming from the top of it, attaching it to the fire escape. It reminds her of the stiff, metal fixtures that let chandeliers drip from ceilings. She takes the dangling thing for an upturned dress form draped in dull fabric.

So humanoid.

No, she stops herself. It is human.

Then she sees the shoes, the tips of shoes reaching for the earth, pitching forward, begging to be put on the ground once again.

She goes to the dumpster and climbs it, knowing how to do so without knowing how to explain it. With her hand stretched up, her arm pulling on its socket, she can just reach one of the shoes. Her nails swipe at it but she only catches some of the sole's tread and comes away with black under her nails. She tries again. Misses again.

Now that she is under it, him, she can see the rod is not a rod, but a rope, and the man has draped himself in a tweed fabric, wrapping it around his head and letting it flow about his body. It could be fabric cut off an old couch. The rope keeps it snug around his neck, secure in place. She figures he must have been a good man, one who didn't want children or garbage men seeing the rigor of his penis or the dribbling of his insides from his mouth when they came across his body.

Aberdeen has convinced herself this man was a good man, an okay man, a man who was sick or tired or insane and done with what he could eke out of this life. A good man needs to be taken down and laid out, she tells herself, and then she reaches up and tries again to grab a piece of him.

After a few more tries, she comes away with one of the shoes. She feels a wetness on her hands and then looks to see the inside of the loafer is full of fluids, some viscous, others oily, runny. She tosses the shoe away and watches the parts of him turning back into the base constituents of life fly out of the shoe in a spray over the bins and brick and asphalt.

It does not upset her, to have the juicy remains of a stranger on her palms. She still feels warm, safe, happy. And she still believes he must come down, even if just so she can lay him flat on his back with his hands folded over his chest.

She takes the socked foot in her hand. It's easier to grab, though the sock is frozen and crunchy. She gives it a sharp tug and hears the metal groan and a popping of the man's spine, the gas trapped there releasing and never building back up again.

This won't work, she takes time to reason. She needs to get above him. Then she can lower him to the dumpster top and roll him to the ground. Yes, she thinks. That's the way.

The ladder up to the fire escape hangs a body-length away from the dumpster. But she is resolved. She puts her hands flat against the building and inches her torso out over the void until her feet are soon to leave the metal bin. Then she pushes off with her toes and catches the ladder in her hands. She says a mumbled prayer willing her strong enough to hold on while the ladder runs on old, ungreased tracks down to the ground. The sides of the ladder hit the asphalt with a thunk and she leans her forehead on one of the textured rungs that is freezing, she knows, but doesn't feel cold to her at all.

She holds the ladder like she would hold Hurt. Like she wants to someday be able to hold Louis. If the boy were here, right now, she could embrace him like that and not feel ill at ease. He would hold her back. She knows this.

After a time, she climbs. The man hangs from the first landing. She looks down on him and watches him do pirouettes from his neck instead of his feet. Then the knot gets her attention. She carefully lowers herself down while holding on to one of the landing bars and takes it in. The thing is thick and solid and pulled taut, without gaps, by the weight of the man below it.

Aberdeen looks around her, as if a blade will magically appear. Part of her thinks one will. She has no idea of what this heroin can really do. It has changed her reality. Why not the reality of the fire escape or the materializing of tools? She waits a moment, the sharp edge does not come, and then she starts to work on it with her fingers. She pulls a nail back but only notices because she is looking at the finger when it happens. A bright red flush rushes into her nail bed and the nail itself splits below the quick, still hanging on with a bit of defiance. There is no pain, so she rips it clean off and lets it fall through the grating at her feet.

Her and the man, they both are pain free tonight, blessed children in a city of sick.

She works at the knot. The tips of her fingers go white, the blood moving out of her extremities to somewhere warmer. She knows it will come back and keeps prying with numb digits until the strength leaves her hands completely and she sits back on the fire escape and rests her palms over the knot. When she lifts them up, she sees that she has not altered a thing. The knot still holds. The weight of the dead is too much for her to win against.

Pirouettes, the man does. Turning and turning though there is no breeze. The slow spin holds her eyes and she is not sad about him but about the fact she cannot release him from his twirling, a winged maple seed never touching the ground.

"I'm sorry," she says to him.

Someone lets out a cat call from nearby and the sound runs up the alley, runs past her, leaves her alone with the man who dangles.

She reasons if she can see his face, then it will be something. If she can see his face, she can take his death with her and know of it and he will not be alone. He can join her in her peace and warmth. It is the new course of action. It is right.

The rope is strong, thick. Her arm will not reach the fabric around his head and even if it could, she has nothing to cut it away with. The rope around his neck holds the fabric closed, the bread tie around the new loaf, twisted tight and secure.

But if she can get right up to him, right up to his face, then she might be able to rip the fabric with her hands and see him.

The rope is strong, thick. She knows she has thought that before, but she thinks it again.

It will hold her.

She swings her legs over the edge of the fire escape and eyes the rope so that it's between her feet. She wraps her feet around it, then reaches down and takes the bit of it emanating from the knot in her fists, pulls her feet away, and then lets her body drop.

A heel takes the hooded man in the head. He doesn't mind,

she thinks, because he's dead. But now his death does not bother her as much. It had to happen sometime. Death happens.

Then it is a matter of her using her whole body to move down the several feet of rope until she can latch her legs around the neck of the man. She can feel her muscles tiring again. Time for another lie down. She works as fast as she can, but she feels like she is moving like the dead man, in slow circles, in uncontrolled revolutions.

The rope makes the metal creak.

She sits with her legs wrapped around his face. She is a woman asking for a reverse shoulder ride, a morbid approximation of a sex act. The wetness is still under her skirt. But the entirety of the situation does not stun her, upset her, repulse her.

It is what it is.

She uses what nails she has left and what strength she has left to start a hole in the fabric above the crown of his head. She pulls out bits of the rough fibers and blows them away from her palm when they stick to her skin. The fabric is gray and black and brown, lines running together like telephone wires in third world countries. Her black hair peaks about her skull from the rubbing of fabric on fabric, a product of static electricity.

Even though the man has no energy to give, there is still a spark.

The hole gets bigger. She gets her fingers in it, two on each side of the rip and tugs. Spreading it wide, she can see the man had a cowlick on the back of his head. The swirl is messed, but she can see the white of his scalp under his light hair. It looks like a crop circle. His hair, the color of corn.

It is the same color of *his* hair. Hurt's hair.

Then the plan changes. She does not want to see his face. What if he has the sloping brow of Hurt, the pinched bridge of the nose, the philtrum, that dent below his nose and above his lips that Aberdeen can perfectly rest the tip of her pinkie in.

What if the dead man has her husband's face?

She no longer cares to see, to take the look of this man with her, to carry it until she dies of the heroin depressing her breathing so much she can't will her lungs to lift anymore. She wonders if this will happen, could happen. Tries to care if it could, if it will. But there is nothing. No concern left for herself.

It's time to get down. Aberdeen puts her hands on his shoulders, moves her legs down like she's a graceless child on a slide, lets her body drip down the shrouded man until her legs hang and hit against his. Then she lets go.

Her tailbone hits the metal of the dumpster. Nothing. No pain. She reaches back to hold it in her palm, but this is just out of habit. Cup the hurt, hold it so that it will go away faster. When there is no hurt, what's the point?

Aberdeen climbs off the dumpster. Time for home, she thinks. She thinks she has had this thought earlier in the evening, but she cannot be sure. So many things have happened to her. They have all come at her like they have walked out of a fog, dallied with her, then walked back in.

She walks in her own fog and finally finds parts of the city she does not need to make up names for because she knows them and can name them.

Things happen to her on the way home. She will not remember them. The only thing she will recall is seeing other people, the people lost in the city like her. None of them scare or alarm her. She considers a passage she reasons is in the Bible, about all people being children of God. Pure and innocent. And she thinks of the big, white tent. Even the people there, especially Janos and Beso and Donation Box and Yellow Eyes.

All she says to herself on her walk home, over and over in her head is this:

Everyone needs hugs.

Her home is to the east and her walking puts her on a pilgrimage into the light of the coming sun. It warms up slowly, a cold bulb with a dim reach, then a flicker, a flash, and full illumination.

The apartment building doorstep is there now. It takes both arms for her to pull open the door. Janos is not there to hold it open for her. If he was, she would probably kiss him and tell him to stop playing with snakes.

Stairs go up and up five floors. It takes effort to get her legs high enough so that her feet clear each step. On the set of steps above landing four, she puts her hands on the steps three above her feet. She rests. Then goes on.

The door to her apartment is open all the way. She is thankful for it. Her limbs are done now. She wants her bed.

Walking in, she turns her head to the light of a lamp in the living room. Louis sits under it, a soft cookie on his jeans, crumbs everywhere. He looks up, jumps up, sends the cookie to the ground where it crumbles on impact.

"Abbie," he says and comes to her and wraps his arms around her. His face is wet and the wet transfers to her cheeks. They are of a height. She reaches up not to wipe her face, but his, keeping her other arm around his back, squeezing.

"It's okay, Louis," she says and she says it because she feels this is true.

"I didn't go to sleep. I couldn't go to sleep. This is the first night in my life I haven't put on my pajamas and gone to sleep. I stayed up and waited for you." He says with his mouth turning up with pride. And relief.

"Where were you?" he asks, still holding onto her.

Do mothers lie? she wonders. Of course they do.

"I got a little sick. I am a little sick."

Louis lets her go and goes back to his cookie. He considers it on the floor but doesn't move to pick it up.

"I'll go get Sani. She can help you if you're sick." His gaze moves from the cookie to the window and the newness of the day. "Even if it's early. I'll go."

"No, Louis. I'm okay," she says and sits down in the entry hallway. Her bed is far away right now. She wants it but can't seem to get there.

"Where is Hurt?"

Louis looks at the wall that separates the living room with the back bedrooms. He doesn't say anything. Instead he goes to the hall closet. He takes out his coat and the ragged, blue hat.

She hasn't knit his hat yet. When she is better, she will.

"He's sleeping?" she asks.

Louis puts on his outerwear and digs his shoes out from behind Aberdeen's back. He slides them on. They don't have laces, the yellow stripes speckled with dried mud.

"No," he says, and walks out the front door.

Aberdeen sits. She begins to pay attention to the noise coming from the other room. It seeps from behind a closed door. But it is there. It is her husband.

She pushes herself up after a time. The bedroom is not that far anymore. She goes to it, opens the door.

Hurt moves around the room making a path around the sides of the bed, across the foot of the bed and back again. She looks at the floor and sees a white powder on the same path, leaving what must have been white footprints at first, but were now just smears of dust with an occasional big toe or an instep well defined in the chaos.

Hurt is talking to himself. He stops and takes in his wife.

"I had a great idea. If I put on a lot of powder while I pace, I can see how much time has passed since you left and came back. It's like leaving a record of time that way. I'm glad you're back, because I ran out of flour. And then Gold Bond."

To elucidate his point, Hurt picks up the plastic container of talc and squeezes it, sending a weak plume of white into the air.

This must make sense, Aberdeen thinks. It's the heroin. The heroin is interfering somehow with her ability to understand him.

Hurt tosses the bottle on the ground and goes to her and

hugs her so that her body folds inwards. Then he lets go, holds her with his arms stiff and begins to yell.

His concern, his worry issues forth at speeds so fast he mispronounces words, slurs others together, chastises her bleeding nail bed absent a nail, takes tight little sips of breath before starting on another point.

Aberdeen closes her eyes, lets the words come at her and absorbs them into the soft force field around her body. She goes limp and lets the strong anger in Hurt's hands hold her upright.

Undetermined time. Again. And when she cannot not be in bed any longer, she says something.

"Stop," she mumbles quietly. "I just need to go to bed now, Hurt. I will explain things later. I just need to get in that bed."

She needs to sleep, give in to the feeling and trust that she will wake up and there will be explanations and Hurt will be communicating with her, not with the heroin. She believes the heroin has taken her ears and her eyes and is hearing what it likes, seeing what it will.

Later, when it is gone, he will be normal to me, she thinks.

He stops his ranting for a moment and picks her up like a bride and takes her to her side of the bed and lies her down on the comforter without touching her filthy clothes or the dried blood on her finger. The depressing of the mattress and pillow under her weight make Aberdeen shiver, her muscles releasing entirely. It is what her body has wanted since the skin-pop, since the needle hovered over her thigh like the only standing pillar among ruins.

"I just need to sleep, Hurt," she mumbles and turns on her side. He stands at the side of the bed still. Aberdeen can smell the scent of talc and menthol.

Hurt starts with her disappearance, his words ticking off, turning into talks of his homework and Louis and then the downgrading of Pluto from planet to planetoid and the way cotton candy tasted when he was younger and on to apocalypse and on and on and on.

Go to sleep, she tells herself. He is just upset. He will be all right when you wake up.

Everything will be all right when we come back from where we all have been.

CHAPTER SIXTEEN

There is no clutching to them, no way for her to describe her dreams. They do not stick around for her to decipher when she opens her eyes, finds Hurt gone, and sees a tall woman rubbing at the powder on the floor with a damp towel.

Sani. Louis went for her. He knew she would need someone. He saw reason even if Aberdeen hadn't.

It makes sense. Things are clearer. And Aberdeen can feel how the connections in her brain are coming smoother now. She's dismounting the chemicals.

And the dread of what she has seen, what she has done, what she has felt, makes her close her eyes, pinch her arms, curl into the tight shape of a newborn. Beso has truly fulfilled part of his quota with his work on her. He has caused one more "small terror" for his superiors.

Yet, she thinks, the ride is almost over.

The only light in the room is from a dim lamp. It creeps under her eyelids making them bloom in a red background, a velvet movie theater curtain. It is night once again. But Aberdeen cannot guess if it is the next night, or the next next night.

Sani says nothing and wipes the floor. Aberdeen can sense her move around the bed, cleaning the pacing path of Hurt.

And when she is done, Aberdeen can feel Sani hover above her. Aberdeen tries not to move. She feigns sleep.

"I can do this until you open your eyes and tell me what happened," she says.

Aberdeen keeps her eyes closed. "Where's Hurt?"

Sani's voice is smooth. There isn't a tone of irritation that Aberdeen can latch onto, feel guilty about.

"As soon as Louis and I got here, Hurt went on about needing to find you a specific kind of jelly donut. He said it was the first thing you ate together when you met in Europe. Something about blackberry filling that isn't really blackberry but some sort of similar berry. Something we don't eat much here?"

Aberdeen can remember the donuts. The café was small, barely twice the size of many of the water closets in the hostels she'd been staying in. She'd saved up for the trip the entirety of her late twenties just to find herself in accommodations swarming with college kids given beer allowances from their parents. She'd gotten some of the black jelly on her chin. Hurt dared to wipe it away with his own napkin stained with his own dessert. It didn't repulse her. She liked the way he was brazen and sincere and already willing to take care of her, hours after they had met.

She got why he went out to find her that specific kind of donut. It was him taking care of her. But it worried her, because she had never seen that specific kind of pastry in America. Neither had Hurt. Yet he was out for one, out to find something that might not exist.

Her eyes open but her body does not move.

"He's acting strangely, isn't he?" she asks Sani.

Sani shrugs. "I can't say I know him well enough to have a baseline. Could be the stress of not knowing where you were. In fact, he might have a better case than you in calling the kettle black when he's the pot, or whatever. Strangeness is all over you, Aberdeen."

Aberdeen tests out a calf muscle, moving it up and down by lifting and pointing her foot. Her body could be what constitutes the jelly in that donut Hurt is looking for. She is limp and soft and done for days, she thinks.

"You don't want to know what happened," she says to Sani, who takes a seat on the bed, nudging aside Aberdeen's legs with her wide hips. Aberdeen knows Sani wants to know. She just doesn't want to admit she was dumb enough to go into the big white tent, get kidnapped, enter the den of giant cats, get shot up with heroin to then wander the streets climbing on corpses and brushing the face of a soldier.

It is too weird. She looks to a fresh Band-aid on the tip of her right ring finger. Even this woman in front of her with the heat in her hands who takes away pain would name Aberdeen an anomaly.

Sani does not press it. Instead she sits with Aberdeen, who closes her eyes once again and drifts back to sleep. She sleeps for a small cluster of minutes before her body jerks, she realizes what has happened and she forces herself to come out of the fetal position, sit up in bed and look at the healer in front of her.

This woman can help her, she thinks. Tell her. It might be the best way to heal.

Aberdeen swallows and notes the dry rough of her throat. She wants to ask for water, but she thinks if she sends Sani away now, she'll lose her command over the story and by the time she comes back, all will have fallen apart. Her resolve will be out of her in sweat, soaking the sheets.

"Where is Louis?"

"Sleeping. He stayed up the other night, all night, until you got in. Then he found me, brought me here and sat on the floor at the foot of your mattress while you slept. When the color started to go from his face, I made him get in his bed. I told him he was too big for me to carry," Sani says.

Aberdeen nods. "I remember he was up. I remember most of it, I think. But memories can be faulty. For sure."

"Of course," is all the healer says and lays a hand on Aberdeen's knee. The warmth slides down to her toes, up to her pelvis, climbs to her head. It helps.

"So there is a tent."

"Uh-huh."

"And it's a front, a way for some assholes to sell drugs to those in a bad way. And if you don't want drugs, there is another part of the tent that's for show. They put on a farce of Pentecostal healing. Spiritual healing."

She decides against telling the woman about Beso's intentions to seed terror. She won't rile up Sani or Louis, perhaps not even Hurt, with fear, anger, worry. Then the "small terror" would spread and Beso, his goons, and the cartel would be getting exactly what they want.

Sani's words are clipped. "No. It's not spiritual. It's faith healing. They are different. One depends on the grace of a beneficent God to cure illness or pain. The other is the energy of life, directed, convocation and invocation and reverence for the spirits who surround us all."

Aberdeen's kneecap is so hot it draws her focus. If she can keep her mind here, with Sani, with her heated leg, she can do this.

"I don't know if the distinction matters too much judging by what I saw. It's a way to make money. They aren't healing anyone. At least I don't think so. Neither by the power of Jesus Christ nor the help of spirits."

"And?" Sani prompts.

"And I was spotted as someone who didn't belong with the druggies or with the healing crowd. Three men took me...," and Aberdeen drifts off. She can see the eyes of the big cats behind the grating. Golden orbs hovering at her mid-section.

"It was unpleasant," is all she ends with.

Sani asks this of Aberdeen, because she is a woman, and it is something that any woman would instinctively ask of any other woman that had been stolen away and returned.

"Did they touch you? Rape you?"

Aberdeen shakes her head no and pulls at the covers. Sani lifts her body off the bed so Aberdeen can get the sheets up to her chin and sits back down.

"You were drugged, obviously," continues Sani. "I'm guessing an opiate. Heroin?"

Aberdeen can feel a sharp stab in her thigh when she adjusts her leg and realizes it's from where they jammed in the needle. It must have ripped through pleated skirt, tights, skin, fat, muscle before Donation Box pushed the plunger home. Her thigh had been attacked and now that the effects of what had been in the syringe were dissipating, the ache and hurt were growing, multiplying, quickening.

"How do you know? Do you see many people on it?"

Sani takes the cuff of her long sleeve sweater and rolls it up to her bicep. Her arms are fragile and their thinness matches the porcelain tint of her skin well, yet they exist in stark contrast to her pear-shaped bottom. The only things that mar the flesh are the puckered scars of past abuse. Metal has been inserted there hundreds of times, worming into veins, delivering relief, sliding back out.

Aberdeen lifts a hand and touches Sani's arm. The woman doesn't pull away. Aberdeen runs her fingers over the tracks and feels how they have healed in soft ridges like the sections of a caterpillar.

After a minute of them touching, after a minute of commiseration, Sani rolls back down her sleeve and speaks.

"It was an entire life ago. It cost me my medical practice, but it was what I needed to do to get me here. I'm not sorry for it."

Aberdeen tucks her hand back under the covers and licks

her lips.

"So you can tell me what to do with what I experienced. On the heroin, I mean."

"No," Sani says. "I can't. Heroin Spirit, rather, Poppy Spirit does different things for different people. It depends on how it *rides* you," and she says this with a bit of lust in her voice. "I could only tell you what it did to me, but that is not what we are talking about. After they shot you up, you came home? They let you go?"

"Yes," Aberdeen says and stops there. "Do I have to tell you what happened before I got home?"

"You only have to tell me what you think needs to be said."

"Okay, then I'll keep it in. For now."

Aberdeen looks at the lamp and blinks. "Can we turn it off? I'd like it dark in here."

Sani gets up, clicks the switch, comes back.

She smirks, laughs a bit to herself. "It's smart. What they did to you. The heroin makes sense."

Aberdeen doesn't need to ask how.

"Poppy Spirit turns those points of anguish into nothing. They hold no sway under it. You become a bit of dough, soft and pliable and left in a warm oven to rise. These people know what everyone wants during this time of chaos if they aren't actually sick or addicted. They want peace. They gave it to you. They knew you well enough to know that was what you were looking for more than anything else in that bizarre circus tent. Even more than a new canister of albuterol for your lungs."

A gift, Aberdeen thinks again. She's glad she got it, in a way. Now if she can just stop herself from ripping open the flaps of the box, opening it again and again, looking for the same thing hidden underneath the tissue paper. She can't want it too badly. No matter the way it makes her melt into contentment. No matter the way it makes pain a negligible thought, a thing to laugh at while sipping an iced tea. No matter the way her underwear grew so wet she could have ran smooth with anything, anyone, for hours.

If she took it again, Beso would win. He would win the game he made the rules for and forced her to play. Fuck him, she thinks. She refuses to be one of the people who tries heroin once and builds a relationship with it for the rest of their lives.

"The man in charge, Beso, he seems smart. But who knows. I was so scared I peed on myself a little. He might have been of middling brain power. It could be that the word *evil* is just too wedded to the word *genius* in my mind. He could be a moron. Fear can distort things so badly."

"Don't go back to it. I can tell you it will not agree with you living life."

"I'll try. I don't think I will," Aberdeen says and only half believes it.

"Was the needle clean? Did they take it out of some sort of packaging?"

Yellow Eyes. The lion rapist. His rank blood is in her somewhere, his platelets dancing with her own. But what can she do about it? There are no drugs to cure her. The hospitals would likely turn her away. All she has is hope she won't succumb to hepatitis C or AIDS. Her thought turns morbid and she thinks of Feline HIV, Feline Herpes. Maybe she'll get those, too.

She decides she will not sleep with her husband. She can't risk giving him something if she has something to give. She'll have to figure out how to stay away from him. She can tell him he was right, that they shouldn't be trying for a child while medical care is null and void for people like them.

It means no chance of a baby. Not until the drugs come back. Not until she is sure as shit she won't be delivering a sick infant into a world without chemicals.

She bites down on the insides of her cheeks, lets out a sigh.

"No, it wasn't clean," she admits and Sani pats her on the leg, leaving her hand there again, the burning running through

Aberdeen, again.

"Let's take you to a hospital and see if they can do something for you. We can see if there is a way to get you a blood test. I've got friends, remember? I can pull some strings."

"When I'm back to normal, we can go. I don't think it matters now. What's done is done," Aberdeen says to Sani. Even when she is back to what she considers normal, she will likely decide not to go. Why know what you are dying of if you don't need to? Aberdeen has always considered herself a woman who likes a good surprise.

"Let me do some work on you," Sani says and puts her other hand on Aberdeen. "Lie back."

Aberdeen goes flat and lets the heat take her over. It reminds her of frying her bare skin on the sidewalk in the summers of her childhood. She can feel the intensity of the sun coming down on her and the radiating warmth of the white concrete penetrating up. But the heat here, now, comes from a woman who wears scarves about her head and shot heroin until her arms became bits of raised lacing, like the yielding bumps on a chenille bedspread.

"I'll burn the stuff out of you," Sani smiles and Aberdeen can look out over her prone body and see the light white from Sani's teeth in a room devoid of warmth in the way of true sunlight. The only draw here, the only radiation comes from the two of them, skin to skin.

They stay in the quiet until they hear the front door open and Hurt call from the entryway.

Aberdeen starts to yell out to him but Sani shushes her. "Focus," she says as she shuts her eyes and keeps pushing out the healing.

Hurt enters the room and flips on the overhead light. Both women recoil, bend their necks downwards.

"I found it. I found the donut. It's not the exact same, but I don't think we can be too picky, can we?"

Aberdeen can't help but think that of course the donut cannot be the same. The donut she ate with him in that café in Brussels is long gone, digested, turned to shit turned to soil. Anything else is just an approximation. Not the original. Right now, the same can be said of her husband Hurt, too.

"It's okay, babe," she says, not believing it. "I can't believe you went out to find me a donut. Thank you."

Hurt moves to the bed and tries to tug the covers off his wife. Sani acts as a weight, keeping them pinned at Aberdeen's waist. He drops them, puts his hands on his hips and huffs.

"Get up. Come and eat it."

Aberdeen looks to Sani. The healer keeps her eyes closed, deep into concentrating on delivering whatever it actually is she is delivering to the wounded bits of Aberdeen's body. It must be energy. Aberdeen continues to look at Sani, look at her eyes, willing her to open hers in return so she can tell Aberdeen what to do with her husband, what to say to the man that makes demands of her to eat pastries after her descent into that dream induced by the brown liquid, the syringe, the spoon, the tuff of cotton.

Sani must know where her work lies, because she does not give aid to Aberdeen.

Aberdeen takes the covers back up and tucks them around her sides. "I'm really worn out, Hurt. And I think that if I eat right now, I might vomit. Not that I don't want to eat. I would love to eat. I just don't think I can eat."

He claps his hands together so quickly Aberdeen pops up in bed a bit. Sani is unfazed. A puckish smile takes over the entirety of his face. He is teeth and gums and lips pulled so tight they are flattened red licorice.

"How are you going to get better if you don't get your energy up? There is enough sugar in the donut to help you cope. It will be a good thing, really," he says and then leaves the room, yelling out for Louis, likely waking the boy from a dead slumber.

Sani keeps her eyes shut but shakes her head from side to side before talking. "Donuts to help you cope."

"Yeah," Aberdeen says. "See? Strange."

"Strange," Sani says as a rush of hot smacks Aberdeen right where the needle went into her thigh. "I see, yeah."

Hurt is back. Louis stands behind him with the hallway light at his back, one fist knuckling his eye, the other, his nose. He still wears street clothes. Aberdeen imagines his pajamas are folded in a tight square on his dresser. She remembers she washed them before she went to the tent and put them there for him to see. But he did not, could not, not with what was happening, not with his tiredness, her tiredness, Hurt's abnormalities. Fresh pajamas, no matter the crisp odor and weft of the fabric, just didn't matter. Aberdeen takes in the sorry state of her own dress by lifting up the sheets. We've become those kinds of people, she thinks, the kind who don't care enough to take the outside world off before giving themselves to the intimacy of sleep.

Another clap. Hurt's smile is still there. With wide, long teeth, big enough to devour the entire room.

"Hit the overhead light, Louis," Aberdeen asks and the boy reaches around the doorframe, inching his hand past Hurt, careful not to touch him, and turns it off.

"No! Up!" Hurt commands, comes to Aberdeen and sticks out his hands for her to take.

Sani gives up, takes her healing away, waves a hand in front of her face, over her head, then says a silent prayer for herself or Aberdeen or in thanks. It is unknown which one. It does not matter.

Aberdeen gives up, too.

"Take them," she says, and puts her arms in the air. Lifting them up gives her the look of a zombie, a mindless one, a victim of plague and death. She owns it; she has come out of her trial not quite alive, not quite dead.

"To the kitchen," says Hurt as he heaves her up. Then he lets go of her, stands in front of her with his arms outstretched once she has her feet. He looks a father, waiting for his toddler to misstep and career into his embrace. Aberdeen shoos him away, shuffles her legs, the legs that are done, to the kitchen, to the dining table, into the reality her husband wants for her.

Louis and Sani follow and take up the other chairs around the table. They only have three. The fourth chair did not come with the set. She asked herself who would ever buy a table set that only had three chairs, but the price was so decent when she saw the oak round-top that she reasoned it away. Why did they need four chairs? It would only ever be Hurt, Aberdeen and someday, a child.

Hurt fetches a pink paperboard box from the top of the stove and opens it. He delivers a donut to each of them. He doesn't place the pastries on a napkin or a tea saucer. They go straight onto the wood of the table, leaving white, sticky crystals of sugar everywhere. The sugar looks like sharp bits of milky ice, like Hurt has rolled the donuts about outside before bringing them in to eat.

Louis picks his up, ready to eat. Sani shoots him a look and he lowers the donut. He puts it back down on the circle of glazing left on the tabletop.

Hurt says, "Let him eat it. We're celebrating."

Sani doesn't say anything. Aberdeen is too tired to object, to get into a fight with Hurt. Her brain isn't quite back to firing right and quick. The boy can have some sweets. It's not like any of them will make it out of this alive. Life will get them all.

Aberdeen nods at Louis and he picks back up his donut, bites it, smiles.

Sani doesn't touch hers. Hurt rips off a piece of his and wads it into a ball before popping it in his mouth. He dips his chin towards Aberdeen's donut. "Go on. Just try."

Louis speaks up during a mouthful of chewing. "What are we celebrating?"

"Aberdeen coming home to us. We're lucky she came back. She could have died." Hurt takes another bit, balls it up, downs it.

Aberdeen is fairly certain Hurt doesn't really know what happened to her. How could he? He hasn't asked. His years as a vet tech can't give him much insight into the effects of opiates on people. And she's sure he's never done drugs, never even touched a cigarette.

"You wouldn't believe where I got these," he starts but doesn't finish. His attention is drawn to the living room. He starts to hum the melody of a song he played over and over again for Aberdeen last summer. Some piece that wowed him with its use of mandolin and fiddle.

She looks at the donut. She can see the indent where the black jelly has been plunged into the fried dough. It reminds her too much of her night. The dough and she have been doped up, shot up, packed full of sugar or heroin, both things that please and kill.

Taking her pinkie, she sticks it into the hole and pulls out a bit of the filling. It is dotted with seeds, black and marquise-shaped like the diamond studs her mother used to wear. Where did this come from, she thinks? Did he cross the Atlantic to get it, flying on nothing but the stuff that is fueling him now, making him babble, dish out non sequiturs, tramp around in enough foot powder to cake a Geisha's face?

She puts the filling to her mouth. It's blackberry, not what they had together in Brussels. This is nowhere near the same thing.

Hurt finishes his donut then moves to the living room. Aberdeen doesn't follow him with her eyes. Instead she looks to Louis happily devouring the thing that will kill him.

"I have something to ask of you," she says.

He stops eating, the pastry squished flat between his fingers. "I don't want you hanging around Janos anymore, okay?"

She's waiting for protest. She's waiting for Louis to tell her that he is his friend, that he has no one to talk to other than adults, that he's sick for his lost grandma, that he's tired of carrot sticks and water for snacks. She's waiting for him to act like a child.

He does not.

"Okay," he says, and goes back to his donut.

The sweet, artificial tang to the filling sits on Aberdeen's tongue. She walks to the sink, takes up a dirty glass with a ring of dried red something in the bottom of it. Turns the water on, fills it, drinks it all the way down. But the taste is still there. It makes her stomach turn. Up comes the vomit. More bile. It smacks the stainless steel sink, dribbles down the drain.

She wonders how her body can keep up with making all the bile she keeps dispelling. These bodies are amazing, she thinks, with their ability to just keep on keeping on. She doesn't mind the throwing up. Like she has been doing. Like she would be doing if there were a tiny mote growing in her uterus.

Hurt is dancing in the living room now. She can hear his feet come up and down on the floor in a quick thumping. Louis pushes out his chair, goes to join in.

Sani comes over to Aberdeen, lifts her hair away from her sticky mouth. A lock of it gets dragged through her open lips and trails away a line of saliva, a thread of spider silk.

"He has no idea what I went through. I haven't told him," Aberdeen says, picks a seed from the tip of her tongue with a pinkie finger.

"Pay no attention to him," Sani says in Aberdeen's ear, her breath close and damp. "We're all just trying to deal."

CHAPTER SEVENTEEN

This must be the way that people become shut-ins. The idea would be laughable to a past Aberdeen, a pre-heroin, pre-abused, pre-abducted Aberdeen. But current Aberdeen gets it now. Walls are the soft chests of mothers, familiar smells the reassuring hands of fathers. Her apartment is her tender, her handler, her defender that pushes back at all that the world is pushing in.

She does not go out for food. Hurt takes up the responsibility and goes gladly when she requests something of him. He attacks the chores she asks of him with verve and a smile. They are just simple, day-to-day tasks that give her a quickened heartbeat and a tightness in her arms. Hurt must not see them this way. He goes at them like errands from a goddess, savoring the commandments, finding pleasure in them. She is happy that he does. She cannot.

Her trauma has brought Hurt out of his sullen cloud. She considers he is moving through his own stages of grief. Stages set into play by LTP and everything that's come after it. First it was anger, then somberness. And now, energy, unbridled, unceasing. Yet she has told him nothing of the needle. And he has not asked. She will not terrorize him with her own tumult and end his new-found joy in living.

She does not go out for air. She has always gone out for air. Air drew her outside the day after the chemicals disappeared for good in the second round of bombings. Now she takes in the same air over and over, never opening windows, only sipping in the exhalations of Louis, Hurt and Sani when they return from the outside world. She gladly takes their leftovers. She likes that the carbon dioxide and a little bit of oxygen has been inside them. She sips the rest of the useful stuff out with her crackling lungs; the air was them, now it is her.

Louis does not mind that she stays in the house for eleven days. Aberdeen becomes his stalwart playmate now that Hurt is preoccupied with an unnatural desire to tend to any need that leaves her mouth when he is not at work or speaking in a heated timbre over his microphone. Hurt jumps at the chance, looks like a dog waiting for a Frisbee. But there are days when she does not play with Louis and instead lies on the couch with her legs cocked to the floor. She thinks of the heroin. She thinks of getting back on the horse and riding it all the way to Louis's father. Once she got to him, she would want to hit him, call him names, but she would not. If the heroin was with her, she would kiss him with genuine acceptance. She would invite him into the same dalliance. He would likely come.

She does not stop to consider that Mr. Dover may be a fine man, a clean man. She needs him to saddle up now, more than ever. Ride out with her. Because she needs the camaraderie, however imagined it might be.

Louis looks out the living room window. Aberdeen feels that it is all they ever do. Look out windows. Like they're in some lame movie that uses far-off looks through clear glass as prognostication of the future. But he does it several times a day. So does she. But Louis looks out for playmates and signs of real snow at the end of winter, not the false winter of swirling polystyrene. What he gets is the back of the billboard, its message pointing outwards to the world and not to them.

Aberdeen looks out for confirmation that the world is still shit. Yes, she notes, it is.

She also looks out for Janos.

The man hasn't been back in the eleven days she's been home. She does not see his familiar bleached hair or the bounce of his body back and forth on the brick wall. Clients wanting what he has to sell just keep walking past her building like it is just a building and they just are walking.

She wants him to come back. She's not sure if she wants it because she could jimmy up the window in such a way that she could stick her head out, squint, and line up his body with the trajectory of a falling box of rocks. She's not sure she wants to punish him.

What she really wants from him is the looks he gives her. More than that, she wants an apology. She wants to tear the snakes from his fingers, rip the top button off his dress shirt and make him go to college somewhere far to the south where it is warm all the time and he has no reason to stand against cold walls in a wide, woolen coat.

She wants to save him. Add him to the list, she thinks.

"How about a walk today?" Louis pushes. The donut didn't treat him well the day that Hurt was insistent on celebration. There were scares. Aberdeen cannot relive them more than that. There were scares for Louis. The small batch of insulin Myrtle managed to save for the day Louis couldn't manage anymore without it, if that day came, were some of the most precious commodities in the apartment.

"Tomorrow I might want to," she says, wondering why twelve days would embolden her anymore than eleven. Or fifty. Even though her body is better, even though she can't feel the places that two needles popped through her flesh, her mind says stay, slow the body, put it on a chair, leave it there for safe keeping.

This is all the discussion Aberdeen has with Louis today.

He is always with her, but he's mute most of the time. He stands like a watchman at a chamber door. None may enter the house or leave it without him knowing. This is how he reciprocates what she has does for him. He is genuinely in the moment, with her, around her. He comes for hugs often, his soft arms flung around her, then pulled back so he can fly off in a stiff approximation of an airplane or a bird of prey.

Louis leaves for toys. Aberdeen goes to the most interesting window. It is her turn to see what she can see.

It makes her touch the back of her neck, then her thigh.

Janos is back.

He looks nothing like a snake handler. He looks like a college kid bereft of personal grooming. The collar is turned up on his coat. From five floors up she can see how his short hair gathers in clumps. It must be unwashed, untended.

Janos, she thinks, you are a piece of work.

She retrieves an old, green afghan from the couch. She was told when she was young that her grandfather made it, pulled it into amassing loops with a metal hook. It made her love her grandfather more when her grandmother told her this each time she would visit them. She felt connected to her grandfather. They were both makers, crafters. It wasn't until she was older that she realized that they were teasing her. Of course he didn't make it. Men didn't do fabric work. When her lips turned down, they laughed. Seriously, they said to her, do you think that is something any man would do?

She supposed not.

Men had more important things to do. Like study for master's degrees. Like sell tickets for drugs. Like force Aberdeen into possible addiction. She looks at the blanket, pulls it about her form, thinks on how the loops and chains would connect done under the relaxed hand of a junkie.

She's back at the window. Janos looks bored, but all she can see of him is the white hair of his head and the span of his shoulders. They slope downward sharply. It gives him the carriage of a person who cannot handle much.

Then there is her Hurt, her husband passing by Janos. She takes in a breath and holds it there. He has a plastic bag in his hand and she waits with a rigid back to see what he will say to the man. There will be words loud enough to come up to her window and enable her to hear. There will be a punch to the side of the head.

These things do not happen. Hurt walks by him, opens the door to the apartment building. Janos turns his head to watch him go in, then brings his hands up to his mouth to huff warmth into them.

Part of her wants to open the door, run down the stairwell in her socks and tell Hurt to do something, anything. She wants Hurt to instinctively know that Janos was part of the gang that maligned her. Yet he doesn't know there was a gang. He knows nothing.

Instead, another person catches her eye outside.

Wheelchair Man. Janos holds the door open for him and gets out of the way of the bulk of the chair and its wheels the same circumference as any found on a cruiser or a ten-speed. She expects that the disabled man will wheel down the street, probably not saying thanks to Janos as would be right for his crusty nature.

But he does not wheel away. He wheels towards Janos. She can see the old, red kerchief on his palm. He's reaching for something within his thin jacket. He pulls it out. Dull green and rectangular. Money.

Janos pockets it and comes out with his own paper. It is the roll of tickets. It is new, fatter, thicker than the tight circle she first saw. He has gone through many tickets. He has gone through enough to necessitate a new supply.

He releases a tail off the roll. He has snakes in his hands again, Aberdeen thinks. He holds the round out to Wheelchair

Man, inviting him. She can only see how the red handkerchief moves to hold the queuing stubs, rip at it, release it. She knows there is a ticket in his hand now, even if she cannot see it from her height.

"No," she says out loud.

"No," she screams at the window, condensation between two panes from a broken seal.

Louis comes for her then. He stands and watches her pound her fists on the glass before moving to her side and wrapping his arms around her waist. A bird, come home to nest. A plane, landed.

Aberdeen imagines the men five stories down looking up at the sound. All they can see is the glint of afternoon sun pinging off the ascending windows, making cubes of white light. Like illuminated tickets, rectangles shown under the light of a lamp meant for authentication. They pocket their illuminations. Wheelchair Man with one. Janos with hundreds and hundreds.

CHAPTER EIGHTEEN

Wheelchair Man is on her list for saving. It is a short list. It goes Hurt, and Louis, and Wheelchair Man, with Hurt and Louis quickly tying for first. Wheelchair Man holds the end of the list strong and in third. But he's on the list, just the same. And it causes Aberdeen to buck up and renege on the role of shut-in.

On day twelve, she puts on snow boots so she can feel the cushy walls of them against her ankles, pulls her hair up in a clip, wears three layers of tops (a wife-beater with holes at the hem, a brown sweatshirt of Hurt's, a zippered fleece) and thick, stiff jeans. They all create a shield, sort of like the heroin made a force field. She will wear it until she is ready to be out on her lonesome.

Hurt watches her leave the apartment. Louis tries to go after her, but she holds up a hand in pause and leaves him on the landing while she takes the stairs down to the bottom floor. To the apartment of the veteran, she goes calling.

But when she hits the bottom of the landing and before she places her fist to his door she stops and considers her movements and her leaving the apartment. What is she doing? Why is she leaving her place of safety when she's so dependent on a drug? When her body sings to her its name, soothes her with remembrances of its ability to spread, inundate and take away?

She is addicted to a chemical.

She wants to walk to the front door, the glass door, and look out it, see Janos in his familiar spot. But instead she goes back up the stairs, Louis watching her, appearing as just eyes and a brow over the metal railing.

The H is calling. It's calling with bullhorns and intimate squares of folded notes slipped into her hand. It's trying to get her attention.

But this is not the chemical to which she is addicted.

Louis follows her back into the apartment and watches as she opens the coat closet and digs around. Hurt comes out to watch, too, and folds his arms over his torso. His foot is tapping at the floor again, but not in a rhythmic pattern. It's staccato, then mucked up with bits of long scuffing with his heel. Then there is a pound or two to complete the chaos.

Aberdeen locates the evening clutch, moves the zipper open but gets it stuck on the satin lining. She doesn't finagle it open with her fingers. Instead she pries the teeth back with her hands, takes what she wants, and drops it to the floor.

Her inhaler of albuterol. Her only expired bit of hope.

She looks to Hurt and remembers how he held it when she located it the day after the chemical plants were bombed again. On LTP. The inhaler was precious to him. Now he looks at it with a calm face. His rapping on the floor stops and he finally asks.

"So the other one is gone?"

"Yes," she answers, thinking of the way it was tossed on the ground in that cage with all the predators. The human predators, not the cats. "I'm down to this."

She wraps her fingers around it so tight the blood goes somewhere else in her body, leaving her hand white. She looks up to Louis and he gives her a wan smile and moves over to her. She wraps her arms around his knees and squeezes him, like she's strong enough to lift him up by his legs, heave him above all the people and chaos so he can see the fucking parade.

"Don't let me misplace this," she tells him, looking up the length of his jeans and orange-striped hoodie.

"I won't, Abbie," he says. "I'll take care of you."

Hurt snorts at this, rolls his eyes, leaves. It is something she has never seen him do in their three years as a couple. That, she thinks, is the look of an asshole. It must be a new stage in his ever-progressing set of emotions. She's already missing his helpful, energetic phase. She feels it lasted no longer than her last bleed.

With the metal and plastic still in her hand, she uses her legs to push up, stand up, go to the kitchen and dig around in the drawer that holds things like scissors, a tea infuser, pads of paper with pithy sayings on them, a bit of florist's wire. She finds the roll of duct tape, just a rim of it circling the cardboard ring five, maybe six times. She takes it out with the scissors.

She unbuttons her pants and lets them slide down far enough to expose the white of her upper thighs and holds them there. Louis puts a hand on his head and goes to his room. Hurt turns up a radio in their bedroom and voices of dissent and anger and emotion flow out of it and take over the apartment.

She cuts a few strips as long as her forearm and puts the inhaler, canister up, against the flesh right under the seam of her cotton underwear. The hair is fine there, so white and soft she never shaves it that high. She knows if she needs the inhaler, no, when she needs it, she will have to rip off the tape and take away some of the down that covers her, shields her, keeps her good and warm.

The tape leaves her hands slightly sticky. The inhaler hovers to the side of her leg like a small gun in an inconvenient holster. At least it's under her clothes. She will be able to get to it if she needs it. If someone else needs it, they will have to get through her. And she is done being poked at.

She tells herself she will only pop the canister out when she showers. Otherwise it will be her new growth of plastic and flexible, metallic adhesion. It is just a different way for the chemicals to ride her now. At least it's outside of her. It's something.

"Going back down," she yells out to the missing boys. They don't come out; Hurt enveloped in the radio's words of conspiracy and chaos, Louis stymied by her show of skin.

Back to the stairs. And back to a kind of peace. Her back is straighter. It only took her identifying what she needed, she thinks, and then she finds herself at Wheelchair Man's door.

There isn't a need to knock because he opens it wide for her. He knows she's coming.

"Ah, Jesus," he says. "I knew it."

"What's your name?" she presses.

"Leave off of it," he says and wheels into his apartment, waves her in.

She closes the door behind her. The apartment smells sour, milky, and is absent of comfortable heat. The man wears three pairs of socks on his feet. She can see three rings up each calf: white on top, brown and fuzzy in the middle, a black, dipping crew on the bottom. She lifts up the hems of her tops in one pinch of fingers and realizes both of them are dressed to fortify.

"I could just look at the mail on your table, see what your name is."

"And I could use my wheels to run over your feet and stop you."

They stay where they are and look over one another. He's thinner than she remembers him being the last time she was standing in front of him. And there is a rigor in his frame that was not there before. The white whiskers around his mouth are stained yellow from coffee or cigarettes or chewing tobacco.

"Shit, I knew you were coming, girl. Figured the other day you were the only one that'd be fucking pounding on windows upstairs. You've got more of a temper than you know. If you just let it out instead of misdirecting it into giving a shit about other people, you'd be better off. So would I."

He squints his eyes, still taking Aberdeen in from feet to head. "You all right? You look tired and worn out in those clothes. Figure fashion don't matter no more with the end of the world? That it?"

Aberdeen wonders if fashion ever really did matter. Probably not.

"I've had other things to worry about besides me."

"Like me?" he says.

She shakes her head and her hand moves down her leg, pats at the inhaler hidden there. He follows her hand, wrinkles his nose.

"How do you get all the way to the tent? That's a long way for you to wheel."

He laughs, turns his chair around and moves into his sitting room. The drapes are pulled and filtered light casts spotlights on the dust motes in the air.

"I was in *Vietnam*, girl. Do you think pussies survived there? Do you think I would have left that damned rice paddy with a shot in my back and pig shit up to my ears if I was a pussy? Once a pussy, always a pussy," he says, looking at Aberdeen's sex, then glancing up to her eyes. "But once a man, always a man."

She can't help it. "A man without working legs."

"My hands work just fine," he says looking at them with their banded palms. "They get me places just fine."

"All the way to the tent?"

He laughs, pulls at one of the drapes closest to him and opens it a crack. A wedge of white spreads out over a brown carpet.

"Ah, I get it now," he says. "You're one of the people that goes *inside* the tent, aren't you? One of them religious freaks looking for salvation. That why you know about the tent?"

"No," is all she replies with. The dust in the apartment is making her nose itch. She suppresses the urge to put her finger up to it. The man might think she has something, a cold, start yelling at her about infections, about her bringing his death straight inside his domain.

"Fuck no 'no' on the matter. You've been there. And I don't see you as a user."

"A user like you? Someone who half a year ago was yelling in this very building about how all the people dependent on medicine were going to rise up and kill the people like you? The clean people, the ones that don't need chemicals to save them from living?"

He drops his head, but it isn't out of shame. He's looking at his crotch. Aberdeen can see that he's hard, filling up his old, ratty pair of fatigues.

He meets her eyes. "It's an effect of the paralysis. Junk still works, just at odd times. Don't be thinking you're helping matters. It's not you, at least not in that outfit."

Aberdeen smiles, feels the canister tugging at the hairs on her thigh, thinks of her other thigh, still carrying the black bruise of where the needle thrust in. She thinks of men jabbing at her with hard things, hard in need. Hurt, Donation Box, and then, Wheelchair Man. She still smiles.

Sexual release is one thing they all still control.

Then she says something to release the tension. "Do you use that to help you get to the tent? A third hand?"

He laughs so that the movement of his chest makes his chair wiggle on the carpet, flattened and grooved from years of his wheels. He holds his head like it will make him stop, but his laughing turns hysterical and Aberdeen can't help but laugh with him.

He takes in a bit of air, wipes at his eyes. "I think I actually like you, you know that?"

"Of course," she says. "So tell me. Why are you going to the tent? The pain in your spine too much without help? No bullshit."

Wheelchair Man shakes his head. "People think paralysis can't hurt much. Parts of your body are dead bits, but hell, other parts," and here he whistles through closed teeth. "The pain has been working me over real good for awhile. So I broke down, talked to the boy outside. He's been helping."

"What's the ticket get you? How do they know what you paid for? It looks like they all come off the same roll."

His shoulders rise. "No idea. I'm not sure. They know, though, when you get there and give them the ticket."

"And what does your ticket get you," she presses.

"We called it the shit that makes you *boocoo dinky dau* when you smoke it. Stuff from the countryside was best. What they gave you in Hanoi was part dried gook shit."

Marijuana.

Aberdeen's nose stops itching. Her body shifts downward, stacking muscles up right, shimming into relaxation.

"Good," she says to him, "that's what I was hoping." She pities the old man, the man who thinks all Asians are the same, all to be reviled, Vietnamese the same as Koreans all put under the hateful moniker *gook*. But still, she thinks, these points of bigotry do not make a man deserving of hot metal in his spine.

"And it's doing the job? You're getting relief?"

"Sure as shit," he says, lets out a guffaw. "Sure as shit."

She thinks of his hollering that day in the stairwell. How his face was contorted in fear. He was the only one in the building willing to turn fear on, give fear the stage, let it be a performance artist.

"Suppose people shouldn't throw stones, then," she says.

"Unless they don't mind getting gun fire in return. That's a learned fact, girl."

A curious jab of pain hits her needle mark. For an instant,

the thin needle is there again, parting flesh. She winces and he notices.

"You all right? What'd you get from that tent? You didn't tell me."

"I got more to worry about," she says. "If you keep getting your pain relief from Janos and whoever you see at the tent, just remember they're wrong people. Bad. They have the right stuff, right now, but they will kill you. They will take your life if they feel the need."

A moustache falling into a trimmed beard, a wooden box, yellow eyes. Parts of her tormentors. She sees them all overlaid on the walls of Wheelchair Man's apartment, transparencies, faint, but present.

He wheels back over to Aberdeen and sticks out a hand to her. She hesitates for just a moment, then takes it. He smells unwashed, like mud dried on boots. The skin of his hand is dry and dotted with mounds, little calluses that keep him able and moving.

"I don't go for social calls," he says, holding her hand stiff in front of him, hers swooping down to him, his reaching up to hers. "When I don't have the cash to pay, they take my credit, so I'll keep visiting their store, okay?"

She wants to ask him what he means by "credit" but she smiles, takes her hand back. She can live with his reasoning. She agrees it's okay. Because what the fuck can she do about it, even if it isn't? He's an adult. Even if he's one of her three, he's conscious and free and she will not scare him, like she has been scared, in an attempt to have him fall in line.

"You've been warned," she says.

He looks to the kitchen, a room darkened, lit only by a nightlight in the shape of the Virgin Mary near the garbage disposal switch.

"Do you want to stay for a drink? I think I've got a little bit of Black Velvet left. And you're my only social experience aside from the white-headed shit outside and the crazies who pass my window and tap on it with their fingers. It sounds like hail on my windowpane, all day and all night."

She wonders if she should, but decides her attachment should only stretch so far.

"I have an apartment to clean up. I need to get cleaned up. I've been out of commission for a little while. I need to get back to a routine."

His face goes soft, muscles weak. "We've lost our routine, girl. The whole nation. Maybe eventually the whole world. We're so lame and hurt right now, America, especially with no help from allies and the enemies waiting like jackals once we expire. Our routine ain't nothing more than survival now. Individual and as a people, a country. We ain't getting out of this with gift bags or Christmas stockings full of little bottles full of little pills."

His rant is right. From what she knows, there is no end in sight. No help from others. That's why she wants to help. Since LTP, America had lost its friends. England gives the Yanks a lift of a teacup with a middle finger holding the handle. China stops talks with American ambassadors on their own soil.

But Aberdeen, Aberdeen can help here. Now.

Instead of confirming his fears with the only knowledge she has, likely the same he's privy to, she takes up his hand again and bends down onto the balls of her feet. They are at a level so their eyes match. His are red-rimmed, gummy.

"Are you ever going to tell me your fucking name?"

He blinks heavily, smiles a grin that gives away what he gets from his ticket.

"What would keep you coming back to see me if I did?"

CHAPTER NINETEEN

Janos is gone. This is the third or fourth furlough he has taken from the block. Aberdeen hasn't spoken to him since the night in the tent, in the zoo, in the city, in her haze of heroin. But he is definitely gone. There is no dealer on the wall, no rolls of rectangles that bring promises of drugs.

This is bad for many. This is bad if Aberdeen ever gives in and wants to pony up. This is bad for Wheelchair Man.

Aberdeen is fully emerged from her time in her cave. She showers each day. She goes shopping and fights for the least stale bread at the store. She is back to operation, even though the itch is there, the thoughts of fine metal making love to her veins, the push in, the warmth.

And though she is back, others are slipping. Wheelchair Man is in a bad way.

Three days after Janos disappears, Wheelchair Man is back at the bottom of the stairwell, taking up his yelling again. This time his ranting isn't about the crazies being the death of him. This time he screams out words condemning religion, government, and society. He lambasts everyone, including the Secretary of the Interior and Madonna. Aberdeen and Louis sit with their backs to the cold metal of the railing, safe on the fifth floor, their heads turned to the sides so his words funnel upwards, direct to their eardrums. They listen and Louis pouts, runs his hands on his thighs, while Aberdeen considers helping, but decides against it.

If she can't get him pain relief, she has no recourse. He would refuse Sani with her unconventional hands. She swallows hard and puts a hand over one of Louis's. She almost can't admit it to herself as she hears the rubber of his wheels squeak on the waxy floor of the foyer as he makes sharp turns, back and forth. But she does, eventually.

She can't help.

"I want to help him," Louis says, scrunching his body up against the metal and looking down the stairs. "He's so sad, Abbie."

"Yes," she says, "he really is."

Wheelchair Man rants for three days and then stops. Aberdeen considers it may have been his way of asking for help. After all, he can't climb the stairs to seek her out. And she is ashamed to admit that she has been stealing past his door whenever she ventures out, sometimes finding herself walking on the tips of her toes like a villain sneaking about, doing ill deeds in a silent movie.

Wheelchair Man is still on her list. But his dependency on marijuana reminds her of her own desires. She worries that interacting with him will find her pushing him out the heavy, glass door to meet with Janos for a new, pink ticket. Their heads bowed, breath puffs of white in the crisp air. No one will need to talk. Their needs will be evident. Especially hers.

So with relief in the form of drugs out of reach for so many, including her, Aberdeen takes up a curious hobby. She begins praying. At first she prays to something she names Creator, asking for guidance and help for Hurt and his strange, ever-transitioning personality and for simple things like an early, warm spring. Then she starts praying to other things, things around her. She prays to her terrariums, the ones she has left, prays they do not molder and can hang on with scant fertilizer (because the fertilizer is gone, too) and she prays to the rug near her bed that it will not bunch up when she steps off of it into bed each night only to stay bunched and trip her up when she leaves bed in the morning. She prays to her cereal and to the strength of the windows that keep out the cold and the 60-watt bulb that flickers in the bathroom and threatens to extinguish.

When the stairwell is quiet again, when Wheelchair Man has likely lost his voice from the booming and calling out, she prays to find Janos back outside. But he is nowhere, at least nowhere to the people of her building and the ones in need out on the streets. She feels morose and abandoned somehow, not knowing where the feelings are coming from, but letting them come over her anyway, flesh out her days with something other than worry and anxiety and her need for chemicals.

At least she has not had an asthma attack. Each night she puts her hands over her chest and prays to her lungs. She offers them any sort of supplication they demand. She gives them praise and honor and expressions of gratitude. She promises them anything they want in exchange for not killing her.

She considers, at night, that her lungs may be her worst enemy. Not the heroin. Not Beso and his tent of addictions. Not her need to help others, regardless of her own issues. But the bellows inside her that find their job somehow *lackluster* and want her dead.

She goes to sleep the night Wheelchair Man gives up his vocals with her palms over her breasts, her intention on her bronchial sacs, and wakes up and prays to them again, a prayer of thanks, a prayer given in surprise that they are so very giving.

And she decides, against all reason, to go and help him, the man in the chair, the nameless one that smells of week-old body odor and has impromptu erections.

She leaves Hurt snoring in bed, gets on her clothes, her real clothes, nice clothes, and goes to wake Louis. He needs to come with her. He wants to help. This is something she can teach him about. Like any good mother would do for a son. She can teach him how to give of himself to others. Myrtle would be proud, she tells herself as she pushes open his bedroom door and finds his bed sheets disheveled, cold and absent of the boy she loves and wants for her own.

She goes back to her own room and pushes on Hurt's shoulders with the flats of her palms. He doesn't wake up. She pushes harder, pressing him into the mattress like she's trying to restart his heart. Eventually he snorts, sits up.

"What?" he says. There are no more *good mornings* from him, no kisses goodnight either. Aberdeen realizes that, right now. She sets her mouth in a line, creases her forehead.

"Where is Louis?"

"In bed?"

"No. He's not. Did he say anything about going down to his old apartment yesterday? He always says when he's leaving. He always has, anyway. Did he say anything last night, before you put him to bed?"

Hurt musses his hair with his fingers and then runs them down his face. Aberdeen thinks he looks younger somehow, more alive lately. He's sleeping less but when he awakens he is up, flying about, working, thinking and talking with a fluidity foreign to her.

"I didn't put him to bed. He said he was going to stay up reading in the living room. So I left him to it."

Aberdeen lets her bottom fall to the bed. Her mind whirls.

"So he may have not even gone to bed. He could have left last night. He could be anywhere, Hurt."

"He's probably downstairs in his old place," Hurt says as he puts a hand on the small of her back. His palm is hot and wet and she can feel the moisture through the fabric of her blouse. "Did you check?"

"I checked with you first. I thought you would know where he is."

"Well, I don't. Why don't you know? You should know."

She downs him with a stab of the eyes. Aberdeen feels her stomach leap, her cheeks flush. The things he is saying to her lately, she thinks, are things Hurt would never say. She says nothing, just holds him with her stare.

"What?" he asks, "it's not like he's our son."

She gets up, feels Hurt's hand peel off her shirt. She walks to the bedroom door, leaves, and shuts it behind her.

Standing in the short hallway, she can see into Louis's room. The new sun is starting to show across his dresser, the antique she used to store her crafting supplies in converted back to its original use, holding Louis's small boxers, his socks with the holes he always orients over his little toe, never the big toe, his five sweaters, all knit by his grandmother, all washed and folded and known now by Aberdeen: the one that pills, the orange one, the one with spaceships at the collar, the old man one, the one with the weak seams.

Aberdeen takes in a deep breath and then lets it out as a scream. It issues forth, fills the apartment. She holds it, extends it until her lungs are empty bags, until Hurt flings open the door and shakes his head at her.

She looks at him as she takes back in air. He still shakes his head, says nothing, keeps shaking. She puts on her shoes, a coat, and heads downstairs.

Then she is in front of the apartment Louis shared with his grandmother. She tries the doorknob but finds it bolted. She pounds on it, yells out like Wheelchair Man. Except she yells out for something important. For someone more than just herself.

She yells but no one comes to the door. She thinks of Louis opening it wide, smiling, taking her hands, but it does not happen. No matter how she envisions it while the meat of her hands goes tingly and then sore from bashing against the hard wood.

She gives up and makes the rest of the trek down the stairs. It is a repeat at the door of Wheelchair Man. She considers if she had the desire to help him, Louis could have had the same desire, but acted on it before her, the night before her, or hours before her. She is both proud he might be in there, helping the man, and scared shitless he is in there, helping the man. Louis is just a boy, she thinks, and Wheelchair Man has broken parts that are in no way healed.

She does not want these broken parts breaking her Louis.

There is no answer and her hands finally give and go numb. She walks to the front door, peers out at the morning and the crust of frost on the metal of the handle outside, on the tips of the tree branches and on a discarded paper cup, crumpled and smudged with black. Real spring threatens, but it doesn't hold sway yet.

Aberdeen considers going out to find him, but then she realizes she would have no idea where to look. The boy she has been caring for, tending and aiding is still a stranger to her. She does not know where he would run if he were to run.

She sits for a time, right in front of the door, and cries. A resident of the building she does not know moves around her to get out to go somewhere, a duffel bag over his shoulder. He does not offer words of concern or help. He moves his legs around her bulk like she is a fountain of a woman crying, inanimate and beautiful, but otherwise of no concern whatsoever and only in his way.

Aberdeen rubs the water into her cheeks, pushes herself up and climbs the five flights of stairs back to Hurt. He's eating three runny eggs on a plate of toast. There is no real plate under the combination. A bit of yolk spills over the crust of the bread and falls to the yellow floor. She looks for it, tries to find it with her blurry eyes, but it disappears, blending into the linoleum too damn well.

"Not in the building. He's not here. Where the fuck is he?"

"Call the police, then. Have them put out an APB for a goofy black kid with self-esteem issues." Hurt takes another bite of his meal. He licks at a bit of crust on his lips. He smiles.

Aberdeen sucks in her cheeks. She rubs her forearms hard and fast so the skin feels hot enough to flame.

"I've got zero words for you right now, Hurt. Zero."

He keeps the bread and egg in front of his face. His eyes fixate on it. He finishes it while Aberdeen watches him ingest a meal seemingly more important and worthy of focus than a missing Louis.

He goes to the sink and dusts the remnants of the toast from his hands into the stainless steel basin.

Hurt tries to move past Aberdeen back to their room but she stands her ground. She decides she does have words for him. They are bubbling up, giant spheres of warm anger that burst against her larynx.

"I know he's not ours," she says, "but he's as good as ours. We are his somebodies. There are no other people for Louis other than a junkie cowboy for a father somewhere out West."

Hurt sighs. "A junkie father? How would you know that?" His eyes narrow. "I'm just..."

"What? An asshole lately? A douchebag I don't recall marrying? What if you had no one, Hurt? Louis has no one. We are it," Aberdeen yells, her hands flying up and contorting to make her point.

"I want to take care of him. Don't you get it," she goes on, "It's the only fucking thing I can do right now. It keeps me from going crazy."

His hands are quick. They dart up and snatch at Aberdeen's wrists and pull them down to her sides. Hurt pins her arms against her body. His nostrils flare and flick like a horse done with its racing.

"You think you're going crazy? Don't toss around the term,

Aberdeen. Some people really are. Some people are out of their minds. Completely out of their fucking minds!"

Aberdeen is frozen. Instantly she thinks of the way Yellow Eyes and Donation Box touched her. She thinks of the way Beso touched her. Now her husband was touching her with the same brute physicality. No more.

She folds her fingers into her palms and thinks of her fists as mallets, the kind that drive in railroad stakes, the kind that flatten and forge.

"Let go of me, Hurt."

Her tone is that of a woman that is *done* and he releases, backs up with his hands in the air and steps into the yolk that had disappeared on the yellow linoleum floor. It distracts him and he lifts up his foot to scrape off the sticky yellow with a thumbnail.

Aberdeen pulls at the bottom of her blouse as if it is disheveled. It isn't, but it feels good to pull it down to reclaim her composure and poise. It is a claim on her own self and on her space. It is hers. No one else's.

"Are you coming outside to help me look for Louis or not?"

Hurt puts his foot back down, his fingers mucked with yolk.

"I have my own projects, Aberdeen. He'll come back. Just like a lost dog. Where the hell is he going to go anyway? If we're all he has? Huh?"

Aberdeen knows all Louis has is her, one, not a *we*. She looks at her husband. She notes his fair skin. She is glad she does not have a child with his features. She suddenly feels blessed by not having a child with Hurt. The elation of this grows until she looks over at the toaster on the counter Hurt had used to toast his bread and smiles at it.

She prays to it. She prays aloud.

"May you always toast Hurt's bread so that he can happily eat it."

He lifts his eyebrows, holds slimy egg in his hand and she leaves the apartment again. She fights back tears. She fights back the part of her that says to turn around and make up and dream of babies again. Babies that possess Hurt's love of animals. Babies with her aquiline nose.

Still, the way he grabbed her and held her is a new thing. A potentially dire, harmful thing.

She's out the door. She's walking, searching. Her eyes well up with water when she thinks too long of Hurt or Louis and so she tries instead to stay present on the walk and take in the things she passes. It helps the water get sucked back into wherever it comes from, sucking backwards into vessels and bits of flesh until her eyes become dry again and no longer red and she does not fear walking past the groups of soldiers who will not mistake her for a woman bereft of her medicine who needs to be taken somewhere, taken away.

The first thing she sees is a bird, a sparrow maybe, gray and very dead. It is flat, run over by a car and left looking like a specimen pressed between the pages of a book. Not a botanical find but one of meat and stick legs and small, minute pinfeathers no bigger than those billowy, false lashes seen on ladies in cabarets and drag queens on stage.

She brings her hands up to just under her chin to pray to it, or rather, to something for it, but a man walks by in a large overcoat. He raises his eyebrow at her, just one, and she tucks her hands in her pockets.

Be inconspicuous, she thinks. Like people that don't pray in public, she thinks.

She walks on, like she seems to always do now after the loss of the medicine, walking towards something, away from something, looking for something. She realizes she's never walked more in her entire life and suddenly she is tired.

A group of children are shouting and bouncing around a fallen electrical wire that zips and spits across the pavement a half-block away from where Aberdeen stands. It reminds her of one of those lame fireworks she always hated as a child, the black discs people light and watch grow, pulse up and out for a few moments before they freeze and a fingertip reveals that they're nothing more than bubbling ash. Except this wire shoots sparks of fire and licks at the ankles of the children that cackle at its attempts to do harm.

Then she sees a boy, one that looks like Louis. It's the slope of his shoulders that reminds her of the boy and she makes for the group, waving her hands at them and shouting for them to move away from the wire. The hum of it, the vibratory aliveness of the thing grows louder as she gets closer. The kids ignore her until she is close to them but still out of reach of the snaking line.

"Get away from that," Aberdeen cautions, looking over the face of the boy that caught her attention. It isn't Louis. Her stomach flips. "It's a live wire. It could electrocute you."

A slip of a girl with a plait of hair running down her back wrinkles her nose at Aberdeen. "It's not alive. What you mean it's alive? You crazy? It's full of fire!"

And the group of children laugh and watch their toes and how the line reaches for their feet and Aberdeen moves off. She reminds herself of what matters. Hurt. Louis. Wheelchair Man.

She says Louis's name to herself over and over until she is back to the apartment building. It's past midday. She stops at Wheelchair Man's door and knocks again. There is no answer. Her feet barely clear the steps of the stairwell as she shuffles upwards. She considers, hopes, that Louis has gotten hungry and will be coming home for a bite of macaroni or a baked potato.

Her head is down, so she doesn't see Louis and Hurt at the top of the stairs. She runs headlong into Louis's soft torso. She looks up the length of his chest and folds her arms around him. He puts his chin on her head and she can feel the beginning of an Adam's apple bob as he swallows hard.

"Where were you?" she says to him in a whisper. She looks up to his mouth and waits for an answer.

"I wanted to help him," he says, not letting his eyes meet

Aberdeen's. Hurt is cracking his neck and steps back from Louis's side to pinwheel out his arms, to toss blood into his hands.

"Wheelchair Man?"

"Yes," he says and hugs Aberdeen tighter to his body.

She lets him hold her for a minute and then pulls away. Aberdeen reaches up and takes Louis's ears in her palms and dips his face towards her own.

"You took him all the way to the tent, didn't you?"

Aberdeen watches as Louis's lips shake and his eyelashes go dewy and heavy.

"He was so sick for help, Abbie. I just wanted to take him where he wanted to go."

"To the tent?" she asks again, knowing the answer.

Louis wipes at his eyes with the back of his hand and nods. "Into the room."

Aberdeen looks over to Hurt. He's bouncing on the balls of his feet and holds his hands up to his chin. He throws out a jab and feigns a strike in reply, dipping his head to his shoulder to avoid it. Aberdeen raises her eyebrows at him and releases Louis's ears.

"What room?"

"Behind the tent," he replies before breaking into a round of heaving sobs. "The room with the cages outside of it. The cages that hold the shelves of medicine."

CHAPTER TWENTY

"We can go get him," Hurt says, his arms still held in front of him. Aberdeen knows he's no pugilist. It's an interesting act but she recalls that the only time Hurt got into a brawl in junior high he ended the thing by defending his head with his arms until he could capture the attention of a teacher to come and save him from scuffing his knuckles.

The thought of storming the tent for Wheelchair Man makes Aberdeen's arms go numb. They will be there. No doubt. Donation Box. Yellow Eyes. Beso. If she goes, she knows they will see her. And if they see her, they might stick her again. Or kill her. Or take her to the lions. Or decide Hurt and Louis and Wheelchair Man could all be used to make a dent in Beso's quota.

She sets her lips in a seal against her teeth and shakes her head. Wheelchair Man was third on her list. There is no way she will sacrifice numbers one and two for number three.

"No," she says. "He'll get his marijuana and come wheeling back when he feels better. He's done it before. He'll do it again."

Aberdeen turns to Louis then and takes his hands in her own. They are cold with old sweat and lightly sticky. "He'll be okay. He really will."

"Bullshit," Hurt says. "You've heard his rants these past few days. He's cracked. He's fucked up and he's going to be so stoned he won't be able to grip the wheels on his chair to roll himself back up here."

"And," he continues, stopping his fighting dance for a moment to raise a finger in the air, "I want to find out what kinds of pharmaceuticals they've got stored in that room."

Aberdeen lets go of Louis, ignoring Hurt's new verve for leaving the house and interacting in other people's lives. She knows that since the protest he's been a homebody, leaving only when necessary to fill his twenty-five hours at the veterinary hospital or to help out Aberdeen with an errand, otherwise spending his time ranting about the condition of the country with his fellow pupils online. She touches the back of her neck and imagines the needle plunging into it, the other one, the one which held a sedative. She can almost feel it scraping the bone of her vertebrae and her stomach rolls once and she tastes bile on the back of her tongue.

She swallows hard and fights the acid back down. "Louis, where is this room? And how do you know they were pharmaceuticals on the shelves and not something else?"

"Abbie," he says, his eyes squinting up at her, "they were in medicine bottles and they all had labels with names on them and I could see the pills in the clearer bottles. It was medicine. I'm sure it was. I saw it all in the hallway leading from the room. I was close to the door that led out. I swear I could see it was medicine."

She nods and looks to Hurt. He's smiling wide and his face is flushed with redness. It makes the freckles on his cheeks disappear in a wash of blood just under the surface of his skin.

"We don't need any drugs. We aren't going into that room. And we are not going after Wheelchair Man."

"You're just scared," he says.

"I am. And I have a right to be scared. Have you forgotten what happened to me? Have you forgotten how long it has taken for me to recover my sanity?"

He snorts and puts his hands over his ears, shakes his head. "No, I haven't forgotten. I'd have to know something first in order to forget it. These people did something to you. That's been obvious since you wandered back home in a drugged stupor that night. Maybe they did make you lose your sanity. That's why I haven't pushed you. There is no recovering sanity, Aberdeen. Once that shit is gone it is way, long gone."

"So have you lost yours?" she finally asks, regretting it as soon as the question leaves her mouth. She doesn't want him to actually answer. She wants to go in the apartment, put on her pajamas and hide in her bed until she hears the screams of Wheelchair Man again down in the pit of the building, blessing her with the knowledge that he is back and safe and still angry as hell.

Hurt's broad smile collapses and he pulls at his earlobes. "I'm sick of hiding away. I'm going after him and I'm bringing him back and you can stay here and cower with Louis if you can't handle it."

Louis looks to Hurt and Aberdeen notices that they are nearly the same height. He is growing so fast, she thinks, and losing weight around his stomach. He is becoming a man.

"I'm going with you," he tells Hurt. "I took him there but I got tired of waiting around for him to come back out so I left. Besides, I knew you'd be upset with me disappearing. But I shouldn't have come back without him. I abandoned him. He is my responsibility."

"You are not going," Aberdeen says and then counters. "I'll go with you Hurt, but Louis, there is no way you are allowed anywhere near that tent. Ever again. Do you understand me? Promise. Promise right now as if you were swearing it to your grandmother."

And she is surprised by his response. It is another indication of his arriving adolescence.

"That's not fair, Abbie. Don't make me think of her. Not right now."

The bile returns, that new, meddlesome companion climbs up her throat and sits in the back of her mouth. "I'm sorry. But you can't go."

Louis turns then, sharp on the heels of his feet, and pushes open the door to the apartment, leaving it gaping behind him as he strides to his room. Hurt steps to it and pulls it closed.

"Let's go," he says.

Aberdeen needs to use the bathroom and badly wants a piece of bread or a handful of wheat crackers to pick up the acid and return it to her stomach. But she sees the energy in Hurt's limbs, the way he can't stop twitching and picking at himself.

She knows that if she goes to the tent, she will be seen. And if she is seen by the men that took her last time, she will be done for this time. She considers the last time she went and how she voided urine onto herself and this time she thinks if they do see her, she will just scream, cling to the other people in the tent with the tips of her fingernails and hope some of Hurt's new verve will mean he will do anything it takes to protect her from the men.

She realizes these are all "ifs" and if they do not pan out she could be dead within the day.

"Let me say goodbye to Louis first because it may be my last goodbye."

"Every single one possibly is," Hurts says and takes her by the arm and turns her back towards the stairs. She doesn't fight it; she lets her body go a bit soft and she runs her palm down the rail on the stairs, praying all the way down that if she does not come back, that the rounded bit of painted metal in her hands always prevents Louis from falling and tumbling and always leads him back up to his home and his place in this mess.

Goodbye Louis, she says in her mind, and they are gone.

The tent grounds are bustling and Hurt's eyes are wide,
watching the scores of people trampling down the dry grass
capping the barest mention of new green and tucking errant hair
behind ears and up into hats decorated with wide ribbons or fake,
fabric daisies. He points to the people who seem out of place, the
ones who have shoulders up to their ears with upturned collars
and glazed-over irises.

"A flock of odd ducks," he says as he watches them circle
the big, white tent and disappear out of sight. "I guess we want
to follow them."

Aberdeen had switched off on the walk over, preferring to
not think of the imminent abuse or the possible reintroduction to
heroin, another acquaintance like the bile, this one with dark
circles under the eyes, a blanket over the shoulder, switchblade
in a leather boot, just a perplexing sight of potential trouble. But
the tent, the milling about of people ready for hope and healing
and the edge of desperation in the circling groups turns her back
on.

Turns the fear back on.

Her arms go tingly and then completely dead as if she has
been lying on them on a hard, wooden floor. She stands as still
as she can get, her reptilian brain at the base of her neck telling
her it does not want to be poked again by a needle, does not want
her to get damaged. If she stands still, she will disappear. She is
a fawn in tall, golden grass. She is prey and she promised herself
she would never be prey again.

Her right eye goes wet and sends out tears but her left
remains completely dry, so dry that it stirs her from her solidity.

"I can't cry out of my left eye," she says in a whisper to
Hurt. "It's plugged shut. It has finally given up. I've overused
it."

He tugs on the sharp, bony bit of her elbow buried

213

underneath her jacket. She looks down at his hand tugging at her limb and she can't help but think of it as bullying. She lifts her arm up and out of his fingers and checks to see that all of her buttons on her coat are buttoned up. It is her oldest jacket, a ratty thing of red and white rayon. But it is not the one she wore to the tent the first time she came. That one sits next to the tall kitchen garbage in their apartment and several times a day she passes it and considers tucking it in the bottom of the sack and burying it with peels of apple and peels of potato.

"I literally can't cry out of it," she repeats and turns her head to her husband. "I'm done. I'm so very much done. Why am I here with you? I'm going to get killed."

Hurt is eyeing the opening of the tent. Aberdeen forces herself to look towards it. There are two men at the entrance; one of them wears a face mask as if he is about to brave a Tokyo subway and the other lifts a dark, wooden box to the sky and yells out something into the crowd.

"I am going to die," she says again and knuckles the tear duct of her left eye. She prefers both her eyes to be dripping water when she gets slammed with the poppy juice again or before getting a slug in her temple.

"We aren't going into the tent. We're going behind it," he says and then he lifts his arm to encircle the top of her back and pulls her in close. "I won't let anyone touch you. I fucking swear to it."

She stays silent and picks at the corner of her eye, trying to dislodge the nothing there, not a bit of hard crust or a goopy plug. It seems clear, but it refuses to demonstrate her feelings of trepidation.

"I can't cry anymore." Aberdeen shrugs and steps forward with Hurt, nestling her face into his neck. He smells of musk, a smell she has never smelled on him before and she mentally conjures a fox and prays to it to keep them both stealthy and quick and sly in this field of fools and illness.

Hurt walks her blind through the throngs of people, using his free arm to push aside those who will not move out of his way. No fights are started like this; they all passively shift as if yielding to a more dominant male on the scene. Aberdeen only takes her face away from the safety of Hurt's neck once and sees a young woman stumbling about the field, her legs splayed awkwardly so that her knees almost knock. She calls out to someone named Ned while parting the clumps of old grass with white fingers tipped with chipped, pink nails.

I will not be that, Aberdeen thinks, and places her head back in the space between Hurt's pectoral and collarbone.

There is a voice, deep, and a laugh, familiar. Hurt keeps walking forward but Aberdeen holds her ground and opens her eyes. Her right cheek is still damp. Her left is dry and wanting.

Donation Box and Yellow Eyes stand halfway around the back of the tent, waving the ones looking for drugs toward them. They hold orange buckets on their forearms, the kind that come from home improvement stores, and the sick and addicted shuffle towards them and drop one, five, fifteen paper tickets into the mouths of the buckets.

Yellow Eyes shakes his bucket and presses a hand into its depths to compact the paper.

Donation Box beckons more in with a flick of his fingers. They keep coming.

Hurt stops in front of Aberdeen and turns. "What?"

"No," is all she can say, again and again. "No, no, no."

Because she can think of nothing else to do, she lifts her hands up to her face and fans her fingers out in front of her eyes, nose and mouth. It is the worst mask imaginable but it is the best one available.

"Those are the men? Those are the men that hurt you?"

Aberdeen turns. She runs.

Hurt is on her immediately, clutching her at her waist and digging his feet into the ground to keep her from bolting. She clamps her hand over her mouth to keep from screaming. She knows she promised herself she would scream, would fight, but now it would call her tormenters to her, not keep them at bay.

Hurt leans in and speaks in her ear. "Don't run. We're going to walk out of here slowly, okay?"

She nods and then the bile that threatened to leave her earlier does, and she pulls back her hand and bends over to leave a small pool of vivid green between her feet.

Hurt rubs circles on her back and hums a song she does not know. She rarely knows his songs anymore.

Then she's up again, the tears coming, unceasing, from her right eye. She looks forward and starts walking calmly. Hurt takes up her arm, twining it in his own, lovers on good terms. They pass the front of the tent and keep walking when a voice stops Aberdeen from moving on.

"He's in there," it says.

She turns and recognizes the man with the respirator on his chin as Janos. She immediately glares at the man with the donation box and does not recognize his pockmarked face, his close buzz cut or his hoop earrings.

Janos waves her over but she doesn't move. Hurt lifts his chin up, stands in front of his wife. Janos says something to the man with the box and lifts his mask off his face, offering it up to the other man who takes it and slips it over his head. Janos moves towards Aberdeen and Hurt. He's wearing the same white button-down he wears on the stage, the underarms ringed with yellow pit stains. His hair is flattened with pomade.

He stops, takes a cigarette out of the back pocket of his slacks and wipes a piece of lint off of it. He lights it and several people in line look at it wantonly. His flaunting of a delicacy in front of so many is callous and brave. He meets their looks, removes a lemon drop, pale yellow, from a cellophane bag and tucks it into his cheek, puffs away on the filter-less cigarette.

He proffers the tobacco to Aberdeen who shakes her head

no and then to Hurt. Hurt takes the cigarette with his index and middle finger and flicks it away into the crowd. It lands at the feet of a woman bent over from scoliosis and she swoops it up, cups it in her hand and inhales with nose and mouth.

"Who is in there?" Aberdeen asks. She thinks of the way Beso blew that kiss goodnight to her as she lost consciousness.

Janos skews up his mouth and then spits on the ground in front of Hurt. "The crusty veteran in the wheelchair. He's paying his way."

Hurt looks at the wad of phlegm at his foot and smiles at Janos. "What the fuck does that mean?"

"She knows," he says, nodding towards Aberdeen.

And she does. And it is enough to get her into the tent, whether Beso is there or not.

She moves towards the opening and Janos goes with her. Hurt is a step behind, his hands in the air, lost in the current activity, the newfound gutsiness of his wife.

Janos hustles to get in front of Aberdeen and nods at the man with the donation box and the small group moves into the tent opening in front of the queue of people in line for salvation.

It's as she remembers from last time. Except the daylight is earlier, stronger and it illuminates the white tenting from outside, creating a glowing canopy above the heads of the people crammed in the tent. To someone easily impressed, the confined area would come off as holy and infused with spirit.

Aberdeen's spirit isn't here. She's not sure where it lives.

She stands on her tiptoes to see over the people in front of her. The smell of the tent is different from last time. This time it's an affront of mingling drugstore perfume and scented hairspray. At first all she can see is the hair and hats and skulls of the revivalists, but then Janos moves in front of her again and begins to walk and as he does, people move to let him through, the snake handler in their midst. Some reach out to touch him. One man grips onto Janos's belt loop. Janos is gentle in prying the man's fingers away and stops for a second to pat the back of his arthritic hand.

Finally, suddenly, the stage comes into the view, that pieced together platform of raw particle board and haphazard trusses. The big man with the tailcoat and the missing eye is there, a Bible tucked up under his armpit. He raises his arms into the air and the crowd, the people that were previously speaking in hushed tones and murmured *amens!* let fly whooping and hollering. The fabric of the tent waves and bucks against its framing at the same time and Aberdeen wonders if their fanaticism can move tents, if not mountains.

She stays behind Janos and looks behind her to find Hurt pressed against her back. He eyes the crowd and sticks tight to her body. When she moves, he moves, torso to back, thighs to buttock. She reaches back and grabs his quadriceps with her hands and squeezes and pulls him in closer, as close as their physical forms allow.

This is fortification enough to take another look at the stage and see what she doesn't want to, but what is there.

Wheelchair Man is parked in the center of the stage. There are small wooden blocks in front of his wheels, preventing him from rolling off the slightly pitched platform. He's sleeping, or unconscious, and he wears a nicely pressed suit with wide lapels betraying its age and era. There is a wig on his head, dark black. Aberdeen is close enough to see his wild, white hair escaping the netting. His handkerchief is missing from his palm and his head hangs slack. His wiry beard dips down, fans out over his groin. The audience stares, hungry at the sight of the man, as if they can see through the wig, to the crown of his head, his fontanel, where all their compacted and desperate hopes might penetrate.

"Holy shit," she says aloud and gets a glare from a woman standing to her side. "Is he dead?" She pokes Janos with a straight finger, hard into his back. "Is he dead?"

The audience tucks in close to Janos, hiding Aberdeen and

Hurt in a mangle of bodies. Janos gazes back and snorts.

"Hell no. It's all part of the act. He's done it dozens of times. Hence the outfit. Each time he gets up there it's harder and harder to disguise him and pass him off as some new soul to save. He refuses to shave the beard."

"So he's acting?" she asks and squeezes her fingers so deep into Hurt she can feel the blood straining to move past her grip and back to his heart.

"Not quite," he says, his head turned back to the stage. Aberdeen leans in to hear him. The crowd continues to yell, flail and prostrate. People are vibrating, others are laid out flat in front of the stage, a ring of others holding strong to keep them from being trampled. The preacher, the mouthpiece keeps his arms up to the heavens.

"What do you mean?" she asks and the preacher lifts his body up and shakes his fists in the air and the noise becomes deafening.

"What?" Janos yells back.

"Not acting," she yells in response. She can feel Hurt's breath on her neck.

Janos shakes his head. "He's had a sedative. It doesn't fool the people unless he's totally out and gone. God has to revive the truly sick and meek or the money doesn't flow in. It's simple."

"It's horrible," she counters.

"But it's his way of paying. We've all got to pay for our shit eventually."

Aberdeen considers that Janos is right when the preacher drops his arms and the revivalists fall dead quiet.

"Brothers and sisters," the preacher starts and then stops to take in the crowd. He meets gazes with several of the people below his feet, staring directly at the woman next to Aberdeen with sight halved. The preacher's other eye socket is shuttered with a sunken eyelid devoid of lashes, dry and sealed against bone.

"The man who sits before you, the wretched soul that God has not forgotten in our time of loss, was brought here by his family to receive the Holy Spirit into his broken body. We do not know if he will walk after receiving the light of God directly into his heart, but he could. He could cast off this wheelchair and walk out amongst you."

The preacher with his thin, red tie moves to Wheelchair Man and puts his hand on his skull, careful not to disturb the wig. "But this child of God has not been conscious for days now. His family is worried he is giving up, passing out of his body to join our Heavenly Father. But NO!" he booms, taking his hand from Wheelchair Man and holding his Bible out to the audience. "If we let him go, we let all of our sick and unfortunates go! It is not his time just as it is not YOURS!"

The crowd responds with a resounding "Amen."

"Watch this," Janos says and points at a man climbing the stairs to the stage. It's the same man Aberdeen saw last time. The faith healer in suspenders, shirt sleeves rolled up his hairy arms. "He's going to wake him up."

"How?" she speaks into Janos's ear.

"With a stimulant straight into his chest. It'll counteract the sedative immediately. His head pops up so quickly I worry sometimes he's going to give himself whiplash."

Everyone hushes for the faith healer. The man is sullen, his face set into a scowl. He rubs his hands together and then places them in front of his heart, palms pressed together. Aberdeen thinks of Sani and wonders if this man has any skills at all in healing.

The healer moves to Wheelchair Man and straddling his legs, places his hands over Wheelchair Man's sternum. Someone's sneeze sings through the tent and then all is quiet.

"Here comes the needle," Janos says, barely audible.

Aberdeen stares hard at the crown of Wheelchair Man's head. Her number three. Her not-so lost cause who hurts so very much.

The faith healer tilts his chin to the sky and presses into Wheelchair Man's chest hard, inching his chair back and away from the wooden brakes.

The same person sneezes. Once, twice, five more times.

And Wheelchair Man does not lift his head so fast his neck will snap. He does not lift his head at all.

Aberdeen can feel something stiff on her behind and it takes her a moment to realize that Hurt has gotten hard and she is confused at his ardor, like the only way his body can handle this display of death is with a countering of life, vital and full up of blood. Still, she takes her hands away from the backs of his thighs and crosses them over her chest, holding her heart in.

Water wells up in Aberdeen's right eye. The left still refuses to go tender. She knows she'll only be counting two now. Hurt and Louis.

"Shit," Janos says under his breath. "Shit, shit, shit."

The faith healer looks to the preacher and purses his lips.

Aberdeen stares at the empty place where the preacher's eye used to be. She wonders if it's possible to still have a tear duct in that fold of skin. And if it is there, can it work, can it start to drip tears into a cavity that is has lost its use, and exists dark and dead?

CHAPTER TWENTY-ONE

Louis is sleeping with an abridged copy of *Treasure Island* over his face when Hurt and Aberdeen get back home. Aberdeen lifts it off of his nose and places it on the floor. He has a bit of blue marker on his cheek and his open mouth shows off his lower teeth, their tips ragged like little castles with little crenellations. She kisses her fingertips and presses them to his forehead and is glad that he does not wake up because Aberdeen would tell him immediately that Wheelchair Man is dead.

Hurt and Aberdeen get ready for bed even though they have not had dinner and the sky is still rosy with the leaving sun. Aberdeen thinks of anything but Wheelchair Man while she brushes her teeth. She spends time considering whether or not any of the snakes Janos handles are actually dangerous or if they are all different colors of passive garter snakes. She thinks of the amber eyes of diamondbacks and the hooded nostrils of serpents that can move through desert sands like quick whips. She washes her face, puts on a ratty t-shirt and some of Hurt's old boxers and cannot remember whether or not she brushed her teeth so she brushes them again.

Hurt lies in bed, his back flat on the flowered sheets. He picks at his lips, pulling them out and away from his gums.

"I didn't know him at all," he says when Aberdeen takes up beside him and clicks off her nightstand light. "So I can't miss him, now can I?"

She says nothing, rolls to her side and sighs out one long breath before sleep comes for her.

Aberdeen dreams of old, tinny pots and copper bowls, rusted cups and metal spoons all bored through with holes and strung up on a piece of fraying twine. They clack and rustle outside of a hut perched on the side of a sloping hill each time a strong gale catches their divots and cavities. The racket is wild and dissonant and it takes Aberdeen staring at the old things that at one time had one use and now had another seemingly for ages before she wakes and realizes that the sound is not in her dream. The dream was a symptom of the banging and clamor coming from within her apartment.

She opens her eyes wide. "Hurt," she says and feels for him next to her while she stares at the bedroom door, willing her pupils to get used to the darkness so they can see danger if it comes.

Her hand finds nothing and she pats around the sheets like he could be lost in their folds.

A light flips on in the hall and illuminates a strip at the base of her door. Aberdeen gets out of bed and goes to it, catching the sight of her unclipped toenails in the glowing strip of white. She decides it must be Hurt making the noise and flipping on the lights. That, or someone is in her apartment and is a real threat to the trio. Either way, she decides to leave her room.

Fright comes and goes for Aberdeen. But right now, the dread is gone.

The hallway is bright and she walks slowly into the living room that butts up against the kitchen and notices that every light in the apartment is turned on. Her eyes catch the electric blue zing of the small bug zapper Aberdeen removes from storage each year when summer comes and the mosquitoes take to her, unquenchable, thirsty vampires. It sits on the stand near the television and buzzes away, the hum never punctuated by a little death. There is nothing to kill before the bugs awaken from the cold season.

"Hurt," she calls out and he emerges from the kitchen, Louis stepping in line behind him. They each hold a dinner plate in their hands; the pattern is a green twining of leaves around the center of the white plate.

"What are you both doing?" she asks. She notes the tiredness in Louis's eyes, the tops of his cheeks capped in puffy flesh. Hurt, however, betrays no sign of sleepiness. His eyelids are pulled back tight, so tight his eyes protrude out of his face in a way Aberdeen has never seen them before.

Louis looks to Hurt and laughs and then holds the plate up high and nods at it. "Watch this, Abbie," he says as he chucks the dinnerware to the kitchen's linoleum floor. It doesn't break but causes a sharp clatter. Aberdeen watches the plate whirl like a gyroscope, speeding up and then coming to rest.

Hurt throws his down then. "For good measure," he says as he does it.

Aberdeen knows the plates won't break. They're Corelle, resinous and resistant to strain. But the behavior. Obviously Hurt and Louis are not resistant to strain.

After the next plate settles and quiets, Aberdeen points out the obvious. "So you told Louis."

"He needed to know."

"He needed to sleep one night without knowing."

She bends down and stacks the dinnerware. She was wrong about their stoutness. There is a small chip off one of the sides of the plates. She runs her finger over it and can feel the raw graininess of ceramic underneath the cured sheen.

"Are you okay, Louis?" she asks and moves next to him, puts a hand on his arm.

He puts a hand over her hand. "I guess. I don't know yet.

Maybe I am?"

"He's totally fine," Hurt says and Aberdeen can hear the energy in his voice. His usual cadence is off. He emphasizes "fine" with the harshness of a judge.

"I told him I got a complete piece of wood when I realized Wheelchair Man was dead. It was fucking weird but there it is. I wonder if that's every man's last physical action before dying. Popping a bone to see if they can keep the genes around. One last ditch effort."

Louis takes his hand away from Aberdeen's and uses it to cover his mouth, cover a laugh. Aberdeen puts the plates on the counter and swallows before speaking. She believes her husband is tired, in shock.

"Completely inappropriate, babe," she says, using his pet name to soften the criticism. There is something about his wildness that keeps Aberdeen from going on the attack. She doesn't feel like prey, but she doesn't feel the predator. Instead, she's some sort of other class of creature, the giraffe that watches the crocodile take the zebra, outside of the fight but helpless to mediate or solve.

"Louis," she goes on, "back to bed. I need to talk with Hurt for a minute."

He goes, without complaint or stifled sighs.

"And shut your door behind you," she calls out to him and then she stays silent until she can hear the wood find its casing completely and click into it. It, too, back to rest.

Hurt moves to pick back up the plates but Aberdeen snatches them away. "Talk to me," she says. "Tell me anything you're feeling. Like what made you throw around dinner plates at one in the morning? Or anything."

Hurt musses up his hair, running his fingers through it so that it stands straight up. He moves to the couch and takes a seat. His eyes seem to be entranced with the light of the bug zapper. He regards it for a minute before shaking his head and adopting a scowl.

"Our sheets are too damn scratchy. I feel like whenever I sleep in that sheet set I'm belly-crawling through a field of prickly pear cactus."

This is the first Aberdeen has ever heard regarding the sheets from Hurt. They've had them for a year, a wedding present from his paternal grandmother. The woman, crippled with arthritis, had added a delicate crochet of lace to the top of the flat sheet. The sheets were precious and beautiful and soft. Hurt's hyperbolic dislike of them was perplexing.

"I can't feel them at all, other than to know they're clean and not yet sticky with my night sweat," Aberdeen says, trying with levity. "Aren't you sleeping much?"

"Only pretending," Hurt says.

"I had to wake you up from a dead sleep just yesterday. When Louis went missing."

"Oh, I sleep sometimes in the mornings. Maybe an hour or two. It's all I need nowadays. Honestly. Anymore than that and my body is just eating itself with sloth."

Aberdeen lifts her brow and moves to Hurt. She sits next to him on the couch, perched on the edge of the cushion, careful not to touch Hurt at all. "Okay," she says, "so what, you just recline there all night while I sleep."

"Yes, but I'm working in my head. Working things out. Tonight was the first night I decided to get up and test some things out."

"Like plate throwing."

Hurt smiles. "Fuck yeah."

"And what else are you thinking about?" she asks, not sure if she really wants to know.

"Shit, everything, Aberdeen. Other than the plates, tonight I was thinking about hugging. Do you know that humans need at least twelve hugs a day to feel good about themselves and connected to others. I figure I only get about three, maybe five hugs a day. I'm practically killing myself. And what about all the people outside? I doubt they get that many hugs a day. It might go a long way to waylaying the sickness out there. Maybe that's what I'll do when it gets light outside. I'll go out and give people hugs. Everyone wins."

Hurt finishes, winks at Aberdeen and then the bug zapper catches his attention again.

"I guess you thought of the bug zapper tonight, too," Aberdeen suggests.

"We can't be too careful," he answers, "with West Nile Virus from mosquitoes and the shit flies have on their sticky little feet. If we don't stay diligent, we could get sick and then we're really screwed."

Aberdeen chances placing the back of her hand to Hurt's head and checking for a temperature. Nothing. He's cold, if anything. "Are you feeling well?"

"I'm fine. Just being me," he says and Aberdeen takes her hand back, puts it in her lap and bites her lower lip.

Hurt starts again. Aberdeen notices his voice, still strange, still too fast, so fast he trips up on some of his words.

"My degree is going to be useless after all this, you know. They won't even have libraries after we get the drugs back and the government figures out how to kill all the terrorists. Libraries are for civilizations. What we are going to have will not be civilized. We will be made derelicts and deviants and all the books will be burned in old oil drums so we can heat up our meth. I should just stop now and start something more important."

"Like what?" Aberdeen decides to play along, to stop her brain from pushing for answers. She chooses to stay with her husband instead. Take in his words. Try to understand.

"I'd be a great pilot. Helicopters, though. I'm not suited to fly jets. Not enough maneuverability for my taste."

Aberdeen smiles and nods. Her husband is so near-sighted

he can't shave without his contacts or glasses. Her husband despises flight; he endures it with the help of tiny bottles of Stoli.

"You would be a great pilot," she echoes. "But an even better librarian."

He lifts a hand and waves it at her in dismissal. "That life is so over for me. Especially since they're all saying that the libraries will be like empty catacombs without any bones on the shelves."

"Who says?"

"Who says what?" Hurt replies and then gets up off the couch and closes in on the bug zapper. Aberdeen notices the blue glow casts an eerie light on Hurt's jaw line. He puts a hand up to the metal cage surrounding the electrified core and scratches at it with his fingernails like he wants in.

He runs the tips of his nails up and down the metal. "They're all gone. I knew it would happen, but I thought maybe it wouldn't."

"The people who talk about the libraries?" Aberdeen says but she knows it's likely Hurt's so shocked at what transpired in the tent that he's thinking about Wheelchair Man and applying his feelings to all the lost and dying denizens of their city.

Aberdeen thinks then of Wheelchair Man's handkerchief. She figures it's in a garbage can by now, thrown out by Beso or one of his lackeys in order to clean up and get rid of any mention of Wheelchair Man. She wishes she had stood her ground in the tent instead of letting Janos usher her and Hurt outside in the clamor and chaos that ensued when the vet's death was noticed by the revivalists. She should have stayed. Found his handkerchief. Taken it home.

Hurt's voice brings her back. "Not people, Aberdeen. The medicine. The pills!"

"People will be okay someday. They'll get their drugs back." Her mind goes to the room Beso must have somewhere near the tent. The room that Louis took Wheelchair Man into, that had the shelves of pharmaceuticals. At least there is medicine somewhere, she thinks. It's something.

Hurt's face folds inward, his eyes droop and he balls up his torso, then explodes his spine up straight and runs his fingers through his hair. Smoothing the follicles, then making them stand on end. Over and over. The hum of the bug zapper plays backup to Hurt's contortions. He looks a marionette under the control of an angry master.

"No!" he shouts and then calms himself by cupping his ears in his palms.

Aberdeen inches back on the couch. She thinks she can hear the door to Louis's room click open.

Hurt visibly vibrates. After a moment he's subdued enough to take down his hands. Aberdeen stares at him. He stares back. Then, he raises a finger to his temple and speaks.

"No," he says, "*the* pills." And his finger points to his skull, indicating himself alone, and Aberdeen now understands, whatever he's struggling with in there, too.

He turns back to the blue light and pulls a hair from his head. He pokes the reddish-blonde strand through the grating on the bug zapper and the electricity takes the hair and curls it up tight, blackens it to an ashy squiggle. The room smells of it.

Aberdeen has nothing to say. She looks at her husband and wonders. There is nothing specific to her wonder. It's all she can do just to have wonder anymore, for him, for any of it.

"So," Hurt says, his nostrils flaring slightly at the pungent scent. "I need your knitting needles, because I think I need to learn how to knit sweaters. No time like now. Right fucking now."

Aberdeen looks past her husband to the hallway where Louis stands, his arms stock still at his sides, trying to disappear in the wide open.

I may just have number two, Aberdeen thinks. Number two might have to be enough.

CHAPTER TWENTY-TWO

Aberdeen and Louis hold vigil for Hurt until the morning comes. Louis says nothing the entire night, letting his eyes close and his head drop every so often, only to jerk awake when his body goes slack and his back brushes the upright pillows of the couch, his eyes rolling and taking in the apartment like he's never seen its contents and woes before.

Aberdeen thinks of how their vigil is similar to those that people used to have, those nights of restless mourning while they sat in a parlor with a dead relative. She was only missing the cloying scent of white lilies and of casseroles of canned tomatoes and browned hamburger.

She was doing that, mourning, in her way, sitting with her idea of who her husband was and what he was now. A shell of Hurt full up on something else. Not decay, not death, but energy, hot and unstoppable.

Through the hours of the night, Hurt does these things: unwinds a skein of Aberdeen's pale, pink lambswool yarn onto the floor, recites a passage of one of his textbooks aloud to Aberdeen and Louis while tucking his hand up against his chest in a mockery of Napoleon Bonaparte, eats five freezer waffles not yet fully cooked and mushy cool in their centers, describes his vision for the walls of their apartment to be covered in bulletin boards so that he can "better organize his mind's jumble," looks up pictures of brindle Bullmastiffs online, curls up at Aberdeen's feet and sleeps in the fetal position for fifteen minutes before waking and leaving to shower while singing "Singing in the Rain," over and over, loud and off-key.

When the clock hits eight, Aberdeen stands up from the couch and digs out her cell phone from her purse. She dials up Sani, explaining nothing, just begging her to come over.

Hurt answers the door in his green bathrobe when Sani arrives, Aberdeen close behind him. When Sani steps in the room, Hurt grabs her rough around her waist and squeezes tight. Sani holds her arms up in alarm, the way she might hold them before jumping into a lake or slipping down a waterslide, and looks to Aberdeen.

"I'm so glad you're here," Hurt says, speaking into the top of Sani's scarf-wrapped skull. "We don't really know one another. That's got to change."

"I agree," Sani says and then gently disengages from his grip. "How are you feeling, Hurt?"

He doesn't consider the question. The answer was there before it was asked.

"I'm fucking wonderful. Amazing!" and then he moves off to their bedroom, knocking the water out of his ears.

Sani takes off her long coat and drapes it over the sofa. "What did he take?"

"I don't think he took anything," Aberdeen says. Louis has finally given into sleep and his body lies prone on the couch, his arm flung over his eyes.

"Okay," Sani says. She reaches up and places her hands on Aberdeen's shoulders. The palms are warm. They are always warm. "Then what hasn't he taken?"

Aberdeen takes a moment to enjoy the radiating heat of Sani's hands before nodding.

"Louis, honey," she says, once, then again a bit louder until his arm slides off his face and he sits up fast, blinking. "I want you to go and tell Hurt it's time to get donuts. He knows the kind I like."

Louis stands, stretches.

"But Louis, your job is to watch him. You keep him away from the soldiers and you just go to the bakery and straight back. Do you understand?"

He nods and makes for the bedroom to gather Hurt. After Hurt puts on a strange outfit of a blue sweater, green khakis and white tennis shoes, the boys leave the apartment but not before Hurt leans into Aberdeen and assaults her with a passionate kiss.

Aberdeen locks the door behind them.

"Let's find the bottle," she says and the two women work over the apartment like amateur burglars. Cushions are tossed, cabinets opened and swiped with forearms until all contents come plinking out onto counters or floors. They bully up the mattress between the two of them and pry up the windows, feeling with their palms along the brick ledges.

The hunt is devoid of results. No pills in bottles and no bottles without pills.

Aberdeen stands in the living room and surveys the mess. There's no way she'll be able to put the place back together before Louis leads Hurt home with their sticky, sugary treats. Her mind reels for a good excuse. She saw a mouse and went after it as it wound its way about the rooms. She had a desperate moment of panic when she could not remember where she had placed her grandmother's old, brassy watch and tore up the place in an anxious whirl.

Or, she considers, Hurt may not even notice or care. This Hurt may not give a second thought about a messy, ransacked home. He may not care about home anymore. Aberdeen has no way to tell, until she gets used to this new man, the one of the crazed disposition.

"Maybe he's not on medicine," she says to Sani. "Perhaps we've got it wrong and he's just caving under the stress of these last months. And yesterday."

"What happened yesterday?"

Aberdeen picks up a pillow and sticks her hand down the pillowcase, feeling around the cushion for any lumps. Nothing. She does not look at Sani. For whatever reason, she is embarrassed to speak of Wheelchair Man. It's like she's failed, let him down by not tending to him and she does not want to voice her inadequacies to a healer like Sani, a woman whom Aberdeen thinks of as a person of real worth.

Still, Sani needs to know.

"Wheelchair Man died," she says, "and we could have stopped it."

"It wasn't natural?"

"No," Aberdeen says, dropping the pillow at her feet. "It wasn't his time. Nothing like that. It was drug-induced."

Sani scratches at her head under her scarf and folds her arms in front of her. "Was it the same men? The ones who shot you up with dope?"

"Um," is all Aberdeen can muster.

Sani says nothing. Aberdeen feels this is the very best thing Sani could say.

Reaching down for the cushion Aberdeen dropped, Sani tosses it onto the couch. "We've got to be as smart, as sneaky as Hurt. If he was hiding medicine from you, he'd never put it anywhere you'd readily look. It's got to be somewhere accessible, but not obviously so. Can you think of where that might be? Think hard."

Aberdeen shakes her head, raises her hands up in premature defeat. "No idea. I guess he spends a lot of time in the bathroom each morning. He wants privacy while he relieves himself, but there are times I have to pound on the door to get in and get ready."

"Okay, that's something," Sani says and moves towards the bathroom. Aberdeen follows and the two women stand on the red, fluffy bathmat in the center of the room. They turn around in circles, looking up and down, eyes scanning every surface. Sani stands on tiptoes and pats around the top of the vanity lighting but produces nothing. Aberdeen takes the Kleenex box off of the toilet and pries off the tank cover. There is only brown water inside, a tan ballcock sitting high above it.

Sani wipes dust from the vanity off on her long skirt and then turns on the water at the sink. She rinses off her fingers and palm and then brings up a little pool of liquid to her mouth and slurps at it. She takes a bit more, pausing before drinking like she's partaking of water from a holy spring. She shuts off the water and runs her wet hand along the back of her neck to wet the base of her hair.

Aberdeen replaces the toilet tank cover. "No go. I have no idea."

Sani watches the drain in the sink. The water does not flow through it easily.

"You've got a clog?"

"Oh," Aberdeen answers, "yeah, ever since we moved in. I've put five containers of Drano down that son of a bitch and nothing. I told Hurt I was going to call a plumber but he said no, that we shouldn't waste money on something that works, even if it works slowly."

"I see," Sani says as she drops to the balls of her feet and opens up the cabinet doors under the sink. All the contents, the little flower-shaped soaps Aberdeen only uses when they have house guests, the unused nylon puffs, errant hair ties, these are already strewn across the floor, victims of their previous attack on the apartment. Sani reaches in and wraps her hand around the pipe that runs down from the drain and out into the wall. She checks the top-most threaded connector, turning it left and it spins easily at her touch.

"Ah." She pulls back her hand and stares up at Aberdeen. "Should we let the water in the sink basin drain all the way first?"

"Fuck it," Aberdeen says. "Open it up."

Sani ducks her head fully into the cabinet and works at the connector with both hands. It comes away and water spills out onto her scarf and spreads across the wooden base of the cabinet, dripping in quick plinks over the side and onto the floor.

"Get your face in here," Sani says.

Aberdeen crouches and leans into the cabinet, her torso smashed up against that of the healer's. Sani's long fingers reach into the top of the plastic piping and snatch out a thin, amber bottle made of plastic. The words on the label are nearly gone, washed clean by the daily drenching with water.

The women stand, the bottle held high up to the light by Sani. She can just make out the name of the medication. There are enough letters left in the name to let Sani feel confident about her deduction. She shakes the bottle for good measure. It's empty.

"Looks like Aripiprazole. I'm guessing Abilify."

"You know prescription medications still?"

"Good to know your enemies, Aberdeen. It's cliché, but it's completely true. Drugs may have been my friends once. But not anymore."

Aberdeen is too nervous to ask. So she doesn't. And a moment later, Sani tells her.

"It's an antipsychotic."

The images strike Aberdeen's mind upon hearing the word "psychotic": Hurt skinning a living dachshund hung up on a meat hook, Hurt raping an old woman in a polyester skirt, Hurt shooting a man through the head with a petite .22. She knows he has not done these things, but she wonders if he could do these things. And since they have already played out in her mind, it is like he is already guilty of the imaginary crimes.

"So he's insane?" Aberdeen asks.

"No, not at all. At worst he may be schizophrenic. I don't think so, though. From what I saw today, he may have acute mania."

Hurt is a loon, Aberdeen thinks. Hurt is a fucking maniac. Aberdeen rubs her bare feet on the bathmat. The tickle of the soft fibers feels good. She's almost forgotten what it's like to feel something soft, yielding, easy.

"He's alluded to hearing voices."

"But that could be either illness. It doesn't mean he's experiencing split personalities or that the voices are internal versus external. I've heard of manic people convinced their getting messages from deities directing their actions. But I don't necessarily think this is wrong or even an illness. Who am I to say they aren't communicating with gods?"

Sani passes the bottle to Aberdeen. Aberdeen scratches off the "e" in Aripiprazole with her thumbnail while Sani fixes the drain and mops up the water with a maroon hand towel.

If Hurt is talking with gods, Aberdeen wonders, then why doesn't he put in a good order? Restoration of social order. Supplies of medicines. Either Hurt isn't asking for the right things, or these gods are assholes. That, or they don't exist.

The front door is flung open and Hurt steps into the apartment, a crumpled white bag in his fist. Aberdeen looks out of the bathroom and palms the medicine bottle in her hand. Louis trails in after Hurt. He holds his wrist up against his chest and pushes the door closed with the flat sole of his foot.

Sani stands up and tosses the soaked towel into the bathtub. She smoothes back her headband and steps out of the way of Aberdeen, who moves towards the two boys, still clutching what she and Sani have found.

"What are you doing in there?" Hurt asks, meeting Aberdeen and kissing her on the forehead. His lips are sticky with powdered sugar. Aberdeen licks her fingers and rubs off the mark he's left.

Sani steps up beside Aberdeen and places a hand on her shoulder. The warmth is there, clicked on instantly, and this fortifies Aberdeen with a shot of heat down her torso.

"We found this," is all Aberdeen says as she opens her hand and proffers the empty bottle to Hurt. "Why do you need it? What's wrong with you?"

And as soon as she's said it she's regretting her choice of words. Hurt's face goes red and his chest pushes out. He takes the plastic bottle from Aberdeen and pitches it hard against the wall. It hits a framed pastel of a mossy stream, and sends the glass shattering against the hardwood floor.

Aberdeen flinches, but just barely. Sani stands her ground. But Louis stands with his back up against the front door, his arm still tight against his body. He's gone motionless and quiet.

"Nothing is wrong with me. Nothing. I'm finally free of those stupid pills. And whose business was it of yours to find them anyway, Aberdeen?" He turns to Sani and scowls. "And who the hell said you could come into my home and destroy it? Huh?"

Aberdeen puts her hand up to her shoulder and grabs hold of Sani's wrist. She gives it a little squeeze. "Calm down, babe. No one has done anything wrong, okay? I'm just asking some questions. Nothing more."

Hurt stalks into the living room, kicking at the items strewn around the floor. "Screw you," he screams. "Screw you all."

Louis doesn't move one bit. Aberdeen watches the boy, sees how he still holds his wrist, how he watches Hurt with a certain look. Like Hurt's a predator. And Louis is prey.

It clicks then and Aberdeen pulls away from Sani's touch and goes to Louis. He takes the last step into her arms and bursts into tears.

"I shouldn't have sent you with him," she apologizes. "I'm so very sorry, Louis."

He holds his wrist up to Aberdeen and she can see the bruise, a fat, black ring where his forearm begins. She doesn't push on it. Instead she lifts his arm up by the elbow and places a light kiss on his wound.

"What happened?"

Louis looks to Hurt, still kicking at fallen blankets, the television remote. He picks a hardcover book about terrariums from off the bookshelf and begins tearing out the pages; he tosses them in the air and watches them drift to the floor.

"I wanted a donut, even if I'm not supposed to have one. When I reached for one in the bin, a cream one, he grabbed my wrist. But then he wouldn't let go. He just squeezed it and watched my face. I did my best not to cry and when my fingers started to turn blue he let go."

Aberdeen releases Louis's arm and pulls him in to her. She whispers in his ear, "But he did it on purpose? The pain?"

"He did," Louis whispers back.

For Aberdeen, this is enough.

"You need to get out," she speaks up. Louis hides his head against her chest. "Until you can tell me what's going on and what I can do to help you, you need to leave. Right now."

Hurt finishes with the last page of the book. He lets the hardcover drop and rips the glossy page into tiny strips. It's a picture of a pothos in a mini glass conservatory. He rips it so fine, so carefully, the picture turns into a pile of unrecognizable green, black and white strips on the woolen rug.

He stretches then, pulling on his fingers above his head.

"I was going out anyway," he says, his voice calmer, slower. "I need my twelve hugs for the day and I'm sure as shit not going to be getting them from you."

He moves to the front door and Aberdeen turns her back on him, hiding away Louis. She has no words of support for Hurt now. Only words that would sting. He pulls open the door and it scrapes along Aberdeen's arm, leaving a ruddy burn on her skin.

And he's gone.

"Let Sani see your wrist," she says, pulling away from Louis. She shuts the door and locks it. She is doing what she's always done. Locking those things she cares for inside, and locking out the bad. She knows Hurt is bad right now and he needs to be on the outside, no matter their promise to one another of them sticking together against the chaos in the city, in the country.

Sani looks over Louis and smiles. "A nasty contusion. But we can do some energy work. Let's get you on your bed."

Louis agrees and sniffs a bit, heads into his room.

Sani asks, "What's he talking about with the hugging?"

"He said something about it last night. How people need twelve hugs a day for optimum mental health."

"He should get twenty-four, then. Maybe thirty-six." And Sani moves off to heal the wounded boy.

"No kidding," Aberdeen says under her breath. She moves to the window that looks out over the front of the apartments. Hurt is there. She watches as a man in a trench coat walks towards Hurt. He looks like the man who yelled at the woman who was taken away by the man in the black-rimmed glasses. Hurt stops him with an outstretched hand. They speak for a moment and then Hurt bullies his arms around the man's shoulders and squeezes.

Aberdeen can hear the loud protests of the man five stories up.

She looks up to the ceiling of the room and eyes a crack that runs from one corner to the other in a diagonal rip. She folds her hands up and prays to it.

"Thank you," she says, "for not caving in on my head."

And then her eyes catch the tiniest of pale-pink triangles poking out over the top of the bookcase where Hurt plucked up and plucked out her terrarium book. She goes to it, pulls on the paper corner. She'd almost forgotten.

It's the index card with George Dover's name printed on it. And from under it flutters to the floor an off-white business card. She's forgotten this, too.

Plains View Ward: Camp 894. And a telephone number.

She turns the little card over and over in her hand, feeling the sharp corners prick at her skin. Not only can she hear the man hollering, but now she hears the voice of Hurt as well. They are trying to outshout one another, a see-sawing of anger. Back and forth. Louder and louder.

But I love him, she tells herself.

But he's dangerous, she tells herself.

She goes for her phone and dials the number. She tells herself that the Plains View Ward is a place that can reign in Hurt and give him the medicine he needs. All designs on the camp being a place of internment are forgotten. In the now, it is a feasible solution. Hurt has caused pain on purpose. He's alluded to other potential acts of aggression to her, to Louis.

She gets a woman on the other line.

"What's the address?"

"Excuse me?" Aberdeen mumbles, thrown off by the lack of proper greeting. "What?"

"The location of the disturbed person. The address so we can send out a vehicle."

She swallows hard and gives out the address to their apartment. "He's outside. He's accosting people."

The woman on the other end of the line snorts. "They typically do. I'm sure we'll be able to pick him out."

And Aberdeen hangs up and goes back to the window. She can't bring herself to look down at her husband, that man she does not know. Instead, she presses her back up against the window pane and listens to the fight down below. She can't make out any words. Just sounds of disturbed people.

She's doing the right thing, she tells herself. He'll get help in the facility and when he's better, he can come home to Louis and her. But right now he can't stay in the apartment if he's violent and he can't stay on the streets, forcing his brand of affection and impassioned ramblings on strangers. Hurt might challenge someone even crazier than himself, and that crazy might decide to put a knife in Hurt's solar plexus for all his forwardness and she would be naming him on a metal gurney in a morgue instead of suffering his scowl during visiting hours at Plains View Ward.

"What's the location of the disturbed person?" she asks herself aloud.

"He's in the head of my husband, my Hurt who loves animals and wants to be a reference librarian. He's in there. Can you just take him out and leave the rest of Hurt?"

As she stands there her back grows warmer from the midday sun. Soon enough, the shouting gets even louder. Now there are new voices in the fray.

Don't you look, she tells herself. If you look, you'll run down and try to save the man who isn't there anymore. You'll be saving a man consumed with mania.

And then the road is quiet. Her husband's wild bursts of hollering are gone.

She presses her back hard against the hot glass until she can feel her skin starting to prick and burn from the rays of light.

"Come on, you new, spring sun," she yells out before breaking into tears. "Come on, you motherfucker."

CHAPTER TWENTY-THREE

The first crocus appears, in the thick of spring, late due to their northern clime, and it's a little thing, weak in its whitish stem, the flower head folded up, yellow petals of the bud so delicate one of them rubs into a slick mess of wet pulp between Aberdeen's fingers. She curses her carelessness, tries harder to lift the small flower from the crack in the sidewalk without cutting into the bulb or the stiff, hairy roots that shoot like whiskers from its base. She digs at it with a tiny, brown-handled spade she uses to carefully maneuver plants around in tight-necked glass bottles. This crocus she wants to bring inside, so no indigent steps on it, no dog lifts its leg and waters it with ammonia. She's resolute in her desire to bring life inside her apartment.

Something, she thinks, should be alive in there.

It has been one week since she called the operator at Plains View Ward: Camp 894 and had them come and take away her husband. And since that day, she has been dead. Aberdeen figures she had to die in order to keep on with whatever she currently was: a woman who would betray her lover, her partner of years, husband of a year, to a sentence of internment in a place she knows nothing of, not its location, not its suitability as a place to house people who are sick and crazy and wild for life.

She noticed her own death as soon as she made that call. It was a small thing to notice, actually. It came in the form of ticking off the things she, Aberdeen, could no longer claim to be: a good wife, a crafter, a dependable friend. She went checking, ticking down the list. Until that list was nothing more than a totality of failures. If Aberdeen had been all those things, then who the hell was the very opposite of Aberdeen? Was there such a person? Or was that still Aberdeen, but Aberdeen, dead?

So she became dead. Just like that.

She stood in that window, roasting her skin for an hour, until Sani came out and took her by her hands and pulled her to the couch. Aberdeen doesn't remember what they talked about, but she does remember that Sani asked her about the candles. She wanted to know whether or not Aberdeen had been controlling her lung strength with blowing out candles moved progressively further away from her body.

"No," Aberdeen had answered, her fingers completely asleep, ten digits of tingling fatness. "I don't need my lungs for anything anymore. They've won."

Since then, Sani has come every day to check on Aberdeen and Louis. She frequently asks Louis if he has any pain in his wrist and he always says no, even with the circular bruising turning yellow and slightly puffy. Sani also asks Louis if he's okay about what happened to Hurt. And Louis always answers the same.

"I hope he's somewhere he can get help. And then he can come back home when he's safe."

"When he's safe," Aberdeen says to herself over and over as she picks around the concrete to get at the crocus from another angle. "When he's safe, he will not want to come home. Because he will be coming home to a place of betrayal."

The day after she had called the camp, she realized while she tucked away all the disheveled contents of their apartment, that she had no way of knowing how Hurt was, what had been done with him. Nothing. In her haste to keep Louis safe, to keep others from Hurt's belligerence, she hadn't considered how she would stay connected with him. So she called back.

"What's the address," the lady on the other phone said again. Same greeting.

"Actually," Aberdeen started, "I'm trying to get a hold of someone that was taken to Plains View yesterday. His name is Hurt Childress. He had identification on him."

"Were you the one who reported him?"

"Sure," she said, swallowed. "Yes, I was."

"There's another number for patient checkups. Are you ready for it?"

Aberdeen took down the number, thanked the woman and hung up. She scribbled it in black marker on the back of the original business card. She wasn't sure she was ready for it. But she called anyway, and her fears were confirmed.

Not her fear that Hurt was truly mentally wounded or that he had accosted someone in his zealous search for hugs outside the apartment door. No, these were the fears she hadn't thought of before calling. The buried ones. The ones that were deeper than what she had been confronted with initially.

Abandonment. Imprisonment. Loss of Rights.

Because all the "Patient Query" number was able to produce was an answering service with a recorded greeting, nonspecific, the robotic voice an annoying tone of placation.

"Please leave your name, the name of the patient you are inquiring after, your telephone number and your relationship to the patient at the beep."

So Aberdeen left the information, choked up on the relationship part. She eventually got out the word "wife" but not without a sharp twinge in her stomach when she said it aloud.

And then she waited. She was still waiting, busying herself with things like digging up spring bulbs. She had yet to hear back from Camp 894. She realized that before, before the medicine had all disappeared, they, the doctors and government, wouldn't have been able to disregard her questions about Hurt. They would have had to answer her. The answers could have been bullshit, but an effort would have necessarily been made.

But now, there wasn't even a fake smile from a mouthpiece in a cheap suit.

The message, though, was clear. Forget whoever you're looking for. They aren't coming back to you anytime soon. And the notion that Plains View was nothing more than an internment camp came back to her and nuzzled her neck and breathed foul air into her ear and she hated herself for believing her initial assessment of the place could have been wrong.

Louis seemed to be better at the forgetting. But Hurt was a new person in his life. He could afford to forget a little. Aberdeen could not. Even though she picked Louis, the new person in her life, over Hurt. She wasn't quite sure why she did that, still. Momentary panic and fear fueled by his hidden medication and the bruise on Louis's wrist. But it didn't matter anymore anyway.

Dead people don't need to question.

Aberdeen finishes digging up the crocus and appraises the roots. There are enough of them to keep the little bulb alive long enough for her and Louis to enjoy the bloom. She tucks the white bulb into a shallow plastic baggie and walks upstairs with it cradled in her palm.

When she gets to her apartment she realizes she has left her keys inside. She raps on the wood with her fist and she can hear Louis lumber to the door.

"Who is it?" he calls out.

"Me."

He flips the lock and lets Aberdeen inside. "I thought you might be Hurt. Or that other guy."

Aberdeen slips off her shoes and walks the crocus to the

kitchen table, laying it on top of a pile of mailing circulars promoting natural healing salves, churches and possibilities for joining litigation proceedings against pharmaceutical companies.

"What other guy?" she asks and Louis comes to her, lays his head against the door jamb leading into the room.

"There was a man wandering around the apartment building. He came to our door and I talked to him through the wood. He said he was asking for donations."

"What kind?" Aberdeen asks as she digs a glass out of the cupboard, an imprint of a sailboat etched into its side. It was a tchotchke from Nantucket she picked up with Hurt. Now it would hold a crocus. New uses.

"Well, I don't know. Because I said we didn't have things to donate and then he kicked the door and went off down the stairs. I could hear his feet clop really fast and really hard."

"Thank you for not opening the door," she says and fills the glass with water, sets it on the side of the sink and turns to Louis. "It's getting worse for people, the desperation."

He knocks his head against the wood lightly, once, twice. It flattens a little strip of his growing afro.

"How many of them do you think there are, Abbie? Of those camps?"

She wonders that as well. Camp 894. Are the numerical designations ordered, neat little plots on the number line, or are they just arbitrary numerical assignments? If there is a Camp 1 and a Camp 2, then Camp 894 would likely be the eight hundred and ninety-fourth incarnation of its kind in the United States. At the very least, there would be that many camps. But there could be hundreds more, thousands in total; centers for storing the lunacy of America who cannot be tamed by their communities. And that beastly thing nuzzles her again, reminds her of her penchant for failing the ones she swears she cares for the most.

"Probably not many. It's probably just a random number," she lies and looks to the top of the bookcase where she replaced the index card with Louis's dad's information on it.

"Do you miss your dad?" she asks, after all those months of avoiding George P. Dover's existence.

Louis picks his head off the wall and looks behind him, like his father might be standing there, waiting for Louis to notice him all this time.

"Why would I?"

"Because he's your dad?" she turns her back to him and dips a finger into the water in the glass. Then she runs it around the rim of the cup and a ringing emanates from it for a moment, a bell to cut the tension. "And I'm not sure you're in the best place. With me, I mean. Maybe we should contact him, let him know what's happened and ask him to come for you."

A deeper voice escapes from the boy, one that Aberdeen has never heard. It carries the weight of all the seriousness Louis is capable of, all the determination and self-assurance.

"I'm not leaving you. You need me, Abbie."

And it is this that tells Aberdeen she has rubbed off on Louis. Now he will always be a giver, always tend, support, care. The smile comes unbidden to her lips and she fights it back down. Why is this a good thing, she wonders, if all it will do is set him up to fail those he loves? Again and again, as all her machinations for good have fallen short, horseshoes that never ring around the stake.

"I do need you," she says, "and thank you for seeing that. I don't think many people have ever seen to that need for me. But now you have."

"I have?" he asks.

She moves to him and takes his face in her palms. They are wet from the water and they make his cheeks shiny with liquid. Planting a kiss on his forehead, wondering why she was ever tremulous and hesitant about touching the boy, she allows herself a laugh and it's enough for her to come alive again, for an instant, before the dead feeling returns.

"You've done so brilliantly," she tells him.

Later, she sends Louis down to get the mail with strict instructions not to leave the building. He's to go nowhere without Aberdeen now. He shrugs at her reminding him of this fact and makes a face that flattens his nose and widens his eyes.

"It's the way of the world now, Louis," she presses and he leaves the apartment.

After twenty minutes, Aberdeen realizes he's not coming back up anytime soon. It should have taken him no more than five minutes to open the little metal box in the wall, pull out the contents, shuffle back up the stairs. Something must have caught his eye. She prays, literally, to nothing in particular this time, that he was not the thing that caught someone else's eye.

She swears to herself that she will never let him out of her sight again. She will be his gloomy, withdrawn companion at all times.

She has her hand on the doorknob and unlocks it just as she feels it turn in her grip. She backs up to get out of the way of Louis rushing in, something orange and fuzzy cradled in his arms.

He's out of breath, grinning wide.

"I found her just outside the door. Look how skinny she is and how her fur is so wild!"

Aberdeen takes in the small, skeletal kitten on Louis's forearms. It clings to his sweater with sharp, translucent claws and stares at Aberdeen with penny-sized, milky eyes. It's definitely blind and its patchy fur is the result of mange.

"Hurt!" she calls out to her husband, for him to come and take a look at the cat, use some of his veterinary assistant skills, but when Louis frowns and looks past her, she realizes that Hurt is no longer there.

She had him taken away.

She shakes her head, shakes away the thought, crooks a

finger and tickles the underside of the kitten's tiny chin. It mewls in protest or perhaps mewls in pleasure. Aberdeen figures that the kitten could be unfamiliar with a world of something other than pain, hardness.

And then Aberdeen sneezes.

"Oh, no. Are you allergic?" Louis asks, turning his body away with the cat so that it isn't pointed towards Aberdeen. "I didn't think. I was just trying to help it. Like we do, you and me. Helping things."

"It's okay," she starts to say but stops, bending over and letting out a quick firing of tight, dry sneezes.

"I'm putting it outside," he stutters and opens the door and places the kitten gently on the landing. "Stay here," he tells it, "and I'll come back out for you in a minute."

After this, he rushes to the sink, washes his hands and strips off his sweater. He balls it into a wad of fabric and digs out a shopping bag made of plastic, shoves the sweater Myrtle made him, the one with the weak seams, inside the bag and ties a knot in the top of it. He puts it under the sink, in the cabinet. Then he comes back to Aberdeen, his chest bare, doughy and hairless except for one or two thick, orange cat hairs stuck to his neck.

Aberdeen smiles at him, tries to pass off the seriousness of the attack, but she knows he won't be fooled. Even if he were to be fooled, it wouldn't last long. Because she can feel her lungs tighten. And there will be no faking her skin riding a color gradation from scarlet to violet to cerulean blue.

Fumbling with the button on her pants, she undoes them, pulls them roughly down to her knees. The canister of asthma medication, the last bit of albuterol she has left, is strapped there. She doesn't take time to tease away the tape but rips it quickly, off like a well-worn bandage, and lifts the inhaler to her mouth.

She takes one hit. The spray is weak, nearly nonexistent, its efficacy questionable.

One might do, she thinks. I should save the rest for another time. Because there will likely be another time. Unless this time kills her.

And because the first spray has no effect, she takes another one.

Her lungs seal up. Another spray. She lets it drop from her hand.

"No good," she says in a tight clip of a voice. "Too old."

She goes to her knees. "Pound," she wheezes and gestures to Louis, "on my back."

He pummels her with his fists, hard enough to bruise the skin. Her chest shakes and pitches but there is no release.

Her head is getting light, her vision slightly blurred. She prays to her lungs in silence. One word, over and over.

Please.

Then Sani's voice pops into her head.

"Candle," she says.

Louis pops up and brings a candle from her bedroom, one that she keeps on her chest of drawers. It smells of limes and she's had it for ten years, never wanting to burn it because then the scent would be gone. It had been a gift from her mother. Of all the candles in the house, Louis runs for this green one, faded and dusty from years of sunlight and display.

He pulls a drawer out of its casing in the kitchen and rummages around in the mess with his fingers for the box of strike-anywheres and races back to Aberdeen. He lights the candle and holds it up to her face.

Concentrate on it, she tells herself. The flame is all that exists right now. See it? Now make it go away.

A little huff, a wheeze *out* more than an exhale, and the fire flickers, disappears. It leaves a snake of black smoke, its wick charred and brittle. Louis strikes another match and lights it again. He moves it a few inches away from her face.

All you need to do in this entire world is this: blow out the candle. Nothing more.

Her lungs get on board for this. Her praying must have helped, a truce called. We can handle this one thing, they must have thought. It's easier than all the other things.

And so it goes. Fire. No fire. Fire. No fire. Until the candle is three feet away and her back straightens and she is exhaling a steady stream of air and it only waves at her, tells her to fuck off.

She's fine doing just that, now that she can breathe again.

Louis pinches out the flame without licking his fingers. He winces, pulls back his lips and stuffs his fingers in his mouth. But he carefully sets down the candle on the floor, the dark green wax pitching a bit over the side and leaving a waxy spot on the floor, quickly turning solid.

"Better," Aberdeen says finally, reaching a hand out for Louis. He holds it tight with his own. "You're a life saver."

"No," he says and the tears start.

Aberdeen reaches over and dips her thumb into the cooling wax. She holds it up for Louis to see and he does the same. She notes the way it sears hot at first before growing tepid, molding to her finger. Before it's completely hard, she works it off with her nails and it comes away with a messy rendering of her nail and thumbprint.

Louis hands his to her and she puts both green, waxy thumb tips into the candle wax and they dry standing up straight. Her little, curvy waxen faux thumb next to his fatter, wider one.

"It's the good job, thumbs up candle," she says.

Louis's tears are unstoppable, landing on the cold wax, his lap, and the floor made of dead trees.

It's four in the morning when Aberdeen rouses and knows that something is amiss. She hasn't been dreaming, tossing around the empty bed since midnight. She sniffs at Hurt's pillow, where his head used to lay, but his scent is gone.

She puts on a robe, goes to check on Louis.

There is little surprise when she finds him missing from his

ERICA CROCKETT

bed. Again.

There is a light on over the sink in the kitchen and Aberdeen goes to it, finds a note. It's written in pencil on the back of an empty cereal box.

I've gone to get you some medicine. Don't come for me. I will come back soon. I can do this for you, Abbie. Love, Louis.

She knows exactly where he has gone. To the cages full of medicine. To the back of the tent. To danger. She throws the box hard but it just sails a few feet to the kitchen table, a clunky rectangle of cardboard never meant for flight. It knocks over the crocus, still packed away in the baggie.

Aberdeen leans down and sees its withered stem, the bloom puckered and browning. It never made it into the glass of water. Instead, it suffocated, its roots finding nothing but plastic chemicals and air.

CHAPTER TWENTY-FOUR

Hurt proposed to Aberdeen while they were fucking. They were sitting up, her legs entwined around his pelvis, her arms propping up her torso. Hurt would nestle into her hair, then pull back and open his mouth big and sigh. All this sensual grandeur on their full-bed with the broken box spring, in their shitty, dark apartment, their very first home.

He took hold of her left hand in his right, binding their fingers together. She had her eyes closed and could feel something cold and hard slip down over the knuckle of her ring finger. She looked, saw the one carat diamond and came immediately, hard, pitching her belly to the ceiling.

He spoke, after. "I had no idea you'd be so receptive. All I'd have to do to get you off like that is put a rock on your hand?"

Aberdeen hadn't wanted him to think she desired the diamond he could not possibly afford. She knew his salary. "No, I was ready anyway. It was just a surprise. Where did you have it hidden? Up your ass?"

"Funny girl," he said, kissing her nose and chin. "What do you say?"

"Yes," she breathed back. "As long as you take it back and

get me a plain, gold band. Then yes."

And she always told anyone who asked about the wedding proposal, that they had discussed it over dinner at their favorite Moroccan restaurant and shopped for the gold band together.

Aberdeen plays with the gold band now as she pulls on a pair of jeans that are days overdue for a wash, pliable with wear and perspiration, and slips on a sweater of crocheted mohair. She wonders if Hurt was manic when he proposed, thinking himself clever and grandiose. But she didn't think so. She thinks he was just in love. The way she was adamantly and solely in love with him.

She'd already called Sani, not waiting this time for the sun to peek out and join the morning. She promised that early morning calls wouldn't become the new norm, but that Sani had to come over, had to come help. She'd agreed and said she'd be there as fast as she could.

Aberdeen puts on her socks, laces up her black leather shit-kickers. She has one goal.

She isn't going to get Louis. She's going to get Hurt.

What she wants, what she needs in order to rescue Louis, is a man that's gone insane, lost all fear of being abused, dives into danger with the gusto of a masochist or a sadist or both. She needs Hurt. And suddenly she is glad he is the way he is now. The old Hurt would not be able to fight a path through drug dealers and thugs to get at a boy who wasn't his own. But this new Hurt would find it fun, challenging, something to get him hard.

"I do need you, babe," she says to the empty apartment.

She can't just sit. She goes down the apartment stairs and pushes open the door to the cold air. It's not as crisp as it was. The warmth is starting to bleed up from the earth, let loose by the concrete and asphalt, meeting the heat from above, shining down with the sun, when the sun does come. For now it is a muted dark, the wisps of clouds in the sky gray and slightly uplit by the approaching light.

And there is Janos, back to his spot, leaning on the brick wall. She wants to hit him, or hug him, or turn, make her way back upstairs and cry under her comforter.

Instead she chooses to say nothing. She scans the street, waiting for Sani to come, rounding a corner, some new, vivid headscarf over her scalp. Then they can go, find Plains View, rescue Hurt and then rescue Louis.

Janos looks at her, takes a cigarette from the inside of his leather jacket and lights it up. He takes a heavy drag and then lets the blue smoke curl out of his mouth, his tongue resting on his bottom lip.

"Look," he starts, but Aberdeen holds up a hand to stop him.

"They killed Wheelchair Man," she says. "And you were part of that whole fucking charade. Or you *are* part of it. Still. I have no words for you. Fuck off."

He takes another drag and offers the half-ash cigarette to Aberdeen. She flips him the middle finger.

"Shit," he says, "you didn't even know his name."

Aberdeen's arms go tingly. The rage is back. The fire. She knows once she has Hurt, the fuckers at the tent are going to pay. For letting Louis anywhere near them. For what they did to Wheelchair Man, even if she didn't ever know his name. For what they did to her. That needle of heroin, that lion's den, that dead man hanging from the fire escape.

"Assholes broke everything, Janos. And I don't need to know his name to know he didn't die right. He was murdered."

"It was an accident, what they did to Walter. It wasn't intentional."

"Oh sure. Probably another 'small terror' to fill quota for Beso's bosses," she snaps but knows she's not making sense. Terrorizing people only works when you leave the people alive to harbor the fear, tell the story.

Walter. Aberdeen slits her eyes, dips her chin to her neck. "He wouldn't have ever told you his name. He wouldn't tell me. Why would he tell you?"

"Because he didn't give a shit if some lout of a drug dealer knew him. He only cared about keeping you engaged and he did. Kept you completely enthralled with his sad state of living."

Aberdeen allows his name to be Walter, believes it because Janos wouldn't know about Wheelchair Man's confession to intrigue Aberdeen and hold her attention unless he told Janos what he was doing.

Walter, the veteran with the faded, red kerchief around his palm, with the soldered spine and the propensity for pitching magnificent fits. She misses this man and the sound of his wheelchair skimming over the tile in the apartment's entry way, the broken spoke and its pitched cacophony.

She misses caring for him.

"Walter? Walter," she tests out the name. She wonders about his last name. The one that starts with the letter H. "I guess it sort of fits. But not really."

She sees Sani then. The woman is nearly breathless, jogging up the street in snow boots and a pair of patched denim. She puts her palms on her legs to take in air and eyes Janos, but says nothing to him.

"You sure he went to the tent?"

"There's nowhere else he could have gone," Aberdeen answers and then considers that Janos might have seen Louis leave.

"Did you watch him go?" she asks him. "Louis? To the tent?"

Janos pitches the cigarette away, a spark flying off and dying before touching the ground. He scratches his palm. "I didn't know. He didn't talk to me."

"Small wonder at that," Sani chimes in. "So why aren't we going directly to the tent to get him."

"Because we don't know what we'll find, what situation we'll be put in. If they intend to keep Louis, we'll need someone as aggressive and determined as Hurt to help us. They'll know me immediately and then we'll be screwed. We need a wildcard, Sani," she says, "and he's that. Oh, he's completely that."

Sani huffs out a breath. "You," she says to Janos, "will they hurt him? Will they keep him and use him?"

Janos hesitates. "If he has money, then no."

"He has no money, Janos. He's ten. A child!" Aberdeen yells. "And I don't have any cash around for him to steal."

Then she sees something she's never seen on Janos's face. Fear.

"They wouldn't use him..." he begins, but Aberdeen completes his thought.

"Like they used Wheelchair Man, no, Walter? Are you kidding me, Janos? Some social worker you'll be. You can't even read people. Or you can, but you don't care. Just stay the hell out of this, all right?" Aberdeen can feel the heat in her cheeks. They are burning, pricks of fire trotting up her cheekbones, down her nose.

He does shut up, watches his feet, takes another cigarette from his pocket and lights up again. Tosses in a lemon drop candy between his lips as well.

Sani comes in close to Aberdeen, opens her arms and Aberdeen walks right into them. The hug is tight and long, a physical condolence for everything, for each of them. The hug makes her think of Hurt. She hates herself for not making him stay inside, for not giving him hug after hug to squeeze out the crazy.

"Do you have any idea where Camp 894 is?" she asks Sani. "Please do."

"I might know some people we could ask. But actual whereabouts? No, I don't know."

They hold one another longer. Aberdeen looks down at the

cracks in the concrete. She doesn't see any more errant crocuses. She owns the fact that she killed the only one she could find instead of leaving it alone and giving it a chance at life. Come in to my heart, she thinks, and take a seat with the other failures. Be welcome. Stay awhile.

Janos clears his throat of a bit of phlegm. "Hey," he says, "listen."

"Fuck off, Janos," Aberdeen says over Sani's shoulder.

"No, listen to me. I can help."

Aberdeen and Sani release one another. Aberdeen glares at him, at his foolish jacket, his bleached hair. He looks a mess of eighties punk and modern asshole.

"Really? Floor me then."

He smiles at this.

"I know where Plains View is. And I can take you there right now."

Aberdeen walks up to Janos, the smell of nicotine heavy on his frame. She grabs him by the tattered lapels of his coat and pulls him to her. She kisses him once, tight lipped and hard on the mouth.

"Finally," she says, releasing him and watching him stagger backwards. "You're taking your heart out of winter storage."

CHAPTER TWENTY-FIVE

It's far, so they must drive. Janos's vehicle is an old Pinto, doors lined with rust at the bottom, nearly invisible the way it blends into the faded sepia paintjob, complete with bucket seats so worn they feel like rails of metal wrapped in pleather sheathing. They go south. In the opposite direction, in the north, are the woods where she camped with Hurt as the terrorists carried out their first attacks. Aberdeen sits on the tip of the seat the entire ride, the hour and fifteen minutes it takes to get out of the city and into the farmland that surrounds them. It's interstate but the ride rattles the car so loudly they cannot talk. Janos keeps his eyes on the road and Sani and Aberdeen watch out the windows. Old, frozen wheat stalks and bare fields click by in swatches of brown, tan, brown, beige.

A trip out in one of those fields would likely give her an asthma attack. And she remembers she is now without medicine of any kind, no chemicals that will zoom through her bronchial sacs, pry them open, and convince them to inflate and deflate with any sort of regularity.

Another attack and the candle trick may not work. Another attack and she may not just be dead in spirit, but truly and well dead. This is nothing she wants. Not, at least, until she can put things to rights with Hurt and Louis. Then, well, happenstance and luck can rule the day again.

It feels good to escape the confines of the city, but Aberdeen is aware the further she gets from the tent, the further she is from Louis. But something in her gut, nestled tight between her intestines and her bowels tells her that finding Hurt is the right thing to do. In fact, the only thing to do.

The terrain is flat except for small mounds that wave up from the earth, crest and fade back into the level ground. They remind Aberdeen of the backs of marmots diving into holes. It sounds like a good idea. To just go underground. Hide away and escape.

"We're getting close," Janos yells to the windshield and Sani and Aberdeen look at one another. There is nothing to either side of the interstate except more desolate land, the occasional pasture for cattle and 30-foot high billboards advertising beer on the chests of buxom women.

"There's nothing out there," Aberdeen says, scanning the fields. "Nothing."

"Just wait," he hollers back. "When we get there, do as I say."

"Right. We follow your lead, don't say anything, yadda yadda. Got it," Aberdeen answers for her and for Sani. Sani just smirks, looks back out the window.

"Are you nervous?" he asks Aberdeen, taking his eyes off the road and glancing at her face.

"About the camp?"

"No, about getting Hurt out of there. How do you plan on doing it?"

Aberdeen smiles, runs her hand over the cracked casing around the door handle. These cars are ancient, all but removed from the road. She seems to remember hearing that if they are impacted from behind, they have the tendency to blow up.

"Oh joy," she says aloud.

"What?"

"No, nothing. No, no idea on how to get him out."

Janos laughs, pulls the ashtray out of its place in the dashboard and finds a half-smoked butt in the ashes. He nods at it. "Light that for me."

She depresses the car lighter, waits until it pops back up and then holds it up to see the cherry red ring of metal pulsing hot in its center. She mashes the tip of the butt into the hot surface. It catches fire.

"Here," she holds it to his lips and he lightly bites down on it, sucks in.

"So you just thought you'd come out to the middle of nowhere, knock on the door of the camp and ask politely for your crazy-ass husband to be let out to play? Wow. That's some ridiculous naïveté."

Sani chimes in from the back seat, leaning her forearms on the back of Janos's headrest. "I've got a medical license. I thought I might know someone in the camp and be able to pull a few strings, as it were."

Janos laughs, sucks all that is left of the nicotine in the cigarette butt into his mouth and shoots the remains out the window. It goes tumbling, sparking onto the highway.

"Know someone at the camp? Shit, unless you had a previous life as a shark in the private sector, you won't know anyone. This isn't some St. Jude's type operation."

"What," Sani frowns, "these places are run by private insurance or health companies?"

"Maybe. Or maybe they're just run by whatever capitalist big shots got the government contract for the facility in our neck of the woods. I don't know exactly who is in charge of it, but I'm certain it's not the mouth-breathers that run Medicaid."

He goes on, revels in the knowledge he lords over Sani and Aberdeen. "You guys would be screwed without me. Medical license or not, there is no way you'd get within a mile of the camp. I'd say it's your lucky, fucking day. You can take me out for a nice meal after we save everyone. Then give me a place to stay and find me a new job."

Aberdeen raises her eyebrow. "So you won't keep doing the tickets and the snake-handling for Beso?"

"After what I'm about to do, I'll be lucky he doesn't fist me up the ass before killing me."

Sani leans away from the seat, closes her eyes. Aberdeen watches Janos, the way his mouth creases when he smiles, the puffy darkness above his cheekbones.

"It was killing you anyway," she says to him.

He nods agreement, stares at the road.

Ten minutes later, they turn off on an exit that doesn't have any signs pointing towards gas or restaurants or minute specks of towns hidden behind the mounding hills. Another turn onto a dirt lane that kicks up loose dust as they journey down it. Then another turn, another dirt road. Then another, and they keep winding along in the desolate fields of dormant earth soon to flush with new life.

Then, it's there. A giant domed building of metal. It reminds Aberdeen of a more cylindrical Quonset hut. It's massive, perhaps the size of a college football stadium. There is no fencing around it. No floodlights or men in uniforms treading a perimeter. Two vans sit parked outside the building, no lettering on their doors, pearly white metal and rounded lines betraying their newness.

"They built this after LTP? That fast?" Aberdeen balks at its size and looming oppressiveness.

"What makes you think they just built it? Haven't you ever heard the camp theories, that our government always has buildings at the ready, places to stack up bodies in detainment or death if shit hits the fan blades? A new construction," he sniffs and then chuckles, "Abbie, doe-eyed idiot doesn't suit you."

Because she knows she is no addled imbecile, she bites

back, her voice cocky with sarcasm. "Gee whiz. We would have never gotten anywhere close to this place." Aberdeen cranes her neck around to see Sani. She tosses her a smile.

"If they don't recognize the car, they shoot. If they don't recognize at least one person in the car, they shoot."

Sani rolls down her window all the way and the sucking, warbling vibration bugs Aberdeen's ears.

Janos slows down the car on the approach to the metallic dome. "I'm letting them get a better look at us."

"Who would shoot? Where?" Aberdeen rolls down her own window and the shock of chill, moving air starts to numb her face.

"There is a sniper on the top of the building, lying under a reflective metal blanket, one of those thin ones they have in emergency kits. She can dole out headshots to anyone that isn't supposed to be here or outside of there," and he points ahead at the gray behemoth.

"She?" Sani looks forward. "So if a patient, wait, one of the prisoners gets out, they shoot him?"

"Sure," Janos says, pulling his Pinto up to one of the vans parked against the corrugated metal structure and lets the engine die. There are no doors or windows in sight. He doesn't note how he knows the sniper is female. "I've seen her do it. Took the back of the skull off a teenage girl that slipped out the door behind some careless orderly. She was running, then a bullet to the head. BAM!" he smacks his palms together, "She fell and that was that. No one came to pick her up. Nothing."

Aberdeen rolls up her window. "Maybe Sani and I shouldn't get out of the car."

"That's a dumb notion," Janos says, opening up his door, a loud creak sounding from the hinges. "They can shear through old metal, those bullets." He shuts the door behind him, bends over and grabs his toes for a stretch.

Okay then, Aberdeen thinks. Might as well be shot

somewhere the dirt can soak up the blood. It would just make a messy slick on all that old pleather.

The women exit the car as well, both moving behind Janos. They stay silent. Aberdeen wonders if Sani is as shocked as she is at the news that private companies are managing the sick and delusional of her city, of all the cities around her country. But then she recalls that Sani turned away from the blood of the ER to the blood and the opiates in her own veins and figures that the woman is likely incapable of astonishment anymore.

"I'll do the talking. You keep up with whatever I say, whoever I say you are. And this whole thing will be smooth. Easy, even."

There is no wind but Aberdeen hears a bit of grass rustle somewhere behind them. She thinks of the girl who tried to escape Camp 894 and had her skull shattered in consequence. She thinks of the girl reanimating, lifting up off the cold dirt and limping back to the building for retribution.

Janos leads them around the metal dome. It takes brisk walking to make it a quarter of the way around the base of the thing before they stop. At first Aberdeen can't see it, but then Janos knocks on a bit of the metal paneling and Aberdeen can just make out a black seam in the shiny siding and the slight bump of nearly-hidden hinges.

The door opens and a thin man in his fifties wearing pale blue scrubs shakes his head at Janos.

"Weren't you just here?"

Janos takes a small, laminated badge from his wallet and hands it to the man. The man pulls a hand-held scanner from off of the inside wall and swipes the card like he's charging a new sweater or a tank full of gas. He hands it back to Janos and nods at the women.

"The cases too heavy for you to lift? Who're your friends?"

Janos looks back at them. "Trainees. Beso's wanting to be more of an equal opportunity employer. He's realized there's too

much cock on payroll. Liza, Becky, this is William. He works
the front door. Obviously."

Sani reaches a hand between Janos and Aberdeen and
William takes it in his own. His face lights up. The tips of his
ears go scarlet.

"I'm Liza," she says. "Pleasure."

Aberdeen just waves. "Hi. Yeah."

William doesn't release Sani's hand and she tugs at it a little
to prompt him into letting go.

"I shouldn't let you in without cards," he says, flustered,
staring at the addict-turned-healer.

"Shit, William, they've got to see the circuit so if I ever
need a sub, they get the program. They'll have cards next time.
You can tell the sniper to shoot them if they don't."

Aberdeen looks to Janos in wonder at the way he balances
charisma and assholery with such aplomb.

"Deal," William says and turns his body to the side so they
can enter through the tight doorway. "But if the doctor gets mad,
you get the blame."

"So we're par for the course, then," he laughs and brushes
past William. Aberdeen moves next and Sani brings up the tail.
She doles out a giant grin to William as she sweeps by him.

The orderly shuts the door behind them and a light comes
on, bluish white, emanating from a series of long tubes that line
the ceiling. "Stand still for a moment," William says and then the
light shuts off on its own. The room is nothing more than a metal
cage with two more locked passages between the entry and a
solid wall with a door set into it.

Aberdeen closes her eyelids together hard. She can see the
yellow glow of the lion's eyes reflecting off the flashlight. She
can feel the warm piss down her thigh.

Janos rubs up on her side, puts an arm around her and says,
"How'd you like your first UV bath, Becky?" And then, under
his breath, he says, "Keep it together; whatever it is. Keep it

inside."

She does. She tucks it down deep, right next to that pinch in her bowels that pushed her to come to this place. Down to her empty uterus. Next to her liver, perhaps contaminated with Yellow Eyes's diseases. They can keep company for awhile: her past and her future.

William uses a key ring attached to his pants by a metal, retracting line to open the series of gate doors. As they move through one, he relocks the one behind them before opening the one in front of them. UV lights and keyed portcullises representing technology both new and old.

Sani presses her palm to some of the grating and comes away with indented lines on her skin, puckered flesh in the shape of diamonds. "This does the job?" she asks no one in particular.

Aberdeen imagines the series of locking gates was put in after the teenage girl got out, got her head exploded into a pulp of bone and gray matter. There would be no other way for someone to follow an orderly out. Not now, not with the metal latticework.

She takes a moment to remind herself there will be no way out for them, if things go wrong. At least in the movies, keypads, scanners can be overridden or sabotaged with a firm hit with a blunt object. But these are old-fashioned locks, ones that take a certain key.

Play nice, she tells herself as they move through the last locked passage and face the solid, wooden door set into the solid, plastered wall. Be the very best Becky you can be. Bring out Sani and Janos and Hurt safe and sound. Bring out Aberdeen when you are on that highway, speeding towards Louis.

"Have at it," William says as he unlocks that final door and opens it for the group. He winks at Sani. "Nice to meet you, Liza."

Sani nods and touches the man's shoulder as she passes. Janos takes the lead and Aberdeen turns to see the door shut behind them. The key clicks the lock home.

They're in a room without a ceiling. The walls are tall, over twenty feet high, and constructed of concrete pillars, studs and sheet rock. There isn't any plaster on the walls, no joint compound. It was put up in a hurry, Aberdeen thinks, and no one saw the need to make it pretty or finish it off. The room is as big as the ground floor of a department store and is busy with other individuals in the same, sky blue nursing scrubs. They wheel around carts with mini paper cups full of water or gather in clusters with arms full of charts attached to metal clipboards, talking adamantly about this patient or that and gesturing to information found within the sheaves of paper. In the middle of the room is a free-standing row of consoles. Aberdeen squints but can't see what pops up on the flat, colored screens.

"I've got to find the doctor on call. His name is Doctor Byrd and he's a gigantic, gaping butthole. But he's the one we need to see. Ask one of these people for a set of scrubs. Get a pair for me, too. I'll be back."

Sani begins to protest but Janos moves away, his wool jacket a shot of black amongst all the soft blue.

"Like these people are just going to give us scrubs?" she poses to Aberdeen. They watch the people move around them, busy with their appointed tasks.

Aberdeen figures that Janos knows what he's doing. She's decided to trust him completely. If he says to ask for scrubs, she'll do it. A man who looks a bit like Paul McCartney carries a load of off-white towels past them. She clears her throat.

"Excuse me, but do you think we could get three sets of scrubs?"

He doesn't look at her or stop, but he does answer. "Sure, just let me put these away first."

Sani gapes at Aberdeen and Aberdeen gapes back.

Minutes later they have three pairs of pants and tops at their feet. They're faded but highly starched, scratchy to the touch.

"Just slide them on over what you've got," the man suggests and leaves.

They do it, in the middle of the wide open room, pulling the white cotton drawstrings tight around their waists.

Janos is back. He picks up his set of scrubs and slides them on as well, the cuffs of the pants getting caught on his heavy boots. He swears, pulls off his shoes, tries again with the thin material. He puts back on his boots and stands back up.

"Doctor Byrd is on his way. You act like you get everything he says, even if it sounds like he's talking nonsense. Laugh at his jokes. Be engaged, but don't steal his thunder. The bastard likes the limelight, even if it's just us fools holding up some tea lights."

"You know what a tea light is?" Aberdeen smiles.

"I'm no heathen," he says.

They can hear the doctor before they see him. He yells out for Janos by name, then comes parting through a gathering of nurses, not moving around them but through them. One of them drops a clipboard, shoots the man a nasty look.

He's young, late-twenties, slightly older than Janos. His nose is flat and wide and he picks at his inner ear.

"I don't have anything else for you today, Janos. What, you're making weekly runs now? We didn't ever discuss that." He nods at Sani and Aberdeen but doesn't ask after then, want to know their names or why they're there.

Janos tugs down on the boxy scrub shirt. "Nah, I'm here for something else. You know, the rare occurrence."

The young doctor looks off, well across the room, to the panels flashing pictures. "Right," he trails off and holds up a finger. "Walk with me. I've got to look at this."

He hustles off and they rush to walk behind him. Aberdeen doesn't make eye contact with anyone and does her best not to look interested in the proceedings around her. He leads them straight to the monitors and a line of people in swivel, rolling chairs watching the screens. Stopping behind a woman with permed ringlets of bottle-red hair, he smacks her on the back of her neck with the flat of his hand.

"Watch number seventeen, Lourdes. Jesus, it only takes him a few seconds to start sawing at his restraints with the side of that fucking metal bed we have in there. Fix it. Take the bed out. He can sleep on a mat."

Aberdeen can see the man on the video screen. There are cloth bindings on his wrists and he runs them over the rail of his metal bed fast enough to saw through wood or catch kindling on fire. His forearms are a blur. His mouth is open and he's yelling something but there is no audio coming through into the expansive room. She takes in the rest of the panels, each screen divided into quarters. Each one reveals a different person, each person solitary. Some rave. Others sit pinched into tight balls in dark corners.

The rows of monitors take up the entire center of the room. There could be thousands of little cells, each holding a different person. Hurt could be in one. Her eyes dart over the screens, looking eagerly for his light, reddish hair.

The lady, Lourdes, speaks into an earpiece attached to a microphone that bounces off her lip as she talks. "Action on seventeen. Action on seventeen."

Blue-clad orderlies enter the camera shot immediately, tugging the man away from the bed. Lourdes looks up at Doctor Byrd. "Sorry," she says, "I'm working a triple."

He doesn't look at her but instead addresses Janos. "If dispatch brings me one more vanload of ducks today I'm going to open an artery. Not mine. But someone's."

Sani titters at this and Aberdeen follows suit. She's laughing at proposed violence. Doctor Byrd stands a little taller.

"Ducks?" Sani questions.

"Fucking loons, you know. Ducks," he explains and waves for them to follow him. He strides off, short legs moving fast.

Aberdeen tries to recall the sound a loon makes and then it enters her mind, the haunting song that pitches up an octave. She imagines all the sick people in this place taking flight, leaving on updrafts and finding a weedy pond somewhere cold where they can land, float, be free to sink or swim.

She looks at where they're heading, to a door set into the unfinished wall. When they get closer she can see a little plaque on the wood that spells out Doctor Byrd, Psychiatrist.

He straightens the plaque with his thumbs. "I'm not good with tourniquets," he says and Aberdeen laughs and wonders how long she'll need to keep laughing at his nonsense.

They file into his office and he shuts the door behind them. There's nothing more than a sad-looking ficus, a heavy, oak desk that looks older than the doctor and a sweeping, panoramic print of a tropical ocean swell hung on the wall. There is a ceiling here, but it's little more than rough wood scaffolding and particle board screwed to the ceiling beams.

"I was going to kick you in the scrotum for coming to me for more drugs," Doctor Byrd says, pointing at Janos's genitals to make his point unquestionably known. "I sell too much as it is to you. I might actually get in trouble for it someday."

Aberdeen forgets herself and speaks up. "The drugs don't go to the patients?"

It's now that he takes an interest in the women. "Who the fuck are you two again?"

Sani speaks up for them both. "Liza and Becky. We're Janos's trainees, if he ever needs a sub."

"No, Liza and Becky. Drugs only go to important people now. And there are no important people in Camp 894," he smirks. "Oh wait, except for me."

"As his minions, I hope Janos has told you that I don't mess around. Turn on me, tell on me, shit, breathe on me after eating garlic and I will have one of the cells cleared out and made squeaky clean for your occupation. You can smear it with your shit after you go crazy in there. You don't have to be crazy to get put in one, but after a time, it's just natural to go that way."

"Clear?" he asks and looks them each in the eyes. His pupils are dilated, deep black.

They both agree. They both smile.

"So!" the doctor leans against his desk and picks up a pencil. "The rare occurrences are my favorite. Who do you need?"

"Beso's looking for a lively one. Everyone who's on our payment plan is meek or disabled or downtrodden enough to agree to what they have to do to get their hookups. He's got an idea for a new healing act. But he wants a livewire. Man, preferably, but I'm not talking a complete nut. No teeth gnashing. He's got to be mildly coherent." Janos looks to Aberdeen and she looks to the floor. It's enough of a description of Hurt to work and she wonders how he knows her husband so well without the two of them ever really interacting.

"Hmm," the doctor brings the pencil up to the dip above his lip. Aberdeen is reminded of how the tip of her pinkie fits into Hurt's lip indent. She says a prayer to the memory of his face, ruddy and smirking, prays that he's here. That he's okay.

"No one in the cells, then." The doctor looks to the corner of the room, squints his eyes at something and then shakes his head. "Hey, did you hear the news about going to war? It's coming. Wouldn't surprise me if they start clearing out the camps and using the ducks as food for cannons."

Aberdeen shakes her head. "War with whom?"

"Ah shit," he replies and tosses the pencil back on his desk. "I never remember if they tell the proletariat or not these days. My dad's high brass in the Navy. I get sneak peeks and all that, even though I sided with the private sector. Could be that the US of A is tired of China stuffing their fat chink cheeks full of the medicines we could be using over here. No sharing makes Uncle Sam get out the belt. But you didn't hear it from me. Oh, and we might nuke Mexico instead of invading them. Payback for the pharmaceutical hits and all the day laborers outside our home improvement stores."

He looks at the group but they don't laugh. Sani has her hands on her chest and Janos's chin crumples into a mess of wrinkles. Aberdeen coughs.

"That last bit was a joke, folks."

So they laugh, not really knowing what the "last bit" was. Whether it was all he had just said, or just the last quip about the Mexicans. They all laugh in horror, from sadness, and at the twinges of spiky guilt in their guts.

"Anyway," Doctor Byrd silences them with pursed lips. "You can have anyone you want outside the cells but my price has gone up two hundred percent. It got a little hairy the last time I had to explain to the higher ups where that one girl got to."

"She wasn't one of mine," Janos says. "She was the one that got out and your sniper shot."

"Oh yeah," the doctor sighs. "Well, whoever the hell it was you took, I had to pull out the big bullshit guns. Beso going to be okay with the price hike?"

Janos smiles. "He'll have to be. Just put it on his tab as usual."

The doctor pushes himself off the desk and puts his arms around Sani and Aberdeen. "Now you ladies might want to stay in my office while Janos does the shopping. Unless you like having bad dreams. If you do, you can come with us. But this is the one and only warning you'll get."

Aberdeen shows him her teeth. "Those are the only kinds of dreams I get, doctor."

He lets go of Sani and runs a finger up under Aberdeen's chin. "I like you...Becky?" Turning to Janos, he adds, "She's a good lackey, Janos."

"Yes, she is," he says and runs his hands through his white hair.

272

"Let's to it then," the doctor says and they leave the office and walk across the length of the open room to a large, metal-hinged series of panels that reminds Aberdeen of a super-sized garage door.

"Open it up!" the doctor yells out to the room and somewhere a button is pushed because the panels roll up the wall on a track and a pad of concrete with metal railing stretches in front of them. Aberdeen can see rows of doors all the way to the end of the giant dome. They are stacked ten high, with walkways at each level, flat-fronted apartment blocks in some desolate, depressed communist breakaway.

"Whoa," she gasps and the doctor looks at her and puts an arm around her again.

"Big, huh? But our little camp isn't even the biggest. I bet you're impressed by size, aren't you?" He winks at her and escorts her onto the concrete. Janos and Sani walk behind them and Aberdeen keeps her eyes forward, fixated on one of the doors within her range of vision.

Hurt could be in any of those, she thinks, and I'll never find him. Never.

The doors are so distracting she doesn't feel the weight of the doctor's arm on her shoulders, doesn't really notice the way Sani takes in a sharp breath when they get out onto the concrete pad.

But then the doctor is pulling Janos up to his side with his free arm and then waving it out in front of them all, asking them to take it all in. Yet Aberdeen can only see the doors.

"Take whoever you want," Doctor Byrd says. "They're all good ducks."

If she squints hard, blinks a few times, Aberdeen can see the number on the door that's caught her attention. 2549.

The doctor's words sink in. She turns to him. "But you said we couldn't have anyone in the cells."

The doctor chuckles and drops his arm from her shoulders

to grab her ass. Using his other hand, he tips her chin downwards.

"But look at all the ugly ducklings in The Nest. Maybe you guys can pick yourselves out a swan!"

And finally she sees it. Dug into the earth, deep down into what once was a field of wheat, past the bedrock and clay soil, is the largest pit she has ever seen. It stretches the length of the metal dome. And in it are thousands of people in white internment uniforms. They light up the dimness of the pit, pricks of white: rice, the leggy tubers of spring bulbs, maggots.

Doctor Byrd leans over the railing and calls out to the people milling around in the deep of the earth.

"Here, ducky ducky," he says, laughing, mimicking with his hands and arms the wide broadcasting of stale breadcrumbs.

CHAPTER TWENTY-SIX

"No," is all that Aberdeen can say. What else can be said at the sight of such a thing? It is a pit of living humans, their bodies surrounded by compacted dirt walls, the overbearing scents of perspiration, urination and defecation wafting up to the platform, spring-boarding from the flip of her upper lip into her nose.

She fully understands now: the travesty of her decision, the horror of what she has done to her husband. Aberdeen grasps the metal railing and closes her eyes. She tells herself that she'll do anything to find Hurt. No matter the price or path. No matter if they throw her in the pit as well. No matter if the consequence is her own sanity.

Aberdeen opens her eyes, looks to Sani. The woman is doing her best not to cry, holding her hand up to her nostrils to block out some of the stench rising from below. Her sleeve slips down to her elbow and Aberdeen's eyes note the old tracks weaved on her skin. Janos doesn't look down but looks up, to the gray metal stories above them. Of course, she thinks, he's seen it before.

Doctor Byrd removes himself from the railing and walks back into the wide room of nurses and orderlies. "I've got to get my things and I'll go in with you. Hold your horsies, everyone," and disappears back into his office.

Sani speaks then, her hand still to her mouth. "This is not possible. They can't be doing this. It's like the old psychiatric wards. Just rooms of anarchy and untended mental patients. My Gods. Who allows this?"

"What choice is there?" Janos asks, still watching the ceiling. "They don't use the medicine on them. Doctors like Byrd sell it to people like Beso or it gets funneled to people who hold government jobs or run corporations. The medicine that does make it out gets swooped up or destroyed by the cartel cells. The rest of the populace gets tucked into a hole, literally, far away from the cities and towns that don't appreciate their shit getting messed up. Even if most of the people in the pit can be managed by their families, communities are tired, shell-shocked and they need scapegoats since the terrorists are proving to be untouchable. So they take it out on these luckless bastards."

Aberdeen forces herself to look and peers downward. The pit is perhaps thirty feet deep. Maybe forty. There is a fine ledge of a perimeter around the entire hole, just wide enough for two to walk abreast. And every hundred feet or so is a ladder on a track system, similar to the railings on the door that opened to the platform. All the ladders are raised out of the pit and Aberdeen can see little pairs of scrub-clad attendants walking the circumference of the hole, ever looking downward, necks bent in to sternums.

She wants to yell out Hurt's name. But there is no use now. Once she's in the pit she'll find him. Because she must.

"Then who do they keep in the cells?" Aberdeen asks out loud and Doctor Byrd answers directly behind her.

"Only the foulest of ducks," and he laughs but Aberdeen cannot bring herself to placate the man any longer. He holds up two cylindrical pieces of metal that look like fat electric razors.

"Scanner and Taser, Becky. The psychiatrist's best friends. Well, after pharmaceutical drugs. But that's gone to shit, now hasn't it?"

She swallows. "Yes, I believe it's all gone to shit, Doctor Byrd."

"Let's get down there then and catch you a good one. I've got other matters on my 'to-do' list today. I wasn't planning on a duck hunt."

They pass back into the room of operations and the massive metal door clinks back down and shuts away the platform. Doctor Byrd leads them through another door that hides a flight of stairs. They walk down it and find themselves on the ledge around the pit. The smell is worse, as is the light; the dim, orangey glow does little to help them place their footfalls and Aberdeen feels as though she is in the center of a massive, plastic Easter egg and the shell is her sky and her ground.

"Orange light works better than fluorescent bulbs or daylight. They stay a bit sleepier," Doctor Byrd says as he waves over a pair of orderlies. "But why the fuck do you guys care about any of that? Right? You're not here for an informational tour."

Two men with broad shoulders and firm arms trot over. They look to be twins with the same arching eyebrows and slicked-back, sandy-blonde hair.

Aberdeen catches herself staring at them and Doctor Byrd sniffs. "They're twins, Becky. Don't ogle them like they're understudies of a Chippendale's traveling show."

"I'm not," she starts to defend herself, but decides against it.

"Get a ladder down for us," he says to the brothers, "and then go down ahead of us. We've got to bring someone up."

One of the twins produces a key from his pants pocket and unlocks a latching system at the base of the ladder. He lifts up a metal bar and the ladder shudders on the track. The other man keeps it from shooting downwards too rapidly. He metes out its speed, like the ladder is climbing down *him*, holding on to each rung of the metal until it finds the bottom of the pit.

The brother who used the key pulls a bright miniature floodlight from his other pocket and shines it down the length of the ladder. A woman, the whites of her eyes gleaming in the light, jumps off the lower rungs of the ladder and runs off towards the center of the pit.

It's then that Aberdeen remembers the woman who was hauled off by the man in the glasses for defending herself from bullying. Is she in what the doctor calls "The Nest" as well? Or has she died, taken her life in one of the thousands of cells, crying, cutting away at her flesh until the sadness flitted away with the last palpitations of her heart and the last firing of her neurons? If she had a way, she'd get her out, too. But Aberdeen replays her list: Hurt, Louis, Wheelchair Man. No. His name was Walter. She's two for three. And she's unable, unready to rewrite her list just yet.

The man with the light goes first down the ladder and his twin follows.

"I'm next," Janos volunteers and Sani waits for him to clear the first five rungs and swings her legs over the side as well.

"Ladies first," Doctor Byrd says and Aberdeen is glad for it. She thinks that if she were to go last, the jerk would be playing grab ass with her the entire way down. And her foot would necessarily have to slip and end up breaking his nose. She considers it easier to play nice.

Her hands are already sweaty. She's not afraid of heights but is certainly uneasy with them. Gripping the first rung she lets her body settle against the metal of the ladder and takes her time moving down, putting both feet on the same rung down before moving her hands. As she descends, the smell of urine becomes cloying, sends her temples thumping and she gags on her own spit. She wonders if the hard soil in The Nest can soak up any more piss or if the ground of the pit is shellacked in it.

She has no idea how long it takes to reach the bottom but Doctor Byrd shows his impatience by shaking the ladder with his hands as he moves down above her. Once they're in the pit, the awfulness truly hits Aberdeen. Sani is already sobbing openly, not making any effort to hide her disgust from the men surrounding her. Doctor Byrd seems unfazed by her emotions.

To say they are unwashed, unfed, unkempt, unloved would be like calling the Milky Way small and unremarkable. The hair on their heads is matted and flat with dirt and oil. The outfits that seemed so white now look like soiled snow, flecks of debris and gross renditions of Rorschach tests splay over the fabric, made of blood or vomit or urine. Eyes are either red with veins or overtaken by wide irises that appear black in the dim light. Some of the people scatter at the floodlight. Others come to it, lunatics seeking out their master, the moon.

"Ah, The Nest," the doctor says and pulls his Taser and scanner out of his pockets. "If only they would learn to use the bathroom in one place, it wouldn't be so fucked up down here. But if you can't teach them they aren't talking to their dead aunt Sally or that they aren't the second coming of Michael Jackson then you can't rightly teach them bathroom etiquette. We must pick our battles here at Camp 894."

Janos looks out at the people around him and then watches his feet. He steps forward, always cognizant of where he plants his boots, a picnicker tiptoeing around watery goose shit in a city park. "We're on a time table, doctor. Beso wants him for tonight's show."

Doctor Byrd explains what they're looking for to the twins and the brother without the flashlight pulls out a touch-screen device from his pocket and types in a few words.

"You've got your pick of about five hundred," he says. "The meek ones, depressives, catatonics, they all stay around the edges of the hole. If you're looking for someone with some energy we should move towards the center. They tend to congregate there. Egg one another on."

Aberdeen waits for the obvious pun to come from the doctor

but he never delivers it.

"Right," says Janos and he steps carefully towards the center. The group moves with him and Aberdeen notes the people they pass. They are all missed by someone. Their families must be calling numbers, searching for them. Even if they don't want them back, they would never want this for them, this place several meters closer to hell.

A man veers close to Sani and the twins move to protect her. But he ends up being harmless, a gaunt old thing with a face befitting a grouper. He moves his mouth up and down, his eyes from side to side. Then he mimics swimming off.

They keep walking and the sounds of sex find them. Closer to the wall is a group of men and women fully naked, their bodies entangled in a clump. Hair is pulled, scratches decorate backsides and the penetrations are hard and violent. The twins say nothing at the rutting and Aberdeen looks up the length of the wall to see several orderlies standing on the ledge, pointing, giggling.

She thinks this is yet another side show. They should buy a big white tent as well. Then she remembers the lack of birth control and her mind turns to the possibility of hundreds of babies being delivered in this hole of filth and insanity, their wails for sunshine quieted by the buffering of earth. She touches her navel, takes in a breath.

They're approaching the middle of the pit and the further they get from the sides of the hole the darker it gets. Aberdeen wonders how they'll find Hurt or if he's even here. Her stomach twists and the things she's put there, the old wounds and the pressing future of Louis's fate take turns raking her with brilliantly cruel claws.

Ahead is what appears to be something of a mosh pit or a dance party sans proper music. But the score is there in the form of several people humming disparate tunes, others clapping to their own rhythms. One woman jumps up and down on the trodden terrain, desperately trying to pound out a beat. The mass of patients writhe and their limbs fling out wild, random circles into the air and into one another. Tops are missing, breasts doing pendulous flips with every exaggerated gesture. There are pantless men, pantless women, fat people with skinny people perched on their shoulders, tongues down throats, the smell of semen and something that cloys like newly-bloomed lilacs.

"Take your pick, Janos. I'll scan 'em, the twins will bag 'em. Have at it."

Sani and Janos take a twin each and walk around the outside of the dancing mass, craning their heads above the revelers, eyes wide for Hurt. Aberdeen is stuck with the doctor. He looks at her pants, specifically at her crotch.

"It can put you in the mood, right?"

She says nothing to him, but stands on her tiptoes and looks at the heads of the people. The tears are coming and she's sure they bubble up from desperation and physical exhaustion because sadness is no longer enough to get her eyelashes damp. Her left eye is still stubbornly dry. She bats her eyelid.

And she can't believe what she sees but she convinces herself it must be Hurt. Near one of the edges of the undulating throng of patients is a torso that wiggles in strange, sharp jerks. The hips buck but the chest stays still and upright. Aberdeen knows this odd dance from a discothèque they went to in Belgium. She was so embarrassed by it she thought of ditching him there with her bar tab of three vodkas sweetened with cassis syrup. But she stuck it out. She'd always stuck it out with Hurt. Until she didn't anymore.

But she was here to fix that mistake.

She goes plunging into the crowd, the doctor not quick enough to grab her or stop her with his protests. She pushes past the sweaty parts of hundreds of people to arrive face to face with her husband. A man without a shirt collides with Aberdeen's back but she bends her knees and will not be moved.

Hurt stops his jerking and takes Aberdeen's face in his hands. His nails are compacted with black soil and his reddish-blonde hair is dark brown from the lack of a bath. He smiles and Aberdeen can see blood at his gumline.

"Hi, babe," she says to him and he smiles. "Your dancing hasn't improved much. What else have you been up to?"

The human noises, the creative percussion is enough to keep their conversation private.

"Aberdeen," he says, laying his forehead to hers, "I've learned that hurt people *hurt* people. I'm Hurt!" And he laughs, whoops at his joke and Aberdeen finds herself laughing as well. She brings her hands up to cover his, to press them harder into her skin, to feel him alive against her.

"That's all the help you got in here, then? Well, time to leave."

Doctor Byrd is pushing through the crowd to get to Aberdeen. Janos and Sani and their companions have spotted her as well and they all converge upon her and her husband. She moves Hurt's hands down to his sides and takes her own away from him.

The same large man who jumped into Aberdeen steps on the foot of Doctor Byrd. He screams and pulls out his Taser. He delivers a volt square into the sternum of the man and the current travels through him and into three other people who had skin-to-skin contact with the victim. They all go down to the dirt, convulse and then lay still.

"Fucking ducks," he says and nods at Hurt. "Why'd you make a beeline for this one? Have a death wish?"

"No," Aberdeen hesitates. "Beso just said he wanted a man who looked a little vulnerable, sad, but one who could clean up well. He's handsome enough. And thin enough he won't be too hard to manhandle if need be."

"Right," Doctor Byrd says, taking in Hurt who's gone back to dancing but doesn't peel his eyes off of his wife. "Except for the gut he's fairly slim. Let's pull him out of the crowd and scan him to see what you're getting."

The twins each put a callused hand on one of Hurt's shoulders. He looks to Aberdeen and she gives him the slightest of nods. He stops his spastic dancing and allows the men to steer him out of the crowd and away from the gyrating mass of people who should have no reason to party at all.

Yet they do, Aberdeen thinks, and she keeps a hand on Hurt's spine as they walk.

"Pick up your ankle," Doctor Byrd says to Hurt. Hurt looks to Aberdeen again and smiles.

"You know him?" the doctor asks. "Or is he just sweet on you? Wants to buy you a chocolate milkshake and fondle your tits?"

Aberdeen shakes her head. "No idea who he is. He just fits the bill."

Hurt laughs, lifts his ankle high into the air so he teeters on one leg. Aberdeen can see the boxy, black square of a unit strapped around his lower calf with a thick strap. There is no buckle, shining in the light, no zippers or fasteners. It's like a giant zip-tie, permanently attached to his body.

The doctor holds his scanner over the black box and then pushes Hurt's leg back to the earth with a rough shove. He reads the information out loud to the group.

"Childress, Hurt. Mid-thirties, no physical problems. No known drug addictions," the doctor stops and looks at Janos. "Well, we know that's bullshit. That's why he's in here. He's been diagnosed with acute mania with psychotic features including auditory hallucinations. I'd throw in a vote for schizoaffective disorder on top of that psych rap sheet."

"So all that translates to a livewire, I take it?" Janos does his best not to look that interested. But Hurt takes his gaze from Aberdeen and smirks at Janos.

"You want to fuck my wife, don't you?" he says to Janos.

His stomach bucks and falls with his breathing, but his chest stays flat. He rubs at his eyes with his dirty hands and leaves a mess of black on his brow bone.

Janos coughs but doesn't look at Hurt. "I don't even know your wife, man. I'm here to help you get out. Don't you want to get out of this fucking pit? You don't belong in here. You're too good for this place."

Hurt nods in agreement. "I was getting tired of this. Yeah. I'm ready to go. But don't ever think you'll fuck my wife. I'll slit your throat before you get a whiff of her hair."

Doctor Byrd admires the exchange and clicks off his scanner. "He really should be in one of the cells, but they're all full of people worse off than Mr. Childress. You think you can handle this one, Janos? We could go hunting for someone a little less belligerent towards you."

"Nah, he's fine. I like a challenge. It'll make the ride back to town more interesting. Liza and Becky aren't great conversationalists."

"No woman needs to be," Doctor Byrd says and winks at Aberdeen. "Looks like you've had your pick of the ducklings, Becky. Don't forget to find him a body of water to float around in. I'm sure Beso can help you with that once he's outlived his usefulness on stage."

Aberdeen doesn't look at Hurt either. She feels they are so close to getting him out that she wouldn't want the doctor or the twins to think twice about her choice. She decides to play.

"I had a husband once who looked a lot like this man. He was a drunk, abusive asshole with megalomaniac tendencies. I think I'll do just fine finding him a pond to sink in. Don't worry about that."

"As long as he doesn't find his way back here," the doctor smiles, "then he can waddle around wherever he pleases, or rather, where it pleases you and Beso."

"Deal," she says and feels compelled to stick out her hand

to solidify the agreement. The Doctor takes it and kisses Aberdeen on the back of her hand. She turns her head away but Hurt watches, laughing.

"Becky?" Hurt asks his wife, "Is that it? You're quite the man-eater."

"Don't tempt me," she says to her husband and pulls her hand back, using it to give Hurt a shove, a command to start walking.

They make their way back to the same ladder. Aberdeen stays close to Hurt and at one point he reaches down with his hand and lightly brushes the side of her hip. It calls up nothing within her other than a feeling of anxiety. Hurt accounted for. Now onto Louis.

When they get to the ladder they find it swarmed with people, men and women making their way up the rungs, hanging on the sides of the metal as other, faster and more determined denizens of the pit swarm up and climb over the slower escapees. The twins begin climbing up the ladder and shaking loose the hands of the patients, like plucking leeches off shin bones. A ring of orderlies manage the top, lifting up to the ledge those patients who make it to the top and then binding their hands with stiff, plastic zip ties similar to those that hold the black boxes on their ankles while workers new to the lackluster pit break come and escort them away.

"I guess I forgot to send the ladder back up," the doctor says, gazing up the length of the ladder. "So what? It gives them something to do, I suppose."

The twins and the other orderlies in scrubs clear off the ladder. Sani gasps when one of the patients, a man with short legs and arms, is startled by one of the twins coming up from below and swings out over the pit with only one hand still attached to a rung on the ladder. But he regains his balance and the promise of a flying, falling loon does not come true.

Aberdeen takes to the ladder before Hurt but he follows on

her tail. His arms are longer than hers and as she climbs, he purposefully sticks close to her, lifting his arms up to be in line with where her torso presses against the metal. She feels secure with him behind her, his body a way to break her fall if she loses her grip. At one point he places his head against her buttocks and leaves it there for just an instant before her legs shift. It makes her think of the way he'd lay his head in her lap when they were first dating and she would run fingers through his snarled hair for hours and hours.

Back on the ledge, the doctor dismisses the twins and then asks Janos, "You didn't need help out with your purchase, did you?"

"Hell no," he answers. "We'll take the side door."

"Yes, you will. Everyone gets bitchy when a duckling gets marched through operations. The smell seems to get in the chair cushions and won't budge. Not for all the Febreze in the world."

Doctor Byrd's eyes go soft and he pulls yet another something from his pockets and offers it to Aberdeen. It's a syringe, the needle capped by a clear, plastic sheath. The liquid in the tube is slightly pink and stunning in its translucence.

"In case your ducky gets to flapping about. Just plant it in his jugular and he'll take a nap all the way back to that tent of holy holies."

She flattens out her hand and he lays it on her palm. It's heavy, the liquid viscous. She wonders what it is, if it's anything like the heroin she's had inside her heart.

"Thank you, doctor," she replies and closes her fingers around the syringe.

"Run errands with Janos anytime, Becky Beck. We have viewings of The Nest from two-to-four in the afternoon on the platform. We even have snacks. Fridays are brie with candied pecans and mimosas for aperitifs."

She doesn't know whether or not he's joking so she just looks to Janos and the dealer-turned-snake-handler-turned ally picks up one of Hurt's arms and squeezes it tight below the bicep.

"Burning daylight, doctor. See you soon enough," and then he's walking Hurt away. Sani and Aberdeen join them and make for the stairs that lead back up to operations. But instead of climbing them, Janos takes them around the back of the bottom steps and there is a door that looks like it belongs in a shopping mall or a grade school, complete with a push bar and a hydraulic slower at the top of it.

They push through it and it leads to another flight of stairs upwards that connects to a passageway to the series of gates manned by William. Aberdeen didn't notice the off-shooting passage on their way in. Of course, she had been preoccupied by the thought of the sniper who menstruates and rescuing her husband.

"Have fun," William says after leading them through the metal grating and out the door to the fresh, chilly air and the dormant fields. He smiles at Sani, closes up behind them, and then they are alone.

"Play it cool, still. There are cameras around us. And the sniper, of course." Janos pulls at Hurt to get him to the Pinto, his steps slowed.

Aberdeen opens one of the back doors of the car and helps Janos duck Hurt's head in and get his lap belt fastened. She scoots in next to him and acts aloof, staring out the window.

"Aberdeen," he starts but she shushes him and avoids his eyes.

Janos turns over the engine and Sani flips on the radio, acting casual. All that comes over the air is static punctuated by an occasional clarion trumpet fronting a few chords of mariachi music. She leaves it on anyway and they pull away from the metal dome and the thousands of people unhurriedly dying inside of it.

No one says a word until they are back to the highway on-ramp and the Pinto's bald tires hum over the asphalt.

Sani speaks first. "I can't believe it. Something like that exists. And we just left them all there."

"Fuck yeah we did," Janos says and cracks open his window. "We're a rescue party for one. Not a SWAT team."

Aberdeen takes in her husband. His face is visibly thinner even though he's been gone only about a week. She wonders what they're fed, how they're fed in the pit. He turns his face towards her and she can see a maroon scab running from one of his ears, dipping down to ramble under his chin. His facial hair is a mass of sharp, short spines of red, gold and black. He smiles at her. She smiles back.

The syringe remains clutched in her hand. She opens up her grip and rolls the cylinder around with her pinkie finger.

"Aberdeen," Hurt says and lays a hand on her thigh. "I didn't punch that doctor in the balls because the voices said I had to play along in order to get out. But I'm not crazy, Aberdeen. Don't worry about me. I'm just feeling spryer lately."

"Good, babe," she says and rolls down her own window. She needs him energetic, without fear, able and wild to take on what stands between them and Louis. Half of the ache in her stomach falls away and now there is only the pulsating, pinching reminder of the quiet boy who hugs so gently, who runs towards danger to find relief for Aberdeen's lungs.

Hurt looks down at the syringe. "Don't put that in me. I'll do my best to hang onto control."

"I would never stick a needle in you," she answers, "and I don't want you to be in control, not anymore."

Then Aberdeen holds tight to the syringe and sticks her hand out the open window. She pushes up on the plunger and the pinkish liquid shoots into the air before taking a sharp right angle and blowing back to plink against the side of the car and the asphalt, splashes of tranquility left behind them.

CHAPTER TWENTY-SEVEN

They can't drive fast enough for Aberdeen. She leans forward the entire ride back into the city, her legs bouncing up and down over the trashed floor mat at her feet. Her soles crunch down on old fast food containers, crinkly wrappers that once covered candy bars, the ink faded from months in the strong sun that streams through the car windows each day, now, and once it's parked again.

"We're going to get Louis because he went alone to the tent to get you asthma medicine?" Hurt asks again; he asks for the twentieth time. It's like the information is delivered to him in an unknown language, ciphers or wisps of smoke fanned out by a blanket. He struggles to decipher it.

"Yes," Aberdeen says and then she folds her hands and prays that the car will somehow become faster, regardless of its abilities or the gas in its tank. She still has the syringe in her hands. She looks at it again. There is a drop of the liquid in the length of the needle. She shakes it but the bubble does not move and she pulls on the plunger, adding more air to the container. Putting it in her jacket pocket, she folds back up her hands, resumes her praying. She thinks, briefly, that to pray is to ask, want, demand, and that this relationship with the things she prays to can only be so one-sided for so long.

Hurt yawns, snuggles back into the cracked pleather seat and lets the sunlight beat on his bare chest. Aberdeen watches as the vibrations of the old car lull and soothe him. He closes his eyes. She can see flecks of something shiny, like mica from the pit, smeared across his left eyelash line.

He speaks without opening those eyes. The shiny speck glints, falls into shadow, comes alive again when a luminous beam hits him just right. "How did you know I was in there? And how did you know to come get me? Unless you put me there, Aberdeen. You put me in that pit, didn't you?"

She looks out the window. The highway is lined with looping vectors of tar used to seal cracks in the asphalt. Wild, sticky lines. "I didn't know. I thought you'd get help. After what you did to Louis."

"It was an accident."

"No," she says, placing her hands flat on her thighs, "it wasn't."

He allows the barest of pauses. Enough for an inhalation. "It wasn't," he agrees without excuses. "But I would never hurt you."

"You did. When you hurt Louis."

"Ah," he says and leaves his mouth open wide. She can smell his breath from where she sits, pungent and sour with old stomach acid and the remains of whatever he's been living on for days in that hole. She imagines troughs of off-white gruel, lumpy with something substantial. Like birdseed.

The car moves on, closer to the city. Sani and Janos stay silent in the front seats. Janos pulls the rest of the smoke out of another butt dug out of the ashtray. Sani stares ahead and rubs the back of her neck. Her fingers tangle in the fine hairs above the pitted nape, wet with sweat from their time in The Nest.

The road hums under them, the song sung by the run of rubber on asphalt.

"That's why I don't want kids," Hurt volunteers and it catches Aberdeen off-guard.

She's wanted honesty from him about children for so long. She thought she'd never get it. He'd been so elusive whenever she brought up the subject and now he was open, willing to explain.

"Because you'd be violent?"

"Not that," he says, "but sort of. I didn't want to pass this on to children." And he points at his head with a dirty finger. "Wait, that's not completely true. I don't want a son or daughter who has to deal with the fallout I used to deal with before they found the right drug regimen to keep my episodes under control. I *would* like a child to feel what I feel when I'm at my most manic. The world is Technicolor and the speakers are on full volume then. You can hear what frogs think. And new snow? It's like pearl barley. It's that heavy and defined. You can see each grain of it. There's no better feeling. None while living."

"Why not just tell me?" Aberdeen asks.

"How many people find out their partner could become a dangerous person, strolling about in a constant lucid dream that happens to be everyone else's mundane reality, and then stay with them?" Hurt licks his lips. "I'm a walker between worlds, Aberdeen. In other places and other times I'd be considered a holy man. But in America, I'm just crazy."

She can hear the pain in his voice. Aberdeen touches him on his chest, right above his sternum. His flesh yields, puts out goose pimples. "But you aren't. You're lucid right now."

He brings a hand up and lays it over hers. "Right now," he says, "I am. But that shifts quickly, like tides coming in. With the drugs, I'd just forgotten how to ride the waves, but I've gotten my surfboard out of storage."

Aberdeen knows she has her Hurt, here, for a moment, perhaps an hour, perhaps weeks. But without the medicine, the other man, the wild one who can talk to thunder and pinch the wrists of children, will come back. She will have to learn to live with him.

"I needed you," she says, finally admitting that she desires him as much as she yearns to be relied upon by others. "And when I needed you most I realized I had given up on you. I won't do it again."

Hurt presses a finger to his ear and nods, as if he has a radio device in his ear canal. "They say I need you, too. I'm glad we all agree."

And like that, the lucidity is over. Wild Hurt is back. And Aberdeen does not ask to hear any more explanations for anything.

"Me too," Aberdeen answers and taps on Sani's shoulder, points to the radio and then gives her the thumbs up sign, jerking her hand to the roof of the car. Sani cranks the radio up several clicks so it drowns out the road noise. There is less static now and more brass horns, Latin *guitarras* and falsetto cries as they cruise into the outskirts of town.

Janos drives the Pinto to a parking lot near the white tent. They all pile out of the car and Janos asks them to lock the doors after them. He's afraid of the radio getting stolen and traded in at the tent for drugs. They shuffle the scrubs off their bodies, shimmying them down to the dirt where they create little pools of periwinkle fabric around their shoes. Hurt follows suit with his dirty white bottoms, tugging at his pants, until Aberdeen stops him from getting stark naked. Janos pulls his scrub pants sharply over his boots and his mouth upturns when he hears a rip as they come free.

"It's happened three times before. The radio theft," he tells them. "I'm there when they try to pawn it for a hit of coke or H and I have to take it back and turn them away. It's fucked up."

Aberdeen takes in Janos, the would-be social worker, the man with the hard exterior, asking them to latch the doors on his piece of shit car while Louis is somewhere in the tent. She knows he will always be an enigma.

And then it's like Janos has heard her thoughts about the boy. Like he has a soul inside to redeem.

"So how do we know Louis is even here? He could have gone home without the medicine."

Aberdeen smirks. "Not likely. If Beso had any inkling he was there for me, he would have kept him. To get me to come to him. To make me a dependent. To continue on with his terrorizing." She is embarrassed to single herself out as someone important to the man, but the Spaniard had said as much about her imminent suitability for his theatrics.

"We all are dependents," Sani says, "but not to that man." She turns to Janos. "Are you ready to stop being a dependent? I'd say that what you did back there makes you *persona non grata* around here."

Janos puts on and then peels off his wool jacket. The day has warmed, the afternoon sun pulses down on the industrial park. He slings the bulky fabric over his forearm and looks to the distance, to the tent.

"Beso cuts the checks. But Louis, that kid, he's something."

"Special," Aberdeen suggests.

"What's the plan behind this?" Sani asks. "Where would Louis be if he were here?"

Janos acts to answer but his words are halted before they're formed. Hurt, in his soiled, white patient scrubs, shirtless and shoeless, bends down to touch his toes and then leans back, his hands on his ass, and cracks his spine.

"I'm fucking ready," he yells, sniffs and rubs at his nose. "Let's do this."

And then he's off running, sprinting to the canvas tent that holds promises of healing, false faith, drugs, and perhaps a boy named Louis.

Aberdeen looks to Sani and then Janos.

"Fucking catch him!" she says, nearly breathless, and Janos takes off at a run after Hurt.

She sets off, too, Sani at her side, striding with the full length of their legs. Aberdeen watches Hurt's legs kick up wildly, his heels coming up to his hamstrings. His hands are in fists, like hammers at his sides swinging in blows meant to fell, over and over.

She already misses him, her husband. The other, wild version seems set on dominance.

But as she hurries after him, she prays to him, thanks him, for becoming what it is she needs now. She does not know if Beso and his men have guns. Or if they're even in the tent. She has no idea what will happen when they get there, but she knows this man who takes over Hurt does not care. He only *does*.

There are lengths between Janos and Hurt and the drug dealer cannot close the gap between himself and the maniac. Aberdeen curses the cigarettes that have marred Janos's lungs and the immune system disorder that cripples her abilities to exert herself. Hurt will get to the tent before them all. So the plan is thus: the plan is whatever Hurt does when he gets there.

Sani takes off her headscarf and Aberdeen sees her hair, the way it's thinning at the very top of her head. "Don't think about running. You're no good to Louis if your lungs are seizing up," she cautions Aberdeen as she wraps the bright, orange and yellow block-print scarf around her right forearm.

"I won't," she says as she watches Hurt and then Janos round the corner of a cinderblock wall.

There are people everywhere, as there always are around the tent. In their finery, in their complete state of faith. And the junkies are there as well, little pinkish-red tickets in hand. Aberdeen lopes by a man who whispers *kiss kiss* as he makes his way towards his own sort of God.

She can hear Hurt before she sees him as she comes to the dry field and the omnipresent queue into the big, white tent. He's somewhere in the crowd of people, whooping, trilling his tongue against the roof of his mouth in some mockery of a Bedouin warrior, the same sound he made during the protest. Back when his ribs were knocked in and he was still relatively her normal husband. An eon ago.

Sani stops as Aberdeen continues forward. Standing her ground at the back of the line, she bends her knees, puts her hands together and rubs them briskly. Then she takes her headscarf from around her arm and waves it in a wide, flowing figure eight above her head, a swirl of patterned infinity. A few people take notice, point, but most stare ahead, distracted by the promise of what waits in the tent and the sounds of a madman ahead of them.

And then Hurt bursts out of the crowd, running alongside the line, Janos just feet behind him.

"No," Janos yells but Hurt pumps his fists in the air and knocks over a small girl in his rush for the tent opening.

Hurt takes a second to look over his shoulder and smiles wide, catching Aberdeen's eye. He sees Sani, too, and screams with all his manic volume.

"Look," he says, throwing his fists towards Aberdeen and Sani, "God!"

Quickly done, he continues on, barreling towards the tent.

The people in the queue mumble and more take in the form of the woman with the flying scarf above her head. A man leaning on an aluminum cane pokes at Sani and her eyes fly open, the scarf drops and she snatches the cane out of his hands. He stumbles and Sani steps in to catch him. And as she does, she wraps her arms around the man and puts her palms to the back of his neck. He doesn't protest; instead, he sighs and goes limp in her embrace.

More people step out of line and step to Sani.

Distractions are usually things of falsity, Aberdeen thinks as she leaves Sani to her healing. This distraction is an invocation of something real. And the people take it in, soak it up, desiccated plants finally being watered.

Aberdeen can see the tent's opening, see that the man with the earrings who stood with Janos the last time she was here is now wearing the respirator. She can also see that the slim, well-built man with sandy hair holding the donation box is, in fact, Donation Box. She can hear him in her head, asking her if she knows what skin-popping is.

Hurt is at the entrance now, running down anyone who won't get out of his way. The man with the earrings tries to block him from going in but Janos waves his arm at the man to step aside and he does, just as Hurt pushes the wooden box out of the arms of the man responsible for injecting Aberdeen with heroin. Hurt disappears into the tent and Janos pauses a moment to say something to his coworker before heading in after him.

Aberdeen steps into the line of people, leaning against a tall man in a baseball cap. She's not sure what she should do. There is a chance that Louis is on stage, but she doesn't think Beso would put him up there when he could be used as bait for Aberdeen. The pain in her stomach returns as she realizes she should be seeking out the back of the tent, using Hurt as her fearless companion to get her where she needs to go. But she finds herself alone in a crowd of the confused.

She can't see in the tent but she lifts her chin trying to hear something, get a feeling for what's happening in there. And then she freezes. Donation Box is staring directly at her. He does not smile, wink, nod. He does not give any indication that he sees her. But she knows that he does.

He locks eyes with her for ten seconds and those seconds contain the possibility of addiction, pain and death. Then he releases his stare, doesn't say anything to the man with the mask, but steps away from the box overturned at his feet and strides with even steps around the outside of the tent.

He's going to the back, she thinks. He's going to Beso.

Her arms go numb and she feels the acid in her stomach crawling up to her throat. She can't go to the back now. She needs to get in the tent. Leaving is not an option. She can almost feel that Louis is here. If she were the biological mother of the boy, she might feel it as a tugging in her uterus. But it stabs at her instead, sharp and methodical, right in her chest. Like a needle embroidering the tissue of her heart with his name. Louis.

People ahead of her are pushing towards the opening. She's certain someone can hear or see something spectacular or odd and the commotion is luring them inside to get a look at what's transpiring. The man with the mask and the hoops in his earlobes and cartilage is left alone to deal with the press of curious folks. He tries to hold them off with shouts and his arms spread-eagle, but their insistence convinces him to finally pull off his mask, step aside and take in the way the queue dissolves into a mass seething into the tent.

Aberdeen goes with the others, with the flow, notices how the metal framing of the tent shakes and creaks as she brushes the canvas, squeezes into the tent and keeps her back against the curving, hard nap. She shuffles to the right, stays out of the swollen crowd. Soon there is no more room in the tent and the opening bottlenecks. Hands and brows of those who cannot enter poke above the heads of those who make up the back of the milieu.

People fan out as best they can. She is pressed against one of the tent struts by the back of a man who has one hundred pounds on her easy. He smells of vanilla custard and his hair tickles her nose he's so close. Her lungs start to complain, about the scent of the tent, the dust of the field and the press of the man's body against her own.

No prayers are said to the lungs now. Her eyes find Hurt, or rather, the arms of Hurt from the elbows up to his fingers. They wave above the crowd and she can chart his progression through the mass by where they stick up and flail. There, then they drop to reappear a few more feet ahead moments later.

He's making his way towards the stage.

Of course, she thinks. It's where a maniac would want to be. The center of attention.

She has no lock on Janos. The drug dealer is gone. For an instant she wonders if he's gone off for Beso as well. She recalls the way he betrayed her to the Spanish man in the nice suit the first time. He could be capable of doing it again to steel himself against retribution. She thinks to curse him but the words will not come.

There are his fingers grasping the front edge of the stage. Hurt pushes his torso up onto his palms and swings his leg high to center himself on the platform. He rolls the rest of himself up on the wood and keeps rolling, his body wheeling towards the center of the raised dais.

The caller, the man without the eye who wears the coat with the tails, stands there, his Bible in his hands. He's frowning, watching a crazy man acting like a rolling pin take over the show. The crowd is stewing, people talking loudly, some of them cursing Hurt, others lifting on tiptoes to make out what will happen next.

Hurt stops and props his head in his hand, assuming the pose of a bathing beauty, a move made popular by pinup girls of decades past. He holds himself there for a moment before swinging his legs around and then hopping to his feet. His hands come out in front of his torso and he shakes his fingers at the crowd. They vibrate and wiggle and then they go still.

The crowd goes still.

Aberdeen pushes on the back of the man in front of her. She uses his weight to steady her as she finds the metal lip that makes up the base of the framing she leans against. She puts her heels on it and it gives her an extra inch to see what she will see.

In the hush, the maniac speaks.

"You all," Hurt yells, "are so royally fucked."

At this, the people scream back epithets, slurs to take down Hurt, drive him from the stage. But he stands there, the ringleader off to the side and out of the way, and as the waves of curses come at him, he welcomes them in, waves them in to his mouth and pantomimes eating them by the handful, stuffing them into his cheeks and chewing, swallowing, chewing some more.

Someone is climbing the stairs to the platform, taking the steps in three long jumps. It's Yellow Eyes and his gaze is focused on Hurt.

Yellow Eyes closes the distance between himself and Hurt, his arm raised as if to punch the maniac who took the stage. He's muscled, hardened, a sharp contrast to the wiry, soft Hurt. But it's as if living in The Nest for a week has sharpened the instincts of Hurt. He easily avoids the punch and plants one of his bare feet into Yellow Eyes's crotch.

The large man folds over, goes knock-kneed and Aberdeen can only think of how comedic his stance appears, this dope-addicted pervert. Then, he drops to his shins and grabs at the zipper of his pants.

Hurt takes the opportunity to bring his leg up high into the air, tuck it against his inner thigh and does a delicate pirouette before bringing his free heel down hard and sharp onto Yellow Eyes's genitals once again. The man missing the eye moves to the stairs, walks down and disappears out the side of the tent.

Yellow Eyes is prone on his back and his mouth works to take in air. His arms are flung away from him and his fingernails scratch at the wood under his body.

Hurt plants his foot on the man's penis and scrotum again. And again. Five more times. Until Yellow Eyes does not move.

All the while her husband chants, "sinner, sinner, sinner" at Beso's lion-raping minion. And Aberdeen knows that Hurt doesn't know what Yellow Eyes was. But then, she considers that somehow, he must know.

ERICA CROCKETT

The crowd is subdued, mesmerized by the violent display.
Hurt picks his foot up to his chest and examines it before putting
it back down on the plywood stage, as if he might find bits of the
deviant's soul upon his heel.

"I didn't want to do that but I had my marching orders.
Literally," he says, laughs. "But self-defense is something each
and every one of you ought to know. Take note of the
destruction that can be done to the genitals of men. There is a
very good chance this sinner will not survive such a brutal attack
on his member."

Hurt looks down at the man and shakes his head, posturing
like he has just found the trounced man, like he's stunned at the
broken form before him.

Then he scans the crowd and smiles. "You get damaged
when you put faith in people like this. You've all put trust and
energy and respect into people to heal you or take care of you or
find you some drugs to take away the pain. But you've all been
tricked! There is only one way to get through this time without
medicine. And it is not this way." He presses his ear and
Aberdeen knows he's receiving what he thinks are messages
from someone, or someones. "You must listen to those that are
off the medicine. You are to take the advice of those you've
called crazy. Because these are the people that will lead you to a
new way of life. They will save you, motherfuckers. Do not
despair!"

At Hurt's feet, a bit of motion, a slice of green, then gray, a
bit of tan wriggles and slithers across the stage. Aberdeen now
knows where Janos has gone. He's loosed the snakes. They take
the stage, perhaps fifty of them, and they weave their way for the
crowd. When the reach the edge, they slip over the side and the
mass of people begin to lift their legs, push back and scream.

Hurt laughs, bends down and takes up three of the snakes.
He holds them aloft and shakes them. A chartreuse snake with a
black stripe on its belly sinks its teeth into Hurt's pinkie. But he

300

acts as if he can't feel it and perhaps he cannot.

"God is casting you out of the Garden of Eden, assholes. He drove out the snake and he drove out Adam and Eve. You are all cast out! Run! Be free!"

Then, the trampling begins.

The people do not know the snakes are non-venomous. That innate, human fear of the legless, the scaled, has them pushing over their own family members in order to run. An elderly man goes down. Then a woman heavy with child. Aberdeen can feel the mass of the man in front of her ease back, bear down and begin to crush her chest.

She cannot wait for Hurt or Janos. She is too slight to fight her way out. She struggles to turn her face to the canvas and then finds her chin smashed against the material. She tries to breathe through the heavy weft, begging the sturdy weave of the fabric to let in enough air to keep her alive. She scratches at the white tent, pushes at it, but the framing holds the canvas taunt and firm.

The heavy man pitches and rolls off of Aberdeen's back. He collides with the tent and loosens the fabric enough to cause a gap near the metal strut. He goes down, his arm flung across his eyes and a deep, bloody rip across his forehead.

She steps over him and squeezes her body into the gap. She pushes her arms out, puffs out her chest, and works the gap open with her maneuvering. Then she is on the other side of the frame, her feet outside the metal base of the structure. She crouches down and slips her palms under the canvas and puts her face on the dirt. She crawls out underneath the tenting, flat on her belly, taking in the cooler air of the outside field, another snake set on escape.

She pops up quickly, takes in the surroundings, expecting to find people running about. But the area is largely vacant excepting a few ticket holders high on whatever their tickets got them, stumbling their way back home.

ERICA CROCKETT

Excepting them.

And excepting Donation Box, standing in front of her.

He picks some of the dirt off her mohair sweater, skimming the line of her bust and then puts his hands on Aberdeen's shoulders, acting the friend newly rediscovered, the lover in an act of consolation.

"Finally a return customer? Or are you gunning to be Beso's next ingénue? Or do you like the attention that comes with the terror?" he asks her as he pinches down on the muscles and nerves that run over her collarbone.

Aberdeen does not fight. She lets him turn her, steer her towards the backside of the tent. She stares ahead, watching the curve of the canvas bend like the long arc of a crescent moon.

"You finally have something I want," she says to the man behind her as she calls up the image of the boy that can claim sugar and love as his two weaknesses.

CHAPTER TWENTY-EIGHT

She wanted to get to Louis, but she'd had something else in mind, not this parading forward, held tight by the hands of the man who injected her full of heroin. She wanted to have Hurt at her side, rallying her, supporting her momentum. They would have found Louis on their own, without incident and she would have taken him in her arms and saved him and made things right and good for the boy entrenched in the muscle of her heart.

But this would do, too. If she could only be certain that she would get Louis and herself out of it alive. That is the variable, the question that mucks about in her skull as Donation Box steers her around the tent. She can hear the shouts of the people within the canvas prison. She knows that people will be trampled to death and that Janos and Hurt are somewhere inside, doing what they can to seed chaos with snakes and prophesying.

She thinks of Yellow Eyes, the way his crotch must be caved in, the form of it collapsed and battered into a pulp of wrecked flesh. Aberdeen is tempted to tell Donation Box what has become of his comrade, but the delight she would take in sharing the information may be overshadowed by the payback he could dole out. That pain, that prick of another needle.

Biting her tongue will have to do but she allows herself the thought of a lioness trapped in that small enclosure, licking her plaque-covered canines, pacing back and forth in front of the wires. If she only knew that she had been avenged. If Aberdeen makes it out of this alive, she swears she will go back to the zoo, meet eyes with all the lions and try to convey what has happened to the offender. They would want to know, surely. Aberdeen would want to know what happened to someone who raped her.

Focus on the walk, where you are heading, she tells herself. There will be time later to think of the cats with the glowing eyes. Now was the time to watch where she was being lead, in case she ever had to escape or come back or lead a battalion of soldiers not on the cartel's dole to the doorstep of Beso's operation.

They reach the very back of the wide tent that holds hundreds only to see there is no back room, no boxed area attached to the pavilion. There are other junkies about, unfazed by the sounds of rioting and bedlam billowing out from the tent. They cluster up in little groups, like to like, scratching at track marks under unwashed sleeves or wiping hands under dry noses. They all stand near what looks to be a steel double door laid flat on the ground.

"Stop here," Donation Box says, tightening his pinch on her frame. The pressure on her nerves sends a sharp ache up into the base of her skull, where it whirls about like a firework nailed to a streetlight pole.

One of the metal doors creaks open and is flung wide. It crashes on the dirt and stirs up a little puff of dust, a demonstration of the warming earth. A group of users, of ticket holders, moves in unison to the opening in the world and a hand emerges from the door, then an arm and a woman comes into view. She has tight ringlets and triceps that sway low and wobble as she climbs out of the horizontal doorway.

Aberdeen recognizes her as the speaker of tongues that went to work on the man that believed himself to be a bird. She spouted nonsense and the audience believed that she was touched, holy, because she said things they could not understand, not realizing that the syllabic nonsense was just nonsense. And that sometimes, there really is nothing *to* understand.

There are little plastic baggies tied off with shiny, green twist-ties in a large plastic bag hanging off her fat wrist. They look to contain baking powder or chalk dust.

"Greens?" she asks the people and they nod and she puts a puckered, yielding baggie into each open palm. The sacks mold to the cupping of their hands, turn into little parabolas, go malleable. As soon as a person gets a supply, they cut out, break from the herd, their needs now completely and soundly met.

Once the last person leaves, Donation Box guides Aberdeen to the door that approximates the entrance of a root cellar, leading to things stored in the cool dark. The heavy-set woman smacks her lips and cracks a wad of gum against the roof of her mouth. Aberdeen can see the bright yellow of it as it shows itself behind the spaces in the woman's teeth.

"That her?" she asks and Donation Box sniffs.

"Get her down then," and she ducks back into the opening, only to keep speaking, her voice a mumble that Aberdeen can only just make out. "Ridiculously easy one to catch, apparently."

And then the same cheekiness Aberdeen displayed the last time she was held by these people comes pouring forth.

"You guys have a crap system for distribution. Tickets you can get playing arcade games? Really?"

"It's not that simple," Donation Box counters, but Aberdeen doesn't want to argue. She just wants to poke a little and she doesn't know why. She tells herself to shut up, to not risk the man's anger when she's so close to getting somewhere.

Then again, she thinks, she may be close to being killed. That will not do.

She digs in her heels then, but the soles of her shoes find no purchase in the hardened dirt. She cranes her neck around to meet Donation Box eye to eye. He pulls on her and does his best not to make contact with her gaze, but his eyes cannot dart about forever, and then their pupils lock.

"Tell me he's here and I'll go down into that hole without a fight. Please."

Aberdeen can see the concrete stair, chunky with grainy ice that runs along the edges, steps that dive down into the earth. A false light, orange and warm shines from below, escaping out into the daylight, into something real. It reminds her of the lights around The Nest. All those helpless people. All those people she could not save. Louis will not be one of them.

Donation Box doesn't respond, instead taking his hands off of her shoulders and pressing on her back to start her down the stairs. He looks around, eyes the groups of drug users that loiter around the door. He's nervous; Aberdeen can feel the shaking of his palm on her skin.

She thinks to run, but with her traitorous lungs, Donation Box would have no problem catching her.

Besides, Louis is likely in the room under the earth, so she places a set of toes on the first step down, wiggles them around to make sure she's got footing and then descends. The carroty light gets brighter while the sun's light dissipates. She stares ahead, her palm pressed to the freezing concrete wall for balance. She hears Donation Box pull the door down upon them, set a bar in lock position and then his footsteps alight behind her own.

Fifteen steps down and they're under bedrock. Her bedrock, her Hurt and even Janos and Sani, are above her now. She's it. She takes a full breath while she can still breathe and says a silent thanks to her lungs.

Another door. This one is wooden with a simple doorknob and lock found in any home on any interior door. The lack of security makes Aberdeen lift her eyebrows, but Donation Box moves past her then, his hand returns to one of her shoulders and opens the door for her.

It's a corridor of cages and dirt hard-packed as walls, railroad ties act as buttresses and scaffolding. In the cages are bottles, boxes, containers holding tiny pills of every color, dropper bottles of bubble-gum flavored penicillin, baby aspirin, blood sugar test strips, gels for acne, Viagra, Depo shots. It is the remnants of the city's permissible drugs not under the control of the government or other small cells of the cartel. They are caged; their imprisonment helps to imprison the people above her, on the topsoil, the ones dying from rioting or cancer or spontaneous terrorist violence or the snort of an amphetamine.

The corridor is so long she can only see the outline of the tongues speaker advancing down the dank row, illuminated by the low light of amber bulbs strung overhead, white wires leading back into the earthen walls. She is a warden of sorts, looking side to side at her charges in their locked cages, telling herself aloud, "All is well."

Aberdeen slips her fingers through the metal grating of one of the cages and pauses. All could be well, for a time, if the drugs could get outside to the people. Of course there wouldn't be enough for everyone, but it could be a way to mollify some, for a time, until the drugs come back.

But war may be coming, not the return of the drugs. Perhaps it's best if they don't know, she thinks, before Donation Box roughly shoves her away from the cage and down the underground hallway. Let them suffer and die thinking they had what they could get, got what they fought for, and did all that could be done.

Leave it be, she tells herself. But then, Aberdeen knows she's never had the ability to leave anything or anyone just be.

"I wish I could just Robin Hood all this outside, right now," she says to Donation Box as she walks. She takes in an entire section of caging stocked with brown bottles of hydrogen peroxide.

"Good luck carrying it," he says, "and not getting killed when they swarm you to get it."

The air in the corridor is stale but smells faintly of mildew and humus. She thinks of her terrariums, those little green worlds she so loved to create. It's the same smell that emanated from her very last terrarium to make it through the winter, the one of Corsican mint and white lanthanum. It had died, like the others, engulfed in neglect and a black rot that took leaves one at a time, turning them soft and then turning them into a pulp and then turning them into soil.

There is an ending to it all, she thinks, then speaks, looking back at Donation Box.

"This isn't the only cache, right? Can't be. With such lax security, with a bunch of employees doubling as stage performers and corner dealers. No one would put all their eggs in one subterranean basket."

"Strategies aren't up for discussion," he answers and they continue to walk.

They catch up with the woman, her pace hindered by what appears to be a bad hip supporting too much weight. She blows a bubble with her gum and it bursts flat against her chin. She reels the majority of it back in her mouth with her tongue but has to pick a spot of chartreuse off her skin with her fingers. She flicks it to the dirt and Aberdeen steps over it.

"You aren't even the mother, are you?" the woman of tongues, of glossolalia, says to Aberdeen and then she knows instantly they are leading her to Louis.

"I don't see how it matters," Aberdeen replies.

The woman smacks her gum and smiles. "It's hard enough taking care of the ones that come out your cooch. Seems foolish to take on one that doesn't even share your skin color."

Aberdeen considers telling the woman that Louis shares her heart, but she's certain it would be lost on her. "I haven't had the pleasure of making any of my own, so, he's it."

The woman snorts and looks to Donation Box. But the man doesn't return the gaze.

"Could have picked a heartier urchin. He's got guts but his balls are soft, no doubting that."

"I suspect they'll harden up," Aberdeen says, "as he becomes a man."

"If he does," is what the woman says, "if he has the chance," and Aberdeen's heart leaps, pounds at her ribs, ready to get out and fight.

Then there is another door, this one metal and set into a frame that appears to be concrete. A doorbell is tacked up with nails directly into the dirt around the doorframe and glows with a red light. Donation Box pushes the bell but no sound finds Aberdeen's ears.

"Say cheese," he says and points to a camera tucked near the last of the cages in the corridor. Aberdeen flips it a middle finger, the door opens, and she is escorted inside.

The room is a concrete bunker, perhaps a hidden location constructed during the Cold War by a man wanting to protect his wife and children from the bombs of communists. Except it's bigger, large enough to house several families within the cinderblock walls. There is a partition against one wall, nothing more than rods and drapes that cordons off a toilet and a drain in the earth with a little handheld sprayer snaking out of what looks to be a water heater tank. Several cots are folded up and stacked against another wall. There is a hot plate, a shelf of canned beans and potted meat. There is a stack of board games, all the boxes with soft, worn edges. There are magazines in haphazard stacks and a docking station for a music player or a phone.

There is Beso behind a desk covered in butcher paper.

There is Louis in a wheelchair, his head slumped down over the collar of his favorite sweater, the blue one, the one embroidered with spaceships that have never flown.

Beso stands and waves his hand at the woman and Donation

Box and they leave out a door set in the wall behind the Spaniard. Aberdeen can see a ramp leading up out of the earth and figures it's the door that Louis must have wheeled Walter through.

Beso turns his head to watch them go and then smiles when the door clicks shut, running his fingers over his goatee.

"Have you changed your hair?" he asks Aberdeen.

She keeps her eyes on Louis. He's not moving. They have him drugged, just like Wheelchair Man, Walter. Then her eyes cast over the spokes of the wheelchair wheels and she finds what she hoped she wouldn't. A broken spoke, collapsed and resting on the hub of one of the wheels.

It's Walter's chair.

"Did you bury him at least? Did you give him any sort of respect after you paraded him on stage, already dead?"

Beso furrows his brow. "Ah, the old soldier? Are you wanting to leave flowers somewhere? Something tacky you get at the grocery store wrapped in plastic?"

"Among other things, yes."

"No," he answers, his face smooth once again. "Unless you plan on getting many, many flowers and placing them in many, many places around this city."

"Enough," she says because it truly is enough to know. It is more, but she will have to digest it later.

Aberdeen doesn't move, but Beso comes around the desk and leans against it.

"Can I touch him?" she nods at Louis.

"No, you cannot. You can stand there and discuss payment. This is what you can do."

Aberdeen smirks, shows her teeth. "Someone always has to be in a fucking wheelchair, right? How about me instead of him?"

Beso makes a shushing sound with his tongue and teeth. "Ah! To see you on stage. Do you remember how I said you had a look about you? Like a heroine? But I am thinking you really would like something else, would you not? We could create a relationship this way."

He walks back around to the desk and lifts up the edge of the butcher paper, pulling out a drawer. Aberdeen watches him while keeping Louis's limp form in her peripheral vision.

His voice is muffled by the paper, but Beso says something about making payments and how it can, in fact, be fun.

Popping back up, he has a black bag in his hands. She's seen it before, or one like it. He sets it on the white, stiff paper and unzips it. He pulls forth a dull spoon, a powder in a baby food jar, a length of yellow rubber.

He pushes the drawer closed with his thighs and laughs.

"What is it that is on the sign boards near dangerous rides in this country? Something about people needing to be so tall and so old before they can have excitement and the ups and downs?"

She holds a hand up to chin level and plays along. "You must be taller than this height to ride this ride."

"Actually," Beso says, spinning the spoon on the table, until it blurs, no telling handle from divot, "this ride is best taken lying down, if you remember."

"Just lie down," he suggests, letting the utensil slow, then stop at the edge of the desk. "Lie down."

Aberdeen stares at the heroin in the jar, the way it coats the base of the glass. She tells herself that she may have to take it in order to get Louis back and she decides if it comes to that, she will do it, without hesitation. But her mind screams at her to find another way. It is only her body, the blood that swells and pools in her cheeks and in her genitals that says *yes,* purrs *finally,* and pulses and beats and throbs and works her entire body into a shivering timbre before her legs fold, she sits on the dirt floor and her chin, just as Louis's, dips to rest next to her heart.

CHAPTER TWENTY-NINE

It takes the barest push of Beso's fingertips on her chest to get Aberdeen to lean back and let her spine touch the earth and her black hair tumble outwards from her scalp, spray across the cold dirt. Beso straddles her, still standing, his knees locked as he tilts his head down to look at her body. There is a strong crease running the length of his off-white slacks, tumbling over his knees, ending at smart cuffs. And there is where Aberdeen starts, at least the form of her, shaking, body hot, hands folded in prayer.

The soul of Aberdeen flees as the prayer ends, seeps out into the ground and granulates itself in order to lie next to the flakes of mica and clods of clay that surround her and Beso and Louis.

Now her body is in charge and it quivers in expectation.

"*Listo?*" He asks and repeats in English. "Ready?"

Her heart stays, though. And this is what speaks.

She keeps her eyes on the crease in his pants, her voice quiet and aimed to placate.

"I can't take it until I know Louis is okay. You wake him up and I'll let you stick me with heroin without a word of protest. But you wake him up first. That's the deal."

The Spaniard, the man whose name means *kiss* doesn't laugh or mock. He looks over to Louis and then looks back down to Aberdeen.

"What is the saying here? That you are not in a position to negotiate with me?"

She remembers the feel of the sepia-liquid in her leg, the way the drug rambled and ran up to her heart and made the moon turn on, become brighter and become her home.

"Come on, Beso," she says. "If you haven't used him already, you'll only get one performance out of him. Your tent people won't forget a boy like Louis. Not the same way they forgot an old man like Walter. It's just the way people are. Besides, he's another duty done in the name of terror. He won't ever forget this, forget the fear. He's used up already. Let him go."

Aberdeen turns her head so her cheek is pressed to the earth and gazes at the spokes on the wheelchair and the shoes on Louis's feet. She hopes she'll have to buy him new tennis shoes, with the way his feet will grow as he ages. She hopes that he will keep on living. She wants millions, billions of things for him.

She knows that there is nowhere, at least not now, where Louis could be paraded. Wild Hurt, Maniac Hurt could have the canvas and dais burning by now, lighting up the tent with one of the old-fashioned lanterns they had placed around the area, the only cessation of flames coming from the stream of piss he'd be lacing over his chaotic work. She wonders why no one has told Beso of the anarchy above them. Where is the phone call or the messenger running into the room, sweat at his temples? Why doesn't Beso know about all the silenced *kisses* and the overturned soapbox?

She smiles, one corner of her mouth attracting loosened soil with her damp lips. She runs her tongue over the clay and it tastes like nothing at all.

Beso reaches down and orients his face to hers by pulling

on her chin. "You are right, Abbie. They will remember him. And I am not such a monster to use a child this way more than once."

There is sand on her front tooth. She swallows it away.

"So wake him then," she says, bringing her hand up to his and squeezing his fingers. She pulls her palms back, places them back into a folded little steeple.

"I am reasonable," he answers, swinging one of his legs wide over her torso so he stands at her side, the heels of his high-shine loafers against her hip. "Anything to get you."

She closes her eyes, places her hands above her heart and wills the urge for the ride away.

"Why? Why do I matter so much to you?"

"You have a presence, a strong character that shines. I saw it after I decided you would be one of my small terrors. I don't see much in the holy sheep and the addicted goats. I like the innocence of you but I like corruption better. I also have the belief that everyone is a person of worth," Beso says, his back to Aberdeen, and lays a hand on top of Louis's head. The boy's brown hair gives, envelopes the man's fingers.

Louis doesn't twitch.

Aberdeen doesn't laugh or smile. "We have that one thing in common, then. But I doubt we are defining worth in quite the same way."

"No," he says, "we are not."

Her stomach heaves, her arms nothing more than numb, heavy weights on her chest. She lets them lie over her heart and then she feels something thin and hard just under the fabric of her jacket.

The needle meant to deliver a sedative to Hurt.

"I have my own syringe. Please let me use it instead of whatever you were planning on sticking into me." She unfolds her hands and pulls out the needle, a bit of the pink liquid still around the rim of the syringe plunger halfway down the cylinder.

Holding it up for Beso to see that she is ready to cooperate, ready to take her medicine, his eyes go wide and he smacks the top of Louis's head.

"This is something, Abbie, like you are a woman that has only fucked once and you come to the bed with a cock ring." He traces the edge of his whiskers with his thumb and index finger.

He doesn't reach for the needle, but instead moves back to the desk and opens the drawer again. He holds up his own small needle, something that could be used to take blood for an insulin test. From the drawer also comes a small bottle of clear liquid. He dips the very tip of the needle in the liquid and recaps the container.

"It is time for the boy to wake up. If he sleeps too long he will not make a thing of himself. At least that is what my *abuela* used to say."

Aberdeen remembers Myrtle then, whispers the woman's name under her breath and hopes that if souls do survive, that Myrtle can hear her name being invoked, come to it, and protect her grandson.

Beso goes to Louis in the wheelchair and Aberdeen thinks of Walter and how his stimulant dose did nothing for him on the stage in the tent. He was already dead. And she wonders, now, if both her and Louis are already dead, too.

She says "Walter" under her breath as well, then "Wheelchair Man." She might as well invite him to the party. They need the help.

Cupping the syringe in her hand, she holds it between her palms, as if the metal and the plastic were the most precious of instruments and she the most admiring of users. She reveres it the way Hurt cradled that expired canister of asthma medication. She speaks to it just under her breath, one of her prayers, asking it to save Louis and to deliver to her the feel of ease and warmth.

She sits up then, so she can watch Louis come back to life.

"He will come back," she says aloud and Beso shrugs,

stands between the boy and Aberdeen and places the tiny needle over the place in Louis's neck where an Adam's apple will someday jut forth.

"I would not like to lose an asset," he says and then pushes the needle in.

Louis's head snaps back immediately, his neck smacking the top of the wheelchair seat. His eyelids part and his pupils are wide and dark. Aberdeen lets her emotions swell and overtake her, the left eye still dry as a single trail of water slips out her right, good eye.

"He is alive," she speaks to her hands, the syringe, Myrtle, Walter, Beso and all things, everywhere.

Beso smacks Louis on the cheek with soft fingers. The boy straightens up, looks around and then down to the ground to see Aberdeen sitting at the base of his wheelchair.

He pulls away from Beso and locks eyes with Aberdeen.

"I was getting you medicine," he says but it is not what he says that causes Aberdeen's soul to return but the voice in which he speaks. It cracks, perhaps out of fear, but possibly because, as Aberdeen has seen, Louis is becoming a man.

And she wants to hear his voice shake in pitch and tone again and again until one day it grows deep and solid and she knows that she must *be* there for it to happen.

No heroin rides. No abductions or abuse. No giving in.

So her hands fold up, no longer into lean steeples, but into fists. Aberdeen is done praying, pleading, asking.

Now she is taking.

She plants her fist into the side of one of Beso's knees, into the soft bit between patella and bone. He screams and collapses immediately, sitting hard next to Aberdeen and reaching out for her torso.

She keeps a hold on the syringe and tries to crawl away from Beso and Louis, but Beso is fast and catches the hem of her jacket and holds tight. Aberdeen looks behind her and sees Louis pushing up from the wheelchair.

"No," she screams and rakes into Beso's forearm with her nails but he's protected by his suit jacket. "Louis, you stay away from him!"

And then she sees Beso's other hand come around and take hold of her hair. She feels sharp pricks on her head as he pulls several strands of hair out of her skin and can see a clump of black in his palm.

He pulls up on his one good knee, his face a contorted mess of pain. Using his leg for leverage, he yanks back Aberdeen's head and then plants her face into the hard-packed earth.

"*Me cago en tus muertes!*" he screams down into her ear, spit escaping his mouth and spraying over her scalp. She hits the ground three times and with the third impact her nose snaps and her mouth is flooded with blood.

Aberdeen gasps at the stinging pain and breathes in her own blood. Her lungs object, seize and she coughs uncontrollably.

Beso's grip loosens slightly, and Aberdeen twists her head away, leaving her hair with him. He puts his hands on his knee and winces while Aberdeen sucks in air, trying to displace the blood in her lungs with what truly belongs there.

But it is all too much and she can feel it coming. The asthma. It is not just the blood. It is the fear and elation and dirt and adrenaline. Aberdeen suspects it may be that her lungs are joyous to have found a partner in Beso, someone else as bent on her destruction as they are. There is a vice around her breasts, a corset made of a disease born within her.

She reaches up for her nose and finds the septum running towards her right cheek instead of straight, a large knot in the middle of the bridge that used to be slender and fine. A wine-red clot slips down her wrist as she tries to stem the flow of blood with her palm. It slicks her lips, stains her teeth and inundates her mouth with the taste of iron.

Beso lifts up his pant leg to examine his knee, his attention removed from Aberdeen and Louis.

This is when she looks down at the needle held so tightly in her palm that her skin has gone white around the knuckles. Her wheezing is audible now, a high-pitched whistle with every exhalation. She draws the plunger out of the plastic syringe, sucking air into the cylindrical chamber. A bead of the sedative rolls about the sides of the compartment, leaving behind rosy legs.

And she hears something soft in her head, a voice raspy with age and tinged with sass. It's the voice of Myrtle and she asks Aberdeen, like she asked her the day they met outside of the pharmacy, "what do you do with an empty needle?" and she finally has an answer.

She lifts the needle and throws herself onto Beso, bringing the syringe down somewhere around his left shoulder. He screams and grasps her hair again. Aberdeen thumbs the plunger into the cylinder, sending air into the drug dealer's blood stream, perhaps straight into his heart.

She wants to say, "There's your holy spirit, Beso. There is the holy air, coursing to your heart. Isn't it funny that it kills you to get air when it kills me not too?"

But she hasn't the energy or oxygen for it. So she simply says what she knows she should say.

"I'm sorry."

His fist hooks her in the jaw and she's thrown off of him. He scrambles to pull the needle free from the folds of his suit. Aberdeen's vision is going, dark rings squeezing her sight down to pinpricks of light and shadow. She lets herself lie back then and places her hands over her ribs. She can't feel her torso expand at all. This is suffocation, she thinks and wishes she had the power to be hysterical, but her body is shutting down. All except for the left eye, which now unplugs and runs clear and sends drops of tears over her broken nose to her mouth to wash away the taste of life.

Any moment, she thinks, he will die from the air in his heart and Louis will be safe.

Then, her vision is gone. She hears Beso start to say something but then a dull smack sounds out, muted by the earthen walls, and she feels someone keel over next to her on the cold dirt.

Louis's voice quivers but sounds more resolute than she's ever heard it sound before.

"I'm going to get your medicine, Abbie. Don't stop breathing."

And she turns her head to the soil, presses her ear there as if she can hear his departing footfalls as clearly as a train running away from her on iron trestles. But she hears nothing, sees nothing, and lets her mouth fall open.

Her soul considers leaving again. For good. She yawns, her body's attempt to pull in as much air as possible, and she thinks how funny it is that things are where they should not be: blood in lungs, air in a heart, Louis in danger, Hurt a maniac and Aberdeen dying, her lungs a straw with holes along the sides of it, then Aberdeen dead, airless cells already entombed under feet and feet of dark, thawing earth.

CHAPTER THIRTY

There is a new taste in Aberdeen's mouth. No longer just iron and salt, but a film acidic and bitter. There it is again. And again. A mist slipping down the midline of her tongue, coursing to her lungs.

It is the taste of chemicals. And it brings her back to life.

She flips open her eyelids and she knows that they are up but at first she cannot see. As her lungs begin to relax, to give up their attack, the light grows, then the shapes and shadows chip themselves out from the general dark, like they've been pressed out with cookie cutters, and she can see Louis's wrist against her chin, his hand holding an albuterol inhaler firmly against the hard palate of her upper jaw.

He depresses the metal container three more times, until Aberdeen has enough strength in her arm to reach up and rest her fingers on the pulse point in his wrist. He pulls back and sits hard onto his butt, leaving the inhaler in her mouth and rubbing at his neck where he was pricked with the needle that brought resurrection.

Her heart is keeping time with the hearts of hummingbirds, of voles, a fast, untamed rhythm. She has no idea how many doses she's been given of the albuterol, but she doesn't care. She prefers her heart muscle beating wildly to not beating at all.

She flips Louis a wan smile, like the slight curve of a slim crescent moon, the spaces in her teeth stained black with blood.

"You're a regular Lazarus, Louis," she tells him, still prone on her back. "Coming back to life and bringing others back as well. So a Jesus, then, too."

The weight of something against her hip causes her to sit up and she sees Beso sprawled out next to her, one of his legs draped over her ankle, an intimate posture, something she would have assumed with Hurt in bed months ago. Beso's neck is turned like he's trying to see the middle of his back and his eyes are devoid of moisture, open and dull.

"I hit him," Louis said, "with a can of food. Beans, I think. I hit him on the head above his ear and I think I killed him."

The boy brings his legs into his chest and grips the toes of his old sneakers, bending his feet up. He keeps his eyes on Aberdeen, never letting his sight slip over to the man who held him hostage.

She puts fingers to the man's wrist to search for a pulse of blood through his forearm. It's missing. She can see the can of green beans a few feet away. There is a dent in the side of the metal tin, so deep and sharp it looks like the can has grown a toothless maw.

Staying on all fours, Aberdeen pushes Beso onto his back. There is a violet pool of blood just under the skin at one of his temples. She pats around his shoulder above his heart, looking for the syringe she stabbed there. But she finds it sticking out of the fabric of his jacket just under his armpit instead. Lower than she'd hoped. If it had hit his heart directly, the air wouldn't have had to travel as far and he would have been put down faster, cleaner.

She wraps her fingers around it and takes in a breath. And then takes in another, because she's blessed that she can.

"No, Louis. I killed him. With a needle full of air to his

bloodstream. I wasn't sure it would work, but it did. You didn't do anything, Louis. You were just saving me, defending me, okay?"

The boy looks to Beso's body then and back to Aberdeen. He twists the skin above his ankles and nods. "You killed him?"

"Yes," she says, "because I had to."

The door that Donation Box and the woman left from opens and Hurt skips in, his knees coming into contact with his healed ribcage, a large stick in his hand, the tip of it set on fire.

"Motherfucker!" he screams, his eyes darting to take in the entirety of the room. When he sees Aberdeen and Louis near the body of Beso, he lets the torch dip, the flame licking the hard-packed floor, searching for something to ignite.

Aberdeen coughs, her chest still tight, her body sore and weak from the lack of oxygen. She looks to the needle and whispers "thank you" and tugs at it to pull it from Beso's chest.

But it slides free only of fabric and she realizes that she missed when she tried to stick him with the needle. It never found purchase in his flesh. There was no sigh of air sent by prayer and justice to Beso's heart.

No. She missed and Louis killed the man for her.

Not that he will ever know this, she thinks, as she tries to stand and greet Hurt. But her legs are weak, they fold like two streamers downed from rafters at a party, and she collapses back to the earth.

Hurt moves past the desk crowned with the jar of heroin and crouches down at her side, holding the fire aloft, like he's looking at a relic from the past, or a new discovery of importance.

"Aberdeen, you missed out. You should have seen it."

Louis scoots over to Aberdeen and takes her head into his lap. She relaxes into it, smells the sourness of adolescent perspiration on Louis's jeans. Hurt seems to notice the boy then, the sides of his mouth turning up into a wide smile.

"You're okay, Louis? She save you?"

"Yes," he says, speaking down into her hair, "she did."

"No, he did, save me," Aberdeen says, looking up into the eyes of her husband who, for the time, is not the man she married.

Of course, they're all different now.

"I killed Beso," she says and Hurt smiles wider in response.

"Sure you did, Aberdeen," he says, his voice quiet but his tone sarcastic. "I guess he shouldn't have said that about your ancestors."

"What's that?" Aberdeen asks.

He shakes his head, shakes his torch at the ground, the fire flicking up the length of the wood, striving for Hurt's fingers. "Nothing. And now we need to go."

Aberdeen notices the slight lift in Hurt's eyebrows. He doesn't believe she killed Beso. And he's right, at least about this.

Louis looks at Hurt and swallows. "Back home?"

The fire that Hurt holds eats away at the club of wood as fat as his arm. It sparks off embers that flit to the ground and die there, next to Beso.

"The voices say we need to leave the city."

Aberdeen thinks of what it must be like above them. Trampled people, some wounded and some dead. Sani healing others. Janos digging through the pockets of the deceased. She wonders at the chaos her husband has caused. She wants to get out of this earthen hole and see it for herself.

"Because of what you've done?" she asks him.

"And because you're a murderer, Aberdeen," he says to her, as if it is her new vocation and it is a fact, even if it isn't to him. "And they will make you pay for it."

Louis's hands are sweaty and Aberdeen's hair gets tangled in the webbing of skin between his fingers. He bends his head down and rests his forehead on hers, puts all his head's weight there, like he could sleep on her face for days.

"They say we should go west. Myrtle and Walter, at least," Hurt says. He finally brings the torch down and thrusts it hard against the dirt, grinding it dead. It sparks, sputters and then the flame vanishes.

Aberdeen touches her nose with her thumb; her adrenaline is wearing off and the pain is blooming across her cheeks and radiating outward. She'd invited Myrtle and Walter to this party. Somehow she wasn't too surprised that Hurt was claiming to speak for them. She was willing to believe anything anymore. She preferred it to not believing anything anymore.

"My dad lives somewhere out there," Louis says, his voice muffled by Aberdeen's black hair. He doesn't speak about Hurt mentioning Myrtle.

The desk is just at the bottom of Aberdeen's vision. She can see the baby food jar and the film of powder that decorates its base. She licks her lips and hates herself for it.

"The moon will be the same wherever we go," she says to Hurt, meaning it to be both a glorious and a sad thing. She thinks back to that night, when she flew to the moon and found it soft and welcoming.

He twirls the stick, drilling a hole into the dirt with its tip. "I'll have babies with you, Aberdeen. But the voices will always have to stay. Even if the drugs come back. They are wise, booming voices."

She inhales and her lungs are back in line with the rest of her body, at least for now. Her heartbeat is still quick, thumping out blood as if she's running for her life. And she might be.

"Hurt," she asks, "will the voices guide me, too? Take care of me?"

He drops the wood and takes Aberdeen's cheeks in his hands. She sucks in air in response to his fingertips pressed into her wounded face, ten points of sharp electricity fan out over her flesh, down her neck, up to the crown of her head. Louis lifts his forehead away from her own and she can feel the cool wet of his tears over the skin of her skull.

"Of course. They'll take care of us all."

Louis looks up to the earthen ceiling. "I don't hear them."

"If you're lucky," Hurt says, "you might someday." And he kisses Aberdeen lightly on the lips and when he releases her, she can see her own blood in the divot above his top lip, the philtrum, the place where her pinkie finger fits perfectly. It is the same on this man as it is on the man she married.

She has covered him with her own life.

She has been the muscle pumping blood and being into both Hurt and now Louis for so long that she does not know where she stops and where they begin. And she is content with this melding into them. She is the heart. Louis is the spine. Hurt is the spirit.

But she takes a moment for herself, pulling away from the trinity she's made out of them, focusing her attention on her head still in the lap of the boy she wishes were her own, noting the infected gash curving up the jawline of her husband's face. Then she goes inside herself, nestles down in the space between her empty womb and her traitorous lungs, makes her mind tight, small enough to fit into a Mason jar next to moss and bright, tumbled sea glass. In here, the world and time is miniscule and quiet, and she prays to the moment's perfection, before they must raid the cages of medicine and she must decide whether or not to take the jar of heroin and they must escape the faith tent and flee the city and journey out west.

It is something, she thinks, to simply breathe and focus on breathing and live if only because of the air in her lungs.

ACKNOWLEDGMENTS

For the cheers and constant encouragement, for the editing and beta reading and reviews, for the evocative cover design, for the suggestions on best practices for bringing a book to life, for formatting and wrangling of minutiae, for music video trailers, for coffee dates and glasses raised high, for interviews, for inspiration, for the support, for the love and belief in what I do and why I do it, a massive, ebullient thanks to my family and friends.

www.ingramcontent.com/pod-product-compliance
Lightning Source LLC
Chambersburg PA
CBHW030559180626
46816CB00005B/1606